BLOOD PRESSURE

Also by Terence Taylor

Bite Marks

BLOOD PRESSURE

A Vampire Testament

TERENCE TAYLOR

 St. Martin's Griffin ⚏ New York

This is a work of fiction. All of the characters, organizations, and events portrayed in this novel are either products of the author's imagination or are used fictitiously.

BLOOD PRESSURE. Copyright © 2010 by Terence Taylor. All rights reserved. Printed in the United States of America. For information, address St. Martin's Press, 175 Fifth Avenue, New York, N.Y. 10010.

www.stmartins.com

Library of Congress Cataloging-in-Publication Data

Taylor, Terence.
  Blood Pressure: a vampire testament/Terence Taylor.—1st ed.
     p. cm.
  ISBN 978-0-312-38526-2
  1. Vampires—Fiction.   2. Triangles (Interpersonal relations)—Fiction.   3. New York (N.Y.)—Fiction.   I. Title
  Ps3620.A978B59 2010
  813'.6—dc22   2009040017

First Edition: April 2010

10 9 8 7 6 5 4 3 2 1

Dedicated to my late therapist, John Edward Ryan, for teaching me to hear through the noise and to listen to what it has to say. Any depiction of psychotherapy in this book is pure fiction and no reflection on mine, which made all this possible. And to the much-missed Octavia E. Butler, whose furor scribendi lives on in us all.

I

DARK MOON

If we must die, let it not be like hogs
Hunted and penned in an inglorious spot,
While round us bark the mad and hungry dogs,
Making their mock of our accursed lot.

—Claude McKay
"If We Must Die"
(1919)

PROLOGUE

5:46 P.M.—Grand Central Station, 18 July 2007

Lopez checked the van's dashboard clock and counted down.

Three. Two. One. The steam pipe under the intersection of Lexington Avenue and Forty-first Street exploded at precisely 5:47 P.M., a time that Clean Slate Global tactical computers had assured them would look random, like a real accident. Even though it was the height of rush hour, there'd still be time to seal off the area before their targets arrived at nine.

The van drove away from the site while Lopez notified the city agency in charge of the evacuation, then sat back to let them do their work. Everything was on schedule. She was pleased with her new unit's work so far and knew that Richmond would be, too. Her only miscalculation as project manager had been the timing of the traffic light that let a truck through too soon and left it stranded in the crater caused by the blast.

She was sorry for the driver, but if anything it made the setup look even more convincing. As planned, news crews gathered near the blast and never went near the staging area where her teams were assembled and ready to go.

Project Steam Clean was on, with no evidence that could ever connect the blast to Clean Slate Global or their client, the city of New York.

They'd get in, do their job, and get out undetected. No one would suspect a thing.

Especially their targets.

As Perenelle de Marivaux watched the news report about the midtown steam-pipe explosion on the small, flat-screen TV in her boudoir, she sipped an extremely old cognac and wondered if it would be a good idea to postpone tonight's quarterly meeting of the Hundred. She finished brushing her long, dark hair and bound it up in lustrous curls on top of her head.

According to the news report, the police had sealed off several blocks around the explosion at Forty-first Street and Lexington Avenue. The Grand Hyatt, where the hundred members of the High Council were to meet, was inside the frozen zone, only one street away.

Perenelle didn't like it. The elected Superiors of the Bloodlines of New York would have no difficulty entering; that wasn't the problem. Any of them could walk past the largest army unseen. Her question was whether the blast was coincidence or somehow tied to their gathering.

Others always said that Perenelle was paranoid and gave the humans too much credit. But those who mocked her most were less than a century old, and hadn't personally witnessed the strides humans had made over the last six hundred years, as she had. They didn't understand or care how shrewd, how dangerous, mankind had become with their modern science. Modern vampires, they ignored the obvious. Humans were catching on to them and in time could find a way to wipe them all out.

Perenelle smoothed her ruby-red velvet evening dress in front of the full-length mirror, slipped on new black boots, and admired her reflection as she added jewelry. She looked young, beautiful, eyes large and shining, lips slim but inviting. It was good to live like this again. As much as she'd enjoyed the last few decades as old Perenelle, her reintroduction to her West Village neighbors as her own young relative—come from Paris to nurse her ailing old great-aunt—gave her fresh pleasure.

The inevitable thought came—*If only Nicolas were here to see me.* Losing her husband in a Himalayan avalanche still haunted her; that it had happened while he searched for a way to cure her made it all the worse. Her search for a better way of life after a century of solitude in America had ended. What she had now wasn't perfect, but it could have been much worse.

At least she was at peace.

Perenelle opened a wireless laptop to check her e-mail as the sun set. There were already posts to the group list from tonight's host. Evidently he wasn't worried. The meeting was definitely still on. Perenelle sent back confirmation, but decided to take extreme measures to ensure her own safety.

Better safe than sorry.

The Superiors of the hundred vampire Bloodlines of New York flickered into view inside the police barricades as they approached the Grand Hyatt Hotel from the street, singly, in pairs, and in small groups. They were bewitchingly beautiful, men and women of all variety from uptown to downtown, east to west, all five boroughs represented in the latest styles.

They entered the frozen zone undetected, clouded the minds of the police as they strolled through armed barricades, past the graceful, classical curves of Grand Central Station to the starkly modern geometry of the hotel next door. Forty-second Street was empty of casual pedestrians and moving vehicles. Except for the bellowing sound of the geyser spewing mud and mayhem into the air a block away, it was a peaceful night in midtown.

Perenelle faded into view and approached the Grand Hyatt with caution. Twin glass towers soared over the dead street. The hotel's glistening walls reflected the dirty plume of rising steam on the next block. Perenelle didn't see any immediate cause for concern, but that didn't ease her feeling that she was on a closed set, not an open road, that they were all supporting players in someone else's show.

Doormen ushered Perenelle in like royalty. When she walked into the lobby, Perenelle saw that most of the hotel employees had been evacuated with the guests. Those loyal to the Bloodlines had stayed, on one pretext or another, to serve them. She strode through the abandoned street level to the empty elevators, took one up to the meeting. Most of the city's Superiors were already there when she entered.

The vampires of New York City had founded the Society of the Veil by unanimous vote in 1937. It was their only judicial body, instituted to keep the secret of their existence safe at any cost. Their territories were divided into one hundred hunting grounds called Bloodlines, since lines drawn on the map of New York City to divide the five boroughs granted blood rights to the territories within.

The Superior of each Bloodline was responsible for protecting the veil of secrecy within its boundaries. Quarterly meetings helped avoid battles between the 'Lines, settled disputes, and aired differences. There were complaints at first, even a few revolts, but in time they'd all come to see how much easier life was in unity.

Perenelle viewed it as a personal triumph. She nodded to her fellows and smiled, blew kisses across the room. Thanks to skills she'd learned from Rahman-al-Hazra'ad ibn Aziz, the Moorish vampire who'd infected her more than six centuries ago, she'd created the imaginary tribunal that brought them together, kept them safe and secure. All made manifest by illusions that deluded even her kind. None of them would ever know what she'd done for them, the sacrifices she'd made over the last century to assure their safety. None of them could ever know.

She tried to look at ease when she saw Dr. Townsend Burke across the room, the one vampire in New York who was in on her secret. Their relationship began in London, in the 1840s, when he used a sample of her blood to infect himself instead of helping her husband, Nicolas, to find a cure for her condition with the new science of transfusion. It had not been the best of introductions. Despite that, he'd shared her belief that the world, human and vampire, had to be protected from the likes of Tom O'Bedlam, the mad vampire whose excesses had inspired them to join with Rahman to form the Veil.

Burke saw her and nodded, made his way toward her. She tensed. They hadn't spoken in some time, had grown distant since 1986 when he took custody of Claire St. Claire, Tom's coconspirator, created in a Berlin brothel in the 1920s.

Burke had petitioned the High Council to free the girl a year early from her fifty-year entombment. As a fledgling, less than a hundred years old, she was entrusted to his care. Her fate since then had been a mystery to Perenelle, of no interest unless the girl fell back into her old destructive ways.

"My dear Perenelle," said Burke as he reached her side. "It has been too long." He bowed low and pulled out a chair for her as he rose. Vampires could sense one another and seldom touched. The low level irritation they felt made contact uncomfortable for most and kept their hunting grounds far apart. That had made it easy to establish borders for the bloodlines when the Veil divided up the five boroughs. Perenelle nodded and sat.

"Through no fault of yours, Doctor. I have found myself preoccupied with other than social matters." She made the excuse only to be polite. There was no reason to antagonize the head of the East Village Bloodline, one of New York's most prominent, by telling him she had no interest in his company, especially when he had the power to expose her sham. "How fares your charge?"

He smiled, rueful. "Caring for Claire is never an easy task. Her"—he searched for the right word—"rehabilitation has been a slow process. But she has grown."

"Cancer grows, Doctor." Perenelle tried to restrain herself, but couldn't. "I would hope for a more qualitative change."

Burke glared at her for a moment, obviously offended, and had started to retort when the overhead lights flashed to call them to order. He nodded grimly to Perenelle, turned away, and went to his seat. She knew she would have to placate him, but there was time for that later. Perenelle let him go, made small talk with those around her as the rest took their seats.

The meeting was called to order.

Other Superiors left their conversations long enough to put down their vintage liquors and stop feeding on fresh blood from enthralled humans provided by the caterers. The long room had been arranged with two rows of tables facing the front. Their cheerful host was a crisp, round vampire in an expensive, custom-made business suit; he occupied a single table centered in the front.

One look at him explained why he'd picked the cleanly corporate Grand Hyatt instead of something more traditional like The Plaza, or the evening Perenelle had assembled them in the Temple of Dendur at the Metropolitan Museum, the unforgettable night when Claire St. Claire had been freed from her fifty-year entombment.

Their host was one of the Wall Street New Bloods who'd bought his way into immortality. He was less than a hundred years old, still living under the supervision of his Old Blood sponsor. Most New Bloods had no real style, no flair. This hall could have housed any corporate retreat; their assembly looked no more remarkable than any mortal gathering of New York's high and mighty.

Perenelle looked around at the bland, smiling faces, the designer clothes and styled hair on the women and the men, and wondered for the first time if she'd gone too far in her attempts to tame them. Was diet the only difference left between them and the humans? Had her creation of the Veil civilized the vampires of New York beyond any ability to distinguish themselves from their prey?

The last human left the room and the meeting officially began. Their host made a brief speech welcoming them all and then in a quiet, trembling voice introduced the Triumvirate of the Veil. Perenelle closed her eyes, prepared to cast her illusion and make it seem to them all that the lights faded, as they always did before an appearance of the Triumvirate. Everyone went silent, even those who'd talked through the host's speech.

The Triumvirate of the Veil appeared at the front of the room and stood behind the table as if in judgment of the assembly. Perenelle always made changes in the Triumvirate after each ten-year election. Currently it was a man and two women, always anonymous, features blurred as if in constant motion. Perenelle kept it diverse and had decided on a female majority for a change, one black. When they talked, it was in three distinct voices that spoke as one.

"Welcome all . . ."

As soon as the last human left and the doors were locked, Lopez moved in the first tier of her team from the service elevators. Black-clad troopers lined up along the outer walls of the meeting room. One member of each team took tripods from long cases, telescoped them out to stand tall, pulled out reflector dishes that opened like umbrellas, and snapped them into place to face the conference-room walls. The other unpacked transmitters and locked them into the parabolic centers of the umbrella dishes, then plugged in portable power supplies. In less than five minutes the site was operational. Each outer wall along the length of the meeting room was lined by a row of six-foot-wide microwave dishes made of thin metal mesh.

Lopez didn't speak. Their targets had inhumanly acute hearing. Everything her team did had been in complete silence, with text-messaged commands. Lopez flipped open her muted iPhone and sent a ready signal from her touch screen to the second tier, got them ready to move in as soon as the microwave pulse was activated. She pushed a button on the master remote that controlled the transmitters on both sides. The assembly squad moved out to make room for the second team.

A red light on top of each of the power supplies went on as the charge built up. The lights clicked to yellow. In a few more seconds the lights would go green and it would all be over.

Then her cleanup crew would go into action.

The Triumvirate vanished amid applause.

The crowd stood, kept applauding as lights in the room rose to normal. Their host held up his hand to silence the crowd.

The Triumvirate had put on a good show, applauded the efforts of those Perenelle wanted to encourage, chided those she felt needed reining in. She always had to resist the impulse to take a bow when her audience was moved by a performance. Perenelle sighed as the host tried to call everyone to order, so that they could deal with specific business. Their host raised his arms and his voice.

"Please, may I have your attention, please . . ."

Then everyone fell to the floor except Perenelle.

It happened in complete silence, with no warning, nothing to explain it. No one moved. Perenelle walked to the middle of the room, looked around in shock. She had an odd psychic sensation, different from the usual sharp, low-grade static of being in the company of other vampires, but it stopped before she could analyze the feeling.

Every door to the room burst open at the same moment on both sides. The operation moved like an assembly line. Pairs of black-clad storm troopers entered on one side of the room, each team with a lightweight metal casket. The first teams opened cases, placed a vampire inside each, sealed the caskets, and carried them out the other side as the next team entered behind them.

Perenelle's immobile peers were efficiently packed up and removed from the room as she watched. The procedure continued as a white-haired woman appeared at the door in the same black coverall uniform as the others, but with a look of command. She saw Perenelle, gaped, and shouted into a microphone for backup.

Perenelle saw fear and confusion in the woman's eyes as she reached up to adjust a small video camera on the side of a headset, recording everything. When Perenelle realized what the woman was doing, she came to her senses and vanished.

Perenelle's astral body dropped back into her real one in her West Village home with a jolt. She opened her mouth and screamed loud and long, wept as she realized that she'd just seen the leadership of her kind across the city either captured or killed. It was only her precaution of using the gift of astral projection tonight that had spared her, learned from Rahman when he'd taught her the illusions she'd used to create the Triumvirate.

It had saved her life in the past, from Rahman himself when he'd turned on her twenty years ago. Now it made her the only vampire in New York who knew what had happened, who could warn the others. She stumbled to her feet from pillows on the floor and poured a cognac.

Her worst fears had been realized.

There was an organized, human task force that targeted vampires, armed with unprecedented weapons to use against them. Not only did the humans know that vampires existed, they knew of their society, their meetings, and had laid a successful trap.

For all her planning and all she'd done to keep her kin from drawing too much attention, she'd done nothing to save them from this. Perenelle hadn't protected her kind at all, only spayed them, pulled their fangs and claws with her dream of peaceful coexistence. When the humans came for them, they'd had no defense, no warning. She'd made them too complacent with a generation of protected peace.

Perenelle tried to focus, told herself that she could correct her mistake. She'd start by using the humans' technology against them. E-mail would warn the surviving vampires of New York. Their communications were safe from surveillance. They'd made sure of that by enthralling the best hackers in the city.

Once the others knew the danger, they could formulate a plan to locate the lost, then save or avenge them. If this were really the first volley of a war with the humans, it would not end quickly or easily.

All the power Perenelle had used to keep her kind in line for seventy years would be unleashed to defeat humanity instead, to restore the balance of power between them. If the mortals wanted to wage a war, they'd get one to remember.

Perenelle would see to that.

II

NEW MOON

There are years that ask questions and years
that answer.

—Zora Neale Hurston
Their Eyes Were Watching God
(1937)

CHAPTER 1

3:32 P.M.—*East Village, 19 July 2007*

Christopher had never been sick a day in his life.

It was a running joke in the family. There wasn't one kid or parent they hadn't carried to the emergency room in the middle of the night, at one time or another, except Christopher. They'd made jokes about his good health all through his childhood, had even accused him of bringing a few family pets back to life before they could be buried. They made jokes, the neighbors made jokes, teachers made jokes, but beneath all the laughter was something darker.

There was fear.

He could feel the shiver under the love, behind the smiles. His adoptive parents loved and cared for him, but the Ross family could sense the same thing he could. Christopher wasn't one of them, even if they couldn't pin down exactly how or why, different in a way no one could define. Despite his dark-blond good looks, his athleticism, the charismatic quiet that drew people to him, they were a little scared by how easy it was to trust him. It was like he was too good to be true, not their son but a confidence man with a practiced pitch they should beware.

No one tried to stop him when he announced that he was moving to New York to look for his birth parents and uncover his history. They'd said all the right things, told him they understood why he had to go, that they'd miss him and he should hurry back soon, but he saw the relief in their eyes, the way their bodies relaxed as soon they dropped him off at the Metro-North train station in Bridgeport.

Once he reached Manhattan, he took the Lexington Avenue subway downtown from Grand Central Station to see the first of the apartment shares he'd found on Craigslist. The layered music beats in his iPod headphones made his walking view of the East Village streets feel like a low-budget, independent DV movie instead of the real thing. People that crowded the streets around him were either tourists or locals. You could tell the difference when one stopped midsidewalk to shop, gawk, or take pictures as the others shoved past.

Christopher kept moving, blended in like a local. His clothing and short, shaggy hair were cool and casual enough that the big bag over his shoulder didn't make him look like he'd just arrived. He moved down the crowded New York streets with what looked like purpose, as if he knew where he was going, when he was completely and totally lost, unsure of what he'd find now that he was here. He'd been to Manhattan only once before, on a high school field trip, and they'd gone no farther than the Museum of Modern Art, on West Fifty-third Street, after leaving Grand Central.

Christopher finally stopped at a corner store and asked the clerk behind the counter for directions, got back onto Second Avenue, and walked south across Houston Street to find Rivington. After the canyons created by towering high-rise condos being built along Houston Street, the neighborhood below Houston seemed smaller, more intimate. He walked past windows filled with hip clothes and small restaurants with free wireless.

The address turned out to be a rusty redbrick six-story walk-up on the corner, with storefronts on the ground floor. It was near a couple of places to eat and a market, not far from the subway if he'd walked here the right way. It would do. Christopher rang the bell and a buzzer let him in the front door without question. A male voice with a clipped accent spoke from the intercom as he entered.

"Third floor."

A skinny Middle Eastern kid a little younger than him opened the door upstairs, grinned, dressed in hip-hop gear, a backward baseball cap worn over a fade with geometric stripes cut into the side.

"Yo, man. Check it . . ."

He receded as Christopher followed him into the corner apartment. Dance music filled the air, pumped from stacks of speakers on shelves that covered the rear wall of the living room. The rest of the space was filled with hard drives, computers, screens, and recorders—reel-to-reel, cassette, CD, DVD—a technological armory equipped for any audio need. It all framed a worn couch that slouched under the window, the only free space in the room.

"My gear," said Spider. "I produce music, so that half is studio space, cool?" Christopher shrugged as he looked over the setup.

"Yours?" he asked, nodded at the pounding speakers.

"Yeah. My girl Vangie's new band, Bitter. They play tonight at a gallery in Chelsea. Come; should be hot."

"Sure."

"Want to see the room?"

"I'll take it. You want references?"

The guy looked at him and grinned. "You're cool, I can tell. Tag's Spider Remix, call me Spider." He held out a fist. Christopher punched back, felt like a liar even if he knew he was "cool." Everyone thought so. Just once he'd like to meet someone who didn't automatically fall for his fatal charm. "First month's rent and half the deposit today, move your stuff in anytime."

Christopher dropped his bag on the floor.

"Done. Where's the party?"

CHAPTER 2

4:17 P.M.—*Red Hook, 19 July 2007*

She wasn't there.

Lopez played the video footage she'd shot at the Hyatt for her boss, Jonathan Richmond, again, ran it slow motion on the big HD screen in his office, over and over, but there was no trace of the woman Lopez said she had seen vanish from the target room.

"Let's look at what we know. Obviously the equipment's working or there wouldn't be any picture," said Richmond. He tugged at his gray goatee. "You say she saw you?"

"Looked right at me. Then vanished into thin air."

"An apparition?"

Lopez frowned. "More focused. Conscious. There was definite interaction between us. I'd say astral projection?"

"Hm." Richmond rewound the video back to before their team had broken in and played it again. If it were anyone but Lopez, Richmond would have written the vision off as job jitters or a stress-induced hallucination. But the teams jokingly called Lopez *La Blanca Bruja*, the White Witch, because she always knew things were coming before anyone else did.

Richmond trusted her gut instincts. She'd been with him since the beginning, a SWAT commander from one of the teams that had cleaned up the quarantine area downtown in 1986. Like him, she'd understood that what she saw on the Lower East Side wasn't the result of an outbreak of plague or a new biological weapon, as the troops had been told, but something far worse, a staggering discovery that undermined mankind's future forever.

They'd fought walking corpses that had risen from the dead to spread their tainted blood to increase their number. No one had ever established the source of the plague. Dismembered remains that burst into flame when exposed to sunlight were found under the rubble of an abandoned tenement inside the zone, a building that had exploded for no apparent reason.

Other strange finds were made in the rubble of a sinkhole under Sheep Meadow that had claimed more than a hundred lives, people with no reason to be there. Richmond stayed in charge of the task force and made sure the excavation was especially thorough. He had kept the results as secret as the ruined subway station they'd found there, one that MTA records said didn't exist.

There were crazy reports from National Guardsmen who'd taken a work train in to secure the station that year. Survivors had come back with unbelievable stories of a subterranean battle with albino vampires, reports that had to be sealed.

That wasn't nearly as interesting as the manuscripts and scrolls discovered beneath the station. Clean Slate researchers were still studying them. What they'd discovered already was mind-boggling.

Mankind was not alone.

Beings walked the Earth that looked human but weren't, unnatural things that fed on people and had to be stopped. It was only a matter of time before vampires or worse tried to reduce humanity to a food source, unless Clean Slate Global stopped them. It was the single most-important job in the world. Richmond watched the video over and over until he saw what he was looking for and stopped the disk. He ran it back and hit Play with a laugh.

"There." Richmond grinned as Lopez looked at the screen. "A lesson from astronomy. You can't see a black hole. You have to look for how it affects objects around it. . . ."

Richmond pointed. On the right side of the screen, one of the vampires seemed to talk to thin air then pulled out a chair, as a gentleman would for a lady. He stood next to it as if in conversation.

Lopez laughed.

"Damn. That's why you're the boss. And they call me a witch." She fast-forwarded through the video footage and found more instances of exchanges with the empty chair.

"You say she looked familiar?" asked Richmond.

"Yeah. I've seen the face, just can't place it yet."

"Where?"

Lopez shrugged.

"Remember. That's priority one," said Richmond. "If she saw what happened and escaped, she'll warn the rest. We have to be prepared for the worst."

"We always are." Lopez headed for the door. "I'll see that our new guests get settled in."

Richmond touched the screen on his desk as she left.

"I'm finished here. Is our friend receiving?"

A voice came from the speakers in his desk: "Ready when you are."

He was in a white room.

It had a sterile medical feel. That was all he knew, and that he was alive when for some reason he didn't expect to be. There was a memory of falling from great heights and enduring great cold. Who he was, where he was, nothing else was clear. Not his own name or who he was. He was weak, barely conscious, but healing, feeling better daily.

The door opened and a tall man walked in. He had gray hair and a goatee, wore a dark suit of an odd cut. For styles to have changed this much, he must have slept for a long time. The man smiled and sat in a chair next to the bed, spoke to him in what sounded like modern English. His head was still too fuzzy for him to translate. When the man realized he didn't understand, he smiled, shook his head, and apologized in French.

"I'm sorry. I forgot myself. You're still recovering. My name is Jonathan Richmond. They told me you were finally awake. As your host, I wanted to pay my respects and welcome you to New York."

New York? He was in the New World? What year? He stared up at the man, tried to speak, but his mouth was dry, his throat didn't seem to work.

"Your body's still in shock. You've been in a coma for over a year after being buried in ice in Tibet for some time. It took us over ten years to find you. It's amazing you're doing this well, after what you've been through."

Richmond poured a glass of water and held it up to his lips, lifted his head so that he could drink. He sipped, felt cool water moisten his tongue.

"Therapy begins tomorrow. I know this seems strange, but all will be explained in time. Rest now." Richmond rose to leave. "We'll talk when you're better. For now, just trust me, Nicolas."

He walked out with a smile and shut the door behind him.

Nicolas. That was his name. Yes. Nicolas. He remembered that much as he fell back into healing sleep.

Nicolas de Marivaux.

CHAPTER 3

4:43 P.M.—Park Slope, 19 July 2007

Lori woke up nauseated from her afternoon nap even though her churning stomach was empty. She jumped up, ran to the bathroom, and crouched in front of the toilet just before the flood. There was more than she'd expected, considering that she'd skipped lunch. It all came up and hit the bowl, but she kept heaving. Her stomach squeezed out everything it could find until only acidic yellow bile remained, burned her throat as she choked it up.

It was stress, that's all. Just stress.

She repeated that to herself like a mantra as she tried to calm her stomach, stop gulping in air that built up the pressure in her gut. Nothing was wrong with her yet. It was just anticipation of the nightmare to come that had her dozing through the day like this. It was how she'd always handled stress, avoided it by staying asleep.

Lori rinsed her mouth, spat again and again to get the bitter taste out, and belched up empty air until she was sure she was done throwing up. She stood up and looked in the mirror to see wet, red eyes, stringy blond hair, and a trail of spittle down her chin. This is what forty-eight looked like. Lori groaned and ran water in the basin. When it warmed up, she rinsed out a washcloth and wiped her face until she felt almost human again.

She picked up her bathrobe from the bedroom floor as she walked in, put on her black cotton slippers from Pearl River Market, and went downstairs to the kitchen to put on water for tea. The robe was thick, plush, ivory terry cloth, a Christmas present last year to herself from Restoration Hardware. Lori was usually more into her local hardware store than expensive designer chains, but she'd found it while she was there with a friend and tried it on. It was almost floor-length on her, soft and warm, like wearing the cotton fur of a skinned, giant teddy bear. She got the biggest one she could to wrap up in while she worked in front of the computer on chilly mornings. It had gotten her through the last draft of the new book.

Not the last draft. The most recent.

It seemed like it would never end. She'd never battled with a book like she had with this one. It was almost six months past the deadline extension, with no end in sight. She still didn't have a manuscript she could turn in, and if she didn't get back to her editor soon with a reasonable explanation why not, she wouldn't have to worry about it. It was too easy for a publisher to lose patience with a writer who didn't turn in her book on time, and this one was so late that she was lucky she still had a contract.

It was only Lori's track record and the subject that had saved her so far. *Zora's Great Day* was meant to be a Harlem Renaissance romantic fantasy. It was about Zora Neale Hurston and a mysterious relationship she'd had after her first marriage ended, which had inspired her to write *Their Eyes Were Watching God* a few years later. Her publisher thought it had bestseller potential, and her editor kept making jokes about slipping the final manuscript to Halle Berry or Angelina Jolie. Neither made it any easier to write.

Lori had done all her research, read the autobiography, all the biographies, and Zora's letters, but still didn't quite buy that she'd gotten the full story. Something was missing, the piece of the puzzle that would let her tell the story of Zora's lost love her own way. She'd gotten all the available facts, and there was every reason for a woman to be attracted to hunky Percy Punter, the Columbia grad student described in *Dust Tracks on a Road* and elsewhere. It just seemed that the heart of the woman she'd met while reading Zora's work was bigger than the *Sex and the City* story of pining and neurotic passion that Lori read in her autobiography.

The mutual jealousy and the desperate longing when apart reminded

Lori of Zora's description of her parents' early relationship. At first she thought that the woman who'd written so accurately about relationships should have had enough self-awareness of her parents and herself to avoid that, but when Lori looked back at her own history, she had to laugh . . . it was easy for smart women to be stupid in love.

She pulled her robe tighter while she waited for the water to boil. The terry cloth had started to fray since the holidays and even washing hadn't removed some of the stains around the sleeves and neck. Her daughter, Joie, sneered whenever she saw it, made comments about menopause and creeping eccentricity whenever Lori wore it outside to get the mail or chat with neighbors.

None of that kept Lori from wearing it while she worked. She insisted that it was comfort clothing, made her feel safe and protected, and that kept her at the computer to write and earn money. Who cared what she looked like as long as the bills got paid?

When the kettle was hot, Lori poured the water into a teapot and looked at the clock. It was only a little after five. There was still time before she had to get dressed for Joie's show. She took her tea to the front room, clicked on the TV, and watched a news report with the latest on yesterday's steam-pipe explosion in midtown. There was never a dull moment in New York. Lori clicked it off, put on a CD of old Kate Bush. That always calmed her down. Let the *Hounds of Love* chase away her blues.

Lori pulled the robe tighter as she drank her tea, didn't mind that she sweated a little. She needed comfort clothing now, any comfort, more than ever. She'd actually retired the robe a couple months ago, when temperatures had risen too high to justify it. It was only in the last week that she'd pulled it out and started wearing it again, day and night, while she slept away her fears.

Ever since the cancer diagnosis.

CHAPTER 4

6:58 P.M.—Chelsea, 19 July 2007

Joie Martin-Johnson juggled her knapsack and a luggage cart loaded with equipment cases, managed to wheel them into the elevator at NYU's Tisch Building just before the doors closed. She'd persuaded one of her professors to let her sign out school equipment for Vangie's show tonight, even though she wasn't in summer session. She was his favorite student and had promised to submit tonight's video as an extra-credit project for the fall semester. He'd set her up with a digital projector, HDV cameras, tripods, and battery packs.

Vangie was supposed to have helped her carry them to the show, but of course, that didn't happen. She was too busy channeling Diana Ross, probably getting her hair and makeup done. Forget rehearsing or moving equipment to the gig. That was for drones like Joie and the band. Who cared what the music sounded like or the staging, as long as Vangie looked great?

Joie hailed a cab outside on Broadway and nearly lost her glasses getting everything in. The gallery wasn't open for hours and she couldn't reach Vangie by phone, which meant that she couldn't even get into Vangie's place to leave everything.

She either had to drag the equipment to Brooklyn and drive it back in with her mom's car or find someplace near the gallery to park her ass until the manager got there to let her in. If Princess Vangie had just handed over her keys like Joie had asked, there'd be no problem, but God forbid.

Joie pulled her cell phone out in the cab and thumbed a text message to Spider. His place was too far south to go there and get back to Chelsea in time, but he could at least get his skinny ass up there early to help her set up for his girlfriend's big night.

The video projector was out of the case and already mounted on its stand by the time Spider got there, wearing an oversized jacket despite the heat. He had a tall, dark-blond friend in tow to help lug his audio equipment. Once she got a good look at him, Joie wasn't sorry he'd tagged along.

"Yo, Joie de vivre!" Spider held his arms out wide for a hug, but Joie smacked him on the head and went back to work.

"Down, Spider. Start connecting."

"Right that. Joie, Chris. Chris, Joie. New roomie."

Spider started pulling cables out of the case as Joie held out a hand to his roommate.

"Christopher Ross," he said with a dazzling smile. "Not Chris."

"Joie. It's spelled French, like *joie*, but I pronounce it 'Joey.' Easier that way, even if I can't get him to say it. Joie Johnson-Martin." She smiled back at Christopher as they shook hands. His was warm, strong, and large, and held hers a moment longer than she'd expected. Joie felt a sudden blush rise up her arm to her chest.

"Back to work," she said, and broke free.

With three of them they got the show up in almost no time. Christopher mounted two HDV cameras on tripods to shoot the show from different angles, while Joie connected her laptop to the projectors that would play the background video. Spider set up his amps, mixing boards, and microphones on a side table with Christopher's help when he was done with the cameras. Joie finished her connections, tested her video footage on the big screen while he watched.

"So this is it, huh? The glamorous New York art world."

"Oh yeah," Joie said with a snort. She pulled down her wire-framed glasses with a pinkie, wiped sweat out of an eye with the back of a knuckle. "This is the big time all right."

"Finito!" Spider snapped his empty case shut, stuck it in a corner of the room under the windows, behind his mixing board. "Think the wine's set up yet?"

The gallery owner, Gala, was in the front room, supervising the caterers as they arranged organic cheeses, crackers, and fruit on platters. She wore her hair in long, thin braids that were twisted up on top of her head; her dress was a traditional African print in a contemporary western cut. She bounced along to sixties' R&B music blasting from earbuds plugged into an iPod shuffle clipped to her belt.

"How's it going?" she shouted, and hit Mute.

"Ready to go." Joie grabbed a glass of Perrier. "Taking a break until the band gets here for sound check."

"You got it, baby. See you then." She went on to the next table. Christopher picked up a cup of the wine with a smile to Gala, who giggled back like a schoolgirl. Spider gulped one down and grabbed two more cups as they all headed for the door.

The hallway outside the gallery ran almost a block to the elevator, harshly lit by bright overhead fluorescents, tall brick walls painted white. They walked until they reached the door to a fire exit. Joie opened it and they walked through to concrete stairs. She sat down in the middle of the staircase, sipped her sparkling water, and sighed.

"So why New York? Of all possible overpriced hells on Earth, why this one?"

Christopher leaned against the wall on the lower landing, eye-to-eye with her.

"Does there have to be a reason?"

"No one comes to New York unless they're looking for something. Money. Career. Or someone. You don't have to move here to see the sights."

Christopher laughed, and for a moment Joie almost bought the casual seduction of it. The laugh that said he didn't care what she said, that he was just here for fun and this conversation was only a lark. She knew it was a lie, even if she didn't know how she knew. Joie usually had her mother's lack of intuition about men, but this one she could read like she'd known him for years. He knew it, too, even if he didn't know that he knew it.

"I'm adopted. Looking for my birth parents."

"Cool. Very Lifetime Movie Network."

The straight truth. She hadn't expected that so fast and easy. Joie raised her eyebrows and peered at him more closely over her glasses. Maybe he did know. Her smile brightened as Christopher suddenly got more interesting. Meeting him might almost make up for a night of Vangie. Almost.

She'd find out soon.

CHAPTER 5

8:12 P.M.—*East Village, 19 July 2007*

A piece of paper gave Vangie the name and address of a building on the south side of Tompkins Square Park for her intake session. When she got there, all she saw on the ground floor was an old dry cleaner next to a clothes shop, Luna X / Styles. The window was filled with hats, tops, skirts, jackets, dresses, all bright red, so much, so varied, that it was hard to take it all in.

The view pulled her in for a closer look as she tried to sort through it. That little coat there, that could look good on her, maybe for tonight's show. Vangie was leaning in for a closer view when a door to her left popped open.

"Looks your size, kiddo, wanna try it on?"

The bleached blonde in the doorway was short, in her early forties, but her clothes and heavy makeup looked like they'd been bought when she was twenty. Crystal-meth skinny, she was dressed like an eighties' music-video vixen in black and red with a lot of polka dots, ruffles, and spandex. The woman pulled up elbow-length fingerless gloves and teetered on black patent-leather stiletto heels, scratched at torn fishnet stockings as she held up a dead, half-smoked cigarette.

"Let me know, 'cause if you ain't . . ." The woman waved the cigarette at Vangie, snorted, and lit up when the girl didn't answer. "Sucks I can't even smoke inside my own store. Damn Bloomberg. My own damn business if I live or die, right?"

"Yeah, sure." Vangie held up her paper. She'd been too surprised by the woman jumping out like a jack-in-the-box to respond immediately. "I'm looking for a Dr. Lazarus?"

"Christ, why didn't ya say so? Hang on . . ."

The woman scowled, stubbed her cigarette out on the wall, and stuck it back in her pack. She disappeared into the shop, came out a minute later with a white smock pulled over her dress, and locked the door behind her. "You're early. Ten minutes later I'da been upstairs to let you in."

"Sorry."

"Whatever." The woman walked from the storefront to a bright blue door covered in marker graffiti on the other side of the display window. She unlocked it and waved for Vangie to follow. "C'mon. One floor up."

They walked upstairs to a wooden door with a brass nameplate, ABEL LAZARUS, M.D. The woman unlocked it and Vangie followed her into a small, white waiting room with a desk and phone. There were two tacky sixties' plastic chairs on the other side of the room, a small white table stacked with old *Interview* magazines stuck between them. The walls were plain and bare, the paint old and cracked. There was a door to a front room across from the desk that had to be the doctor's office. A little red light above it shone like a ruby eye. The bleached blonde sat down behind the desk and held out a card and a pen.

"Just fill this out. The doc will be with you soon."

Vangie nodded, took what she'd been given, and checked out the room between answering the usual questions about name, address, and medical history. The walls were bare of anything but two posters. One was a rainbow at sunrise, the other a kitten dangling from a clothesline with HANG IN THERE! written underneath in big letters. *That was from the seventies, right,* thought Vangie and almost laughed. If that was the level of therapy she could expect, she might as well leave now.

She handed back the completed form and the receptionist looked it over. "Evangelyne Withers . . . I'm Luna X, but you know that." The girl looked at Luna, blank. How would she know that? "My shop downstairs? The sign?"

Vangie smiled, not sure what to say. She didn't know if the woman was as odd as she seemed or if it was the hash she'd smoked at the apartment before she'd left. She knew it was stupid to get stoned before her first session, but she'd never been to a therapist and it kind of freaked her out. If he was going to treat her problems, he might as well see what they were.

Luna stared out the back window at the sky as it darkened, hummed while she filed deep-red fingernails. It took Vangie a minute to realize Luna was humming "Don't Fear the Reaper," a song Vangie was going to sing at the show tonight. Weird.

A little machine on the floor near the door to the inner office hissed with pink noise to mask any sound from inside. Vangie fidgeted. She didn't want to be here. Her adviser had sent her in for therapy after she'd flunked a couple of classes that got her stuck in summer session. Some colleges had lost a few kids to suicide in the last ten years and she guessed they weren't taking any more chances.

The counselor was convinced that Vangie must have something seriously wrong to go from straight-A grades to total failure in one semester. Vangie couldn't admit she was skipping classes to play in an art-rock band in the hopes of breaking big downtown and dropping out. He'd just think she was trying to screw her parents out of tuition money while she partied in New York.

Which she was.

The light over the door clicked from red to green. Luna snapped to attention and put down her nail file, walked to the door, and nodded to Vangie.

"This way."

She opened the door and walked in. Vangie rose and followed her, not sure what to expect. Luna stood proudly next to a long, low couch under the two windows that faced the street.

"Meet Dr. Abel Lazarus," she said, with all the breathy excitement of someone introducing a rock star. "Doctor, this is . . ." She checked the card again. "Evangelyne Withers."

Luna X scurried out of the room and closed the door behind her. The doctor's office was totally different from the spare and tacky waiting room. It was warm and inviting. The walls were creamy white above dark maple wainscoting, and the lighting was low, almost romantic. The furniture was sleek and modern, wood polished to a fine luster; the fabrics were luxurious weaves she'd seen in design shows that her mother took her to when she was young.

The paintings on the walls were originals. Some seemed familiar. She moved next to one and looked more closely. It was by a local artist whose work she loved. She recognized another from a show she'd seen a few weeks ago. Vangie had wished then that she could afford to buy it on her budget. The doctor was doing well to afford it. Good thing her parents' insurance was footing the bill.

She looked around for a chair.

The only seat in the room seemed to be the sofa under the windows, and the doctor was on that. It looked comfortable, large, curved, with a low back, but would leave her a little too close to someone she was supposed to open up to—unless that was the idea.

"Just have a seat on the other end of the couch. Sorry. I know it's unconventional, but you'll find many of my methods unorthodox." The doctor smiled. Vangie sat down and took a good look at Dr. Abel Lazarus for the first time.

He was beautiful.

There was no other word. He had close-cropped auburn hair and wore a loose, black silk shirt and slacks. His face was sculpted like a model's, with high cheekbones and a flawless complexion. His wide-set eyes were the most beautiful feature of all, eyes you could swim in, one gray, one blue.

Eyes you could trust.

She must have gasped, because the doctor chuckled and looked down with affected modesty. Vangie blushed and giggled. "I guess you get that a lot."

"Enough." He grinned back at her. "I hope I'm not too distracting. We're here for you."

"I think I can deal." She laughed again. The room was so comfortable that she could have decorated it herself, and the doctor was a hunk. If she had to go anywhere once a week to keep her school counselor happy, it could be worse than here.

They sat angled on the couch, facing each other as they talked. At first she babbled about meaningless details, thrown in to fill up the time, then talked about her past, her feelings about school, losing her father, and about her mother and stepfather. In no time at all it started to seem more like a chat with an old friend than a therapy session. She looked away and held her breath as she carefully considered what she wanted to say next.

"I have a confession to make." She hesitated.

"It's okay, Vangie." She'd already given the doctor permission to use her childhood nickname. "You can tell me anything." Dr. Lazarus's arm lay along the back of the couch. It didn't take more than a twist of the wrist for his fingers to take hers in a tender clasp. His skin was cool and dry. She sighed.

"I don't know what I'm doing. I want to be in the band and all that, but . . . I am wasting my parents' money. I hate it, but I can't help it and I've done worse, things it would kill them to find out. It's like I'm trying to get back at them. . . ."

"Why is that? What could make you so angry?"

Vangie frowned as his fingers pressed hers tighter. "I don't know. They were okay, I guess."

"Just okay? Your stepfather didn't raise you, did he? What happened to your father?" Vangie's head swam as Lazarus leaned closer. The hash wasn't strong enough to have this effect. She felt more like she'd taken acid or ecstasy. Her mind expanded, her senses heightened. Dr. Lazarus's beautiful face filled her vision. He was all she could see as the rest of the room seemed to dim, grow darker until it faded out completely.

"My father?"

"Yes. How did he die?"

The doctor's office was gone. Vangie floated in a void and heard Lazarus's voice echo as if it came down from a great distance. Had he hypnotized her? Was she in a trance? Before she could think more about it, the emptiness was filled with another place, another time.

Vangie heard a dull hum as she rose in a small wooden chamber. It was an elevator, the one in the building they used to live in on Park Avenue before her daddy died and they moved to Park Slope, where Mommy met and married Mr. Withers. There was a little fish-eye mirror in the elevator that passengers used to check inside before boarding. Vangie looked up and saw herself reflected in it behind the elevator operator, a small man in a doorman's uniform. She was eight, in a frilly, light blue dress, on her way home early from a party.

Vangie knew the day now. It had been lost in a maze of other memories, pushed down and away, out of sight, to the back of her mental closet. A bad memory, not a day she liked to remember, but here she was again.

Her mother had dropped her off at the Felders' for their son's birthday party. Jerry went to the same school and his mother had invited everyone in his class to the party. She had no idea which of them might be her son's friends, and he'd just shrugged whenever she'd asked him which kids to invite.

Vangie didn't want to be there and had insisted all morning that she had an upset stomach. She didn't like Jerry, no one did, and he didn't like her or anyone else, either. Her mother insisted that it would be fun, her way of saying, *You're going whether you want to or not, I have things to do today.*

Vangie made it all the way through the birthday presents before the butterflies in her stomach burst free, along with her ice cream and cake. The front of her lovely light blue dress was ruined, a widening trail of chocolate syrup and dried sugar down the front. Jerry's nanny was sent to take her home in a cab; she turned her over to the doorman's care before she raced back to deal with her own charge.

"*Where are we?*"

Dr. Lazarus spoke, stood next to her in the elevator and held her hand. This was new. She'd been alone in the elevator that day, except for the doorman. It made her feel better to know the doctor was with her this time.

"Home," she said. "We're home."

"That's right, honey," said the doorman as he stopped the elevator and opened the gate. "Let's get you inside."

He walked her down the hall to her door, didn't seem to see Dr. Lazarus, only her. All the way down the hall Vangie heard the dogs yap, her mother's three Yorkies—Maisie, Belle, and Fernando. She heard their tiny claws scratch the inside of the door as they leaped up against it, frantic. Daddy usually made them stop when they did that. The doorman rang the bell, smiled down at Vangie while they waited. The doctor smiled at her, too.

"Somebody sure can't wait to see you," the doorman said with a grin to Vangie. They waited and waited, until he frowned and rang the bell again. The doorman looked at her with mild concern as he fumbled in his pocket for his passkey. "Now, I know they didn't go out. Guess your folks are . . ." he began, but couldn't think of a way to finish the sentence. He put his key into the lock and turned it, opened the door only a little.

"Mr. Curtis? Mrs. Curtis?"

He stuck his head in the door while the dogs ran out and raced around Vangie, leaped up and down at her feet, then ran back inside. Vangie pushed the door open and followed them. The doorman came in with her, walked in front of Vangie as if he wanted to see whatever was ahead before she did.

"Hang on, hon, just let me see what's up."

He walked down the hall, looked in the living room and dining room and checked each empty room as they progressed. The dogs lost patience, left their side, and scampered down the long hall to the bedrooms. Dr. Lazarus looked down at Vangie.

"I guess we should follow," he said.

Vangie squeezed his hand, started to remember what she was going to find there. "Don't want to."

"It's okay, Vangie. No matter what's waiting there, I'm here to help you through it." He looked into her eyes and smiled, reassuring. She relaxed, trusted him, and slowly walked the rest of the way to her parents' bedroom.

The doorman reached the bedroom first and walked in after a discreet knock. He stared in shock at what he saw, stood still long enough for Vangie to enter before he could stop her. She saw her mother on the bed, her father on the floor.

At least she thought it was her daddy.

When she got a better look, she saw that he had a mask over his head made of black leather, strapped on like a helmet. Other leather straps, some kind of harness, crisscrossed his body, and he wore tiny, black leather shorts that showed her more than she wanted to see. Vangie squeezed Dr. Lazarus's hand. She'd never seen Daddy dressed like this before. At first she thought he was asleep on the floor, except that his arms and legs twitched like he was electrified.

Vangie looked at her mother, who wore nothing but a black leather dog collar decorated with shiny metal studs. Her wrists were handcuffed to the bedposts; arms spread wide, mouth plugged by a bright red rubber ball, wet with spit, held in place by a leather strap. She twisted her bare legs, clenched her knees together and pulled them up into a fetal position to shield herself as best she could. Tears ran from her eyes as she tried to scream, to tell her daughter to look away, get out, but the ball gag muffled anything she said. The mascara and eyeliner that she'd taken such care to apply before taking Vangie to the party was smeared, ran down her flushed cheeks as she wept.

The doorman roused himself enough to grab the phone and call 911. He gave the operator the address, then turned and saw Vangie inside the room, staring at the scene. The doorman dropped the phone and reached for her.

"Shit! Hey, you don't want to be here right now! Wait outside, okay? Just . . ."

As he moved forward to turn her away, Vangie watched him slow down until he came to a complete halt halfway to her. Her mother was frozen on the bed as well, her last attempt at words cut off. Fallen tears hung in mid-air. Dr. Lazarus stepped forward and crouched down by little Vangie's side.

"Can you see this day, this moment clearly?" he said softly. *"Can you show me what it did to you?"*

Vangie stared into her mother's eyes. They still seemed to see her, even though she couldn't move a muscle. Vangie looked down and saw a cat-o'-nine-tails whip on the floor, near her father's hand. She picked it up, lifted it, slapped it down against her bare leg hard enough to score her skin, and watched a thin line appear on her mother's leg at the same time. Vangie kept whipping herself. Lines appeared on her white skin with every stroke, each matched on her mother's bare flesh, whipped herself harder and harder until they bled, faster and faster as blood flowed down their legs.

Dr. Lazarus took Vangie's hand and stopped her as she was about to lose control. He pulled the whip from her skin and aimed it at her mother's instead, used the straps to trace a long line along her mother's intact skin instead of Vangie's. She followed his lead and pulled it back, slapped it down on her mother's thigh to release lines of blood that oozed to the surface.

The doctor turned Vangie's gaze from her mother's thigh to her own. She could see that her flesh was intact, unscarred by the lashes on her mother's skin. Vangie looked from one to the other, whipped her mother a few more times to be sure that what she saw was true.

She smiled back at the doctor and they laughed as Vangie swung and swung again, punished her mother for killing her father with her sick sexual appetites, released the secret rage Vangie had carried inside for years and turned on herself. Her mother writhed in slow motion on the bed, skin flayed from muscle, unable to feel, to act to save herself.

As blood ran and their laughter rose, Vangie watched the bedroom around her dissolve back into the warm, safe womb of the doctor's office. She stopped lashing out at the shredded body, which had disappeared with her vision; her hands were empty, clean, and adult again. Only the vivid memory of that red rubber ball in her mother's mouth remained.

Vangie had never gotten that ball and the matching, wet red lips wrapped around it out of her head. When she'd started wearing lipstick, she'd worn the same shade to shame her mother daily with the memory of the night she'd killed Vangie's father. It didn't matter if her mother said that it was all her father's idea, his desires that she was fulfilling. It was sick and her daddy wasn't sick. Mommy was. She had to be. Mommy was sick and she had to pay for what she'd done to him.

Vangie had made her pay the only way she knew, but no more.

"You can survive your past, Vangie," said Dr. Lazarus as his fingers pulled her wrist closer to his cool lips. "Work with me and I'll help you find your peace. . . ."

His teeth grazed the tender skin of her inner wrist, then closed down hard. There was the slightest sweet sting as sharp fangs pierced the vein, then a delicious warmth and inner peace ran through her head and body as he fed. Vangie swooned with pleasure, felt a sense of belonging like none experienced before as she was bonded to the doctor, body and soul.

She savored the glory of his power as she felt it take control, craved it for herself as she realized what he was, that he was real. Vangie saw a miraculous new road open ahead of her as he fed, a road that rolled out to forever. Her head was clear for the first time in years, clearer than sex, drugs, or rock 'n' roll had ever made it.

Lazarus had freed her.

Vangie didn't have to hurt herself to injure her parents. It was time to skip the middleman. She'd take time to avenge her father, pass her classes while she played with her band. When her life was the best it could be, when she'd exceeded all her parents' expectations, she'd take away what they valued most and kill their darling daughter just when they were proudest of her, when everything finally seemed to be okay.

While they reeled from the tragedy, the doctor would bring her back to life. She'd take her mother and stepfather's lives one at a time, save her mother for last and make sure to enjoy killing her slowly, as much as she'd enjoyed killing her daughter a day at a time. Then would live forever young and beautiful, rich on her daddy's money, finally hers after she'd visited the family lawyer for a quick bite.

She laughed as the doctor finished his work and wiped his red lips. The ever-smiling receptionist delicately bound Vangie's wrist with a sterile white bandage and scheduled her next appointment, sent her off happy and light as a cloud as she dreamed of a better day.

She danced down the sidewalk with the red jacket from the shop window in a bag, on her way home along Tompkins Square Park to get ready for the best show of her life. Vangie didn't know why she'd ever had doubts about going to see a shrink. This had gone so much better than she ever could have dreamed.

She was definitely going to like therapy.

CHAPTER 6

8:29 P.M.—*Fort Greene, 19 July 2007*

There was something both liberating and degrading about doing your own renovation. On one hand, Steven Johnson felt a sense of power as he physically re-formed his own space with his bare hands, ripped out walls and put in new Sheetrock, plastered, painted, and changed the shapes and sizes of rooms. He had a vision, or at least enough of one to start demolition.

On the other hand, he was living like an animal in chaos and debris until he was done. Steven stood covered in Spackle dust in the middle of his latest circle of Hell, coughed, and reconsidered hiring someone to do this. He pried the lid off a new five-gallon tub of wallboard compound from Home Depot. The stores had sprouted all over New York while he was in L.A. Steven could find almost anything he needed nearby and get it delivered to Fort Greene to rebuild his home, but he was going to need more than wallboard compound, trowels, and sandpaper to reshape his new life in Brooklyn.

Steven had felt like the survivor of a train crash since his return to New York to be closer to his daughter, Joie, realizing that even with residual checks from L.A. jobs and the book still coming in, he'd never be able to survive here if he hadn't bought this building for nearly nothing twenty years ago. A cheap place to hang his hat was all that had let him survive in Brooklyn while he reoriented his life, found a new direction on the East Coast.

In the eighties he'd worried about taking on the burden of a bigger mortgage when he was offered the chance to buy out the rest of the building. The only thing that had made it possible was the surge of cash when the *Bite Marks* book was optioned for a movie. It never got made, but the studio paid big bucks every two years to re-up the option, just in case they worked out the right package to make it happen.

Even Lori had paid off her house in Park Slope by taking a crack at a screenplay. There had been almost ten in all by different writers and writing teams over the years. Steven had been hired by three different directors to work on production designs as they each searched for a "visual language" to tell the story, even if they weren't sure what story they wanted to tell.

He'd given them high Gothic, street punk, and fetish, had ran through every possible combination of looks for a vampire society, and it had all still ended up looking like *Underworld*, *Blade*, or a hundred other vampire movies.

In the end, along with fifteen years of work in L.A., the movie deal had left him comfortable, something he'd never thought he would get from a life in art. For once, he didn't shudder at the thought of old age; he saw himself selling his building for enough to live happily on his savings at the most luxurious retirement community out there, with paid companions to wipe his ass.

He went back to work on the wall again, smoothed Spackle on in broad strokes and feathered it back and forth with the broad flat tool until the edges were smooth. Wall repair was ideal work for an anal compulsive and brought out the best and worst in Steven. He stepped toward and back from the wall as he worked, to see shadows that betrayed uneven surfaces, dents, scratches, and other flaws that needed touching up.

Steven was angry that his city had turned its back on all but the landowners. He was safe and sound, unless his property taxes rose beyond his ability to pay them. Even then, he could still jack up the storefront rent or add roommates. That he was okay haunted him, as neighbors he'd known since he'd moved here disappeared when their leases ran out and rents rose. Older owners around him had sold out, tempted by inflated prices for houses bought a lifetime ago, their mortgages paid off in the seventies. He'd come home to a city of strangers, including his daughter and Lori.

An Internet station blasted vintage eighties' hits from external speakers plugged into his laptop. Grandmaster Flash's "White Lines" pounded through the room and lightened his mood despite the subject as Steven smoothed white lines of plaster. He had to laugh at how different his life was now from what it had been when the song came out, how different everything was. Back before he'd known Lori, before they had faced down the forces of Hell on the Lower East Side in the winter of 1986. Nothing, not even the last fifteen years in L.A., had changed his life as much as that one nightmare experience. He shook his head to clear it out as he reached for more Spackle.

But that was over.

The demons had been vanquished. He was in a spanking new Brooklyn that was changing faster than the Los Angeles he'd left behind. All evidence of everything that had driven him from New York fifteen years ago was long gone. As soon as he'd erased any last trace of the way the loft had looked back then, he was convinced that he could be happy here again.

A part of him knew it was childish, like a kid covering his eyes to make monsters disappear. Steven knew that erasing the way the old loft had looked wouldn't clean away everything that had happened in it back then, but pretending it did gave him some sense of control, enough to finish the work.

He cleaned off his tools and went to the bathroom to shower and change. It was almost time to head into town for his daughter's show, the first time he would see Lori since his return. They'd talked briefly by phone a few times. She hadn't sounded unhappy to hear from him when he told her he'd moved back to Brooklyn. She hadn't sounded happy, either. He would find out for sure tonight. Steven shook his head as he climbed into a hot shower and scrubbed himself clean.

His walls weren't all that needed repair.

CHAPTER 7

8:36 P.M.—*West Village, 19 July 2007*

The remaining leadership of the New York Bloodlines signed on to the online videoconference one by one, appeared in windows on the wall-mounted, seventy-two-inch flat-screen TV in Perenelle's parlor. The seconds in command and those who'd missed the meeting at the Grand Hyatt were all who remained to make decisions on how to handle the crisis.

Perenelle took a seat in front of her webcam as they assembled on the screen. She still didn't have a plan of attack. Today's meeting would have to provide a strategy by its end or they were already lost.

"I sent you all a synopsis of the events of July eighteenth. If you understand the situation, I suggest we address questions after we discuss what to do next."

"*About what?*" Claire St. Claire represented the East Village now that her Superior, Dr. Townsend Burke, was one of the missing. "*This imaginary war with humans you've hawked for years? You bore me. As always.*" She sneered with black-painted lips.

"*So what happened then? Who took our Superiors?*" Perry Dean took Perenelle's side. He was one of the New Bloods, another Wall Street broker who'd traded his skills at amassing wealth for eternal youth. His sponsor, Marianne, was one of those Perenelle had seen taken away in a sealed metal box. He still looked shaken, left to manage the Battery Park Bloodline by himself. *"Do you think they vanished on their own and she made the whole thing up?"*

"I don't know what happened!" Claire flipped him the finger, folded her arms, and scowled. *"I only know I don't trust that bitch's word about anything."* There was a chatter of angry responses from all windows. Perenelle shouted them down.

"Silence! This benefits no one!"

"Who put you in charge?" spat Claire.

"The Triumvirate. Would you like them to pay you a visit and confirm my appointment in person?"

That shut them all up, even Claire. No one was willing to take the risk of crossing them if they'd survived the attack.

"Now," said Perenelle. "We're up against a cunning and vicious enemy. We need to identify who among us informed them of the time and place of our meeting."

"One of us?" asked Perry. The thought seemed to scare him.

"Vampire or human, someone who knew about the meeting gave away its location with enough notice for the block to be sabotaged and sealed off. We need to identify an enemy capable of this," she said. "We need to know who betrayed us to do that. When we find the traitor, they'll tell us before they die screaming."

"Agreed. But one question needs be asked first, Madame de Marivaux." The speaker was Wilfred Adderly, one of the oldest of the survivors, though still two centuries younger than Perenelle. He'd been elected Superior of the Upper West Side many times since the birth of the Veil, had stepped down in the last election to give way to his New Blood protégé, Cybelline Smith, now numbered among the missing. Perenelle respected him more than she did the rest, bowed her head to give him the floor. *"How did you escape? Of all the Superiors of all the Bloodlines of New York, how is it that you alone survived to tell the tale?"*

There was a predictable rumble of mutters among the assembly. Perenelle didn't even pause. She already knew her answer. "It's clear that one among us may be a traitor. I can't tell any of you how I escaped without giving away the only advantage we have. Until we know better, anyone who didn't attend the meeting is suspect."

"What about you?" sneered Claire.

"Pardon?"

Adderly spoke up before the fight began. *"Understand, we have only your word for what happened. You can't, or won't, explain how you escaped. What assurance do we have that you yourself aren't a Judas goat sent back to lead the survivors into a trap?"*

Perenelle clenched her teeth but kept her silence. They were right. Until they found the guilty party or parties, she would have to be under suspicion. It was that or reveal more of her secrets than she dared.

"Agreed. I must prove myself as well. For this reason, all decisions to move forward will be by majority vote. I propose we make a list of Superiors who missed the meeting and humans involved with the event. We'll start with the mortals. If we eliminate them as suspects, then the list is reduced to members of our number. Agreed?"

The proposal passed. For the rest of the meeting they discussed how to conduct interrogations and make sessions available to all, gave out assignments, and set deadlines. By the end, they all had jobs and had agreed to consult the following night with progress reports. Perenelle breathed a sigh of relief as she signed off. Progress had been made.

The war had begun.

CHAPTER 8

9:12 P.M.—*Chelsea, 19 July 2007*

The neighborhood had changed big time in fifteen years.

Steven got out of the Eighth Avenue subway at Twenty-third Street and walked the long, hot blocks west to Tenth Avenue. There had been a time when the only thing that brought him anywhere near Chelsea was an early-morning meal at the Empire Diner after a night of clubbing. Now, it was a hardworking neighborhood of trendy bars and expensive restaurants, towering luxury condos and high-priced art galleries.

He walked a little slower while he dug through his jacket pockets for the brass pot pipe he'd stashed there on his way out the door. He'd quit smoking weed almost two decades ago, but had started again in Los Angeles, needing a buffer other than booze or coke between himself and the bullshit. It was easier to sit in rooms and smile at the inane comments those people made about his work if he saw them through dope goggles. Now he was using it to put a little distance between him and current reality, in case his re-union with Lori was as strained as he feared.

Steven looked around as he crossed Tenth Avenue to make sure no cops were in view, lit the bowl with the blue flame of his windproof lighter, and filled his lungs. Even as he inhaled he mentally kicked himself, knowing that smelling like pot wouldn't endear him to Lori. He held the smoke in.

Too late was too late, and if he was going to be damned for one hit, he might as well relax and have another.

A rattling old freight elevator packed with a rainbow coalition of young artists and fashion designers took Steven to the fifth floor and let them all off in a block-long white hallway, lit by glaring fluorescent bulbs overhead. He followed the pack of kids out of the car and down the length of the hall to a door labeled GALA(RY).

Gala, a delighted black woman his age in long braids and African textiles, whirled from guest to guest as they came in, greeted old favorites and introduced new faces to one another. Steven moved up in line as if meeting the queen. He shook her hand when his turn came and dutifully wrote his name and e-mail address in the guest book behind her.

The crowd was mostly black, in their twenties and thirties, wearing a range of modern styles from hip-hop traditionalist to jazzy new beat and other artsy variations of casual chic. Steven couldn't make fun; he'd taken too long to decide which face he wanted to put on for the evening.

In the end, he'd gone low key, chosen black jeans washed out to dark charcoal, a bright yellow T-shirt, a black blazer, and pricey running shoes. He wore a string of wooden prayer beads looped in strands around his right wrist, his Tibetan mala. In times of stress he pulled it off and thumbed through its 108 beads, chanting "Om mani padme hum" at each, a mantra for love and compassion. He was usually chilled out by the time he got midway, kept the beads handy like an emotional life preserver. He hadn't gotten too deep into Buddhism in L.A., had just taken what worked for him, as he'd done with everything else in life.

Tonight he went for wine instead and sipped a plastic cup of red as he looked around at the art. The large pictures on the walls were complex photo collages by an artist he'd known when he lived in New York. It was good to see artists his age still getting shows in trendy new Chelsea. Steven kicked himself for feeling old as he approached forty-eight. It was too Hollywood and he'd left that behind.

"Dad!" Joie came out of the other room, tried to hide a big grin and look blasé as she hugged him. "Glad you made it."

"Wouldn't miss it," he said. She rolled her eyes.

"God, you flew in once for a fifth-grade dance recital. It's okay to miss one show. I'm not a kid anymore."

"Don't I know it." He sighed and looked around. "Your mom here yet?"

"She's driving in. Play nice when she gets here."

"Hey, I'm always nice. . . ."

A tall, light-haired boy approached Joie with a smile. He reminded Steven of someone he couldn't quite place.

"Dad, this is Christopher, Spider's new roommate. He helped set up. My dad, Steven Johnson."

"Nice to meet you." He shook Steven's hand.

"Same here. You an artist?"

"No," said Joie. "He's here on a mission. A quest." She exchanged a look with the boy that said there was an inside joke to that. Steven still had an odd feeling that they'd met, but before he could ask any more questions, Lori appeared at the door.

"Uh, excuse me a minute," he said.

"Be nice!" Joie whispered after him.

Steven moved away from her and headed toward the front of the gallery. Lori looked around and saw the wine, then Steven, and headed for the wine. He joined her at a table.

"Got another?"

Lori turned to face him, cup in hand.

"Get your own."

"Thanks . . ." He picked up a fresh cup, threw his empty into a trash can. "Hey."

"Yeah." She stared at him, her eyes narrowed. "I swear to God, I never know whether to kiss you or kick you."

"Start soft." He leaned forward and gave her a peck on each cheek. "Sorry I haven't come by. I've been rebuilding."

"You're already a coward. Don't add liar." She said it with a straight face, but her eyes twinkled. "How long?"

"Only two years. Not since I divorced Tanya."

"Yeah . . . How is she these days?"

"Her meds seem to work," he said, tried not to crack a smile. "Don't know if the restraining order's good in New York. Hoping she can't get a gun; I think I could dodge a knife. I'm only half kidding."

"Sure can pick 'em."

"I picked you."

"I picked *you*." She poked a forefinger into his chest. "Everything after that was your fault."

"I can deal. If you can."

She started to retort, then the lights flashed.

"Saved." Lori laughed. "Showtime!"

Steven followed her into the front room, where the band was set up. As they entered and saw Joie getting ready in a corner, it felt like they were a real family for a moment.

"Ladies and gentlemen . . ." The gallery owner called the assembly to order. People moved into the front room.

The show was about to begin.

CHAPTER 9

9:32 P.M.—*Chelsea, 19 July 2007*

It was the moment of truth.

Joie sat in front of her laptop near the power strips that connected all their equipment, a third HDV camera in her hand. She grabbed a few shots of the band as they got ready. Glenn, wearing a black leather kilt and a fishnet T-shirt, tuned up his guitar in a corner. Vangie was at the microphone, doing a last-second sound check before Spider turned his attention to his keyboard. She had on high stiletto heels and the tiniest of black dresses with a tight little long-sleeved red jacket that looked new, buttoned tight at the waist. It flared out over her full hips.

Jak was at the drums, her A-shirt already wet, tattoos shiny. She tapped out riffs on the high hats to remind everyone else that she was ready and waiting. When Spider and Vangie seemed to agree on the levels, she nodded to Gala.

"Ladies and gentlemen," Gala said, as she flowed in front of the microphone. "I'm so happy to welcome you all to tonight's event, a moment of shared glory, if you will." There was loud applause from the eager crowd.

"You've been able to enjoy the art of Kass Runyan as we premiere her new exhibit tonight. We've already found homes for quite a few of the pieces, so enjoy them while you can." There was light laughter. "In honor of tonight's event, we also debut a new performance project by Vangie

Withers . . . y'all seen her work here before. I know you saw the last piece she did. The fire department still reminds me of that night every time they do an inspection . . ."

The room broke into laughter and Vangie grinned, curtsied.

"But she swears no pyrotechnics tonight, aside from the usual conceptual ones. Vangie?" The manager bowed out and turned the microphone over to her.

"Thanks, Gala. I promise not to raise your insurance rates. Tonight we're doing something new. It's a band thing I call Bitté. Or Bitter, depending on my mood."

That got too big a laugh. Vangie was getting popular downtown and was hot enough to charm even those who didn't know her. "We only have three songs, so far. If these work . . . we'll see."

Vangie nodded to Joie and she started the video, ran cartoony images of exploding stars and whirling constellations over Vangie and the rest of the band while they did a Japanese pop-style cover of Bowie's "Starman." It got a round of polite applause and they rolled into an original dance number written by Spider. Joie played sixties' beach-movie footage, Frankie and Annette in the surf cut between Betty Page bondage clips. It was a bouncy track that got Vangie's jacket off and thrown to the side. She ended the song panting, a light sheen of sweat on her perfect skin. Joie could see guys in front itching to lick it off. Vangie pulled her tiny skirt back down over damp thighs.

"Next is more of a performance piece. . . ."

This was the main event. Drums and piano started a steady beat in the background that built up to a dark rhythm. Vangie took a few deep breaths as house lights lowered, thin pin spots kept band members lit from above. Glenn started to play a familiar, repetitive riff on his guitar. The audience burst into applause, cheered as they recognized the opening notes of "Don't Fear the Reaper." Jak kicked up her drums and cymbals, as Spider brought up his organ. Vangie smiled.

"I call it 'Mommy, Please.' . . ."

Vangie and Spider started to sing together, then Vangie took over as she stepped forward. It was a smooth, melodic start; she crooned into her microphone like a Vegas lounge singer, eyes closed, while Spider hunched over the keyboard, growled into his microphone like Tom Waits.

Joie kept shooting, stopped only to click the laptop's keypad to run a montage of clips from every version of *Romeo and Juliet* she'd been able to find. Leonardo DiCaprio and Claire Danes rolled into Leonard Whiting and Olivia Hussey, all the way back to Leslie Howard and Norma Shearer. The bass organ went deeper as the song got toward the instrumental break; death scenes from *Sid and Nancy*, *Rope*, *The Honeymoon Killers*, *Bonnie and Clyde*, *Thelma and Louise*, and *Badlands* flowed over them.

"Don't fear the reaper," sang Spider.

"Baby, he's my man," sighed Vangie. "La la la la la . . ."

The guitar took over for a long, low, instrumental passage, a trickle of music that ran like an icy stream through the room. Trembling organ chords rose to follow it as the lights went off on everyone but Vangie. She pulled an iPhone from the back of her braided leather belt and made a call, switched the phone to speaker mode, and held the microphone between the phone and her mouth as the beat continued.

"Mommy?"

A woman's voice came from the phone, echoed through the room over the speakers. *"Yes . . . yes, dear. What is it?"*

"Mommy, it's Vangie," she said, her voice a little girl's.

"Yes. I know."

"You said you'd come to the show tonight." The room was silent except for the drum and guitar, low in the background.

"Vangie . . ."

"Where are you?"

"I don't know why you do this."

"You said you'd come."

"I said we'd try, but we can't."

"Mommy, please." Vangie sank to the floor, knelt with her head down, face in shadow.

"Your father won't come, Vangie. There's nothing I can do." The voice was flat and cold; fell from the speakers into the air like ice.

"You promised!"

"Not after that last show. Not after what you did. My God . . ."

Vangie started to rock back and forth.

"Mommy, please."

"It was in the papers. On the news! You call that art?"

"You promised!" Vangie lay the iPhone and microphone on the floor next to each other, untied her belt from her waist, her face down. She whipped the belt out and down on the ground in front of her, hard. The braided straps broke free to reveal that it wasn't a belt but a cat-o'-nine-tails whip.

The crowd gasped.

"*What is that? Dammit, Vangie, why do you do this?*"

"Mommy, please . . ." Vangie slowly began to whip her bare back with the cat-o'-nine-tails.

"*You're on stage now, aren't you?*"

"You promised!" The strikes came faster, harder.

"*Why do you play these sick games with us?*"

"Mommy, please . . ."

"*How dare you make me part of your sick show?*"

"You promised!" Vangie's voice got louder, more desperate, as the whipping intensified. Red stripes appeared on her pale skin. Joie was a little scared, even though she'd helped stage it. There was a long silence from Vangie's mother while the music built and Vangie whipped herself, faster and faster. Images of mothers from *Mommie Dearest, Gypsy, Psycho,* and both versions of *The Manchurian Candidate* flashed by while REAL? and TRUE? flashed over the clips.

"*You little bitch.*" The voice didn't sound angry anymore. It sounded resigned.

"Mommy, please!"

REAL? flashed on the screen.

"*You're sick, Evangelyne.*"

TRUE? flashed on the screen. The cycle continued.

"You promised!" Vangie started to weep.

"*You're just sick to do this. I can't help you.*"

The phone disconnected with a click.

"Mommy, please!" Vangie kept talking over the dial tone as the music rose, rhythm built. "You promised! Mommy, please. You promised! Mommy, please! You promised!"

She'd started out Marilyn Monroe–breathless, childlike, but as the cat-o'-nine-tails flew faster she cried out louder, chanted the words over and over like a prayer as the music hit maximum and cut to silence.

Thin lines of blood crisscrossed Vangie's back as she dropped the whip. Spider sang into his mike, low and husky. Vangie whispered the last lyrics into the microphone, rose from the floor to her feet, whipped back her hair, and leaned over Spider as they screamed together.

She stood upright, frozen for a moment as if she saw someone out beyond the crowd, the specter of death, her demon lover. Spider's words broke the spell and brought Vangie back.

"Saying don't be afraid . . ."

She shrieked out the rest of the stanza, and at the last line she put the microphone back in the stand and reached behind her. Vangie pulled two open straight razors from behind her and raised them overhead, gleaming. Joie switched on red strobes and the blades flashed like lightning. Vangie swung them down one at a time to slash each wrist.

Blood poured down her bare arms as she dropped the razors and gripped the microphone stand, slid down to her knees, and shrieked the last line of the song, "Don't fear the reaper," repeated it as the flashing red strobe slowed to a stop in darkness.

There were nervous stirrings and murmurs in the quiet dark as the audience wondered what they'd just seen. Joie shivered. She'd never seen Vangie so convincing. Even knowing what was coming, the wrist slashing had scared her for the first time. She wondered for a moment if everything had gone right, if she'd seen an act or the real thing, if Vangie had finally gone too far on stage.

Then she turned on the lights.

The crowd went wild with applause when they saw Vangie on her feet, alive and well, now sure that the bloodletting had been faked. She laughed and bowed as the crowd went wilder than ever. Joie watched, impressed. She'd seen real star power in Vangie tonight, believed for the first time that she might actually have the talent to make this thing work.

Vangie shook hands as the fans gathered around to see how the razors pumped blood from the handles and apologized for stains. Joie started unplugging and rolling up cords and cables so they could be wrapped out by the time Gala was ready to leave. Spider's dance remix of the last song played overhead as he handed out sample CDs to the crowd.

"Need help getting stuff home?"

Christopher loomed over Joie, one of the cameras and tripod in her hand. She looked up at him and half grinned. "That's either really generous or the slickest line I've ever heard."

"Either way, you get your stuff home."

She sighed. He really did have the most ridiculously perfect smile she'd ever seen.

"Let's find my mom and her car."

CHAPTER 10

Questioning had begun by the time Perenelle arrived at Perry Dean's penthouse overlooking the newly begun Freedom Tower construction site. Their suspect was bound on his back to the long dining-room table, shirt ripped open to expose his bare white throat. His skin was pale; spilled blood trailed down his neck from twin punctures, and a small puddle pooled under his head. He was ready and willing, newly re-enthralled by their host, their control reinforced by fresh infection.

The man was the caterer for their evening at the Grand Hyatt, had hired most of the staff and provided willing victims for feeding, handled all dealings with the hotel. If anyone had had contact with a human traitor, it was he.

Perenelle leaned close to his ear, spoke softly.

"*Bonjour,* Monsieur DuMaurier. Do you remember me?"

"*Oui,* Madame de Marivaux."

"There is not a mortal who worked for us that night you did not hire, *c'est vrai?*"

"*Oui, madame.* True. I vouch for them all. None would dare betray us. All were enthralled or . . ."

"Or? What?"

A tear worked its way up from under his lower eyelid, trembled on the edge as he strained to hold it back. Perenelle reached out a fingernail, touched the glistening sphere with a razor-sharp tip, and released it to run down his cheek.

"I see. Someone you trusted. A bond stronger than ours." She shook her head. "So stupid of us. So obvious."

"Please, madame. You must understand. . . ."

"*Je comprends*, DuMaurier. We are not without feeling. I know the strength of family, how often love can lead us to make foolish choices. Your son? Daughter?"

He wept despite their power over him.

"My son. *Mon Dieu*, my son Xavier . . ."

"Of course. He returned home after a long absence, ready to join you in your work. All was forgiven. You were so proud."

"Please, no . . ."

"It's our own fault for not reinforcing your loyalty before the event. We've grown careless. Complacent. We won't repeat that mistake."

"Mistress, mercy . . . I would die for you."

Perenelle leaned down and kissed his lips.

"*Oui. Vous mourrez.* After you give him to us."

She bit deep into his throat and drank the first blood she'd drawn in decades, fed on his life energy as her mind joined with his, forced him to scream out his son's address, phone numbers, how they could find him, when and where, pulled it out of his mind like family pictures from an old scrapbook. Perenelle saw it all as clearly as if she'd been there herself, then took the rest of his life, fed as if she'd never fed before and drained him almost dry.

She stood up, intoxicated; blood stained the corners of her mouth. Her skin was flushed with heat, her eyes lit from within with the traitor's life.

"Bring me the son."

DuMaurier's body was carried out for disposal while she gave the others their instructions. They flew to do her bidding as Perenelle retired to a nearby lounge to absorb the rush of human sensations running through her after the feeding. She let her mind wander over the range of possibilities ahead.

The son was only the first step. He would lead them to the next level of the conspiracy, which would lead them to the next, and the next if need be, until they had its leader by the throat. It wouldn't take long to identify their enemy. They had at least one advantage when it came to interrogation. She smiled.

It would not be as easy for the humans to get answers.

Over the last two decades, Jonathan Richmond had become something of an expert on the subject of vampires. He'd never dispatched one personally; that wasn't his job. He was an administrator, the idea man who kept the company together and moving forward. He knew his business, understood the enemy they fought, but when it came to extermination or enhanced interrogation, he left the nuts and bolts to those with expertise in those areas. He was concerned only with results.

That didn't mean he took no interest in procedure.

He was on his way to the interrogation wing. Richmond almost never went into the field but often attended in-house operations. The rehabilitation of Nicolas de Marivaux was a pet project, but he also found himself drawn to the debriefing rooms when the latest subjects were being questioned. Seeing what it took to break the immortals strengthened his resolve and reminded him how much force was needed to defeat the enemy.

These were not ordinary terrorists. Methods employed to break them were more sophisticated than any used on humans and had to engage both their minds and bodies. The vampires' own extraordinary physiology provided innovative methods that would be useless against humans. Today's technique was one of their more successful.

Richmond entered the darkened viewing room, masked from the interrogation chamber by blast-proof one-way glass. He stepped close to the window to take a look inside the chamber.

The subject stood chained, spread-eagled, her arms pulled out tight on either side, with remote sensors glued strategically to her skin. She looked like a young woman, with shoulder-length, straight black hair, her complexion golden brown, violet eyes large and cold. There was no anger there, only contempt.

She had been stripped bare for the procedure. Her nudity was utilitarian. Richmond took no pleasure in it, though it enhanced their dominance over the subject and established who was in charge from the start.

The vampire's smoky brown body was athletic, lean but solid, breasts small and tight, hips round and hard. Richmond preferred his women softer, with more flesh on their bones; Marilyn Monroe was more his type. As he watched, the vampire's body changed shape, filled out.

Her breasts grew, skin and hair lightened to take her from an exotic Indonesian waif into a full-figured all-American fifties' bombshell. Richmond backed away from the glass, shuddered. Even with the telepathic dampeners in the chamber on full to keep vampire subjects from mesmerizing them, she'd picked up his desires, transformed her flesh to match them, a standard vampire lure.

She looked like she was in her midtwenties, though who knew her real age. With a combination of vampiric suggestion and chameleon like control of their physical bodies, they could look like almost anything or anyone. Richmond had seen captured vampires over a hundred years old that looked like children, their births and identities confirmed with carbon-dated records and DNA testing.

The subject stood on her feet in the center of a spherical room lined with alternating lights, fluorescent and ultraviolet bulbs. Only the fluorescents were on now. The vampire glared at the one-way glass with a seductive sneer on her new face. The vampires had senses beyond the human range. She knew he was there. For all Richmond knew, she could see right through the mirrors. Let her look. All she'd see was the strength of his conviction.

The interrogation team entered, a man and a woman dressed in white, like clinicians, as Richmond felt they should be. This was nothing more than a surgical procedure to extract information.

"Sir. Lead Interrogator Munder, my technician, Dr. Geist. With your permission." She bowed stiffly. Munder, in her late twenties, with short, dark hair and horn-rimmed glasses, addressed Richmond with respect. She seemed a little nervous, though he suspected that she was affecting it as emotional camouflage to make people underestimate her on first meeting. He never made that mistake with anyone.

Richmond had met her only once before, when she started here a year ago, recruited after several years of exemplary service in Guantanamo Bay. No one had ever released photos or videos of her treatment of prisoners, or information on how she got more effective intelligence than most, though there were those who tried. They'd failed. Her team had been handpicked to make sure of that. She'd designed today's enhanced interrogation system during her application process, a coup that put her above all other candidates and won her the job of running it.

Richmond nodded with a smile to relax her.

"Just observing, Interrogator. Go about your business."

She sat down at the front table and the doctor sat next to her with a wireless keyboard and mouse. Lead Interrogator Munder looked over a list of questions listed on a touch screen pad in front of her, then nodded to the doctor. She dropped the docile role of respectful employee she'd adopted with Richmond. Her face took on the impassive hard lines of a trained professional about to do a difficult job, one she knew well.

"Let's begin."

Munder pressed a button to activate speakers in the chamber and spoke into a microphone in front of her. "You are the vampire known as Superior Cybelline Smith?"

The vampire lifted her head and gazed at the glass as if she could smash it with a look. There was no reply. Munder turned to the doctor and nodded. "Demonstration mode."

Dr. Geist typed a setting on the keyboard in front of him, pushed Enter, and the ultraviolet lights pulsed on and off. The vampire shrieked in pain as searing artificial sunlight hit her skin. A puff of smoke rose from her body as an outer layer was burned off and her hair sparked. When the lights went off, she reverted to her original appearance. Richmond assumed it was her real one.

Munder leaned closer to her microphone.

"Each time you don't answer, we raise the intensity and duration of the ultraviolet lights. We continue to do so with each inquiry until the question is answered. Do you understand our terms?"

The vampire nodded.

"Are you the vampire known as Superior Cybelline Smith of the Upper West Side Bloodline?"

She glared, but answered, slowly.

"*Yes.*"

"Do you know why you're here?"

"*The usual? From your methods, I assume you know what I am and want to know more about us.*"

"That would be?"

"*Our numbers, our organization. Do we mean you harm . . .*" She laughed at that. "*Anything else you could tell by vivisection or autopsy, yes?*"

"You are ruled by the Veil?"

"*Know that, do you? Then you know I can't say. It is our one law.*"

Munder nodded, and the doctor clicked his trackpad.

The chamber lights flashed, brighter and longer by a measured increment. Cybelline screamed as her body convulsed. When the lights faded down, her hair had been burned shorter, her eyebrows were gone, and her skin was scorched.

"Tell us about the Veil."

She said nothing, clenched her jaw and closed her eyes. Munder nodded. The doctor did his job. Cybelline lost her eyelids and stayed silent as her head was stripped bald, skin burned raw, cheeks worn away to expose her teeth in a death's-head grin as she twisted in the chains, flesh tattered.

Her eyes were gone, but what was left of the vampire's features still faced them in defiance. Richmond sighed. It ended this way too often. Whether the penalty for telling was worse than death, or whether it came from a loyalty he could only envy, too few of the vampires had been persuaded to give them anything but the most limited intelligence.

Richmond gestured for the lead interrogator to end it.

Smith couldn't tell them anything now, even if she'd wanted to, with no tongue to speak with, no ears to hear questions. The observation window darkened to protect them as the doctor followed Munder's orders and raised the ultraviolet light to full, ten times the equivalent of high noon on a sunny day in Central Park.

The vampire's body absorbed as much as it could, then ignited, burst into bright white light and burned to a fine ash that settled to the floor of the chamber. Disposal was never an issue when dealing with vampires.

Vents opened and blowers raised the dust to be sucked into secure containers for safe disposal after deeper analysis. Everything taught them something. Today Richmond had learned that he needed a new approach. If they couldn't persuade the imprisoned vampires to tell them what they needed to know with torture, they had to find a willing Judas.

What he needed was the right vampire at the right price for betrayal. If Clean Slate could use one of the Veil's servants to capture a sizable gathering of vampires, he could use one of their own to get them all. He knew just where to start looking.

The Sheep Meadow Station library.

Rescued from the ruins of the secret Sheep Meadow Station, over a thousand years of Rahman's journals found with his scientific and alchemical studies would contain something Richmond could use, a chronicle of some old vampire enmity or other rivalries between the immortals. He'd find someone in their ranks he could turn against them. If Jesus had a Judas, then so could the Devil.

Richmond headed for the research wing and called ahead on his iPhone with a chuckle. He knew they wouldn't be happy to hear from him, no matter how interesting the project was.

They were about to have a long night ahead of them.

CHAPTER 11

Traffic was light crossing the Manhattan Bridge.

The boys had helped Joie lug her video equipment down to the car, then piled into the backseat while she drove them and her mom back to Park Slope. After they helped her unload, Joie talked Lori into letting her drive them home. She found parking near their apartment and they walked down the block from the building to a late-night café for decaf latte.

The place was small and already packed with young people like them, making an end to the night or powering up for more party ahead. They managed to find a spot near the counter to stand while they ordered, took over a table as soon as it was vacated. Christopher bought another round as they settled in while he tried to make sense of the show.

"So that wasn't Vangie's real mother on the phone?"

"Like she'd answer for her!" said Joie. "Vangie's mom has said every line in the show. It's all true, even if it's really a Guild-minimum actress with a script saying it on the phone."

"'Real or True.' Got it. And you're the tech wizard who pulls it all to-gether."

"Yeah, a regular Mindfreak. Vangie gets enough from her trust and grants to pay my bills."

"I thought you lived at home?"

"That only saves rent. Mom can't afford NYU, all her money goes to the house. I have loans, want them low as possible."

"Makes sense." He leaned forward. "Could I kiss you?"

"What?" The question popped up out of nowhere.

"I just . . . I don't know. It seems so inevitable."

The weird thing was that Joie agreed. Her lips were on his before she knew what she was doing. It was like she'd been waiting for him to ask all night. His mouth was smooth, soft for a boy, but firm, and he applied just the right amount of pressure and moisture for what could very well be the best kiss of her life.

When they pulled apart she was a little breathless, like the kiss had lasted longer than she'd expected and she'd held her breath too long for it.

"Huh," she said.

"Yeah . . . I was going for 'wow.'" He smiled at her with that stupidly perfect lopsided grin that she knew had probably melted every heart from here to Connecticut.

"No, I . . ." Joie started to explain, not sure what to say. What she thought was, *I know that kiss. I know you.* She could still feel his warm lips on hers, as if they'd never left. It was nothing she could put into words without feeling naked. "It was fine."

"Damn!" Spider laughed. "Why don't you just cut 'em off while you at it!" She kicked him under the table.

"I've got to get the car home. See you?"

"Yeah. Call me."

"Punch in your number."

She handed him her cell phone as she stood, took it back after he'd entered his number, and pushed Send. His phone rang and she saw her number pop up on his screen as he opened it. "Now you have mine."

Joie waved, out the door before they could offer to walk her back to the car. Christopher looked around as if in the wake of a tornado.

"She always like that?" he asked.

"Not totally sure what you mean, but, yeah." Spider laughed. "Always." He laughed harder.

Christopher sipped his decaf cappuccino, still tasted Joie's lips on his.

He definitely wanted to see her again. There was something about her that attracted him more than any girl he'd ever met. Like it was more than a coincidence that they'd met tonight.

Like it was destiny.

CHAPTER 12

There was nothing like looking into a bathroom mirror at one in the morning after an evening spent staring at the young to make you feel old. Steven winced as he faced down his ragged reflection, tried to convince himself it was the harsh lighting and late hour that made him look as obsolete as he felt. He brushed his teeth and made a resolution to go straight to bed in the future after nights like this to avoid self-confrontation until after a good night's beauty sleep.

Of course, Lori had looked great.

She'd hit the peak they say women reach after forty, looked better than ever, her girlish good looks filled out with maturity into a more alluring, sensual woman. He felt his cock harden just remembering her. What was it about them and galleries? All he had to do was picture Lori standing in one to get a boner. He wondered if he'd looked as clumsy as he'd felt while they talked, like a high school nerd asking out the prom queen.

Steven flexed his arms, checked out his abs in the mirror, sucked in the inch he couldn't quite burn off anymore. His work on the loft was helping to reshape his body along with his home. By the time he was done, maybe they'd both be more presentable as he dove back into the dating market.

Was that the only reason he felt so drawn to Lori, because it was easier to reclaim an old love than to risk exploring new territory? Why should that scare him? He was a single, straight black man in New York, still under fifty, with an Oscar nomination, two Emmys, and a paid-off mortgage on his own building in Brooklyn. That should count for something, right? He didn't have to settle or apologize. He was a catch, dammit.

Steven relaxed his belly, scratched it as he ambled back to the bedroom, tried not to admit it was himself he really wanted to convince. He lay on his mattress in the dark and looked out the window at the park. Then there was Joie. Conceived during Steven and Lori's last lay, the night they'd officially said goodbye. They'd had one final fling in the same gallery back room they'd screwed in the first night they'd met. His baby girl had grown into a young woman without him. The child he knew in New York and from her occasional visits to California was a total stranger to him now, working, making art, and meeting boys. . . . What was that kid's name? Christopher?

He reminded him of someone, but a face he hadn't seen in years. Steven had sometimes wondered if familiar young faces on the street were the kids of friends he'd known in high school or college. Could Christopher be the son of someone he'd known, or grown up with? Anything was possible, stranger things had been known to . . . He stopped, sat up, and put down his beer as his heart raced. He knew exactly who the kid looked like.

Jim Miller.

Nina's big brother, her vampire son's uncle: the baby cured by Rahman's alchemy. The one they had turned over to the city twenty years ago to put up for adoption. Baby Christopher. Shit. He picked up the phone and called Lori despite the time.

"Steven?" She sounded drowsy, not surprising considering the hour.

"Yeah, it's me. Who's this Christopher kid?"

"You call me at one in the morning for this? Christ, Steven, you're in no position to tell Joie who she can and can't—"

"Stop. His name's Christopher. He looks about twenty and she told me he just moved here, that he's on a quest."

"Fuck." She caught on immediately, a big reason why he'd always loved her. "A quest? Like looking for his long-lost parents? Shit, Steven. How is that possible?"

"You know New York's not that big, especially downtown. Maybe they were pulled together, I don't know, connected by what happened that night."

"To him?"

"To him? To all of us! Sheep Meadow burst into bloom in the middle of the worst blizzard in New York history, and we were at ground zero of whatever did it. You had a baby after that you couldn't have before. Did you think Joie was a coincidence?"

"I tried not to think about it—not after I saw she was okay and didn't glow in the dark or anything weird. . . . Oh, God, Steven, if it is him, what does this mean? Christ, she just drove him back to the city. What do we do? Fuck! I can't deal with this now!"

"What do you mean, now?"

She didn't answer him.

"Tomorrow morning," she said. "Here. We'll go over everything." She hung up. Steven put down the phone, wondered what she'd meant by "everything," but let it go and went to bed.

He'd find out in the morning.

CHAPTER 13

2:39 A.M.—*East Village, 20 July 2007*

So the butler had done it after all.

Claire St. Claire read through Perenelle's mailing to the Bloodlines detailing results of the Veil's interrogation of their caterer whose son had friends with an interesting hobby.

Vampire hunting.

She sat in Burke's big leather chair in his wood-paneled home office, with a muscular local teenager curled naked under her bare feet, waiting for her to feed again. The library, as Burke had called the room before his abduction, was lined with his books, medical and otherworldly, his two major interests of study. Burke had pursued a cure for their "condition," as he called it, long after they'd lost any interest in finding it. The search had become a kind of hobby, like stamp collecting, something he played with in his spare time when he wasn't handling the menial affairs of the East Village Bloodline.

Burke took it all so seriously, that and her reeducation. She still looked barely sixteen, the age she'd been when Tom O'Bedlam had found her in 1920s Berlin, working as a professional virgin in a whorehouse, and given her the means to escape. She'd followed him for more than a decade before his last mad scheme had gotten them both punished by the Veil, newly formed just to deal with their crimes.

It had been such a silly thing, really. Tom had only wanted to enthrall the leaders of New York City in politics and law enforcement, anyone who could stop them from having their way with the citizenry. He'd created a cadre of fresh vampires in Germany, young Nazis bored with the slow progress of the new reich. It wasn't strong enough in 1937; they wanted more power, faster. Tom was happy to oblige them.

It all would have gone smoothly except that they'd run into Perenelle de Marivaux on the Hindenburg as she was heading home from Tibet after washing away her sins. She'd arranged a reception for them by radio-telegram to Burke. It was really Perenelle's fault that Claire had been forced to blow up their ride as it landed, so that she and Tom could escape, one of her earliest efforts in large-scale pyrotechnics.

Led by Perenelle, Burke had been one of those who'd championed the formation of the Veil and the new Triumvirate's verdict of entombment against her and Tom after they were caught. She was to be sealed away for fifty years, but he'd be entombed forever, solitary and starving.

It took most of Claire's sentence for Burke to feel enough remorse to arrange for her early release into his custody—in 1986, only a year before Claire would have been freed from her iron vault anyway. It had been hard to feel much gratitude.

In the beginning she'd roamed the East Village streets at night like something out of her beloved movie *Nosferatu*, as she lured children from their rooms at night and seduced young men or women into alleys to feed on them. Burke finally tired of covering up her crimes to placate the Veil, imprisoned Claire in his home, and found ways to punish her. He'd trained her like a dog, rewarded obedience and punished bad behavior until he could trust her to act like a civilized human being, even if she'd never actually become one.

She'd had to accompany him on his rounds, as he called them, watch him settle disputes or cover up crimes beyond the norm, both frequent in the East Village. The neighborhood had grown and changed in the last decade, high-rises had sprung up around them like giant redwoods to claim seniority over smaller, older buildings below.

The flood of new tenants smelled like fresh prey to the Old Bloods in the East Village Bloodline. Burke had to remind them that the drug-addled slum that had provided easy hunting had changed. Police presence had increased to keep affluent newcomers safe enough to sell more real estate to Euro-rich immigrants or wealthy escapees from the Twin Towers area.

Vampires had to be more discreet these days, a term seldom applied to those who'd made the East Village their home in the sixties and seventies, mortal or immortal. The vampires who had moved there had blended in with the Goth and punk crowds that had filled the streets until dawn. Now they stood out like aging, overdressed rock stars in the swarm of suburban hipsters that had poured into the area of late as New York University expanded to consume it.

Claire had enjoyed the change, adopted the styles of the new kids, looked their age, and had easily been accepted. She'd learned her lessons well from the good Dr. Burke, made sure not to do anything that would endanger their secret. She'd learned to contain her baser instincts to keep Burke happy while she looked for her Tom. He was out there somewhere, locked up as she had been, dreaming the dreams of the damned. Perenelle and the others had sentenced him to eternal entombment, but even vampires knew that forever was relative.

Now that Burke was gone, Claire was in charge of the East Village Bloodline and all his holdings, and she was free. Claire gave the naked boy under the desk a little kick to wake him up for another nibble. No more surveillance, no more supervision, no one to stop her. Free to do as she pleased. Free to search in earnest for Tom's burial chamber, free to release the one great true love of her life from entombment, that and more . . .

Finally free to punish Perenelle for putting him there.

CHAPTER 14

10:00 A.M.—*Park Slope, 20 July 2007*

The doorbell rang at ten sharp.

Lori was barely up, not even through her first cup of tea. She was still in her ragged white terry-cloth robe, had been up late like most nights, wrestling with the damn book she'd worked on for the last year. Steven used to be a night person, too, had slowly dragged his ass into the day by her side while they poured down enough caffeine to talk to each other by afternoon. Fifteen years in Los Angeles had reset his clock, made him relentlessly energetic way too early. It was only one of many bad habits he'd picked up out there that annoyed her. His ex-wife Tanya was another.

Steven had two paper bags of groceries in his arms when Lori opened the door. A part of her wanted to feel insulted, but the smart half wanted to eat. She let him in with a grimace. "You've been talking to our daughter."

"Bullshit." Steven laughed as he handed her one of the bags and went to the kitchen, started unloading. "Just known you too long. Never nuttin' in yo fridge but batteries and beer." He opened the refrigerator door with a flourish as he nodded at its barren depths. "Not even batteries!"

Lori pulled a half-empty carton of milk out of the sparsely populated refrigerator, made a fresh cup of tea while Steven put away what he didn't need immediately. He pulled out a frying pan and put it on the stove as Lori sat at the counter on the other side of the island.

"Where's Joie?" he asked.

"Returning video equipment, out for hours. So you think Joie's Christopher is our Christopher?" asked Lori as she dived into the biggest topic of the day. "From twenty years ago?"

"Enough to want to be sure."

Steven pulled a mixing bowl down from the cabinet, pulled a whisk from a drawer, found everything as easily if he'd been there yesterday instead of two years ago. While they talked, he chopped mushrooms, scallions, onions, garlic, and other ingredients for an omelet, tossed them into the pan to sear as he whipped eggs to foam, then flung the froth on top of the sizzling vegetables.

"And if he is? What then?"

"We worry about that then, after we find out more about him. Where he's been, but more important . . ."

"What he is?" She'd worried since Steven had called that their daughter might be dating an ex-vampire. Lori had pushed most of the events of the winter of 1986 from her mind, but the image of the glowing vampire baby, possessed by Rahman, stayed stuck in her dreams.

The sight of the undead infant floating above them in Central Park, powered by Rahman's alchemic elixir and charged with more than a hundred lives, ready to kill them until the sun rose and transformed Christopher back into a human baby . . . How ex a vampire was he, really? She sipped her tea and tried not to fret, almost laughed. Fret? You fretted about your daughter's dress for the prom. There was no word for this.

She tried not to scream instead.

"He's either human or he's not," said Steven. "If not, we need to know what we're dealing with and how to deal with it."

"Perenelle?"

"She's the only one who knew Rahman and what he did to cure the baby. She knows more than we do, whatever it is." He folded the omelet, cut it in half, and split it between two plates. Rahman, the thousand-year-old Moorish vampire who'd killed and revived Perenelle more than five hundred years ago, had witnessed the birth of alchemy and mastered it over his lifetime with help from Perenelle's late husband, Nicolas. Perenelle had told them that much after Rahman was gone, but not enough to help them now. "She said she'd keep an eye on the baby."

"You think she knows he's back?"

"Only one way to find out." Steven handed her a fork.

Lori shuddered. They hadn't seen Perenelle de Marivaux in twenty years. The idea that the vampire probably hadn't aged in all that time was a little freaky. "You think she's still in the West Village?"

"Why would she move? New Yorkers never give up a place, even if they live forever. . . ." That gave them a laugh, at least. "I'll go online and track her down."

They ate in silence for a few minutes. Steven knew enough to let Lori bring up anything else she wanted to tell him. When they were done eating, Lori took the plates and forks from the table to the sink and washed them. Somewhere in the middle of that he heard her say something under the running water.

"What?"

She turned off the faucet, but kept her back to him.

"I have cancer."

Steven tried to rearrange his face to look like he'd taken the news well, but knew he hadn't. All he could think was, *Ohmigodohmigodohmigod*, but what he said was, "What kind?"

"Ovarian. I think there's some kind of cosmic irony there, but it escapes me at the moment. Like limiting them to one miracle baby pissed them off."

"Any prognosis?"

"Bad. Still working on it, but we started a little late. I'm looking at surgery and chemo. At best. Soon."

Steven had to give the universe credit for timing.

She'd broken the news just when he'd started to feel there was some tiny, infinitesimally slim chance that they could get back together someday in the future. Now she might have no future, with or without him. He'd be tempted to laugh if he didn't want to hit someone, or curse the heavens. Instead, he stood up and wrapped his arms around her from behind.

"I'm back for good. Anything you need . . ."

Lori turned around before he could finish and held him tight, shook as she wept, probably for the first time since she'd gotten the news. They stood at the sink for what seemed like years, while he let her cry herself out. Steven stroked her hair and said nothing, held back his own grief and fears. There was time for that later.

For now, he had to be here for Lori.

CHAPTER 15

2:26 P.M.—*Lower East Side, 20 July 2007*

"Why can't you just tell me what this is about?"

Joie was hot and tired, complained as Spider pulled her inside the building and up the stairs to his floor. The weather had gone humid again overnight, and everything Joie wore seemed to stick to every square inch of her flesh. All she wanted to do was strip to her panties, lie under a fan, and drink a tall glass of iced tea, hold the icy glass against her jugular to chill the hot blood pouring into her brain until she cooled down and could think again.

"I can't, I have to show you!" said Spider. "You have to see this shit to believe it. I need you to test it."

"Test what?"

Spider pulled her onto his landing and through the open door of the apartment. The living room was filled with his usual mess of electronic equipment, music magazines, and free downtown newspapers piled everywhere. Christopher was already inside, seated on the couch under the window, the coffee table in front of him piled with the remains of a take-out Chinese dinner. The windowsill was lined with withered potted plants, all dead from neglect. Christopher grinned up at Joie; she scowled back. He looked taken aback for a second, as if no one had ever looked at him in anger before.

"Are you in on this crap fest?"

"Innocent. No idea what he's up to," said Christopher.

"Yo, check it," said Spider and pushed the space bar on his computer keyboard. He had twin flat-screen monitors on the table in front of him, set up for video editing. "This is footage from the other night."

Joie stepped closer to the screens.

The same image filled both. It wasn't performance footage of the band but raw footage of Christopher and Joie breaking down the show. At Vangie's request, the cameras had been left running to catch some of the postshow reactions. When they were over, Christopher and Joie had taken the equipment down together, one holding the cameras while the other unscrewed the mounts.

As they walked to the first camera, Joie watched them both go out of focus. At first she thought it was that the automatic focus had just shifted when they walked in front of the lens, but there was something wrong. She knew the editing program Spider was using. Without thinking, she reached out and rewound the footage, played it again at a slower speed.

She saw what it was that had bothered her. The only thing that changed focus in the frame was them. Everything else stayed the same. It couldn't be the lens.

"That doesn't make sense," she said.

"Duh, Einstein! I said you had to see it to believe it. Lookie. I cut it together from each camera. . . ." He played a montage of shots from the other two static cameras that showed the same thing. The closer Joie and Christopher got, the more out of focus they were. As soon as they moved away from each other, they went back to normal. There wasn't much footage but it was enough to send a chill down Joie's spine.

"What is that?"

"I want to see if it happens again here. I already got the camera set up." He jumped up and turned a video camera on a tripod behind him in their direction, picked up a remote control, and turned on a flat-screen TV mounted on the wall, surrounded by audio equipment. The room appeared on the screen as the camera swung from her face to Christopher on the couch. Spider locked down the tripod head. Joie had a sudden, dangerous thought and started hitting Spider with her bag.

"You shithead! Is this some fucked-up way to trick me into some sick

Internet porn scam? Did you fucking photoshop those blurred frames? What did you use? After Effects?"

"No! I fucking swear, Joie! Chris, man!"

Christopher had been taken off guard, laughed too hard to stop her. "Joie, wait, he's not lying. I don't know what's going on, but it's not that."

Joie stopped, looked at the boys with suspicion as she pushed back her hair and adjusted her glasses.

"Just go sit on the couch next to him," said Spider. He focused the camera on Christopher, left room in the shot for her next to him. She glared at Spider, but walked across the room, sat on the far end of the couch, and looked at the TV.

"Nothing."

"Get closer." Spider looked at the camera's screen, then up at her as she glared back, still suspicious. "Don't give me that. I swear to God, you got to get close for it to happen."

Joie sighed. She bounced a foot closer to Christopher and looked at the screen. The focus did look a little softer, but the couch fabric was still sharp. Christopher slid closer. There was a definite change. Spider's jaw dropped.

"Shit, man," he said. "Closer."

Joie was almost afraid to, but as she and Christopher moved closer, she could see their image on the TV get fuzzier until they formed one big, amorphous, blurred blob in the middle of the screen on a couch that was otherwise in perfect focus. She flung herself away from him, suddenly afraid her body would merge with his in reality as it seemed to on the screen.

"It's okay," Christopher said. "Try again."

They moved closer together, then farther apart, and watched the results on the TV screen. It was always the same. The farther they were from each other, the clearer the image. The closer they got, the more they blurred into one unrecognizable mass.

They watched the effect live, then examined the tape playback together, but couldn't explain it. When they substituted Spider for either one of them, there was no reaction at all; both stayed in focus no matter how close Spider got, even when Joie had to kick him in the nuts to get him off her.

"I want to try one last thing," said Spider. "Sit close, but, like, I dunno, concentrate on each other or something. Anything to ramp it up."

"We are not making out," said Joie.

"Christ, lose that, will you?" Spider pouted, dropped his hip-hop affectation. "Just stare into each other's eyes. Hold hands and wish for Never Never Land. Try anything. This could be big, like *Paranormal State* big. We could get a fucking reality show on MTV out of this shit."

"God, Spider. If this is really one of those stupid hidden-camera shows, I will fucking kill you," she said, and turned to face Christopher. "Now what?"

"I don't know, mind meld or something," said Spider.

Joie giggled, felt silly as she took Christopher's hands. They both looked at the TV and saw that they were out of focus again. She looked back into his eyes. That wasn't hard to do: they were damned pretty, liquid pools of blue light. She shook her head, got back on track.

"Okay. We'll try to read each other's minds. . . ."

They stared at each other. Joie felt her palms moisten, her heart beat a little faster, but that had happened holding a boy's hand before. She tried to let go of her thoughts and concentrate only on Christopher. The room seemed to fade around them until all she could see was him. She heard Spider speak, but he sounded far away.

"Shit . . ."

"What?" Joie said. Her voice sounded thin, too, even to herself, as if they were under water.

"Nothing," Spider answered. "Watch the tape later."

The TV wall looked bright in her side view, brighter by the second. Joie didn't look away, still stared into Christopher's eyes, but wasn't even seeing him anymore. She'd left the room behind, fallen into a kind of waking dream.

She was on her back as a young woman looked down at her, smiled, and lifted her up into the air. The woman vanished as the image faded, slid into another view of her in attack, teeth sharp, face distorted with hunger. Joie's vision faded into abandoned downtown buildings, crumbling walls, other hungry faces in tiled underground caverns filled with pale beings that stared with worship-filled eyes; then bodies piled high under her as she was filled with a sense of power and life, lifted up to rise through earth into open air, into the light of the sun, burning bright as a supernova while she watched the world explode into pure energy around her. . . .

"God!" Joie flung herself away from Christopher.

She shook her head and looked up, vision blurred with tears she didn't remember crying. Christopher looked shaken, too, stayed on his side of the couch as if being any closer might pull them both back into whatever it was she'd seen. Somehow, she knew he'd witnessed it, too, and that it wasn't the first time for him. She could tell by the guilty look on his face, as if he hadn't just shared her vision.

More like he knew he was the cause.

It wasn't until they had a few minutes to recover, until she was ready to leave, that she noticed the potted plants on the windowsill behind them. When Joie had come in, they'd all been dried out from lack of being watered.

Now every dead plant was green and in full bloom.

CHAPTER 16

9:47 P.M.—*West Village, 20 July 2007*

Life went on.

Despite the ongoing search to discover who was hunting the vampires of New York, they had no choice but to go on with their lives. Ironically, for Perenelle, that meant planning her own funeral. Having established herself in her West Village neighborhood over the last few months as the young Perenelle, named after the aged "relative" she'd come from Paris to care for, she'd announce soon that her ailing great-aunt had passed away in the night.

There'd be a discreet private service for the benefit of old friends in the neighborhood and her clients, a chance for young Perenelle to assure them all that she'd continue her aunt's work. A decorative antique marble urn of ashes from the fireplace would be interred in the back garden, and young Perenelle, her beloved great-aunt's namesake, would take over the house and her relative's spiritualist practice.

She'd begin a new life span in her old home, pretend to age and die, again and again, mimicking her human neighbors as well as she imitated the dead in her faked channeling sessions. Her future life didn't start until next week. Tonight she had an appointment with the past, the capture and interrogation of the man who'd betrayed them, DuMaurier's son. The New York Hunt Club had been dispatched as agents of the Veil, led by the rebellious Claire St. Claire, regrettably the most qualified to lead them. Perhaps it would give her a place to vent her anger.

It was time to find out the name of their enemy.

Xavier DuMaurier knew it was coming.

As soon as he heard that his father was dead, he knew they'd be after him. His father didn't have the protection he had from the vampires and had been their slave for years. It would be impossible for him not to betray his son. Clean Slate had known that from the beginning, when they'd recruited him a year ago.

But Xavier was ready for them.

He'd stayed away from CSG/Red Hook and communicated only by encrypted means. If the vampires were observing him to uncover who or what he worked for, he wouldn't make it easy for them. It was on his way home after dinner out with friends that he saw the kid.

Xavier was walking down one of the last DUMBO streets not filled with trendy eateries and high-priced shops. It was one of the few blocks near the river with enough old industrial buildings for him to live in relative isolation. That's what he liked about it. If he brought his work home, like tonight, there was less chance of anyone else getting hurt.

When he'd signed on for the mission, they'd told him to be prepared for anything. The vampires could control men's minds as well as transform their own bodies, and the element of surprise always worked to their advantage. It was still jarring to experience it firsthand. Xavier slowed as he approached his street and took a closer look.

Seeing a kid this young on the street after midnight was already an alarm that something was wrong. He was about eleven, sitting on a loading dock across the cobblestoned street. Xavier almost expected him to be crying to lure him in. Instead, the boy looked up from an old Batman comic book with a grin on his face. That was when Xavier felt his heart jump.

It was his best friend in grade school, a kid named Teddy, killed in a traffic accident when he was almost exactly this age. Teddy looked just the way he had the day he died, navy Catholic-school blazer, gray slacks, white shirt, and black tie, down to the comic book he'd waved at Xavier just before he turned and walked in front of the truck that killed him. There was no question of who it was. The streetlamp lit up his face clear as day.

Xavier broke into a light sweat and started a prayer in his head. He'd seen a lot of weird shit in the year since Clean Slate had recruited him after his last tour of duty in Iraq, but never this personal, this intimate. His loft was only half a block away, filled with weapons, but right now it could have been on the moon.

"Hey, Teddy, how you been?" asked Xavier.

The kid laughed, pulled a pack of cigarettes out of a blazer pocket, and lit one. Teddy always had been a bad boy.

"We both know the answer to that, don't we?"

He laughed and blew smoke out of his nose.

"Yeah, guess we do . . ." said Xavier. This had to be a distraction. He was supposed to stand here and chat with a dead boy while the real threat came at him from behind. Xavier glanced around, tried not to be too obvious.

Teddy stood up and hopped off the platform, onto the sidewalk.

"We need to talk, kiddo," he said, and walked into the street toward Xavier. A truck flashed by him before Xavier could react, slammed into Teddy and drove him into the ground. The vehicle was gone as quickly as it had appeared, with only a distant rumble giving any hint that it had ever been there.

Xavier stepped into the street and stared in shock at the bloody body of his best friend as he did the day it had really happened. Even knowing that it had to be an illusion, his eyes filled with tears as he looked at the crumpled young body at his feet. Before he moved away, the corpse rolled over and Teddy's battered eyes opened. He grinned, teeth broken, face shattered, and pulled himself to his feet like a puppet on strings, as if lifted from above like a marionette. Teddy lurched forward at Xavier, lit cigarette still in his hand.

"Gotta talk," he said, words slurred by his broken jaw and torn lips. Smoke poured from holes in his cheek and the side of his neck as he exhaled. Xavier remembered the last time he'd heard him say those words, the day Teddy had pulled him into an alley by the school to blurt out that he loved him, that he wanted to hold Xavier and touch him.

He'd been angry, repulsed, had shoved Teddy away and told him he didn't want to see him again, that he wasn't his best friend if he was a faggot. Teddy looked sad, said nothing, just walked away and waved with the comic book before he walked into a truck. Xavier had never been sure if it was an accident or suicide, if Teddy hadn't paid attention or had walked into the street on purpose. Never been sure if it was his fault.

A body plummeted from the roof of the building behind Teddy and hit the ground with a loud, wet thud. It didn't stay there but struggled to its feet, too, as Teddy kept stumbling forward. Xavier watched his college girl-friend, Sophie, stand upright, half her face smeared into jelly by the fall, the same side of her body smashed and broken, arm dangling as she staggered toward Xavier beside Teddy. A broken phone was clutched in her hand, beeping loudly like it had been off the hook for too long.

"We need to talk," she said, voice hollow. It was what she'd said the last time they'd talked over the phone, at the end of his freshman year. *"I need your help. . . ."*

He knew Sophie was troubled after their first few weeks together, but their relationship had been so passionate, the sex so good, that he'd over-looked the obvious. She wasn't just wild; she was seriously disturbed. Xavier didn't remember her exact diagnosis. Her family had told it to him when they called to tell him she had to go away for a while, but it had slipped his mind when they told him she'd locked them out. They wanted him to get her to open the door.

Sophie had called on the other line while he was still on the phone with her folks, hysterical, said she was under attack and needed his help. Said he had to come rescue her. Her family and the men from the clinic were breaking in with the dorm-room monitor's passkey. She wouldn't let them take her, told Xavier she loved him as she went over the railing of her bal-cony to get away from them.

He'd listened to her last scream as she fell, the call cut off as the phone shattered against the pavement. Xavier had always been sure that if they'd waited, or called him sooner, he could have somehow saved her from her delusions, led her back to them, the clinic, and salvation. It had taken him years to convince himself of the truth, that she'd taken the only path she could. But here she was, pointing the broken phone at him, accusing, as if it really was his fault that she was dead.

He backed away, saw the stones at his feet shift and push aside to reveal dirt beneath. The earth loosened and fingers sprouted like new growth, rose from the soil to expose hands, arms, and a head, the face tilted down as shoulders shrugged free. Arms reached out like the spindly legs of a spider and bony hands settled on either side of the hole, pushed hard to raise a withered body out of the ground. His dead father stood up in front of him, freshly exhumed, feet planted on either side of a mound of displaced cobblestones, his suit filthy from the grave.

"*We have to talk, Xavier,*" he said in a raspy voice, his throat torn open as if a wild animal had attacked him, his head almost severed. "*They did this to me because of you.*" He stepped toward him as Teddy and Sophie moved forward at the same time, in unison. Xavier backed up as the three specters of his past sins shambled at him, muttered his name, glared at him in accusation. Xavier felt his heart pound as the weight of his guilt slowed him down, left him vulnerable to their attack.

Xavier had a simple job to do here: he only had to be captured and make sure the vampires didn't realize he was a decoy. He just hadn't expected their assault to be so sadistic, so personal. It was more than he could take. If they were going to take him, they were going to have a fight on their hands. It wouldn't endanger his mission, only make his capture look all the more convincing.

Xavier turned to flee, right into the gloved fist of a young Eurasian girl dressed in black leather. She hit him hard, took him down with the first punch. Her voice was the last thing Xavier heard as he passed out.

"Enough of your stupid hunting games. Just take him."

CHAPTER 17

All was fair in time of war.

Perenelle told herself that as she prepared to question their new prisoner. Use of force in this situation was a necessary evil, she told herself. She had no choice but to sacrifice her higher standards for a greater good, the survival of her kind.

The last interrogation had taken her to a place she'd sworn never to reach again, a level of savagery that frightened even her. She'd sunk to that only once before in more than six hundred years, at the end of the nineteenth century, after she lost Nicolas. She'd become a killing machine for decades, wanted the world to feel her loss, her pain, had performed acts that disgusted and shamed her now.

It was in those dim, lost days that she'd killed a boy named Frederic and brought him back to life as the monster that became Adam Caine. That was only the beginning of a descent into deadly despair that came to a head in 1931, a fateful evening in Harlem that finally showed her the demon she'd become. Memories of that night haunted her still; acts so heartless they drove her away from New York to seek redemption.

It took years for her to pull herself out of a downward spiral back to a semblance of her old humanity, but she'd succeeded and founded the Veil as a reflection of her new self-control to benefit others. She could hold on to that, at least, as she moved forward.

They'd changed the location of the interrogation. It seemed best to avoid predictable patterns, meeting in sites that could be tracked or betrayed more easily after repeated visits. Instead of Perry Dean's stylish Battery Park penthouse, Wilfred Adderly had provided them with an empty apartment on the Upper West Side better suited to their purpose. It was an empty building scheduled for demolition the next day, already set with explosive charges for the morning's work. Abandoned and secured from trespass, it was ideal for their work tonight, protected from curious eyes.

Perenelle stood inside the interrogation room while members of the New York Hunt Club carried the prisoner in, bound to a chair. They placed him in the center of the empty room. She nodded to them and they left. The last to exit pulled a small woolen cap from the prisoner's head to expose an X-shaped scar across the back of his freshly shaved head.

His shirt had been torn away to reveal a deep bite in his neck. What Perenelle could see of his muscular torso was covered with a maze of runic tattoos, ornate glyphs that reminded Perenelle of symbols in some of Rahman's more arcane alchemic scrolls. If they were intended to protect him from harm, the markings were of little or no use. He was theirs now, and they would do with him as they pleased.

The young man glared at her with cold pride as she walked around him. He had the eyes of a career soldier. She'd faced many of his kind over the centuries, their lives dedicated to something greater than themselves, to causes they felt worth dying to defend. He would reveal nothing to an ordinary interrogator, but her methods were far from ordinary.

Something had told her before they began that it would be best to proceed with caution. The enemy knew they'd be looking for them. The capture of this agent had been too easy, as if he'd surrendered himself voluntarily. There could be only a few reasons for that. Either he could tell them nothing or his leaders were using him as bait to track his captors. That was why she was the only one still present, the only one among them who could escape capture even if she wouldn't share how. Her real job tonight was to force the enemy to make the next move. The vampires had made theirs.

All she had to do now was wait.

The vampire was already in the room when he was carried in.

She was petite, pale, brunette, and beautiful. They were always attractive. Vampires had the power to look irresistible, the one unholy ability that Clean Slate techs couldn't neutralize. Her outfit was modern, stylish. She looked as appealing as any well-dressed young woman out for a night on the town. If he'd spotted her in a local bar, he would have made a point of starting a conversation. She stood in front of him, her head cocked to one side, with a sad smile.

"*Bonjour*, Xavier. I knew your father."

"You killed my father." He spat the words out.

Her gaze didn't waver.

"That would be the fault of your friends who used him to betray us."

"To save lives."

"Your lives. And the lives you took from us, do those mean nothing?"

He was silent.

"*Mais oui*, but of course. We are monsters. I forget."

She walked around him, brow lightly furrowed. He didn't follow her with his eyes, unconcerned about an attack at this stage of the game. He could feel her eyes on the X-shaped scar they'd found when they cut off his hair and shaved his scalp. He'd heard his captors inform her about it by phone after they couldn't enthrall or mesmerize him.

"You have protection from us."

"You can't control me, no."

He said nothing more. The device implanted in his brain by the Clean Slate lab geeks worked with neurochemical blockers injected daily into his bloodstream to deaden the areas of the brain vampires used to control humans when they linked minds to feed. It had activated automatically by remote control when he failed to check in, which told them he'd been captured and was in play, giving them a way to find him.

Over the last five years, Clean Slate researchers had figured out how vampires controlled human minds, what parts of the brain were affected. They'd devised jamming fields to block the vampire wavelength, the basis of the dampeners used throughout the CSG/Red Hook complex that made it possible to imprison vampires without their being able to hypnotize guards into releasing them. It had taken until now to find a way to miniaturize a dampener, make it undetectable to their prey by implanting it in an agent's skull.

The process was dangerous, still experimental, and the miniaturized dampener needed injected chemical enhancement too toxic for long-term use. He couldn't stay on the formula long, but they knew he wouldn't have to when they began. It was the only way they could allow him to be captured, to be sure he wouldn't tell the vampires everything while they had him.

Their powers couldn't force him to talk, and Xavier had survived the worst methods of human torture as a prisoner of war in Iraq. He could hold out as long as necessary, until reinforcements followed the tracking device built into his internal dampener. The only thing that disturbed him was that he did not see more of them.

The vampires who had brought him here had left. He didn't know if they were nearby with others or gone from the building. Clean Slate's hope had been that the vampires would bring him back to their headquarters or somewhere central. Though they would get his interrogator, this project wouldn't be completely successful unless they made a bigger catch.

"Your friends left you alone with me?"

She shrugged, back in front of him.

"Is my company so unsatisfactory?"

"Just thought I was of more interest, with all the trouble you took to get me here."

"No trouble at all." She smiled at him, didn't seem to be in any rush to get information from him. What was she up to? "Don't worry. They'll return when they're needed."

Something in the way she said that triggered a realization that he wasn't bait to catch them anymore. They'd turned the tables and were using him to lure his team in for the kill.

"No! Cancel Project! *Cancel!*"

The vampire shook her head.

"We are not without skills in this area. We have the advantage of being able to enthrall anyone we need to help us. Surgeons. Electronics experts. You were asleep long enough for us to detect your communication link and divert it."

"Divert?"

She frowned. "It may not be the right word. Even after hundreds of years of speaking English, words occasionally elude me. We have 'replaced' your signal. With one of our own, the sounds of a plausible interrogation."

Xavier paled more than he had when they'd bled him. His team was on its way into a trap, one he couldn't warn them about. He heard noises in the hall outside; footsteps moving in a familiar pattern of ordered invasion, the sounds he'd heard his team make in the past in the middle of an operation.

The vampire looked regretful as she stepped away from him. "I am sorry. This is not the world as I would have it, but it is the world your kind have made for us."

"Get out! Get out!" Xavier shouted as loud as he could to the team outside the room as it moved closer.

More than twenty armed men and women in full gear, prepared for anything but this. They came through the doorway just as he saw the vampire fade and vanish into thin air. There was a series of low booms, distant explosions downstairs. Xavier saw buildings outside the windows start to rise, floor by floor, moving faster, until he realized that they weren't going up.

He was going down.

The building beneath his team collapsed, carried them all down screaming to street level. A cloud of dust and smoke rose to fill the room; the walls and ceiling shattered into flames around them as the roof of the building reached the foundation, buried them beneath a burning pile of stone, steel, and concrete rubble.

Perenelle opened her eyes, safe at home in her parlor.

Escaping capture twice wouldn't make her look any less suspicious to the others, but she was glad she could astrally project to the interrogation rather than attend in person. She'd been sure that any organization capable of the first attack could easily use the capture of one of their agents to track them, and she'd been right. Again. Perhaps this time her associates would start to understand the severity of the threat against them. She tapped the Bluetooth headset in her ear and redialed the vampires assigned to wait in hiding outside the site.

They had accomplished their mission. When the building came down, taking most of the assault team with it, they'd moved in to capture the drivers and backup squads left outside on the ground. Their shock at seeing the building they'd come to invade collapse beside them, with their compatriots inside, gave the vampires an element of surprise and time to restrain them and capture their vehicles as well. They were conducting interrogations and examining the contents of the vans now, but they had already found the name of their enemy on registration papers—Clean Slate Global.

Perenelle went to her laptop as they sent her a link to their Web site. She had to laugh. It was a new age in warfare when you could go online to find your opponent's resources outlined for you, as if on a take-out menu. There they were, logo and all. Their slogan: "When Ordinary Security Is Not Enough."

They were a high-priced, private mercenary group that provided solutions for "extraordinary situations when traditional security measures have proven ineffective." Their clients were billionaires, royalty, corporations, and countries. They boasted that they could have anything built for any need, transport anything anywhere, and do anything anyone wanted done, for what she imagined was a substantial price.

It seemed their specialty this year was hunting vampires. Perenelle couldn't help but wonder who their client was. She forwarded a link to the site and an update to the members of the War Council, then sat back to read more about their enemy.

CHAPTER 18

8:07 P.M.—*Red Hook, 21 July 2007*

It had been a long busy day at Clean Slate Global.

Richmond had pulled in every favor he had coming and made a few threats, but last night's explosion on Broadway was finally old news and off the front pages and TV news leads. The premature building collapse had been explained away all day as a construction accident by authorities for both the city and the site, just as Richmond had instructed them to as soon as he'd heard about it.

He read through the stack of the day's newspapers brought to his office, listened to the television news coverage on multiple windows that floated on the shiny black surface of his desktop screen. As the sky darkened, Richmond looked up from *The New York Times* to the view through his floor-to-ceiling windows, which included lower Manhattan. Gray smoke was still visible in the sunset over the Upper West Side from the explosion and resulting fire.

On TV, the mayor and other city officials repeated their speeches about investigations and crackdowns on construction safety, added empty assurances that the accident was unlikely to happen again, that city residents should go back to their usual routines and how lucky they were that there had been no casualties.

There was no mention of Clean Slate, his lost team, or their mangled bodies, which were still being recovered from the wreckage. It was a hard choice for Richmond to make, but that was the way it had to be. With a few phone calls to the right people, he rewrote reality to tell the world that last night's catastrophe had been only a careless mistake, with no loss of life. Time would pass and the city would forget, even if the loved ones of the men and women killed in the operation that night would feel it for some time.

Their unselfish sacrifice would be kept secret, unknown but not unmourned. The company would make sure their survivors were compensated financially, but Richmond knew that no amount of money could ever make up for their loss. All that could come close would be for Clean Slate to track down and exterminate the monsters that had done it. That he could do.

Richmond stood silently at the Red Hook facility, lost in thought, with Lopez by his side. He took the loss hard, felt personally responsible as the master planner. Overlooking the obvious had been a stupid mistake on his part. The building was a demolition site. It should have occurred to him that the vampires could blow it up. Their actual plan had been hidden in plain sight all along, to lure his team inside, explode it, and capture the stunned survivors for interrogation.

Richmond's real mistake had been in underestimating the vampires' astounding disregard for human life. Killing twenty-five to capture four and a handful of vehicles made perfect sense to them and would never have occurred to him. He wouldn't make that mistake again.

They watched the translators at work through sealed glass windows from the manuscript room's observation lounge. Richmond knew they'd find what he needed. He hired only the best. That's what made his company what it was today.

Clean Slate was based in New York City for the same reason that Area 51 was in the middle of nowhere: that's where the work was. UFOs show up in the middle of nowhere, while vampires and other supernatural predators gravitate to big cities as ideal feeding grounds, large enough to blend in.

It had made sense for him to start here.

There had been ample evidence of vampire activity on the Lower East Side and under Central Park in 1987. Richmond had resigned his post as deputy mayor to take a commission from the city to start a long-term task force to monitor and clean up future activity. He formed Clean Slate and in time developed sufficient staff, reputation, and resources to take on other clients with equally unusual problems that required discreet handling.

As his organization and its funding grew, Clean Slate went global, opened facilities around the world, expanded the range of services they offered. Clean Slate Global's project-planning division found innovative ways to handle delicate situations that no one else could. As they grew, the Manhattan office they had started out in was reduced to a decorative corporate lounge for meeting clients. The warehouse facility here in Red Hook was the real heart of the operation.

It was a massive steel-and-concrete bunker on the Brooklyn shore, disguised as a rundown block-long factory building with a rooftop heliport, its concealed subterranean depths filled with high-tech facilities and a submarine base. It held a research lab most nations would have killed for, high-tech holding cells to contain and restrain any nature of unnatural subjects, and enough exotic weaponry to overthrow a small country. Any country, if you used it right.

Richmond's favorite feature was their reference wing, and the star of that collection was the private library left behind by the vampire Rahman-al-Hazra'ad ibn Aziz. Excavated from the ruins of his secret subway station under Sheep Meadow, the collection rivaled the greatest scientific and historic discoveries in recorded history. It was a shame that it had to be kept secret, but it was for the best. Mankind wasn't ready to hear even a fraction of what Rahman had to tell them.

The translators wore surgical gloves, sterile white body suits, and filtered face masks in a climate-controlled room to preserve the fragile documents as they pored over centuries-old scrolls and journals, separated pages, and vacuum-sealed them in protective plastic sheets. The delicately drawn words traced Rahman's life from his North African birth as a vampire in 701 A.D. to his end in New York's Central Park more than a thousand years later, in 1987. All that time, he'd meticulously recorded his experiments, his results, and, most important, his life and those of the vampires he'd met in his journeys.

The collection was perhaps the only millennial history of vampires in the world, written in Rahman's distinctly precise handwriting in the ancient Arabic text of his youth. It gave away many of their secrets but still contained countless more, locked in language. Over the years, Clean Slate had hired the best and fastest to translate them, many fired from the U.S. military for being gay. The government's narrow vision had been his gain. He had a crack team that was the envy of Homeland Security, fast, accurate, and for hire at the right price.

It would take far more than the twenty years Clean Slate researchers had already been working to translate, much less understand, all the pages. A rudimentary database had been made that finally put the warehouse of material into a chronological order that made searches easier. They could sort Rahman's texts by era and subject and were concentrating only on the last two hundred years.

Researchers were looking for any grudges or rivalries among the vampires that might still survive, a way to exploit some weak link in the armor of their damned veil of secrecy. If they could crack that, they could bring them down. There were plenty of candidates . . . vampires didn't get along any better than humans. As yet, none of the rivals seemed powerful enough in the vampire world to make a difference in the war. They needed a big target and the right weapon to hit it. It was just a matter of finding the right combination.

Lopez spoke up. "Got stopped again on my way in this morning. Yuppies."

Richmond chuckled. "What did they want?"

"The usual. 'What's with the helicopters?' 'What are those screams in the night?'" She cracked a smile. There were screams all right, but their walls were soundproofed many times over. Nothing escaped the CSG/Red Hook facility, not even sound.

"What did you tell them?"

"The usual answer. 'Homeland Security.'" She winked broadly. "'Keep it quiet.' They eat it up. Can't wait to run and tell their Manhattan friends that their borderline Brooklyn neighborhood is safe after all. . . ."

Richmond laughed; but in the last decade it had been an increasing problem to stay secret as their remote location by the river started to gentrify. They had a popular Fairway Supermarket a few blocks down and a new Ikea under construction not far away. Newly imported young professionals had started to wonder why a run-down warehouse needed a helipad on its roof, or why all they ever saw enter or leave were large black vans and armored limousines. Their old neighbors either assumed it was none of their business or didn't want questions asked about what they were doing. It had been easier to operate out of Red Hook then. In time, Richmond planned to move the whole operation except for their corporate office out of New York, maybe offshore to Cuba.

A low alarm broke the silence.

Richmond looked to Lopez, who'd already snapped to attention, pulled out her iPhone to check the steady stream of data coming in on her screen from every outpost.

They were under attack.

CHAPTER 19

The building was formidable.

That gave Claire St. Claire a secret shiver of delight as they approached it. A challenge. It had been a long time since she'd been able to cut loose, operate at full tilt instead of act the docile, born-again virgin that Burke had tried to turn her into over the last twenty years.

After the success of their first mission, Claire had volunteered to lead the team on a foray to Clean Slate headquarters to test their defenses, see what they were up against. She was almost surprised that Perenelle had trusted her enough to vote yes with the others. At this point, she realized, trust wasn't the issue. Survival was. About now, if the Devil himself had offered to save Perenelle and the rest of them, they would have agreed. She felt a pang of longing for her long-lost father, lover, brother, her maker, Tom O'Bedlam.

If ever a devil there was, it was her Tom.

The team consisted of members of the New York Hunt Club, vampires who laughed at the idea of peaceful coexistence with humans and still believed in using them as prey. They'd been the only ones to challenge Perenelle back in 1937, the night the Veil had been formed, to question the Triumvirate's judgment as the others voted to entomb Claire for fifty years, Tom forever. For all the good their protest had done.

Their club had evolved since those days. For years they'd haunted Central Park and the riverfront at night, preyed on muggers, prostitutes, and hustlers, or closeted straight men seeking sex with one another in the bushes; people who could disappear without anyone knowing where they'd been that night.

As the city became safer, more patrolled, and closely monitored by video cameras that vampires couldn't delude into seeing nothing, the Veil had kept them from pursuing their blood sport near home. They'd settled for safaris to distant countries.

As the world's population increased, more and more of it was poor and disposable. With so much ready material, the market for cheap flesh had grown. In the same way as degenerate humans took sex tours of the Far East and South America to have orgies with children, bloodthirsty vampires had organized private clubs to provide them with human hunting stock in exotic settings.

Claire had never been able to persuade Burke to let her go on safari, even when she justified it as a good way for her to release her more violent nature, to see it clearly as she put it aside under his tutelage. No amount of pseudopsychological babble could get him to budge, but she'd heard enough over the years to know that the Hunt Club membership would be her best backup when the Veil needed a crack assault team to catch DuMaurier's son and then break into his headquarters. She'd been right. The idea of Veil-sanctioned mayhem had appealed to them immediately. The only problem was keeping them focused and under control.

There were thirteen in this team. The number had seemed poetic and practical, enough to divide into units, not so many that they'd be easily detected as they closed in from all sides. Most were members of the Hunt Club. Two were Clean Slate drivers, enthralled with a bite and brought to help lead them inside.

Four at the front door, Claire, her thrall, and two hunters as backup outside; four coming in from the river through the submarine port, three hunters, and their human guide. The rest split to drop onto different ends of the roof on black hang gliders, masked from Clean Slate radar, a three-pronged assault.

Their captives hadn't been able to tell them much.

The higher-level agents blown up with the building would have been better informed. The drivers turned out to be new hires, didn't know much more than how to get to work in the morning and which company card to charge their gas on as they drove all day. It wasn't their job to know anything more.

It seemed that Clean Slate was structured like a 1950s Cold War spy cell. Each agent knew only the agents he or she dealt with, none of them with enough information beyond their function to glimpse the big picture. It forced the vampires to improvise as they tried to break into the enemy's headquarters, with no idea of what to expect. Claire had to smile as she walked up to the main entrance with her slave, her backup sliding unseen along the perimeter. There was one good thing about it.

She hadn't had this much fun in years.

CHAPTER 20

2:14 A.M.—*Berlin, 2 April 1922*

Life was shit for a child whore in 1920s Berlin.

To young Claire, it was home, a town unlike any other, save perhaps Sodom or Gomorrah before the blast. In the postwar era of the new Deutsches Reich, established in 1919, Berlin was a city of soaring intellectual achievements and the basest of human desires. Artists were stretching the boundaries of style and taste to find truth. The art of cinema was being reborn through the expressionistic eyes of new visionaries, as Bauhaus architects raised Modernist buildings that reflected a brighter future. Inspired writers were exposing the failures of society and exploring the depths of the human soul, while their neighbors gave them material by endangering their salvation with the most depraved of sexual appetites.

Many men flocked to Berlin to pay a high price for a variety of perverse pleasures, but none paid more than those in pursuit of innocence. Men who wanted the thrill of deflowering a girl's maidenhead were willing to cough up extra for the honor and usually couldn't tell if she used a few clever tricks to fool him into believing that he was her first. Claire still looked years younger than sixteen and had become a professional virgin, one of the best in town.

Her real first time had been the worst and had taken place at the hands of a judge, the night of her mother's death. His wife had learned long ago that if her husband satisfied his lust elsewhere, he left her alone to her shopping, ladies' clubs, and operas. He'd been loud, fat, smelly, and brutal, a memory relived as Claire re-created it four or five times a night for the next ten years.

She was the bastard child of a German prostitute and a Japanese businessman, born in a whorehouse. Her mother had died when Claire was five, her father gone minutes after he'd washed himself off and left her mother with child. Since being orphaned, Claire had been raised by the house madam to work off the last of her mother's debt.

There was money to be made by a young girl with the right attitude and skills. In the depressed economy of a nation that had just lost a world war, inflation was out of control, the German currency almost worthless. Prostitution was the only option for many women left widowed with hungry mouths to feed, young mouths that often ended up working alongside them for their food.

Claire was one of them. Before prostitution was legal in Germany, her house had operated under Reglementierung, a state license that registered prostitutes while granting them no rights. The compulsory tests for venereal disease were helpful, but prostitutes couldn't travel without a permit, live outside of approved housing, or work without a house to sponsor them. It was a neat little trap that kept the city's economy going as all of Europe filled Berlin's renowned brothels, one to suit every taste, and so reasonable.

Claire got good at playing her part, feigning resistance while she gauged whether the customer wanted a seduction or a rape, willing compliance or panicked resistance. She'd become expert at breaking a hidden blood capsule to stain the sheets and her thighs as the client climaxed, pretending to weep quietly in a corner of the bed as the customer left, convinced that he'd gotten the real deal.

To survive, Claire moved through her nights in a kind of dream. As her body went through the motions, her mind went elsewhere, lost in the books she kept in her room and read before bed each morning, after the last customers vanished with the sheltering dark of night. Books she'd gotten from a regular client, sent one by one as gifts after each assignation.

She'd developed a considerable library before his wife found out about his child concubine and threatened him with public scandal and divorce if he didn't stop. As their money was hers, he agreed, but Claire got to keep the books, lovely leather and gold bindings filled with tales of genies and gods, wizards and witches.

That was the magical world she escaped to in her head as she mouthed the words and went through the motions of her job, keeping a perverted proletariat pacified. The part of her that she wanted to protect from the real world roamed wild woods and hidden dells in her head, talked to trolls and danced with demons.

So it came as no surprise to her when she met a vampire.

CHAPTER 21

The entrance to Clean Slate headquarters looked like a big corrugated metal door at the end of a long driveway. A little rust peeked through weather-worn gray paint. It was tall and wide enough for a truck to drive through when raised; a smaller door had been built into the left side for foot traffic. Claire St. Claire pulled up in a stolen red Mercedes convertible that couldn't be traced to her. She turned off the engine, got out, and went to the small side door.

There was a battered video camera mounted above the entrance. It watched while she helped one of the enthralled drivers out of her car. There was a card slot to the left, and the driver slid his ID card through when they got to it. Claire stood by his side, his arm around her shoulder as he leaned on her for support.

He'd been worked over to look convincing, perhaps more than necessary, his face bruised, one leg broken. The LED light on the card reader clicked from red to green, but the lock didn't budge. The camera repositioned itself with a dull mechanical grind as the lens zoomed in for a better look at them.

"Can you help us, please," said Claire as she looked up. "He needs a doctor, but made me bring him here instead. Said he works here, that you could help him? Hello?"

She waited, alert, tried to stay in character, both concerned and annoyed, very *I'm trying to do the right thing here, but it's eating into "me" time*. Claire was dressed like local Brooklyn gentry, dark business clothes, Bluetooth phone in her ear, and a Louis Vuitton bag slung over one shoulder. She'd even fed on a live victim provided by the hunters after they'd assembled. Her skin was still flushed and warm, her green eyes bright with humanity.

They hoped she'd be lifelike enough to fool whatever sensors Clean Slate might have set up at the door to detect cool-blooded vampires. The others had fasted, wanted to stay as unnoticeable on thermal detectors as possible while they staked out the building. Claire was the only one who had to fool them face-to-face.

"Hello?" The driver slumped as if on cue while she struggled to hold him up. "I need help here . . . oh, for . . ."

Somewhere inside, a decision was made. The smaller door in front of them buzzed and popped open. The driver stood up again, looked pained as Claire pushed him through the door and led him inside.

The interior of the main entrance reflected Clean Slate's true nature, a two-story-tall reinforced concrete bunker. Just inside the big corrugated metal door they'd seen from outside were the edges of two massive, floor-to-ceiling steel doors recessed into the walls. Two guards in crisp black coverall uniforms stood inside a bulletproof Plexiglas booth between her and a long white driveway that led down a brightly lit tunnel into the heart of the complex.

Claire could feel something in the air as soon as she was in the chamber, a frequency or energy of some kind, nothing she could define. When she tried to reach out to the guards in the booth, to connect to their minds and control them, she couldn't get a lock. It was the strangest feeling, so odd that she almost fell out of character. She'd never had trouble feeding before, and to be cut off like this was something she'd never experienced. But she'd heard of it.

It was the same problem that the vampires who had captured the butler's son had encountered before they'd blown him to kingdom come, the tattooed boy with the scar on the back of his head. She looked around and saw devices scattered overhead that could be generating the signal, then watched the guards confer, oblivious to her attempts to control them.

One pressed a button on his console.

TERENCE TAYLOR

"Chris?"

The driver looked up, one eye swollen shut. He nodded. The guards waited for Chris to respond further. The first pressed the button again.

"You know the drill, buddy?"

The driver seemed sluggish, but nodded, lifted his battered right hand, and placed it on a flat panel on a shelf built into the front of the booth. The panel lit up red as his hand hit it and a brighter beam of white light slid down the length of his palm. Claire assumed that it was just a standard print reader, until an alarm went off overhead.

"Infected!" she heard one of the men say before the microphone cut off. Taser wires shot out of the wall of the booth and into the driver's chest. He shook with electricity and hit the ground.

Others shot at Claire but she dodged them easily, shouted into her Bluetooth earpiece to tell the others in her team to retreat. Claire spun around and ran for the door as one of the guards flipped a switch. The inside blast doors slammed shut.

Claire stopped immediately, cursed as she spun back to the booth. She'd never have thought that doors that big could move so fast. The guards inside the booth were both on headset phones, barked updates back to whoever was commanding them.

They didn't flinch until she pulled the large, hemispherical black plastic buckle from her belt and slapped it onto the center of their glass wall. The shaped charge inside was sealed tight, invisible to most explosives-detection devices on her way in. It stayed stuck to the glass as she backed away and pressed one of the stones on her bracelet.

The Plexiglas wall blew inward as the guards fled. Claire reached inside the shattered wall to push the button that opened the inner doors, then tossed her purse into the booth and ran for the exit. She pushed another stone on her bracelet as she got outside and the security booth exploded as she ran for the car.

Other explosions went off along the building's perimeter, planted by the rest of the team as they'd made their entrances, to use as distractions to give them time for escape. It had been her specialty even before she'd blown up the Hindenburg, ever since her first demolition. She'd kept up with new technology over the years but rarely got a chance to play with her toys. Despite the danger of the getaway, it was nice to see them in action.

Claire made it to her convertible, started it, and took off for the rendez-vous with the rest of her team. The mission was still a success. She might not have made it all the way inside Clean Slate, but she'd learned a lot. After the other survivors compared notes, they'd have a better idea of their enemy's defenses, and they had given the enemy a taste of what they faced as well.

The top was down and her short black hair whipped in the wind. Claire floored the accelerator and raced up the Brooklyn–Queens Expressway to-ward the Brooklyn Bridge at high speed, changed lanes to dart past slower cars like a video-game driver. Claire didn't care who saw her tonight, knew she could still control any ordinary cops that pulled her over for a ticket now that she was away from Clean Slate's evil little gadgets. She deserved a treat. Claire had accomplished the War Council's goals for the mission, but she'd also achieved one of her own.

She felt alive for the first time since she'd lost Tom.

CHAPTER 22

2:36 A.M.—*Berlin, 2 April 1922*

The madam told Claire that she had a new client.

"Herr Tomas von Durcheinander. A showman!"

Claire was told that the client was very rich, and if the girl did right by him, he'd be back again and again to fill Madame's coffers and move Claire closer to freedom from her debt. The girl ignored the last remark, knew from the way the madam kept the books that her mother's debt to the house would never be repaid in Claire's lifetime.

The new gentleman had asked for her specifically and said he'd had his eye on her for a while. That worried her; she'd had obsessed admirers before and it was never Claire they wanted, but someone they thought they could shape to fill some twisted hole deep inside them.

Claire took a long hot bath and let the madam groom her hair and make up her face while she babbled on about the new client and how Claire was expected to act. When she was done, Claire looked in the mirror to see a virginal young girl in lacy petticoats and corset, ready for her first kiss—the same face she saw every night. Already she could see traces of maturity creeping in. She wasn't growing old, just up, but wouldn't be able to play the virgin child much longer. That meant she'd have to find another way to keep the customers coming in, reinvent herself as a dominatrix or other extreme specialty.

As she got older the stakes would rise, and what she had to do to keep the customers coming in would get increasingly degrading until she killed herself to avoid some last indignity, too much for even her soiled soul to stand.

But that was tomorrow. Tonight she had to glitter and be gay for her new suitor. Who knew? Whores had caught the eye of clients before and been bought out of bondage by becoming wives or mistresses. She was young, beautiful, and exotic. If any of the girls in the house had a chance to seduce a customer into a commitment, it was Claire. Perhaps her prince in shining armor was waiting downstairs.

She went to her room to wait and see.

Claire wasn't afraid when Herr von Durcheinander came into her room, though the part of herself that had kept her alive this long told her she should be. He was tall and handsome, but his eyes were completely mad. She didn't know how she knew, except that when she stared into the deep black pools of his dark eyes, he wasn't the only one looking back.

The man's clothes were expensive if a trifle avant-garde in their style. His hair was purest white, but he was a young man, thirty or nearly so, some small comfort in her line of work. The madam ushered him in with a great show of servitude, as she always did when she got around big money.

"Herr von Durcheinander, meet Claire St. Claire, a young lady only recently brought into service. I'm sure that a gentleman like you can appreciate what a special privilege it is for you to be the first to introduce her to the pleasure of a gentleman's company. . . ."

The gentlemen in question nodded and smiled at Claire as he took off his gloves, ignored the madam as she sang the girl's praises and continued her veiled assertions that the maiden before him was indeed a maiden and had previously worked here only as a maid or servant. He would have the distinction of making her a full member of the madam's stable, a distinction that carried with it the expectation of a larger than usual honorarium for the house, of course. . . .

Herr von Durcheinander flung a handful of gold pieces over his shoulder at the woman and Claire watched the woman's eyes goggle, almost burst out of her head as she fell to the floor and scrambled to collect them all. Whatever country's coin, gold was assuredly worth more than the inflated deutschmarks they used to wipe their asses with in the privy. The madam bowed out with grateful reassurances that they would not be disturbed, for him to take his time to enjoy the evening.

The man tossed the gloves into his top hat and set it down on a small table near the door. Claire snapped out of the spell of his stare and rushed to help him with his coat.

"Herr von Durcheinander, allow me . . ."

He pulled his coat off before she could reach him, tossed it onto a chair, and caught her by the elbow, escorted her back to the sofa.

"Please, call me Tom." He sat her down and poured them each a glass of the cognac that had been left on the table for them along with other expensive treats for her guest. "What a sow that woman is!"

Claire laughed before she could stop herself and held a hand over her mouth, as the madam had taught her long ago, so as to seem more demure and innocent. The man laughed with her, handed her a glass, and they clinked them together in a toast.

"Let's make a promise, shall we? As we begin what I hope will be a long and pleasant association. A pledge not to suffer fools gladly."

They drank and he took her hand, not with the usual, rough start of business, but gently, the way a friend would. She didn't understand what was happening. This was not how her nights usually went, but she felt comfortable and safe for the first time in a long while and relaxed, sipped her drink.

"The madam said that you asked for me."

"Yes. I've been watching you for some time now. Not in a bad way," he said quickly as she let concern flash into her eyes. "Say rather that I've taken an interest in your case."

"Are you a doctor?" she asked, puzzled. Her case? He made her life sound so clinical, so easily diagnosed and cured, like a dose of the clap. He bellowed with laughter.

"A doctor? No, rest assured that I have no great love for their lot. Think of me more like a guardian angel."

Claire frowned and bit at the rim of her glass. "It's cruel to joke of such things. If there are angels, I assure you that none of them are concerned for my welfare."

"Oh, but you're wrong, my dear. I've lived your pain myself and am here to tell you there is a way out. There is freedom. You have but to die to this world to live again, as I did."

His words chilled but excited her even as they frightened her. The idea of death and rebirth was common in the books she read, part of a world of magic she'd always wished she could live in instead of the drab, dull streets of Berlin. She'd asked for a Prince Charming, and Tom certainly fit the bill in every other way. Claire held out her glass instead of retreating to a corner in fear of a man who could be a common killer.

He might also be her savior.

Tom refilled her glass and told her a story about a boy who was raped by a manservant and punished for it, sent away to an asylum so that his conservative religious family wouldn't have to live with the constant shame of seeing their soiled son. The servant had only been fired, but the boy was raped regularly in the asylum as he grew up, lived through decades of sexual, physical, and mental abuse. One night he told his story in a puppet show to a Dr. Townsend Burke, a man with the power to do something about it, a man who was something more than a man.

A vampire.

When Tom said the word, his face mere inches from Claire's, she gasped. It was clear at that moment that he, too, was a vampire, one of the undead she'd read about in Bram Stoker's *Dracula* and seen at the cinema in F. W. Murnau's *Nosferatu*. The doctor had saved Tom from damnation with the gift of a new life, as predator instead of prey, an eternal life of feeding on people too venal to live. Like those who'd made her life what it was now, a living Hell on Earth.

He'd taken the name Tom O'Bedlam, avenged his own death, and begun a new life as one of the undead. "Tomas von Durcheinander" was only a playful German translation of his new, true name; he'd discarded his old so long ago that it was forgotten, thrown it away with his humanity.

Claire threw herself into Tom's arms before she could stop herself, kissed him hard on his cool lips and clung to him, as if he were a long-lost lover, father, or brother. He kissed her back, overjoyed at her acceptance, nuzzled her ear and nibbled at her neck, opened his mouth to bite.

Sharp teeth slid into Claire's throat as she moaned in fear and pleasure, surrendered to the sensations that filled her head and body, saw visions of his life and hers blended into a stew of pain and confusion, abuse and injury that showed her how truly alike they were, saw all the reasons he'd picked her as a companion to share forever with him. The room vanished as her vision faded with her life. For a seeming eternity there was nothing but darkness until a voice called her name, once, twice, thrice.

"*Claire.*"

Not a question but a fact.

She'd been dead a moment ago, but now she was Claire again, reborn cool and beautiful to see herself alive again in the mirror he held up to her face.

"Do you see?" he said. "Mine now, a daughter of the dark. My light, my love, my life, now and forever."

She looked the same, only better, prettier than ever. More than that, she found she could bend her features to disguise them or improve them at will, reshape her appearance. Her body was stronger, more powerful, as if she could leap a wall or smash through a door. Her senses were sharper than they'd ever been in life. She could actually detect the other human lives moving in the building, hear their voices, smell their blood, and feel their passion.

Claire felt so much pour in that she wasn't sure how to begin trying to understand it all. Tom took her in his arms again, held Claire more tenderly than she'd ever been held in her brief life. He stroked her, which soothed, despite an odd feeling when he touched her skin that was almost irritating.

The madam had left them alone all evening, sure that Tom was taking his time to get his money's worth. He put a long-playing record on the new Victor Orthophonic Victrola in the corner. He took Claire's hand and pulled her into a waltz as the music started, whispered into her ear.

Tom explained the strange sensation: vampires could sense one another and usually spread their territories wide so as not to live under the disturbing feeling of constant surveillance, the perpetual awareness of other hunters. It was something he was sure they could learn to live with if they stayed together—both had experienced far worse, for much less. It didn't take him long to explain the rules of her new life, what she could and couldn't do, what could hurt them and what couldn't. The games they could play with mere mortals . . .

Then the real fun of the evening began.

CHAPTER 23

9:07 P.M.—*Red Hook, 21 July 2007*

Richmond and Lopez were in action as soon as they'd heard the alarm. The research team was packing the documents for return to secure storage and Lopez was ready to escort them downstairs herself. When the first bomb went off, they stared at each other, shocked, as the building rocked.

"Well," said Lopez, "ain't yer daddy's vampires!"

Richmond headed for his office, talking rapidly into his earpiece, while Lopez met the research team as soon as they left their airtight workroom. She led them to an elevator to the subcellars, where everything was stored. The lifts had their own backup power. Even if the building was blacked out, the elevator batteries would still get them where they had to go.

Lopez opened the sealed doors to the archives downstairs with a palm pressed to the sensor pad outside. Lasers identified her print, measured her body temperature, and vaporized a thin layer of her skin to DNA test for vampire infection before it opened the door. No vampire or anyone bitten by a vampire could get through the reinforced steel vault doors, any more than they could get in upstairs.

The researchers filed the documents they'd been working on and uploaded updated records to the database as Lopez locked the cases. The researchers finished quickly and left to find safe quarters until the red alert was over.

Lopez lagged behind as she followed them out.

She felt like she'd forgotten something as she walked through the shelves and stacks of materials gathered from Rahman's lair and dozens of other vampires over the years. It was a treasure trove of history and art that spanned centuries and would take human lifetimes to catalog.

She walked through the collection several times a week as she led researchers in and out. Lopez had seen this room and everything in it a hundred times. What made her feel like she was forgetting something as she walked through it tonight? What was in here that she was trying to remember?

As Lopez neared the door she walked down an aisle of paintings and spotted her mystery woman in the last place she'd expected to find her. She stopped as she walked past, turned back, and saw the face she'd been trying to recall for days on a small canvas stacked against the wall with some others. It was the vampire she'd seen during the raid on the Grand Hyatt, the one who'd disappeared before she could stop her and left no image on tape.

Of course she'd looked familiar. She was in front of her every day, as she'd been every time Lopez went through the archives with the researchers. Lopez pulled the painting out of hiding, lifted it up into the light.

The woman in the decades-old portrait smiled at her as if in mockery, dressed in a style Lopez put somewhere in the late 1920s. The subject's name was engraved on a small brass plaque at the bottom of the frame.

It was Perenelle. Perenelle de Marivaux.

"Chief . . ." said Lopez. "You gotta see this."

"Don't call me chief," answered Richmond with a smile from his desk as he wrapped up the evening's crisis, reviewed updates from all posts on his desktop screen. There'd been only two casualties, but they'd captured three of the intruders. Two were their lost men, and even if they were infected there was still some reason to rejoice tonight.

He looked up to see Lopez come toward him with a small painting and the biggest shit-eating grin on her face he'd ever seen. He could use a break and Lopez never called him chief unless she had something good to tell him. It was a dumb private joke between them, so old that neither remembered how it had started. It had gone on for so long that he answered more by reflex than anything else.

"You're gonna love this," she said.

Lopez laid the antique oil portrait on his desk.

It was of a woman in her late twenties, perhaps early thirties, sensual, but an intellectual. You could tell from her eyes. You saw them first: dark, seductive, they held you like twin magnets, pulled you in closer. Then you saw the smile, *Mona Lisa* subtle, ageless, and ironic as if she knew the punch line to a joke you'd never get in a million years. It was an expression that said she'd seen more of life than you could imagine, more than you could ever know.

Her hair was styled simply; her black velvet dress was unadorned but elegant, the kind of timeless fashion only the very rich can afford, a style to survive the ages. She could walk down any street dressed like this today and still turn heads for all the right reasons.

Richmond had confiscated the painting from an estate sale in 1987, when he found out that the owner, Adam Caine, had disappeared from his Upper East Side penthouse around the same time as the zombie incident downtown. Probate court had put the contents on the market when no one claimed them.

The missing man's lawyer had put Caine's financial holdings into a special trust, per his instructions, money that later disappeared into a dozen accounts in as many names. But after it was officially cataloged, with a few odd exceptions, the apartment and its contents had been abandoned. When Richmond got wind of it he sensed a connection to the downtown case and had the city take it all in for further study. He felt vindicated when an illustrated book, *Bite Marks*, came out a year later with a thinly veiled version of the same man as its villain, portrayed him as a vampire who'd destroyed a young woman's life.

The book stayed ambiguous about his true nature, but it was enough to confirm Richmond's suspicions that the man could have been connected to the downtown events of the winter of 1986 and enough to put the writer and artist on his radar. He'd had reports of two civilians matching their descriptions going into the Sheep Meadow Station with the head of the KnightHawks. They knew more than they'd put into their book.

He read the brass plaque at the base of the frame again with a smile as he called the research department to tell them to send up all they had on Perenelle de Marivaux, his key to unlocking the secrets of the Veil.

It took no time at all to read what they'd found on her and, more important, to find out about her relationship with a vampire by the name of Claire St. Claire. Their conflict had come to a climax in 1937, when Perenelle had been instrumental in having Claire sealed up for almost fifty years after she'd blown up the Hindenberg with a cohort, still entombed.

Rahman's last entry on her had been made not long before his death. He described how Claire had been freed from her iron tomb a year shy of her fifty-year term by the Triumvirate of the Veil and put under the care of a Dr. Townsend Burke. Or, to call him by his official title, the duly elected Council Superior of the East Village Bloodline.

One of their guests from the Grand Hyatt raid.

It looked like his protégé, Claire St. Claire, had been free for about two decades. Maybe she'd had time to give up thoughts of revenge against Perenelle. Maybe not. Richmond could scarcely conceal his pleasure despite events earlier tonight. They'd found their weak link. All he had to do was find a way to put the pressure on until it snapped. The war was escalating and humans had to win or die.

They had to find and recruit Claire St. Claire.

Perenelle's scouts reported back to her and the War Council of the Veil within a few hours of their departure. She knew they'd know quickly if they'd succeeded or failed. Either their scouts could enter as effortlessly as they walked in and out of any other building in the world, or Clean Slate had indeed found a way to stop vampires from controlling the minds of their guards.

Detection had never been in question. It had always been easy for humans to set up equipment to tell if someone at their door was a warm-blooded human or a cool-blooded vampire, if they knew to look. That had been the whole point of the Veil, to keep them from knowing to look in the first place.

That seal would be broken unless Veil enforcers wiped out the entire Clean Slate organization and everyone who'd ever had contact with them. It wasn't entirely out of the question. If they could exterminate them and get hold of their client list . . . Perenelle stopped and shook her head. Madness. It would take centuries of killing and she'd already had enough.

Perenelle sighed as she poured cognac, wished for a brief moment that it was blood. Vampires enjoyed the flavor of rare liquors, but they had no other effect. She craved intoxication, the ability to forget, even if only for one night. No matter what the ultimate outcome of the war between humans and vampires was, one battle had been lost forever. Too many humans knew that vampires were real now for their secret to be kept from the public for much longer. Proof would come out. They'd deal with that later, if they survived.

Clean Slate was every bit as strong as she'd feared. The remnants of the Veil would have to bide their time before another assault, wait until they could find an effective way in. There had to be a way. There was always a back door. They would find it eventually. That was the only good thing about this war.

Time was on the side of the immortals.

CHAPTER 24

11:12 A.M.—Lower Manhattan, 23 July 2007

The woman behind the counter at the Social Services office didn't want to give Christopher what he wanted, but she did it anyway. Most people did. Men or woman, young or old, few seemed able to deny Christopher anything. It had gotten him into trouble when he was a boy. His three younger siblings had always resented that the adopted kid got special treatment, always got his way and never seemed to get punished.

Like the time they'd snuck into a neighbor's yard, stripped their bushes of berries, and got caught. Their faces were smeared with juice, hands still wet with the evidence. Even though Christopher was the oldest and should have been more to blame than the others, the younger ones were blamed instead and made to clean messy handprints from the fence and hose the dirty footprints off the driveway. Christopher was given a stern talking to, then forgiven and treated to a piece of berry pie on the porch while his sister and two brothers working out in the hot sun glared at him.

Of course, they couldn't do anything about it.

All it took was a smile from Christopher or a touch on the shoulder for the angriest of them to melt into bashful reconciliation. It got pretty *Brady Bunch* at times, warm and happy group hugs all around until he broke it up.

Only later, after he was long gone, would they come to their senses and realize that nothing had been resolved. He'd gotten off scot-free again, pulled another fast one over them all. That was what scared them. The fact that they didn't doubt him for a minute when he was around, couldn't feel what they really felt about him. It wasn't charming. He didn't have charisma. It was more like Jedi mind control.

When he was a baby, everyone dismissed such concerns as silly. All babies are irresistible, they said, when his mother wouldn't or couldn't leave his side. Even when he got everything he wanted, friends and family insisted that toddlers are just so cute, who can deny them anything?

By the time he was a teenager, a repulsive age even for Christopher, people could no longer kid themselves that they gave him what he wanted because he was adorable. It was clear that he had a gift for making them see things his way, no matter how much it went against their own impulses.

Christopher had been a bright boy and caught on quickly.

The wonder was that his stepparents had instilled in him a strong enough morality to keep him from taking over the town and declaring himself its god. Instead, he'd dated any girl he fancied, negotiated the best car deals ever for friends and family, never failed a class, and had never been turned down for a raise, no matter how many days of work he'd missed. He'd lived a normal life for a boy who could talk the shine off a shoe.

What no one knew through all the years he'd been a poster child for normal was that he had nightmares about an infancy his adoptive parents didn't know about, the one he'd come to New York to uncover. His brief life before they'd taken him, a hidden past he had to dig up to bury the bad dreams.

He'd put the search off since his arrival. Meeting Joie, getting settled into the new apartment, and finding a routine to his new life in the city had distracted him. He was also afraid of what he might find. It was one thing to live with a cloud of doubt about who he really was and where he'd come from, who his parents were and why they'd given him up for adoption. Living with the truth could be worse.

Christopher started at a Social Services office. The woman behind the counter had tried to blow him off, explained that all adoption records were sealed unless both parties filled out a waiver and filed an application with the Adoptee Registry.

He leaned forward, flashed a big smile, and told her some bullshit story he made up on the spot about a medical problem, needing information about his birth parents for treatment, blah, blah, blah, kept talking until whatever powers of persuasion he possessed could kick in and get her to act on his behalf. Sure enough, after a minute or two, she smiled and wavered.

"Look," she said. "None of those files are computerized yet, anyway. I couldn't pull them up even if I wanted to. They're stored downtown."

"Any idea where?" asked Christopher.

She looked at him for a moment, eyebrows arched as if she couldn't believe what she was about to do, then turned to her computer. After she found the address of the records-storage facility and wrote it down for him, the woman wished him luck and waved the next person on line forward as if he'd never been there.

It wasn't easy for Christopher to find the building.

Most of Manhattan is organized on a grid, until you get downtown to streets built along old cow paths and dirt roads paved over when the city grew up around them. The neighborhood around City Hall was broken up into winding streets that seemed to fold in on themselves and the named streets were harder to locate than numbered. Christopher found the warehouse, the right floor and office, and then talked the attendant into going back and pulling out the file for him to see.

The man came back with an aged brown folder, handed it over to him after exacting his promise not to leave with it. Christopher sat on a bench outside the counter window and stared at the worn folder in his hands, a series of numbers written in faded ink at the top next to a name.

Baby/male: Christopher Jude Miller.

He opened it, fingers trembling. There were only a few sheets of paper inside: a report from the caseworker that brought him into the system and placed him with the adoption agency, a birth certificate, and a death certificate. The birth certificate was his. Christopher Jude Miller. Born August 15, 1986. Mother: Nina Theresa Miller. Father: unknown. So he was a bastard after all.

The death certificate was his mother's. Christopher's throat constricted, and his eyes began to tear before he could react to the news any other way. His mother was dead. Immediate cause: evisceration. Manner of death: homicide.

Murdered. He dropped the report to the bench, closed his eyes. At least he knew she hadn't wanted to give him up. When he found the strength to look through the file again, there was no more information on his mother or family, but the caseworker's report said that he'd been found in Central Park. A young couple had found him and turned him in to the police. There was no name or address.

If they'd found him in the park in the middle of winter, it was possible that they knew something about how he got there. The report identified the police precinct that had handled the case. All he had to do was go there and get a copy of the police report. Christopher took the file back to the clerk and asked for a phone book to get the address of the Central Park precinct.

CHAPTER 25

"I think I need therapy." Joie stomped into the bar, threw her bag down on the window seat next to Vangie, and flopped down, limp, on the chair across from her. Vangie had invited Joie out for drinks to hear an update on the video. As long as she picked up the check, Joie could drag herself into town for a few hours. "My parents are driving me crazy."

"That's their job. They say we drive them crazy, but it's really the other way round. My shrink says that's part of the mind fuck they feed you." She poured the last of her drink down her throat and waved to the bartender for two more. "You should go see him. He'd fix all your problems, just like that!"

She snapped her fingers and laughed a little too much. It was obviously not her first drink. The drinks arrived and Vangie slid one over to Joie, who glanced over at the bartender.

"He doesn't ask for ID?"

"Not from me," said Vangie. She wore a smile that answered any questions Joie might have had about why, but she told her anyway. "If I'm old enough to do what he likes in bed, believe me, I'm old enough to drink." He winked and waved at them; Vangie blew a kiss back.

Joie shook her head, sipped her drink, and almost choked. She didn't drink often, but she knew this was strong. One of Vangie's bartender specials should be more than enough to drown her sorrows.

"What are the robo-parents doing to piss you off?" asked Vangie. She settled back. Joie watched her friend keep an eye on the door by reflex, as she always did in case someone more important entered. Such a diva.

"The usual. It's not their fault. Mom's still dealing with the whole cancer thing; we don't know where that's headed. Dad's back for good and getting nostalgic. I know they had a good time in the eighties, but if I have to hear again how much better downtown was then . . . I mean, I've done Pyramid Club on 80s night, it's no big deal." She rolled her eyes and took a bigger sip as Vangie checked her makeup in a compact mirror.

"Think your folks will hook up again?"

"Whatever. I've never been all that *Parent Trap*. Maybe I'm just pissed because he took so long to come back. I mean, why now? What if she . . . Fuck." Joie stopped. What if she dies? She couldn't even say the words out loud yet.

"Sorry," said Vangie, considerate for once.

She gave Joie a few minutes while they finished their drinks and ordered another round, then asked about the progress of the video. Joie took the second drink when offered even though she knew it was a bad idea.

"It's going okay. I have a rough cut done with Spider. He found something weird on the tapes and got all caught up in that for a while. You know Spider."

"What weird? Does it work?" Joie knew that Vangie really meant did it make her look good and dismissed the question.

"No, it's nothing. I'll have a cut for you next week. You look great. The blood stuff looks totally real." There was no point to trying to explain to Vangie that when Joie put her head together with Christopher's they blurred videotape, revived dead plants, and shared nightmare visions. It was too much like some stupid reality show Spider would watch on the Sci Fi Channel and had nothing to do with Vangie, who was downing her drink and packing up her things to go.

Joie didn't find out that she hadn't paid for the drinks until they'd said goodbye and Vangie made her usual rushed exit, this time to her shrink. Their friendly bartender was nowhere to be seen, and the smiling but chilly waitress that caught Joie on her way out made it clear that he hadn't said anything about the tab being settled.

Stuck again, Joie cursed Vangie under her breath, pulled out her debit card, and asked for a receipt. It was worth at least trying to get the money back from Vangie, along with other expenses. She would claim that she had meant to pay but had forgotten, like always, and come up with excuse after excuse not to give her the cash. She'd offer drinks instead, then invariably leave it to someone else to pay for them. Joie didn't know why she'd let a supposed friend get away with this all the time, when Vangie had more money than any of them.

They'd met in junior high in Park Slope, when Vangie's mom bought a brownstone near Prospect Park to lick her wounds between husbands. Vangie was the new kid at school, still reeling from her father's death. Everyone had seen the stories in the papers, heard the rumors. She'd come into class to whispers and sideways looks until Joie walked up and loudly introduced herself. She led Vangie through her first day, made sure she spent time with kids who wouldn't judge her. Joie was quiet but confident, knew the neighborhood and the ropes at school. She'd taken Vangie under her wing, even if there were times later when she regretted it.

Once Vangie got the lay of the land and a few months of therapy under her belt, she'd blossomed into the queen bee she remained through high school. Her breasts seemed to develop overnight, along with long, lustrous hair and a low, sexy purr in her voice. Suddenly she was head cheerleader and the basketball team captain's girl soon after, as she climbed her way to prom queen. So what if she wasn't a valedictorian like Joie.

Joie had always been amazed that they'd stayed friends, maybe the only reason she thought there might be hope for Vangie. And Vangie, beyond all the A-list events and closed cliques, still considered Joie her closest friend, if not her best. That title had always been reserved in public for girls from the in crowd.

Joie shoved the receipt for the drinks into her wallet with her card, knew she'd never be repaid except with a wave and a laugh, like Joie was another one of Vangie's adoring fans. She sighed as she walked out and headed back to Brooklyn, broke again. Why did she put up with Vangie?

Maybe she really did need therapy.

CHAPTER 26

8:33 P.M.—*East Village, 23 July 2007*

The young man on the couch was in tears.

Dr. Abel Lazarus handed him a tissue as Kent tried to pull himself together before the end of his session. He'd just reexperienced a critical moment in his childhood, the day he'd found out his father was leaving home; the same day his mother had first tried to kill herself. It had been the worst day of his life, coming home from school at the age of twelve to find out that his father was gone and not coming back, then waking up a few hours later to find his mom passed out on the living-room floor, empty bottles of pills and vodka beside her.

He'd called 911 and held his unconscious mother, sobbed on the phone with the operator as he'd waited for help to come. They'd arrived in time, but after his mother's release, their relationship had never been the same. She'd blamed him for the fact that she was still alive, abandoned, and in pain. He'd blamed her for trying to leave him as cruelly as his father had left her, only with no hope of return.

Kent had swallowed his emotions, as so many children do, choked them down like the poison his mother had swallowed. To keep living at home with her he'd had to act like nothing had happened. Once he was old enough to leave for college, he'd picked New York University, far enough from her that he could start to forget.

But, of course, no one forgets, no more than the doctor could forget his own haunted past. Sad, twisted memories had followed the boy like a fog, shrouded his days and nights in a haze of pain and misery that had led to an attempt on his own life after a year at school. He'd been sent to Lazarus for counseling and from his first session had seemed to respond favorably.

The reason was obvious to Abel if not to school administrators. He'd bitten Kent on the wrist at the end of his first session and fed. It took no more than a simple command after infection to make the boy act lighter, happier, and go back to his studies with renewed vigor. Of course, he still had weekly sessions, which gave Abel a chance to feed regularly on the boy's blood, but also to dig more deeply into the reasons for his chronic depression. Abel regressed him to key moments pulled from the boy's memory, helped him see them clearly and relive them the way Kent wished they'd gone, if only to see that his wishes weren't the problem.

The boy would have a very real therapy despite the blood loss, a deeper treatment than anything a human therapist could provide. When Abel was finished, the boy would see that no matter how painful his relationship with his mother had been, it wasn't worth throwing his life away. Then Abel could send him off to live his life, to forget about Dr. Lazarus until the doctor needed him one day and reestablished his control over the boy. His practice wasn't entirely altruistic. New patients would arrive as the old passed through, and the cycle would continue as long as necessary, until he was whole again.

Abel's new identity and practice had begun as an easy way to bring victims to him while his body was shattered. He'd needed to bring prey to him without the hunt. Opening a psychotherapy practice in the late eighties had seemed the perfect solution and had provided a steady supply of clients once they heard his low rates.

It was easy to gain influence over the right people to provide him with credible documentation. On paper he was a licensed therapist the night he opened the office almost twenty years ago. It took him less than a year to realize he was good at it; that even without using his considerable powers over the human mind, he had an intuitive gift for uncovering a patient's deepest fears and phobias.

The same skill that had made him a master torturer as he dragged his victims down to levels of desperation so deep that they begged him for death gave him amazing insight into the sources of his patients' pain. Turning that gift to healing rather than torment made him want to know more about the human mind and his own.

He did the required coursework for a full degree: read all the assigned books, sat in unseen on night classes at the best local universities, absorbed everything he could on the subject. In time, he began to use the control he had over his clients' minds to let them vividly reexperience incidents from their pasts, to see and change their memories, resolve them, and let go in a very real way. Abel could pull up the most obscure experiences or erase the deepest pain with a word. He'd found a real life again, one with purpose.

Becoming Dr. Lazarus had raised him from the dead. Adam Caine had died and been reborn, understood more in his new life about people and how they worked than ever before. Even his relationship with his own mother, how she and Perenelle had loved him, but had tried to mold him into what each wanted him to be, not who he was. He was free of them both, finally his own man, and he knew who that was and what it meant.

There was nothing left of his first life as Frederic Hartwell, no more Adam Caine or any of the other identities he'd created in between. He was Dr. Abel Lazarus, licensed psychotherapist, and had no desire to become anyone else again. His journey was finished. He'd found a home in the East Village and liked it.

He was more powerful than ever in hiding from the Veil. Using his reputation at NYU for success with even the most difficult cases, he was able to assemble a network of thralls that gave him more power and influence than he'd ever had as Adam Caine. It pleased him that in his misfortune he'd found a way to improve his lot in all ways but one.

After twenty years his twisted body was still recovering from his assistant Marlowe's revenge, and he had to find a faster way to make it whole again. He had to give that boy credit for exceeding even his own capacity for cruelty when he got the chance to punish Adam for his misdeeds.

In his life as Adam Caine, he'd done more than feed on his victims. He'd entered their worlds unseen and manipulated events, controlled circumstances, unraveled the fiber of their lives, and left them with little or no choice but to accept the merciful deaths he offered. He'd molded Marlowe to be his future henchman when he was still a child, took his parents away one at a time along with all his other options, until when they met there was no other path for the boy.

In the end, he'd had to sacrifice him for his own survival when his reserves were exhausted from an earlier assault, had been forced to use Marlowe's blood to revive himself after a brutal attack that had left Adam's body wasted and weak. At the time, it seemed the sensible thing to do. The boy had failed to retrieve the vampire baby he'd been sent for, and worse, had made a deal with Rahman to bring him the child in exchange for his vampire blood.

If Adam had known that Marlowe's veins flowed with the blood of the ancient Autochthones—vampires older and more powerful than any he'd encountered—he would never have killed the boy, certainly not without proper disposal. Marlowe had risen from the dead without Adam's help, already infected by his allies, and had used his superior strength to get revenge.

Adam had been decapitated, but his heart and spine were preserved to keep him alive, curled into a sack of flesh sewn under his jaw, heart still beating. He'd been presented to the vampire baby as a living toy, doomed to live until the baby ended his life. Only Adam's ability to draw strength from new victims brought to feed the baby's growing appetite had allowed him to send a mental summons for help, a call that brought Luna X and others.

She'd found him and carried Adam away to safety, fed him as well as she could on her own blood until she was able to bring him other victims to feed on. His vampire metabolism did the best it could, but the ability to quickly heal bullet wounds or knife attacks wasn't sufficient to re-form his entire body from scratch.

In twenty years he'd regained much of his flesh, but he was still dependent on Luna to get him from place to place. She carried him like a doll, while he projected the illusion to any who saw them that he walked by her side, arm in arm. More than anything, he longed to be whole again, to end this life as a hideously mutated freak.

He shook off the rising tide of self-pity. Every day he reminded his patients that there were lost souls in the city of New York with far worse problems. Nothing he faced was insurmountable. Life went on, even for him, and one day he would find a solution to his problem.

After all, Abel had all the time in the world.

CHAPTER 27

9:01 P.M.—*East Village, 23 July 2007*

Vangie made it to her session in plenty of time, arrived just as the sun was setting. Luna let her in with a smile, and her beautiful doctor was waiting, hers and hers alone for the next hour.

"The show went really great," said Vangie, legs curled under her on Dr. Lazarus's couch. She smiled at him with love. "I thought of you the whole time."

Abel smiled, rubbed her shoulder.

"I'll see the next one." The enthralled were always like this at first, loopy with unabashed adoration of their new master, as devoted as puppies. After twenty years together, Luna could be overly maternal in taking care of him, but at least she didn't hound him for attention like this one did.

"Yeah. I guess." She looked down, and pouted just a bit. "I just wish you'd seen this one."

"Would you like to show it to me?"

Vangie looked puzzled, then smiled as she remembered who she was talking to and held out her wrist. The doctor took it in the soft palm of his hand and lifted it to his lips.

"Think back to that night. Take me there," he said softly. His teeth sank into her skin and the room melted around them as he slipped into her mind and her memories. The room ran like water into a new shape with different lights, resolved itself into the gallery the night of the show.

Abel stood in the audience and watched Vangie prepare to go on. He looked over the crowd—her crowd. As the show started, they burst into applause. Most seemed to know her from before, and she did not disappoint. Vangie had talent and mesmerized them as he had her, but using her body, face, and voice. He wondered if any of her allure that night was the result of her recent infection, if it made her natural charisma even more seductive. She spotted Abel and played to him as he nodded and wandered the room, watched the faces of listeners as they became fans.

Abel walked through Vangie's memory of the room that night as if through the actual past, every detail reproduced more accurately than she herself could ever remember. He never tired of exploring the literal psyches of his patients, actually reliving re-creations of their best and worst moments with them.

It was the ultimate voyeurism, even he had to admit that, but so compelling that he could never resist the opportunity to explore it when he was there. More than once he'd found the key to a client's trauma waiting to be discovered just out of sight on the other side of a door or outside a window, the key to recovery after he pointed it out.

Abel had fed enough and was going to take Vangie out of her trance when he saw a familiar face, a black man in his forties with close-cropped hair. He'd been talking earlier to a light-skinned black girl working on video for the show. Abel didn't know why the man seemed so familiar until he saw the blonde beside him and put their faces together, remembered the night they'd met at Café Piranha, almost twenty years ago, when he was Adam Caine.

The night they'd tried to burn him alive.

Granted, he had been about to kill them. Steven and Lori? Friends of young Jim Miller, Nina's brother? The sight of them recalled the year when Nina's damned baby had brought the wrath of the Veil down on his head. The pain flooded through him with a fresh sting as he moved closer to the couple to get a better look to be sure he was right.

There was no question. They'd aged twenty years, as had everyone but his kind, but it was definitely them. What was their connection to Vangie? He rewound her memories, ran them backward until the black girl left the stage to go back to Steven's side, just before Lori entered. Abel let the moment play out as she gave the man a kiss on the cheek and he heard her say, "Love you, Daddy."

Steven was her father. The blond woman, Lori, must be her mother. There was too much family resemblance among them. His mind raced. They'd written that damn book about him, *Bite Marks*, gotten a bestseller out of his pain with lies he'd been in no position to contest. Setting him on fire had been bad enough, but publishing the book had added insult to the old injury. He'd put off thoughts of vengeance until he was whole, but for them to come into his life like this seemed to provide an early opportunity.

He released Vangie from her vision, woke her, and asked about her friend. She confirmed Joie's identity and answered his questions about her. Her father's recent return, her mother's cancer diagnosis, all made it easy for him to instruct Vangie to stay on the idea of sending her to see him, now that she'd raised the topic over drinks. Once the girl was here, he could decide for himself the best way to use her.

He sent Vangie home happy and went to look through his old files, one of the few things he'd salvaged from his penthouse before he'd abandoned it. Abel hadn't pursued any of Adam's old art projects in some time, but there might be fresh inspiration in his past. If he was going to have a chance to get even with Steven and Lori, he wanted it to be good. Something special.

Something fun.

CHAPTER 28

9:17 P.M.—*East Village, 23 July 2007*

The Pyramid Club, on Avenue A, was Claire's favorite hangout when she was in her early stages of recovery, after nearly fifty years of entombment by the Veil. In the eighties it had been what it remained today, a black brick hole with booze and music, lively, but with an air of the pit. It provided the kind of dark, claustrophobic confinement she was used to after being entombed for so long.

Claire was out on the crowded dance floor in the back of the club. It was filled with its usual eighties night mix of downtown kids in their twenties looking for a piece of the club's past glory. Pierced and tattooed dancers bounced around in black jeans, T-shirts, and the occasional kilt. They wore too much makeup, skirts too short, pants too tight, and jackets too leather. Either the styles hadn't changed all that much in twenty years or this was their homage to the past.

Claire flowed like smoke, moved around the dance floor almost out of the range of vision of the humans around her. She still enjoyed the music, a sense of nostalgia, but she was losing interest in this scene. Even if the Pyramid was one of the last holdouts of eighties' club royalty to survive, it had become a faded cartoon of its old self, no matter how sweetly reminiscent. Now that CBGB's was slated to reopen as a John Varvatos rock-and-roll boutique, the East Village of the eighties was officially dead to her. She spent more time below Houston these days, anyway.

Twenty years ago, Claire had felt danger in the air of the East Village as she stalked the streets this far east, even if it couldn't touch her. Now the greatest threat was boredom. The club where famed drag queens once danced on the bar, avant garde theater was performed in the back, and drugs of all kinds were inhaled freely, had turned to kitsch.

Loud music filled the air around her, an old favorite, Talking Heads' *Remain in Light*. Claire whirled, refreshed by life despite her mood as she fed on the youth around her. She enjoyed their energy as an appetizer, wondered which one to lure away from the herd for a late-night bite.

Burke had kept her on strict rations, forced her to feed from a select pool of willing thralls whose continued servitude was of use to them. She'd never been allowed to follow her head like this, to sniff out potential victims on the street and take them like the creature of the night that she was.

But Burke was gone, whisked away with the rest of the Council's Hundred to the impenetrable depths of Clean Slate headquarters. Despite the crisis caused by his capture, it gave a lightness to her step to know that she was not only free of Burke's restrictions, she was standing head of the East Village Bloodline until he returned.

If he ever returned.

The song ended. Claire retired to the bar in front and ordered a shot of tequila, her old club drink of choice. The bar always kept at least one excellent bottle in stock for her, thanks to an understanding reached with the owner on the night of her first visit. Vampires couldn't eat, but enjoyed the flavor of fine vintage liquors even if they couldn't get drunk.

Claire sensed something odd as she sat at the bar, something out of place or missing. Usually, she could locate everyone in the room, could lightly touch and connect to any one of them. Tonight, there were bodies she could sense but not connect with, a feeling she'd had only once before.

In Red Hook, at Clean Slate.

A Latin woman in her forties with white hair stepped up to the bar next to Claire, dressed in simple black slacks and a turtleneck with a crisp, short jacket, almost a uniform. She wore odd headgear under a knitted cap; black bands wrapped around her head like a laurel wreath that ended in lightweight disks that cupped her temples. She adjusted the cap to better conceal it. Claire was sure it was a portable version of the device she had sensed in Red Hook. She could feel its signal jamming her connection to the woman's mind, and life force.

The woman ordered a Heineken, smiled, and nodded.

"Claire St. Claire? My name is Lopez. I have a message from you from our guest, Dr. Townsend Burke."

"Like I care," sneered Claire.

"He said that might be your response." The woman picked up her beer and drank from it, took her time to speak again. "You should know that Burke made it clear that you're in no way to speak to us or share information, as per the laws of the Veil. It was the only message he was interested in sending to you."

Claire couldn't stop the smile that spread across her face. She had never been any good at poker. The woman smiled back.

"Nice hat," said Claire.

"Before you consider removing my headgear to influence me, consider that I am not alone, and my associates are more than capable of taking you down from where they are without harming a hair on any bystanders' heads."

Claire knew the woman was right about backup, had already felt the helmet's field coming from other parts of the room. She knew she couldn't move fast enough to take them all out alone, but could move fast enough to evade them. Still, if Burke didn't want her talking to them, she felt compelled to hear them out.

"Let's chat," said Claire, picking up her purse.

"My boss would rather speak with you himself. At headquarters." She stepped back and motioned to the door. Claire hesitated. It was one thing to hear them out; it was another to walk alone into the belly of the beast.

"How do I know I'll get back out once I'm in?"

"Trust? Faith?"

Claire laughed.

"I was told the topic of the meeting would be enough to convince you," added Lopez.

"Which is?"

The woman leaned closer. "Perenelle de Marivaux."

Claire moved to the front door so fast that she seemed to blur, looked back when Lopez didn't follow immediately with her team.

"Where's your car?"

CHAPTER 29

9:32 P.M.—*Lower East Side, 23 July 2007*

The long black car rumbled through the night like rolling thunder, down Bowery toward the Manhattan Bridge, then across to take the Brooklyn–Queens Expressway to Red Hook. Claire ignored Lopez on the ride. The woman was a lackey; conversation was pointless and would tell Claire nothing. She looked out through shaded windows. Her vampire vision could see through them easily as she watched Manhattan recede into the distance.

This was the kind of situation she'd always shared with Tom. They'd had a special bond from their first meeting; more than a team, they were an entity. Two minds, more, if you included all of Tom's personalities, two bodies that functioned as one, like an oiled machine. As she rushed into the enemy's clutches, she let her mind wander back to happier times than these.

Back to their first night together.

"What do you wish, more than anything else?"

Tom had finished revealing the secrets of her new life. He stood, one hand in hers, the other resting lightly on her cheek as he gazed into her large green eyes with a warm smile. "What would make you happy?"

Claire thought about it. Tom had freed her of all restrictions, of any mortal cares, but she didn't want to just walk away from her old life. She wanted to start fresh, erase her past pain from the face of the Earth with fire and begin her new life rising like the Phoenix from the purging flames.

"I wish . . ."

She thought of the best way to ask, how to express her wish in the proper words. In her books, genies and devils could twist your words to ruin your ends. She wasn't sure how many wishes she had and didn't want to mess up. Claire thought carefully, took her time until she was sure she had it right.

"I wish to see all this disappear, as if it had never been. I need to erase my past to claim my future, want to obliterate this house and all within."

Tom beamed at Claire as if she'd passed her final test into a secret society. "Well done! Precisely spoken! So we shall."

They danced their way downstairs, sang an old ballad that Tom had taught her. She had learned it the first time he sang it, her memory as accurate as a long-playing record, remembered everything instantly now. Though the song was strange, the chorus was funny, and made her laugh as they moved through the halls of the house, unseen.

"Bedlam boys are bonny," Claire sang, "for they all go bare and they live by the air . . ."

"And they want no drink nor money!" They sang the last line together as they burst into the first room in the hall.

Helga, the madam's favorite, straddled a stout bald man on his back on the big bed, naked except for his socks. They thrashed like farm animals. Neither of them saw Tom or Claire until they wanted to be seen. Helga looked up in anger.

"What are you doing in here? Madame! Come fetch the brat!" Helga shouted as soon as they appeared, without even questioning how or why. She was jealous of the younger girl, always told the madam of any infraction of the rules and had often added to Claire's burden with punishments she otherwise could have avoided.

The girl stepped closer to the bed as the man swung at Helga's enormous breasts, tried to push her off so he could defend himself. Helga kept calling for the madam, until Claire gripped her windpipe and closed it with a single squeeze.

"Shut up for once, you stupid cow. You always talk too much." Claire shoved her away and the woman fell off the bed to the floor. The man climbed to his feet and held up a sheet to cover his body.

"Get out of here! Out, or I'll—"

Tom snapped his neck with a backhanded slap.

"Claire? We don't have all night," said Tom.

The girl turned to the shocked whore on the floor, the sorry bitch who'd wielded so much power over her until tonight. She cringed on the floor in tears; her makeup ran as she whimpered and pissed herself. A wet stain spread across the madam's imported Persian carpet. Claire laughed.

"He's right, you know. You aren't worth the time."

Claire was a quick learner and snapped the woman's neck as Tom had the customer's. She took Tom's hand as they continued their song and dance, left the first bedroom to go to the next and the next, visited each in turn and rained death down on them all.

She'd never known that she'd kept so much hate and anger buried inside her, built up like a stalagmite in a cavern, drop by drop, night after night of being raped for a living. It was as if vast untapped reserves of rage were being unleashed at once, sent her through the house like an avenging fury.

No one saw them as they went about their work. They willed them not to as they entered each room, picked out their victims, and dealt with each in turn. For this one, a knife in the chest; for that one, a bludgeon to the head; a rope around this soft white throat; snap this skinny neck.

All through the house they went, bed by bed, did a merry jig between each as they sang the song Tom had taught her, the ballad of Mad Maudlin, about a maiden searching for her lost love, Tom. They shared loving glances over the dying, as they consecrated their union in blood and saved the best for last.

The madam sat at her desk, counted the night's receipts before she locked up. The sun would be rising in a few hours, and while there were a select few clients who stayed in their rooms, most would vacate soon and creep back to the lies of their everyday lives.

She was happy to provide her customers with the imaginary landscapes they preferred and a cast of able-bodied characters to inhabit them. If her clients' families and professions were truly satisfying, there would have been no profit for her in providing temporary alternatives. She was grateful, either that so many women were unable to provide for all their men's erotic needs, or that so many men didn't appreciate what they had at home.

Her coffers were full no matter which was to blame.

Something flew through the open door, fell to the floor with a thump, and rolled. It hit the front of her desk before she could get a good look. No one was supposed to be back in her part of the house during working hours. If the girls were having fun at her expense, instead of working, they would pay for their play.

Madame stood and walked to the dark doorway, glanced behind her to see what had rolled in. The light above her desk shadowed the floor in front. Before she could look more closely into the murk, something else bounced through the doorway and rolled to a halt at her feet. The madam shrieked.

"Helga!"

It was her head, at any rate, eyes still wide with fear.

"You can't scare me!" Madame yelled at the dark hall, and ran behind her desk. Other heads pounded into the room after her, customers' and call girls, rolled around the floor like billiard balls. Madame opened a drawer to pull out her pistol. She kept it handy when she was here until she got her cash locked away into her safe and even after that, on her way to bed for the night. Claire and her new customer followed the heads into the room, stopped inside the doorway.

She waved the pistol at them, hammer cocked.

"A showman! You certainly put on a show for me, *mein herr*! What is this, a rescue? You want her? You can have her!"

The man shrugged, lifted his hands as if to say all this had nothing to do with him. It was the girl's business. She could tell from the way Claire looked at her with glittering eyes and her sharp, feral grin.

"I'm here to pay my debt."

"Your . . ." She paled, as she thought of all the years she'd held a dead mother's debt to the house over Claire's head to bind her, as imaginary as the games played upstairs. Even if it had existed, it would have been paid many times over by now. If Claire was upset only about that little subterfuge, there was still hope. "Consider it settled, then. There is no debt!"

"No?" Claire stepped closer, and that damn smile of hers was even brighter. "That is good, Madame, very good. Now that my debt is settled, we are free to discuss one last matter."

Madame shuddered as she considered what that might be.

"Your debt to me . . ."

The gun had no effect on them as Madame fired it. They descended like a cloud, pulled her mind apart slowly as the two of them fed on her body, paralyzed her with visions of Claire's childhood violations, all pouring through the madam's brain at the same time, a simultaneous psychic gang rape that surpassed any other atrocity performed in the name of sex in Berlin that night or any since.

As Tom and Claire left the building they set it ablaze, Claire's leather-and-gilt-bound library of fantasy carried out safely in their arms. As they walked away, lamp pipes, punctured to fill the rooms with gas, exploded and the blast leveled the building. Claire had brought down the house, like the newly born star she was, with her very first homemade bomb.

The car arrived in Red Hook, at the same main door Claire had tried to enter the previous night. The corrogated outer door rumbled open, and they were admitted without incident, rolled down the driveway she'd only glimpsed before. The car descended three levels before it pulled into a chamber with a locked door that led inside the complex.

Lopez and the guards with her went through the same test that the driver with Claire had failed the night of her break-in. Once they'd proved they weren't infected, the door opened. Claire was waved in, untested. The results would be obvious. She followed Lopez down a brightly lit white hallway, the guards behind her. They stopped at another locked door; Lopez opened it with her palm print and led Claire inside.

A tall man in an expensive business suit was seated at a large, curved black desk. Its glossy monitor surface was covered with live windows of security-cam shots and text documents. He looked more like a corporate executive than the leader of a military organization, but, of course, that's what Clean Slate would need. He wore wire-rim glasses and a goatee, waved her to a chair across from him as he shut down the moving desktop.

"Ms. St. Claire. Glad you could join us. My name is Jonathan Richmond. Welcome to Clean Slate Global."

"You said this was about Perenelle." She saw no need to waste time.

"In part. I'm sure you and your—people—know by now who we are and what we're trying to do."

"I know that we are at war."

"After centuries, probably millennia, of humans being fed upon by your kind, like cattle. It's only a war now because we've developed better defenses than stakes and crosses."

Claire St. Claire shifted in her seat and looked around in annoyance, like a socialite forced into conversation with the help. Richmond watched the teenage-looking girl in the seat across from him, knew from Clean Slate's files that she was really over eighty. He kept his foot pressed on the dead man's switch under his desk that would fill the room with ultraviolet light, lethal only to vampires, if his foot came off. They needed her, but he was ready to use it if she even sniffed at him too hard.

"Semantics. What has Perenelle to do with us?"

"She was the only one who escaped our capture of your leadership. We understand that you and she have been in opposition in the past."

Claire snarled.

Richmond stiffened, felt the low end of the sound rattle his diaphragm as he instinctively pulled back into his chair. The sound was savage and the sheer strength of it was unexpected from someone so petite, delicate as porcelain. Something. He had to remember that; she wasn't someone, she was something.

Claire sat back, smiled.

"I'm sorry. Yes. We have a history."

"She did you an injustice?"

"She separated me from someone I love."

Richmond leaned forward ever so slightly, just for the body language, not daring to approach.

"What if I could help you find him? Punish her?"

Claire's oval eyes narrowed as she seemed to consider what he might have to offer. "You're asking me to betray the Veil, my kind, and all I am sworn to protect as a standing Council member," she said.

Richmond smiled. She hadn't said no.

"Let me show you something."

A wall panel opened to reveal a screen, and he played the video of the

Council's meeting at the Hyatt for her up to the break-in, pointed out the movements of the chair that he'd noticed, the way people addressed it. Claire watched the tape twice.

Her eyes narrowed again, this time in anger.

"I don't understand. I don't see anything."

"Then you do understand," said Richmond. "The Triumvirate of the Veil introduced by the host is a collective hallucination. You can't see them on camera. You all know that, they state it freely. I'm telling you that the presence of the vampire called Perenelle de Marivaux at the meeting was also an illusion. Neither showed up on camera.

"You know that the Triumvirate is a psychic projection. If Perenelle is, too, it explains how she avoided capture. She was never really there."

"Astral projection? But only the Triumvirate . . ."

He watched as her eyes widened. Her face twisted as she processed the same information he had and made the same connections. If Perenelle knew secrets known only to the Triumvirate, then she was the Triumvirate. Perenelle ran the Veil. It wasn't a democracy but a puppet government, with her pulling the strings. As Richmond watched Claire he realized that he'd be the only thing in the room when her rage hit.

He signaled for backup.

Doors behind her slid open as Claire bared her fangs in fury. Her head whipped around as armed agents entered in time to distract her from Richmond. She turned back to him with a slow smile, composed herself as her body relaxed.

Claire slid back into her chair.

"That fucking French bitch," she said. "She's played us like children all this time!"

"Will you help us get her?"

"Find Tom O'Bedlam. You found me, you can find him. Free Tom and we'll get you Perenelle, all of them, what do we care?" She stood, went to the door, and looked back at him.

He nodded. The agents retreated, made way for her.

Richmond couldn't take his eyes off her as she swept out. The damn things were beautiful. She threw her last words over her shoulder as she went down the hall.

"Find Tom, then we talk."

CHAPTER 30

3:16 A.M.—*Park Slope, 24 July 2007*

Joie didn't know what woke her up, the sound of a passing truck or an urge to pee; all she knew was that she couldn't get back to sleep when she got back from the bathroom. She lay in bed with her heart pounding, her stomach in a knot. Not so much a knot as a hard, hollow sphere where her guts should be that felt like it could never be filled. The void her life would become if she lost her mother to cancer. It was a panic attack. She'd heard her dad talk about the ones he'd had in his twenties often enough to recognize one when it hit. They were getting more frequent and worse.

Her mom's surgery was coming up soon and each day was like waiting for a reprieve from the governor, for the call that said it had all been a terrible mistake. Lori was fine, they'd just gotten her test results mixed up with someone else's. She was going to live a long and full life, see her daughter marry and make babies between making films, live long enough to see the first colony on Mars.

Joie always threw in the last because it seemed impossibly distant, something that kept her mother alive in a future that was still grand and unpredictable, a world where medical science would have licked simple problems like disease and aging, where old people lived full, rich lives. A world where girls didn't lose their mothers while they were still teenagers, when they needed them more than ever even if they never told them that, even if they told them to mind their own business and leave them alone.

Joie felt tears rise and fought them back.

To cry over her mother while she was alive was wrong. You didn't grieve the living. Mom was just having surgery. She had to think about that and only that, not the bigger picture of cancer. Baby steps. Her mother was having a hysterectomy. That's all. Just because her grandmother had died of cancer didn't mean that her mother would. Take your medicine slowly, a spoon at a time, and it won't choke you.

Maybe a couple of hits of weed would help.

She climbed out of bed and went downstairs. Her mother kept her pot in the basement. She'd started smoking again when she married Fritz and after the breakup smoked more than ever until she finally went cold turkey. She kept a little in the house for the days when she was throwing up, or when the book wasn't going well and needed lubrication.

Lori had always thought she was being clever by hiding her stash in the basement and smoking in an old rocking chair on a Persian carpet, kept down there for no apparent reason. Unfortunately, the ceiling wasn't all that airtight, and by the time she came out of the basement she was always too stoned to notice the light scent that drifted up into the kitchen behind her. By the time Joie was old enough to recognize the smell, she was old enough to want a taste, and used to sneak into her mother's stash on a regular basis until she took too much and got caught.

After that, they had The Drug Talk, and Lori had to face the fact that her generation was hard-pressed to tell their kids that drugs were bad when most of them had been conceived under their influence. They'd worked out a deal to be honest with each other. Lori told Joie her obligatory, cautionary drug-horror stories, about her friend Karl, who had fried his brains on bad acid, and her first roommate Maylene's descent into speed addiction. She also admitted that some drugs had been fun, in small quantities and under safe conditions.

In turn, Joie had promised not to use anything stronger than pot without discussing it with her mom and promised not to completely bake her brain with weed before it was finished growing. Lori kept smoking in the basement out of habit and warned Joie not to smoke up the curtains and furniture in her room.

"My daughter's room is not going to smell like an opium den," she'd said, and gone downstairs to smoke a bowl after the ordeal of their conversation.

When Joie got to the kitchen she saw a dim light under the basement door and smelled an old, familiar scent. Her mom was awake, too, and already down here for the same reason.

"Mom?" Joie pulled the door open a crack and heard a violent fit of coughing from below. She opened the door and went downstairs to help. Her mother was doubled over on the chair, a wooden pipe in one hand, the other on her chest.

"Jeez," she said when she'd recovered enough. "You scared the shit out of me!"

Joie tried not to laugh, but couldn't help herself.

"Sorry. Trouble sleeping." She sat on the bottom of the stairs. Lori reluctantly passed her the pipe and disposable butane lighter.

"This is a first. Don't get used to it."

Joie lit the bowl and took a hit, passed it back to her mother. Lori scowled.

"You do that far too well."

Joie smirked. "You should see me roll a blunt."

Lori smacked her playfully and took another hit herself.

"So. Surgery." She spoke with her lungs full, blew the smoke into the air, and passed the pipe.

"You scared?"

"Duh." Lori grinned, then dropped the pretense. "Yeah. Not so much about the surgery. That's simple enough, I guess. Chemo doesn't sound like much fun." She pulled her robe closer.

"No."

They sat quietly for a while, passed the pipe back and forth. Joie began to feel the effects kick in after the third hit, a pleasant easing of the tightness in her gut. Her dad had once called it instant meditation in a bowl, when he didn't know she could hear him. It did make her feel calmer, if a little distant from real space-time, but that was the point, wasn't it? To push back the world long enough to see it clearly, if used properly. Her mother smiled at her and Joie smiled back, both a little bleary-eyed.

"These stairs are hard," said Joie.

Lori put the pipe and lighter down on the shelf next to her and held out her arms. Joie stood and turned to sit on her mother's lap. Her mom grunted as she landed, laughed, and they threw their arms around each other as they settled in to keep her balanced.

"My little baby girl," said Lori, in a strained voice under Joie's weight. They both giggled and hugged, squeezed into one soft mass as Joie felt the tears rise again and let them fall, felt Lori's splash onto her arm as she cried, too. It felt good after holding back for so long, not hard sobs or tragic tears, just a little shared weeping, a release of pressure that could get them back to sleep and through this panic attack to the next. The flow ended as quickly as it had begun and Joie felt Lori shift beneath her weight.

"Oh, God," she said. "Don't take this the wrong way, honey, but you are so too big for this. . . ." They both laughed until Joie fell off the chair and Lori slid onto the floor beside her. They lay on the carpet for a moment, laughed until they couldn't breathe, clung to each other for a moment before they tried to stand.

"Know what I need more than anything?" asked Lori.

"Häagen-Dazs," said Joie.

"You are so your mother's daughter. Come on."

She got up and helped her daughter to her feet and they went upstairs to raid the refrigerator, demons of the night banished for the moment.

But they'd be back.

CHAPTER 31

9:03 A.M.—Park Slope, 24 July 2007

The sound of banging on the front door and the bell from downstairs woke Lori up, then she heard her daughter shouting as she piled down the stairs.

"I'm coming, dammit! Fuck!"

Lori pulled on her robe and put on slippers as she listened to Joie open the door. She ran out of her room in time to see Christopher burst inside, sheets of paper in his hand, his face flushed red, as if he'd run all the way there from the subway.

"Why didn't you tell me!" he shouted up at Lori when he saw her. "How could you not tell me?"

He pushed his way inside and went to the living room, flopped down on the couch. Lori got to the bottom of the stairs and joined her daughter.

"What are you talking about?"

Lori sat on the rocking chair and leaned forward, her face concerned. Joie sat on the footstool and reached out to take Christopher's hand, but he pulled it away, threw the sheets of paper down on the coffee table.

Lori picked them up, pulled eyeglasses out of the pocket of her robe to get a better look at them. Her face fell as she examined them. She almost gasped. It couldn't be.

"Oh, God, Christopher . . . how did you—"

"Mom? What is it?"

"A police report," said Christopher. "About a couple of Good Samaritans who found a baby in Central Park and turned it over to the police, even said they thought it might have something to do with the hooker that got killed, the one whose baby disappeared. Lucky guess, that . . . At least I got to keep my real name."

Lori was at a loss for words. Neither she nor Steven had had the time since meeting him to find out if he was the same Christopher they feared he was. Getting it confirmed by him didn't help.

"We weren't sure. I didn't want to say anything until—"

"What? You were sure you could get away with acting like we just met? Like I was a stranger to you?"

"Christopher . . . it's complicated," said Lori. He slapped his head into his hands and groaned loudly. "I know, believe me, but we can explain if you let me. Please."

Christopher sat back, glared at her, his eyes red. He must have been up all night with this news, waiting for the sun to come up to come over and confront her. Lori wished that she knew how much he knew, suspected it was more than he realized. The memories of that week had to be buried in his brain somewhere, waiting to come out. She didn't want to be the one to unlock that door.

"Let me get Steven over here; let's make breakfast and we can fill you in on what we know. Please."

Over omelets and bagels, Steven and Lori kept their history of events down to the short version of the story, one that left out any mention of vampires or alchemy. Fortunately for them, they'd discussed earlier what they would tell Christopher if it turned out that he was the one they'd saved, so their lies came out naturally and sounded as much like the real truth as they could have hoped.

"We knew your uncle Jim, but never met your mother. She wrote us, but died before she could call us back. That's how he found us, through the card we sent to her. We were helping him find her killer." Steven looked uncomfortable. "It sounds crazy to say it out loud now, but we were just trying to help."

"So you wrote a book about it?"

Lori winced. This was the hardest part to explain.

"Yes. Jim wanted Nina's story told, and we rewrote the book we were working on when we met. The money we sent you, the trust fund, was from your share, payment for the rights to her story. That was the deal we worked out with Jim. Their share of the money would go to you."

"Why is it about vampires?" He had the book open on his lap, flipped through the large, glossy pages of Steven's artwork between blocks of Lori's words.

"That was the book we were contracted to write. It had to be. We just adapted her story to fit into it," said Lori. "It became a metaphor."

Joie sat quietly beside Christopher and looked like she was having as much trouble absorbing her parents' story as he was. The bestseller she'd grown up with, the book that had paid for their home and her education through high school, was about the mother of the guy she'd just met. Someone she'd thought she shared a special bond with, but it was starting to look much bigger than that.

"So, my uncle asks you to help find my mom's killer, you stalk this Caine guy for a week, Jim dies, Caine disappears, and you write a book that becomes a bestseller and send me money for the rest of my life."

Lori and Steven looked at each other and sighed.

"What was I doing in Central Park? How did you find me?"

"We had to tell the cops something," said Lori. "Jim found you with some junkies and rescued you, but he left and never came back."

"We were told he died in an explosion in an abandoned tenement downtown, tracking down a lead on Nina's killer," added Steven. "Maybe a meth lab. There wasn't enough evidence to charge Caine with anything. We did what we could, made sure you'd be provided for, the way Jim wanted."

Steven poured himself more tea and clenched his jaw. Lori could tell he was going into shutdown mode and soon would refuse to answer any more questions.

"Christopher," she said, trying to organize her thoughts and feelings. "You have to understand that it was a hard year for all of us."

"For all of *us*? I was orphaned! The only two people who knew anything about my mother turned it into a picture book on vampires! You tell me my uncle died, but can't say where or how. What am I supposed to take from this? Where does it get me?"

"There's nothing more we can tell you."

Lori knew that anything more would only make things worse. How could they tell him he'd spent a week as a vampire, that he'd been rescued from a hidden subway station that was secret even from the Metropolitan Transportation Authority? That his uncle had died in a fireball he'd set off to incinerate all traces of the nest of vampires that Christopher had created? That he'd been responsible for hundreds of deaths and had started a plague of undead zombies on the Lower East Side? That only thousand-year-old alchemic secrets had saved him? Even if he believed any of it, how could knowing it help?

He glared at them, knew they were hiding something, but there was no way to get any more out of them. Lori hated lying to him, but had no choice. She had to protect her daughter, and that meant finding out what Christopher really was before they got any closer. Before he found out what he'd been.

"That's it, then." He stood up, threw the book down on the table, and headed for the door.

"Christopher—" Joie rose to follow him.

"Don't! Don't tell me to listen to them. They're liars."

He shook her hand off his shoulder and left, slammed the door behind him. Steven shook his head as Lori winced.

"That went well," he said.

CHAPTER 32

"Wow." Tasha finished off her fruit smoothie at the new Dojo's restaurant on West Fourth Street with a last slurp on her straw. "Have you talked to Christopher since then?"

"I tried. But, you know, caller ID. If he wants to screen, he can." Joie poked at her fries and burger, but had no appetite. This morning with Christopher and her parents had been bad enough, but it was also one day closer to her mom's surgery. Her stomach was clenched like a fist.

Tasha was Joie's real best friend, more than Vangie. They'd met in a freshman film class at NYU, teamed up on their first project, and realized that even though they'd grown up in different boroughs, Queens v. Brooklyn, they'd had the same lives. Mostly. Details differed, but emotionally, they were sisters.

Joie had filled her in on the morning's events because Tasha was a fixer. She had a natural instinct for how to put things right, even if no one in her own family listened to her. If anyone could come up with an angle on how to fix things between Christopher and her folks, and, more important, Christopher and her, Tasha could.

She watched her think about it as she chewed on her straw.

"I've got it. You know what you have to do?" she said. Then her face fell. "Damn."

"What?" Joie felt like she'd had a tarot reading interrupted just before the last card was turned down. "What?"

Tasha pointed to the picture window beside them, but Vangie's voice cut through the air behind Joie before she had time to turn and look.

"There you are! I was hoping to run into you."

Joie frowned. She was still pissed about getting stuck with the bill yesterday. "Hey, Vangie."

"Hi. I wanted to give you this. . . ." She dug inside a purse that easily cost more than everything Joie and Tasha were wearing. "Here." Instead of money, she pulled out a business card and handed it to Joie.

"Your shrink?"

"He thinks he can help with your panic attacks."

"You told him about me?"

"I was telling him about me. You just came up. See, you do matter in my life!" She giggled and turned to go. "Catch you later."

Vangie breezed back out the door, fast and loud, like a summer storm, left the room with the same humid sense of disturbance in her wake.

"I never thought I'd see the day," said Tasha.

"What day?"

"The day that Vangie and I actually agree." She tapped the card in Joie's hand. "That's what I was just about to say. You need to talk to a professional, baby. You got too much to carry alone."

Joie looked at the card again. Maybe a little therapy was a good idea for a while. Her mom and dad had done it often enough, and the sessions she'd had when Fritz and her mom were breaking up had helped her get past her anger. Yeah, what the hell. It was worth a call.

What did she have to lose?

CHAPTER 33

7:45 P.M.—West Village, 24 July 2007

The phone rang while Lori was in the kitchen, making a sandwich and heating up soup. She wasn't all that hungry but knew she needed to eat; some animal part of her brain kept reminding her each day to put food into her stomach or die. There was no good reason to beat cancer to the punch by starving to death.

"Lori?" Steven was at the other end. Miles Davis blasted in the background. "I found Perenelle."

"Great," said Lori. "We could use some answers about now. Where is she, still in the West Village?"

"Yeah," he said, with a laugh. "Sort of. Get dressed. We have to get there by nine."

"Get where?"

"You'll never believe it. . . ."

The Greenwich Village Funeral Home on Bleecker Street was just off Sixth Avenue. It had been in business for three generations—not as long as Perenelle had lived in the West Village, of course, but there were only a handful of institutions here with that distinction. The funeral home was light and airy. The creamy rooms were restored prewar architecture, with high ceilings and golden chandeliers. Wide doorways with stained-glass arched windows led you back to the memorial chapel.

Perenelle stood just outside where the evening service was to be held, accepted the condolences of Perenelle's old friends and neighbors for her loss. She was gracious with a tinge of sadness in a stylish black dress and antique black lace mantilla carried out of Spain hundreds of years ago. Her outfit was one she could never have enjoyed in her senior guise, but had taken out dancing in the East Village on rare nights off from playing the elder sage. It was stylish but demure, modest enough to see off a beloved aunt.

She'd always looked good in black. Perenelle had considered shopping for a new outfit, but then the whole thing started to feel as if she was taking her faux funeral a little too seriously. She had to remember that it was only a means to an end, throwing off her aged identity to start a new life in her old home as her own great-niece. It was a ploy she should have thought of sooner, one she could repeat indefinitely.

Perenelle kept her delicate features arranged in a mask of stoic grief while she took notice of who was there and who wasn't. It was a rare treat, to see who would attend your own funeral before you were actually dead, and she'd had a few surprises. One neighbor she'd thought despised her had sent a huge bouquet and a highly complimentary note on her character to her niece. Either she had misinterpreted his feelings or he was sucking up to the survivor for reasons of his own. Others she'd thought were good friends had begged off on one pretext or another, more interested in enjoying their remaining days in the Hamptons or at home than to pay respects to the end of hers.

The doors in front opened again and she looked up to see two familiar faces. They'd changed in the last twenty years, but she still recognized them. If nothing else, the big grin Steven was trying to hide when he saw her would have given him away, dreadlocks or no dreadlocks. In many ways, it was still the face of the boy he'd been when she met him.

Lori looked slightly strained, as if she was living under more of a burden than her ex-partner. Perenelle felt something awry in the woman's body. Not even her vampire senses could isolate the exact problem, but, based on past experience, it was cancer. She wondered if Lori knew, then looked into her eyes and could tell that she did.

"I would not have expected to see you here tonight," Perenelle said to them quickly, when they reached her side. "I had no idea my aunt meant so much to you."

Steven's eyebrows shot up.

"Your aunt? Right, yes. We lost touch over the years, but heard about the memorial just in time. I found a condolences posting on the funeral home's Web site when I googled her name to get back in touch."

"Yes. The Internet is a blessing." She smiled thinly and pulled them aside, out of the hearing of others. "After all these years, I can't imagine you came only to pay your respects."

"Christopher is back," said Lori. "We need to know anything you can tell us about what to expect."

Perenelle would have paled if it were possible. The cured vampire child was back in New York? Rahman's folly had come home to roost. His last words the night she saw his departing spirit appear to her filled her with foreboding. What he had warned her of could still come to pass.

"We have to talk. After this is over." She handed them a card with her home address, a habit carried over from a gentler age. "Please, do stay for the service. There's a lovely video tribute I'm rather fond of that captures my aunt's legacy, set to her favorite music."

She smiled and rejoined the mourners.

Steven remembered the book-lined parlor. The room in Perenelle's home where they'd met with her the first time. It hadn't changed much in twenty years. There were a few new books published since then on the occult and spiritualism, a new painting or two, and a wall-mounted flat-screen TV.

Perenelle poured them glasses of cognac, didn't bother offering tea. This was not a teatime conversation. It deserved a drink.

"You're quite right that Rahman told me more than I told you that night," said Perenelle. "It wasn't time yet. There would have been no point to burdening your years since then with knowledge you could do nothing about."

"Burdening?" Steven narrowly avoided doing a sitcom spit-take.

"I'm sorry. This will not be easy to hear."

The story Perenelle had to tell was long and grew more discouraging by the minute. It began with Rahman's early days as a vampire and the birth of alchemy as he roamed the Arab world, seeking a cure for his condition. She recounted the story of her own infection in Paris, how Rahman had turned her into a vampire to force her husband, Nicolas, to complete the elixir of life.

"The last stage of the formula must be fed to an infant for the final distillation of the Philosopher's Tincture. The child is then sacrificed. It was the reason Rahman had to force us to continue. The child's drained blood, purified by its metabolism, becomes the elixir of life.

"Nicolas and I experimented for years with the quantity we created with Rahman in Paris. At full strength, it gave my husband virtual immortality. Diluted a thousand times, we were able to cure any ailment, sometimes even restore lost youth. Our supply lasted for centuries, and we'd only just begun to discover its limits when we ran out."

They had succeeded in distilling the elixir of life, but the formula was useless as a cure for vampirism. It wasn't until a vampire child, Nina's baby, was accidentally created by Adam Caine that Rahman had hope for a new distillation of the formula, one that might have an effect on them.

"You saw the result," said Perenelle. "The child was transformed to feed on life beyond all reason and absorbed all it could, even Rahman's. His spirit stayed conscious in the child's body, the only one that did. He could only control its power until the sun rose."

"The explosion," said Lori.

She remembered the moment well. The demon child had floated above them, ready to take their lives. Before Rahman could strike, the sun came up and distracted him. He'd thought his new body could survive the dawn, but instead, the energy of the morning light had pushed the baby's system into overload.

"The sunlight triggered a last reaction, one Rahman didn't anticipate. The formula went critical, threw off the excessive energy the child's body had absorbed into an explosion of pure life. Snow melted away and grass turned green, flowers blossomed. The infant was restored to human as if back to its default setting, but at the same time, something not quite human. Something more may have been buried inside, waiting to be released."

Lori's head was spinning.

"But what does that mean? Is he human or not?"

Steven and Lori accepted a refill of cognac, waited for her to finish. Perenelle sat back and stared into her glass.

"Whatever he is, Christopher's blood is still the elixir of life. He is unprecedented. No one in the history of alchemy has been infused with the pure liquid essence of life in their veins and been allowed to live to adulthood.

"At the very least, I'd say he's an immortal of some kind, or will be soon. Rahman thought that the child's growth would stop when it reached maturity."

"Maturity?"

"Seven times three. By the end of each seven years of life, the human body has replaced every cell. New cells develop until the end of the third cycle, when a body's reached full maturity at age twenty-one. That would be his birthday this year, would it not?"

They nodded, then finished their drinks before they dared ask any questions.

"Could he still be a vampire?" asked Steven.

Perenelle shrugged. "He seems human, from what you say. He walks by day, eats food; neither possible for us. What concerns me is not what he is, but what he may become. Rahman had more to say. . . ." She leaned forward, looked as frightened as they had ever seen her.

"There's another possibility—that the elixir has continued to evolve in his body. If it hasn't been detected in him so far, it's possible that it's become ordinary human blood, that the power of the elixir is temporary.

"The other possibility is that over time it's fused with his body, that the elixir has grown up with him into something new, something we can't foresee, something that can hide itself." She paused, almost as if for dramatic effect.

"As an infant, anyone who drank Christopher's blood at full strength would conceivably live forever. There's no telling what the elixir could become in two decades. Rahman was afraid that his twenty-first birthday could bring on a complete rebirth as something we've never seen on Earth, a being of potentially infinite power over humans and vampires."

There was silence when she finished speaking. Steven finally found his voice.

"How do you stop something like that? If you have to?"

Perenelle refilled all their glasses.

"I honestly don't know."

CHAPTER 34

10:33 P.M.—Lower East Side, 24 July 2007

Christopher sat in the lotus position on the floor of his room in blue boxer briefs, hands on his knees, palms up. His eyes were closed, and soft sitar music played on his iPod earbuds, a CD by Anoushka, a daughter of the famed Indian musician Ravi Shankar. Soothing. Spider was out of the apartment or he'd be in the other room, blasting his latest dance-music mix.

"Can't, bro," he'd bellowed over his wall of sound, when Christopher had asked him to work with headphones. "Need to hear the resonance of the bass in the walls!" It had taken Christopher almost a day and all his exaggerated powers of persuasion to convince him otherwise. Spider still wanted to use his speakers for work, obviously a compulsion even Christopher couldn't break down, but he agreed to limit his mix time to when Christopher was out.

He pushed that thought aside and listened to the sitar and tabla drums, tried to empty his head of consciousness and fill it with an awareness of everything around him, the sounds, the smells, the now of the room he was in. Mindfulness meditation wasn't about blanking out so much as tuning in, grounding yourself in a present reality so immediate and real that you didn't let your mind drift to fears for the future or regrets of the past. It wasn't easy today, after all he'd learned.

Meditation had become a part of Christopher's life in high school after he'd discovered a CD in the library and taken it home to check out. It hadn't taken more than one party for him to find out that booze and drugs had no effect on him. He could drink or smoke anyone under any table, but when it came to finding a way to fight down the nightmares that had plagued him since childhood, he had to look elsewhere. The meditation disk had actually worked, calmed him, and he'd dug deeper, found books, other recordings, and took classes.

His parents had been grateful that he'd found something. They'd tried all the traditional approaches to deal with his nightmares since he was a child, counseling, medication, and psychotherapy, both individual and group. They'd gone through deep feelings of guilt and fear that they were somehow responsible, to worry that there was something very wrong with the stranger's child they'd taken into their home.

If none of the professionals they'd consulted could define his nightmares or their cause, if pills didn't help, if Christopher couldn't find any other way of self-medicating his way out of it, then the only explanation for his haunted dreams could be something no one could explain. The inexplicable was always frightening. Christopher found meditation before his family could start looking for an exorcist.

They supported him, even if they didn't understand it. It had helped him sleep through the night, with no more screams that woke up the rest of the family, and given him a way to soothe himself back to sleep if the dreams did wake him up.

Christopher took his meditation deeper and listened to sounds in the room; let them flow through his head as he cataloged his body, let himself feel each part fully before moving on. He didn't adjust, didn't judge. Just observed, took deep, regular breaths in through the nose, out through the mouth, and oxygenated his brain. He let the range of his senses widen, heard sounds from the hall as a neighbor left his apartment and went down the stairs, traffic on the street, cries of vendors, shouts of children chased home to bed.

Still, his mind went back to the police report, to Steven and Lori's lame explanation of their involvement in his mother's death, in his own rescue, from—what? What was so terrible they couldn't just come out and explain it? Christopher gave up trying to forget about it, opened his eyes, stood up, and looked out the window to the street.

It wasn't too late. He could go out and run. Sometimes exhausting his body took his brain down a notch, let him sleep better than usual. Something had to, or he'd be tempted to go back out to Brooklyn to have it out with them again. He had to gather more information before he did that, enough to force them to spill the rest of what they knew.

He'd talk to Joie first. She had to understand how he felt. She'd shared his visions on the couch in front of the video camera. Whatever it was that had connected them at that moment had opened his mind and let her see a glimpse of the nightmare he'd grown up with, the one that still hounded him. Whatever it was that her parents knew, it was the key to the weird images that whirled through his head nightly, visions that made no sense of a decaying subway station, ruined tenements, pale bodies that moved through the night in silent worship of . . . him. It was madness.

He pushed the images from his head and pulled on shorts, a T-shirt, and sneakers to go out and run until he could forget again and sleep. Spider came in the door just as he was headed out. Perfect timing. Christopher hoped that the rest of the night went as well.

Meeting Joie when he had couldn't have been a coincidence. They'd been drawn together. There was some larger purpose to their meeting, and even if Steven and Lori didn't know what it was, they could help him to find out. That was probably why they were so freaked out. Whatever that purpose might be was out of their control. They just wanted to protect their daughter. If that was their problem, they didn't have to worry. Christopher would make sure nothing happened to her. That was the one thing he did know. No matter who he was, whatever they were to each other, Joie was his to love and protect.

CHAPTER 35

It was almost done and just in time to close up shop.

Luna adjusted bows at the back of the little black dress she was working on and tightened the seams. The sun would be down soon and it would be time to open the upstairs office. As important as her design work was to her, the doctor's was far more important. The master's work was more than a job. It was a mission. He was shaping a new generation.

She put away her needles and threads, swept scraps of fabric from the floor, and slipped on her white, office smock uniform. Luna didn't dress for the office the way she did in the shop. She wore only white upstairs, even if she wasn't really a nurse. It was a fashion statement, her way of dividing her time into day and night, black and white. When she was in the right clothes, she knew who she was, what to do. It made it easier, gave her one less thing to think about. Thinking was hard around Adam after so many years . . . no, not Adam, Abel. Dr. Abel Lazarus now. The doctor. It was easier to call him that than to remember which name he used.

Luna fastened the last button on her smock, put on her sensible but still stylish office shoes, and left the store. She went out to let in a new patient, the first of the night, a young friend of Vangie's. She'd waited patiently outside for entry, a tight smile on her face when she saw Luna. Luna smiled back as she opened the front door and led her upstairs to the waiting room for her intake session.

"Have a seat and fill this out." Luna handed the girl a card and waited for the red light to turn green to indicate that the doctor was ready to receive. "The doctor will be right with you."

Dr. Lazarus's office didn't look the way Vangie had described it. Joie didn't know how he could have redecorated since her friend's last visit, but maybe this was a different room. His furniture was Danish modern, like her mom's at home. The walls were creamy off-white, all right, but there was no wainscoting, and all the art on the walls looked like it was by the same artist, maybe even the doctor's work. He had an easel set up in a corner of the room, a cloth draped over the front of the canvas to conceal the work in progress. The smell of oil paint and turpentine was somehow reassuring, reminded Joie of time she'd spent in her dad's studio as a kid in Brooklyn and later in L.A.

"You keep your painting covered? I guess it wouldn't do for the patient to get a good look into the doctor's mind. . . ." Joie smiled. He seemed nice. She was relaxing already. He was every bit as cute as Vangie had said, but he wasn't just a pretty boy. Like Christopher, there were depths here, so deep you could get lost.

"Not so much that. More not wanting people to see my work until it's ready. I prefer response to the final work, not to the progress I'm making."

"Only children need encouragement?"

"Not necessarily. Do you feel a lack of encouragement, lately?" He smiled. "See how smoothly I slipped that in?"

Joie laughed. He was funny, too.

"Slick. Yeah, Vangie said you were good. . . ." Her smile faded after the laughter. "It's not encouragement. I lack courage. I feel so afraid, all the time. . . ."

Abel listened with half his attention.

The girl was every bit as appealing as Vangie's memory of her had been. She had no idea of just how enchanting she was. Joie sat on his couch, nervous, not knowing how nervous she really should be. She talked about her mother, her father, her studies, the boy she'd just met. Abel lost track at a certain point, let himself get lost in the scent of her golden skin, the warmth that rose from her in gentle waves, the pulse he could sense at her throat, wrists, and temples. Humans were intoxicating even before you fed. The allure of life was as attractive to him as he was to his prey.

Abel considered how long he should take to bring her parents in for a session. Once they'd all arrived, he'd reveal who he was and wipe them from the face of the Earth, as casually as a small boy crushes bugs beneath his foot. Or, better yet, bide his time and find a way to turn them against one another, until he took the last survivor after the others were dead . . . His reverie was broken by talk of a fight between the boy she'd just met and her parents.

"Wait," said Dr. Lazarus. "He was adopted and they're the ones who found him and turned him in twenty years ago?" Abel paid attention again. He'd listened enough to know that she was talking about this new boy, Christopher. Could this be the same Christopher he remembered? Nina's vampire baby?

"Tell me more," he said.

Joie's first session ended after a full hour instead of the usual fifty minutes. Abel sent her off unharmed, much to Luna's surprise when she came in with a roll of surgical bandage. She covered up with a joke, followed the doctor's instructions to set a regular appointment for the girl the next day, and showed her out.

While she was gone, Abel tried to think back to his final days as Adam Caine, to the last time he'd seen the vampire baby.

It was in Rahman's Sheep Meadow station, at the top of a hill of live bodies piled up high to feed it, just before Luna X picked him up and carried him away to safety. The baby had rolled him away as it fed on new life, bored with its toy. Adam had tumbled to the bottom of the heap, seen Luna's face as she picked him up, kissed his lips, and packed him into a canvas bag to carry away to her downtown studio apartment.

Before that, he'd seen the baby fed vials of Rahman's formula by the Autochthones doing his bidding. He'd watched the infant change from a withered, dying husk recovered from the Lower East Side into a plump ball of energy, feeding on life from bodies brought down into the Sheep Meadow Station. There had been a struggle; National Guardsmen had fought his disciples and the Autochthones. So many of his memories were distorted or lost—he'd been barely alive for most of his time underground.

Perenelle would know everything that had happened that night, but, of course, he didn't dare reveal to her that he was alive. She'd have the Veil enforcers on him before he could explain what he wanted to know. Rahman was dead, as far as he could tell, which left only Steven and Lori, and they'd put all they knew into their book. Maybe not all, but it would take him time to find out.

Luna was the only other person there that he knew.

"Last one for tonight, Doc. Anything else you need?" She'd popped into the office doorway, as if on cue. Faithful Luna X, always there when he needed her, no matter how insane. She entered the room, now empty except for the couch, a single floor lamp, and a plain oak coffee table. Luna had cleaned the room up and painted it for him when they moved into the building. She had no illusions about what it looked like, the way his patients did.

Every one of them saw it differently, thanks to his influence over them, and shared their visions of the room with him as they were invented on the spot, filled with whatever they needed to feel comfortable and relaxed. Luna saw only what was really there.

"Luna. I need you to remember something for me." Abel motioned for her to join him on the couch. "Take me back to the night you saved me."

Abel lifted her wrist to his lips.

He'd not fed on Luna for some time, had satisfied himself for years with blood from his practice. She trembled like a schoolgirl on a first date, seemed to feel a special thrill at being joined again with her master. Luna stiffened as his teeth penetrated her skin, then relaxed into a swoon while he drank, as his link to her mind and body made their minds one.

He felt the pleasure of feeding, too, but, more important, he saw the subway station rise up like a stage set to envelop the room, restored everything around them as Luna called up her memories of that night. She was gone from his side, running in front of him toward a monstrous pile of still-breathing humans, the vampire baby balanced on top.

Luna X called out Adam's name, her hair wet, makeup smeared, face flushed, but twenty years younger. It was odd to see her that way again, like looking at a scrapbook of barely remembered old photos.

Abel stayed alert, scanned the re-created battle that raged around him. Luna's point of view was every bit as chaotic as he remembered. He examined her memory for clues to the fate of the baby, to see what had saved it from certain death or destruction. There was a flash of fresh rage as he saw his own severed head through Luna's eyes, freshly mutilated at the bottom of the stack of bodies, discarded by the baby like a shell after eating.

Luna lifted his head lovingly, pressed her lips to his, still stitched shut, one eye gouged out. No one else had gotten near him. If not for her, he might have died there that night. For a moment, Abel felt something almost like gratitude, then reminded himself that she was enthralled, his willing slave. She'd done nothing he hadn't commanded her to do.

Once Luna X had carried him away from the station, her memories of the escape and route home were of no use to him. Abel released her, sent Luna back down to her shop while he racked his own mind. He remembered seeing one of the Autochthones climb the hill and feed the child a vial and a second, both sent up by Rahman while he chanted from an ancient book, then his rescue and nothing more.

Abel had to find out what had been done to the child.

He knew from Perenelle's stories that Rahman had helped her and her husband create an elixir of life. It had kept Nicolas alive for more than five hundred years, until Perenelle lost him in an avalanche. If the vials and feedings were part of an alchemical experiment Rahman had tried to repeat with the vampire baby and that baby was alive and human today, its blood might still be infused with the elixir of life. If ordinary blood couldn't heal Abel's shattered body, surely blood infused with the secret of life itself could. He had to know, and there was only one way to find out.

He had to bring Christopher here and feed on him.

CHAPTER 36

2:19 A.M.—Fort Greene, 27 July 2007

It was hot, the sky was cloudless, with no chance of rain, and the air didn't move. On nights like this Steven was always sure he couldn't possibly be the only one still awake, that some bruise to the psyche of the city or even the country was keeping everyone up this night, all pondering the future in fear for their lives.

It wasn't the war, the gas prices, the economy, or even the impending presidential election. It was a subliminal feeling that the world we saw and walked around in every day was just a stage set and some darker drama was being played out behind the scenes. We were all just extras, waiting for our big moment to run and scream as the big awful thing we'd all waited for in dread crashed down around us. Tonight, it was Lori's cancer.

Steven opened another bottle of beer, his third tonight and not his last, the real reason he'd needed to go back to the gym. He always forgot how many empty calories there were in beer, wondered why they were called empty when they always seemed to fill him out. He'd have to make sure to work extra hard on the walls tomorrow.

He knew he should pull his mala from his wrist and chant instead. A string of 108 beads, you held each one in your hand, chanted the mantra "Om mani padme hum," then moved to the next. It translated to "all praise to the jewel in the lotus," a prayer for purity to the Buddhist god of love and compassion, a spiritual cleansing that led one down the path to enlightenment.

Steven had never managed to stay disciplined enough to be a real Buddhist. He still pulled them off and chanted every now and then to center himself when he was stressed, but beer and pot were always faster and easier. Steven took another swig of his beer and felt around next to the couch for his stash box. As he filled the bowl of the pipe, he thought about Lori again.

Cancer. Son of a bitch. He remembered the stories Lori had told him about her mother's death from throat cancer, a long, lingering illness that had left Lori at twelve with a new stepmother and a dead father who'd shot himself in the head to rejoin his wife. Cancer had always been Lori's worst fear, the bad thing she kept locked away inside where she couldn't see it while she did all she could to avoid it.

Not enough. It seemed impossible after all they'd been through that this was how it would end. Steven shook his head and refused to go there. She wasn't dead yet, dammit, and if there was anything he could do to help her, he would.

Why had he left New York? He didn't have any illusions that staying in Brooklyn could have prevented her illness, but if he'd been here maybe he would have seen the signs, gotten her to a doctor sooner, so she'd have a better chance of survival. If he lost her now, just when he'd started to realize how much he'd missed her, what she meant to him, how right they'd been together . . .

Steven stopped. He had no right to think about that when her health was all that mattered. At the same time, he couldn't deny his feelings. It wasn't her cancer that had brought them up. He'd spent most of the last year thinking about her, wondering if she'd found someone since Fritz, or if she'd written all men off as a lost cause. He was afraid that if he told her how he felt now, she'd think it was only because she was sick, that he felt sorry for her. Even though it wasn't true, he knew enough about Lori's character to know that her pride was strong, even if her body might be failing.

He tried to distract himself with TV until he was stoned or drunk enough to sleep. There was nothing on, as usual. He flipped through his DVR list, saw a few shows he wanted to watch, but they all required thought, documentaries or news programs. Thought was what he was trying to escape, the continuous grinding of mental gears that kept him up as it always did when he was stressed. No matter how bad things were, he knew Lori was out cold right now. No amount of pressure could keep her awake. He'd always envied her that.

Ordinarily, he'd put on some porn and pleasure himself to sleep, but sex was the last thing on his mind tonight. Lori's cancer, Christopher's anger at them for concealing what they knew of his past, even Joie's pain and confusion at dealing with both—they filled his head, left no room for anything, even his own life.

Except that they were his life. He could no more ignore Lori and Joie's lives than he could his own, and Christopher—he'd known that they hadn't seen the last of the boy when they turned him over to the city. His return had been inevitable. There was no way any child could have survived what he had without scars, and Christopher's had to be deeper than most. Why wouldn't he search for their source?

The beer and pot finally kicked in hard enough to slow down his head. Steven went to his bed and lay down, left off the top sheet. It was too hot to sleep covered up.

Steven's mind drifted as he tried to sleep, sweaty. He remembered running down a steep hill for the first time when he was a boy. It was exhilarating, the closest he'd ever come to flying. Each step flung him forward by feet, hurled by gravity, farther than he could ever have run on flat ground.

The only problem was that as he built up speed, at the point he felt the freest, he knew the slightest misstep would throw him off his feet to the ground, to roll and tumble head over heels the rest of the way to the bottom of the hill into a crumpled heap, afraid to look for injuries.

It was exactly how he felt about seeing Lori again.

He closed his eyes and saw her face as she'd looked at the gallery, the bemused smirk, the twinkle in her eyes that said her cutting comments were only jokes, that beneath the crust was a sweet, luscious filling. Steven smiled at the memory and realized that no matter how much of a mess they were all in, at least one thing was clear as he fell into dreamless sleep.

He was still in love with her.

CHAPTER 37

Joie let his phone ring a few times, not sure if she was doing the right thing. She hadn't heard from Christopher since the fight with her parents and wasn't sure if she was ready to talk to him yet, but there was no point in putting it off, either. Christopher finally answered, just when the call seemed about to go to voice mail.

"Hey, Joie."

"Hi. I don't know what to say, except that we should probably get together and talk."

"Yeah. You know that I don't blame you for any of this."

Joie hesitated, a little put out that the word *blame* should come up at all. Whatever had happened all those years ago, she was sure that her parents hadn't done anything wrong. Even so, she knew something had happened, something big and awful, remembered the shared dream with Christopher when they'd done the experiment with the video camera.

Those images had to have something to do with what had happened to him when he was a child. They hadn't made much sense, but if she'd had that dream every night since she was a kid, she'd probably be more screwed up than Christopher seemed to be.

"Okay, look," she said. "I have a therapy session today. Why don't you meet me there and when it's over we can go somewhere and talk."

"Sure. Just tell me where and when."

Dr. Abel Lazarus patiently listened to Joie as she filled him in on life since her intake session. There wasn't much new, and though he pushed for more information about Christopher, she hadn't talked to him yet, hoped to find out more tonight.

"He's meeting me downstairs after this session."

Abel tried to disguise his excitement. The boy was coming here? If he was going to be that close to him, there was no reason not to bring the boy even closer, upstairs and into the office.

"It might be a good idea for me to talk to him while he's here. For your benefit and his." He pushed lightly with his mind. She still looked dubious.

"I don't even know. You can try. I can ask him to come up when he gets here."

"That's all I suggest. He should know what resources are available to him in his search, bureaucratic and therapeutic." Abel almost trembled with excitement. If Rahman had actually managed to create the elixir of life, a body filled with it was on its way to him now. The thought of being returned to full strength, his body healed, his mobility restored, was almost more than he could bear. It took all his concentration to get the girl through the rest of her session. Fifty minutes had never gone so slowly. By the time he looked at the clock and told her their time was up, Abel felt that hours had passed.

"I'll see you next week. Don't forget to ask Christopher to come up before you leave." As he said it, he implanted a command into her subconscious mind, the sense of urgency he felt about meeting the boy, to make sure she would do as he'd asked. He had to make sure that the boy came upstairs before he left. Once he was here, Abel could do the rest, lure him to the couch and in range of his fangs with all the persuasive power at his command.

Joie left, and smiled sadly as she said goodbye. Abel smiled back, hid his hunger as he sat back and waited to see what would happen next.

. . .

Christopher found the office easily enough, on the south side of Tomp-kins Square Park. He waited outside the blue door that Joie had described, tried to read the illegible marker graffiti that covered it. The door opened before he could make any sense of it and there was Joie, every bit as beau-tiful as the last time he'd seen her, no matter how bad that day had been.

"Hi," she said.

"Hey, Joie." He felt awkward, had thought he'd be able to handle this better, but his feelings were still mixed. Anger at her parents and a deep longing to carry her far away from all this so the two of them could get to know each other better, find a new life together that wasn't stained by the past.

"My therapist wanted to see you before we go. He thought he might be able to help you with the dreams and my parents."

Christopher almost laughed, but saw how serious she was.

"I don't know. . . ." He stared off into the sky. "I'm sure he means well, but—"

"Please? Just for a minute. If you don't like him, if it's not a good idea, we can forget it. What harm can it do?"

She looked at him with warm eyes that could melt glaciers. Whatever had happened between him and her folks, she'd had nothing to do with it, and if she was as important to him as he thought she was, it didn't make sense to start their lives together by dismissing her concerns. He sighed and smiled.

"Okay. One minute. I can give him that at least."

"One floor up! Abel Lazarus!" She shouted out directions as he went in-side and bounded up the stairs. There was a door there, a nameplate with the doctor's name on it. He knocked and opened the door. The woman in-side, dressed in a white smock, stood and looked at him, a question in her eyes.

"Christopher?"

"Yeah." He looked around the shabby outer office. It didn't inspire con-fidence, but it didn't have to—Lazarus wasn't his shrink. This was only a courtesy call. If he didn't like it, he never had to come back.

"Come this way." The woman, a skinny bleached blonde, looked like she'd be dealing drugs in the park if she weren't working here. He stifled a grin at the thought. Maybe she was an ex-patient working off an old bill. She walked to a door under a green light on the other side of the room and nodded for him to follow.

Christopher walked behind her and she opened the door, stood inside, and announced him like she was a butler.

"Dr. Abel Lazarus, this is Christopher . . ."

"Ross. Christopher Jude Ross."

He stepped into the room and looked around, not knowing what to expect. It was disappointing. The walls were plain white, the room bare except for a plain pine coffee table in front of a sofa, a floor lamp next to it. Thick red-velvet curtains covered the windows. There was nothing on the walls or floor, nothing that gave any indication that the room had been really lived in. Joie hadn't said much about her doctor, but it was hard to believe that she wouldn't have commented on such stark surroundings.

Then he looked at the man on the couch.

Christopher had never been startled by anything in his life. Maybe it was the nightmare visions that haunted his sleep or some other inner strength that made him immune to the things that most people are afraid of, but he'd never seen anything like what he saw now. It repulsed him, even as he searched his mind for some explanation of what he was seeing.

The thing on the couch didn't look quite human.

He couldn't put it any other way. The man's head was perfect, even attractive, with a dazzling smile and close-cropped auburn hair, eyes sharp, one gray, one blue. But the body! It was stunted, misshapen, as if someone had squeezed him like clay, grabbed and twisted, squashed, pushed and pulled until the result looked barely human at all.

The doctor had the right number of arms and legs, a body, and a head, but everything below the head was distorted, warped. It was a broken doll of a body, not a midget or a dwarf or any other body type he'd seen in nature. Lazarus was like a surrealist painting of a cubist portrait, body parts thrown together every which way, as if the confused artist had lost interest in the work halfway through and given up in defeat.

The right arm was almost whole, but the left was a twisted knot of fingers and melted flesh, legs uneven, short and thin, one larger and longer than the other, but no logic, no purpose to the distortion. It was like someone had been given the parts of a human being and asked to assemble them with no idea of what one looked like, except for vague instructions on paper. That it was alive seemed impossible until it spoke.

"Hello, Christopher. Joie's told me a lot about you. . . ."

The doctor smiled at him until he saw the horrified look in Christopher's eyes and on his face. Christopher turned to run when he heard the doctor bark.

"Luna! Luna!"

Before he could finish turning, Christopher saw a glimpse of the blond nurse as she rushed up from behind, swung the heavy base of a lamp from the outer office at his head, and caught him on the temple as the room around him went black.

CHAPTER 38

Lori was in front of the computer when the doorbell rang. She'd been wrestling with the Hurston book all day, looking for a thread that could pull her through to the end. This was her third draft—she'd abandoned the first halfway, started fresh, and had almost finished the next version before she decided that it wasn't working, either.

When she'd pitched the book to her agent, it was as a fantasy romance, a fictional account of a relationship the Harlem Renaissance writer had with a younger man while working on a musical revue in 1931. It was to be a musing on art and love, how each affects or inhibits the other. The title was *Zora's Great Day*, but so far it had been anything but that.

This was the first time she'd had the problem that other writers she knew often complained about over drinks, the curse of starting something they weren't sure they could or even wanted to finish by the time they got halfway through.

Writing had never been easy, even when she'd been prolific. Lori enjoyed the work, loved it on the good days, hated it on the bad, the same way you enjoy a hot boyfriend who always argues but is too good in bed to dump. Her relationship with writing was the longest of her life and the least functional; pretty much an addiction, with all the same benefits and problems.

She'd been lucky so far. Writing had been good to her, kept her busy, paid her bills, and even bought her a home. This was the first time the relationship had seemed one-sided. She was giving the book all she had, but it wasn't giving an inch back. Every chapter was like digging through stone with a spoon. Worse, there'd been so much hullabaloo when the contract was signed, so much press, that everyone knew she was writing the damn thing. If it didn't turn up soon, all the people who'd said she couldn't pull it off would be happy to dance on her literary grave.

There was a panel on Zora Neale Hurston coming up at the Schomburg Library in Harlem. Lori had agreed to be involved when she was in the middle of the second draft and sure she'd be done by now. Instead, she was looking forward to a night of explaining why she was taking so long. It was too late to cancel. If she could get a few more chapters done before then, maybe she could muster enough enthusiasm to look like she knew what she was doing or where she was going.

The doorbell rang again as Lori reread the last paragraph she'd written, waited to see if Joie would get the door, until she remembered that her daughter had already left the house. Lori grumbled as she stood up and headed downstairs.

When she opened the door she found Steven on the doorstep. She could tell from the look on his face that something big was up.

"What happened? What's wrong?"

"Nothing!" He smiled, as if he was surprised that she'd think there was. "Nothing's wrong. We just need to talk. . . ."

When he was finished, Lori didn't know if she wanted to smack him or kiss him. He'd told her he was still in love with her and didn't want anything to happen without him saying it to her out loud. It was incredibly sweet and incredibly stupid at the same time, and he couldn't have said it at a worst time.

"Steven—" she started, but he cut her off.

"Look . . . I'm not saying we need to get together, now or ever. It's been a long time since . . . I'm not dropping this on you to add to what you already have to deal with or to say I'm any kind of prize or solution. I'm saying you're important to me and I'm here for you, any way you need me. Not because I feel sorry for you or guilty, or because we have a daughter. Because we have a history together and for the last year I've been hoping it might not be over."

"Did this start before or after you broke up with Tanya?"

She was sorry she'd said it as soon as it came out of her mouth, not soon enough to stop it. Steven looked at her like she'd just spit in his soup.

"Thanks. Yeah. You're my rebound. I moved everything I own three thousand miles back to New York because I couldn't get a date in L.A."

"Steven . . ." She grabbed his hands, squeezed, and wished that she or the world were in a different place, that an announcement like this was something she could celebrate or take joy in, instead of poking at his profession of love like a dead mouse dropped at her feet by the family cat. "It's not that I don't have feelings for you, too. Dammit, I think you're the first, maybe *only* guy I ever really loved for who he was, not who I wanted him to be."

She felt him relax a bit as he smiled.

"Warts and all?"

"Baby, if only warts were all that was wrong with you . . ."

Steven winced, grabbed at his chest like he'd just been shot. She slapped his shoulder as he fell back against the couch, laughing. It was too easy to fall into this kind of banter with him, too comfortable even after all the years apart. There was a bond between them that had never snapped, no matter how strained by distance and time. It wasn't just the winter of 1986 and the crisis that had brought them together to conceive Joie before they'd finally called it quits. Steven was a major part of her life and always would be. In a lot of ways, despite all their problems, he'd been the best part of her life, one she'd missed when he was gone, when they were over.

Except they weren't over, and before she knew what she was doing Lori leaned forward and kissed him on the lips, the way she used to kiss him when love was new. It felt the same. *Damn*, she thought, as he pushed forward to meet her lips and wrap his arms around her. *Damn.*

They fell back onto the cushions like a couple of high school kids on Lover's Lane, mouths open, fingers searching as he pulled her ratty terrycloth robe off her shoulders. She pulled his T-shirt up and off, felt the soft, curly hair of his chest lightly stroke her nipples as the robe fell open.

Damn, thought Lori, *what are we doing?* They fell deeper into the kiss.

This wasn't going to fix anything; it was just opening the door to a whole wing of confusion she'd locked off years ago. While her head was shouting *Stop* her body was saying *Shut up,* and for a change she listened to her body, pulled Steven closer and let her fingers do some walking of their own as they slipped down the front of his jeans. *Damn . . .*

How were they ever going to explain this to Joie?

CHAPTER 39

9:37 P.M.—*East Village, 27 July 2007*

Abel couldn't understand it.

Judging from his reaction, the boy had been able to see what was really in the room, with no illusions, something that no one except Luna X had ever been able to do. If Luna hadn't been at the ready, as always, Christopher would have run out, gone downstairs, and dragged the girl away, told her what he'd seen and who knows what after that.

No matter whom they'd called, even if he brought the girl back upstairs to prove to her what he'd seen, Abel could have maintained the illusion over Joie; but why couldn't he fool the boy? It had to be the elixir, or something else Rahman had done to him. Further proof that there was something unnatural about him, further proof that he was, indeed, more than merely human.

Luna X dragged Christopher's unconscious body closer to the couch, lifted Abel like a ventriloquist's dummy, and lowered him to the floor at the boy's side. Abel pushed himself up on his good arm, rolled the boy's head to one side with his other to expose his throat. He looked up at Luna for a second, as if for confirmation that this was a good idea, then bit, and drank deeply as the boy moaned lightly in his sleep.

He almost swooned with pleasure. The blood tasted richer, different from any other he'd drunk, and he'd had more than a few flavors to choose from in his last twenty years in this office. It was unlike anything he'd experienced. Though he could feel a surge of strength and power from it as he drank, he felt none of the usual connection to his victim's life energy, his vital essence. It didn't matter.

He drank his fill and pushed the boy away when he could drink no more. When he woke up, Christopher would be enthralled, under Abel's control and no threat to him. They could send the boy away, back to the girl downstairs with no fear of discovery. Then he would see if the elixir of the boy's blood had any effect on his own body beyond that of normal blood.

Christopher woke up and saw the doctor and his nurse looking down at him. They didn't seem to mean him any more harm, looked at him with disinterest.

"You can go now," said Lazarus, as the receptionist lifted the doctor from the floor and placed him on the couch like some grotesque doll. "Tell no one what you've seen here tonight. If I need you again, I'll summon you."

He gestured, dismissing him, as the woman opened the office door. Christopher stood slowly, looked from one of them to the other. Was he kidding? They'd knocked him out cold and now they were letting him go? What kind of crazy game was this? What had they done to him while he was out?

Christopher reached up, and pulled his fingers away. His neck had been bandaged. He could feel two bite marks underneath, already healing. A vampire. The doctor was a vampire. Christopher didn't know how he knew, couldn't believe it was really possible, but realized that they must think he was under the doctor's control now that he'd been bitten. Wasn't that how it was supposed to work?

Christopher nodded, playing along, and left as quickly as he could before they realized their mistake. He headed down the stairs, decided to get Joie as far away as he could and then warn her not to go back. If she hadn't been bitten already, he'd make sure that she wouldn't be. He'd come back during the day and see what he could do then to make sure she was safe, even if it meant driving a wooden stake through her shrink's twisted heart.

Abel sent Luna X off to bed and lay back on the couch to rest and consider his next move. If the boy's blood had no effect on him, there was no point in pursuing him. But if it seemed like he'd grown at all during the night, if Abel found any benefit to drinking Christopher's blood, he'd bring him back for more and drain him until he was whole.

Before he could finish the thought, Abel felt his body burn with pain, every nerve ending on fire. He gasped, unable to speak, reached out as he fell from the couch, found only the curtains that kept out the sun during the day near his fingers, grabbed them and dropped to the floor.

Abel felt the drapes tear free of the curtain rods over the windows, fall with him to the floor as he writhed in an agony unlike any he'd experienced. He tried to scream, to call out to Luna for help, but instead curled into a fetal ball on the floor, overcome by whatever it was the damned boy had in his veins, whatever Abel had drunk his fill of before sending him away into the night. He couldn't end this way—not after so long, not like this. With his last strength, he prayed as he hadn't prayed since childhood, not sure if there was anyone left who would listen to him.

The last thing Abel saw were the bare, exposed windows, felt his protective curtains spread on the floor around him as he tried with his last ounce of consciousness to pull them over his stunted body before he was caught helpless on the floor, exposed under the burning rays of the sun at dawn.

III

QUARTER MOON

To find me Tom of Bedlam
Ten Thousand Leagues I've travelled
Mad Maudlin goes on dirty toes
For to spare her shoes from gravel

I now repent that ever
Poor Tom was so disdained
Me wits I lost since him I crossed
Which makes me thus go chained

—author anonymous
"Mad Maudlin's Search"
(circa 1615)

There are two tragedies in life. One is not to
get your heart's desire. The other is to get it.

—George Bernard Shaw
Man and Superman, act 4
(1903)

CHAPTER 40

2:18 A.M.—*Midtown West, 28 July 2007*

Lopez led her project team into place as they marched down a service shaft in the Lincoln Tunnel. It had been completed and opened to automobile traffic in December 1937, the winter of the year that the Hindenburg exploded. It was the same year that Claire St. Claire and Tom O'Bedlam were captured and held for trial for its destruction, by the assembled vampires of New York, the year that the Veil was formed to condemn the pair to entombment.

Claire had been freed almost fifty years later, but had never found out where she or Tom had been buried. That information had lain hidden in the journals of the Moorish vampire Rahman-al-Hazra'ad ibn Aziz, now in the hands of Clean Slate. Their researchers had combed through them since Claire's meeting with Jonathan Richmond in Red Hook and found the entries that described Tom and Claire's trial and sentencing.

Rahman had described how they had been sealed separately in iron vaults covered in concrete and buried in different locations. Claire was entombed in a pit dug deep in Central Park as she was to be freed in fifty years. The Veil knew that they'd be able to recover her body at any time, excavating the park under one pretext or another.

Tom was another matter.

There had been no intention of ever recovering him, so the Veil had tried to seal his body away safely, with no chance of accidental discovery. The new Lincoln Tunnel under construction between New York and New Jersey had seemed the perfect spot, connecting the city he'd wanted to conquer and the state where his crime had been committed. All they'd had to do was find a location in one of the service tunnels that would remain isolated and undisturbed indefinitely.

There were passageways off the main tunnel that led to rooms for storage and other maintenance purposes. That was where Lopez's team was now, following Rahman's directions. His scientific precision had made his journals invaluable. As usual, he was right on target. The metal detector used by the techie from Clean Slate labs beeped as they located the iron safe. Sonar readings confirmed that it was what they were looking for, buried just where Rahman had said it would be, six feet on the other side of one of the side-tunnel walls.

The Port Authority had given them approval to excavate by order of the city of New York, and as soon as everyone was in place the work began. It took hours to cut through the wall into the chamber on the other side. Not even the original architects of the tunnel had any idea that their plans had been modified to add a hidden cell designed to hold a monster of a magnitude beyond their imagining.

Lopez stepped into the dusty chamber, barely big enough to hold its tenant. She contacted Richmond as soon as they confirmed their find. A huge monolith, ten feet tall, twelve feet long, a concrete coffin built to withstand the ages. It was still intact, with not even a crack in the cement. Lopez wasn't sure which was worse—the idea that anything inside the vault could still be alive after all this time, or that this was the only way to confine it.

She gave the order to start opening the wall to move the package out, unsure for the first time if Richmond was doing the right thing. Maybe some things were better left buried. Her sixth sense told her that no matter how important this thing was in the fight to save mankind from vampires, it would be better to find another way.

She'd learned as a child that if you played with fire, you could get burned. Playing with dead things, or things that should be dead, could only bring down worse on them all, but she was a good soldier.

She did as she was told.

. . .

Claire St. Claire had gotten the call from Richmond an hour ago on her cell phone. They'd found Tom's tomb and wanted her there when they opened it to help control him. She'd hoped that they'd bring her to the excavation site and unseal his coffin where they found it. That would have given her a chance to wipe out the team and take him away to recover until they could resume their love affair with the dark, wherever they pleased.

Richmond had been too clever for that and had obviously assumed that escape would be her first thought. He wanted to contain them both until he was sure they posed no threat. No matter. The one advantage that vampires had was time. If they'd had to wait this long to be reunited, they could wait a little longer for liberty.

Clean Slate had sent one of their cars to pick her up from the East Village. As she entered their headquarters in Red Hook for the second time, Claire was almost starting to feel at home. The bulletproof black limousine pulled inside the building, all outside evidence of her explosions erased, and rolled into its depths.

Claire laughed. She'd accomplished what the Veil couldn't: found a way into the heart of the enemy's domain. If Perenelle had even a clue about what she was doing, the bitch would be livid. That alone made her betrayal worthwhile, but Claire reminded herself that there was a much more important reason to be here than to piss off her rival.

They'd found her Tom.

Her heart beat a little faster, as much as it could, as she drew closer to him. Claire could feel him here, even through the thick, brick walls of the complex, through the cement and iron that sealed him in his tomb.

Tom was here, and soon he would be free.

CHAPTER 41

3:23 A.M.—*Red Hook, 28 July 2007*

Their facilities were state of the art.

Claire could tell that. Even though she knew nothing of the technology they used, or what their innumerable rows of shiny metal and matte black machines did, she was impressed. Their dampeners were everywhere here, kept them all safe from her mental influence or feeding. Armed guards followed Claire wherever she went, dressed in discreet black uniforms that could be mistaken for workmen's coveralls on the outside.

She sat in a sterile white observation room and watched them work through an airtight plate-glass window. Technicians in the next room cut through the cement block that encased the vault that held Tom captive. Claire watched with a shudder as the shape of the massive safe was revealed, remembered how she'd felt the day they'd opened hers and brought her back into the real world. She'd been comatose after being alone in the dark for nearly fifty years, starved, her flesh dehydrated, a step away from mummification.

The only thing that had kept her sane was her hatred of those who'd put her there, her determination to make them pay once she was released. All that had stopped her then was her sponsor, Dr. Burke, and her knowledge that those who'd entombed her were the only ones who could tell her where they'd put Tom.

The search for him, her desperate need to find out his whereabouts, was all that had kept her in check. Now that he was here in front of her, it was all she could do to contain herself. She had to wait to see him, make sure he was safe and alive again before they could consider themselves truly reunited, before she could strike.

There was no way to know what his condition would be when he was released. Clean Slate had the best facility in the world for this kind of work, and since she needed them to resurrect her beloved she would stay silent and still until their work was done.

The last of the concrete fell away and welding torches were brought in to cut away the door of the antique safe revealed underneath. There had been a combination engraved on the face of the safe she'd been buried in, the code to unlock the tumblers after the spot welds that kept the door shut were removed. Tom had not been so lucky. Eternal entombment, the ultimate punishment in the vampire world, meant that his door had been welded all around, combination dial as well. It would take hours to cut through the thick metal that imprisoned him.

Claire sat back and let them do what they must while she mused on how she'd get Tom away when they were done. She wasn't sure of the details but already knew that her plan needed to be violent and cruel, something Tom would enjoy. He should be baptized in blood and fire once he was reborn. The thought made Claire smile as she closed her eyes, waited for the safe to be opened, and wondered what was going through his mind inside the vault, whatever was left of it.

The wet streets ran crimson in Blood World, glistened like freshly opened veins. Thick smoke poured into the sky from the burning rubble of crumbling midtown skyscrapers. The howls of wild dog packs could be heard far and wide, up and down the abandoned boulevards, from the highest floors of the remaining buildings to the deepest cellars. His children of the night.

Tom O'Bedlam sat on his ivory throne built from the bleached bones of the dead, on top of the cracked steps of the ruined Forty-second Street library. He was warmed by the heat of books that burned in a bonfire piled behind him, centuries of human knowledge bound in dry leather and cloth. No more than kindling now, reduced to fuel to light an eternal night.

His armor-plated street demons carried screaming victims up the stone stairs to him in tribute. Tom accepted graciously, crushed throats with a clawed hand, and fed on their lives as he felt his strength grow with each one he devoured.

His long robes were dirty and ragged, but royal. His crown was a wreath of long thorns that pierced his skull, kept his mind as sharp as the points that pressed through bone into his brain. He couldn't die, not here, not ever, and the constant sensation of pain from the piercing was all that had kept him focused and alert for the decades he'd lived here, if this could be called a life.

Tom O'Bedlam's body had been buried for almost a century, but his mind had gone elsewhere, created this place for his multiple personalities to inhabit, unfettered by the iron walls that bound him. During his confinement, he'd gone into a meditative state and dug deep inside himself to survive, like a bear buried in hibernation for a long winter.

He'd created an internal landscape of a Manhattan inferno, the city devastated, smoldering buildings reduced to rubble, the streets filled with dead bodies and screams of the tortured dying. It was a faithful representation of his rage, his hatred of those who'd put him here, directed at his imaginary world as he'd torn it apart a piece at a time.

There had been plenty of time for Tom to think in the womb of his imprisonment. That's what he'd called the vault after his first year there; had chosen to see it not as a prison but an incubator. That had kept him—not sane, it had been far too late for that—safe and sound, gave him a way to focus his energies instead of seeing them dissipate over time.

It was his innate ability to survive by retreating into fantasy that had saved him, the gift of being able to flee into his mind for sanctuary when he'd been abused in Bedlam asylum. He'd been fragmented over his years there, broken into lunatic little pieces, a new personality formed to shield the young Tom from every fresh act committed against him.

It was King Tom who had wanted to rule like Napoleon, and make men bow down to his glory; angry little Tommy Boy, who was so cruelly treated by the world that he'd wanted to make it scream; Weeping Thomas who'd devised the methods to do so, learned from his own pain at the hands of others. Then there were Laughing Tom, Tom the Ripper, Doubting Thomas, and many more, each with his own face and name, the bastard children of his shattered psyche, too many to count. One born for every beating that young Tom had suffered, every rape, every humiliation, each intolerable act fathering a new personality to populate his inner Hell.

Dr. Townsend Burke, his vampire redeemer, his dark savior, hadn't taken the time to see that before he'd bitten Tom, killed him, and brought him back to life. Becoming a vampire had driven Burke mad and he'd wanted to see if the same curse could drive a madman sane. Out of his own temporary insanity, he'd unleashed Tom's permanent demons; had given them an immortal body with a relentless hunger for blood and vengeance against those who'd made him mad.

So Tom had plenty of company in his iron womb to while away the decades as his many personalities kept one another company, mingled long enough for Tom to see their roots in his history as they told their stories. Some were more human than others and were killed off quickly by those less so. When all else had been washed away in his isolation tank, the strongest personality had taken control. He'd had time to understand and dispose of all his weaknesses, mask after mask murdered and consumed by more powerful personas who fed on one another, until he fed on them. Over time, his madness had distilled into a singular, crystalline purity.

The one left in charge was the face he'd taken on in jest, that of Tom O'Bedlam, an enigma even to himself. The last of his lesser personalities were hunted down and dragged shrieking to him by his demons, to add their life and strength to his.

He'd never felt better.

Tom O'Bedlam was beyond human concerns like joy or sorrow. He was the sole survivor of his own shattered mind and lived in a city aflame with fires that would never burn out, whose avenues ran red with the blood of his murdered multiples. Over decades he'd embraced his Blood World as a new aesthetic, grew to love the sights and sounds of fury and fear that filled his endless nights.

Tom knew he'd been saved for one reason and one only. His life-long torment, ending in this entombment, had shaped him, forced him to grow into something greater than himself, more than he could ever have achieved on his own. What he was now, so pure, so perfected, he could never have become without the sum total of his pain.

It was a revelation he wanted to share by reducing real life to the disordered nightmare of his Blood World. If he could turn his dream into a global reality, everyone on Earth would learn the same lesson he had. As the planet fell into pandemonium and struggled to survive, the weak would be consumed or become strong, growing ever stronger, as they were transformed by their epic ordeal.

The world as they'd known it would end, not all at once but over time. Life on Earth would trickle out like sand through an hourglass. Those who survived would greet Tom as a liberator welcoming them into a new age of possibilities. A new order would rise from the ashes of the old.

Whatever was left would be worth saving.

His imprisonment had made Tom the embodiment of entropy and anarchy. Chaos was all he knew and it was his comfort, his bliss, a gift he'd share with the world if he were ever freed to do so.

It was a grave responsibility to be the bearer of the end of all things. Even if Tom had his doubts, he was sure that whatever power had given him this renewed purpose would bring him forth from the grave and show him how. No one ever said engineering your own apocalypse would be easy.

But he'd find a way.

CHAPTER 42

9:26 A.M.—*Park Slope, 28 July 2007*

Joie woke up and heard voices downstairs, her mother's and a man's. She pulled on her robe and went to see what was up as she thought about her evening with Christopher.

He'd looked shaken when he'd come down from Dr. Lazarus's office and had refused to talk about what had happened upstairs. They'd gone to a café nearby and sipped latte while he calmed down and told her he wasn't sure she should see the doctor again.

"Are you kidding me? I just started!"

She'd been pretty sure that Christopher wouldn't want to start sessions, but she'd never thought he'd try to get her to stop. Their conversation hadn't continued much longer than that. What to do about Christopher was only one of many issues in her life, and as long as she was trying to sort them all out she was going to take all the help she could get.

By the time she got to the bottom of the stairs she could identify the man's voice. It was her father's. When she got to the kitchen she saw him and her mother sitting at the table over dirty breakfast dishes, laughing. Her mom was in that ugly, worn-out terry-cloth robe she insisted on wearing around the house like it was glued to her. Her dad was barefoot, in a T-shirt and jeans, his hair uncombed. From the guilty way they looked up at her when she walked in, she could tell that he had spent the night.

"Oh, my God. You didn't," she said, wrinkling her nose. "Gross." They looked at each other and laughed.

"I could point out that if we hadn't at least once, you wouldn't be here to make that face," said Lori.

"Yeah, twice in the last twenty years. We're animals," added Steven with a laugh as he poured more tea.

"Actually, three times," said Lori. "Or was it four?"

"God!" Joie rolled her eyes and went to the fridge to look for food while her parents cracked up and gave each other a quick kiss. "You people need help."

"We did just fine on our own." Lori grinned at Steven over the top of her mug.

"Maybe she's right. You up for a three-way?"

"Dad!"

Her parents roared while she made a bowl of cold cereal and carried it back upstairs to call Tasha. She could hear them laughing and talking downstairs as if he'd never left, like they were a real family. She was surprised to find that no matter how long it would take to get the image of them in bed together out of her head, she kind of liked the idea of her father being home again. For a little while, at least, they were all thinking about something other than cancer.

CHAPTER 43

10:23 A.M.—East Village, 28 July 2007

Abel woke on the bare wood floor of his office and felt sunlight on his body, the liquid warmth of it running up the skin of his legs and arms. He panicked, pulled away and rolled over before he realized with amazement that he could. His hands pushed him easily and his legs moved in concert with them to carry him out of harm's way. Except that there was no harm. The room was filled with light from the sun. It bounced off the white walls, so bright that Abel should have burst into flames, but he didn't.

He sat up and lifted his hands to see that they were whole, his legs, too, flesh restored, his fondest wish come true. His gamble had worked. Christopher's blood—Rahman's elixir—had healed him. It was hard to tell which astonished him more, that he could feel the sun without burning or that he had the body to feel it with. Both were unbelievable. Abel stood up and walked to the window, looked out to see his view of Tompkins Square Park in daylight for the first time ever.

The trees were bright green, a shade he hadn't seen since his youth. The kind of green only the sun can make by shining down on the leaves of a living plant. The sky was blue, but such a blue! How long had it been since he'd seen the daytime sky? Eighty years? Ninety? Abel looked down at the sunlight on his bare skin, left nearly naked, as his growing limbs had ripped through clothes custom-made by Luna X for his previous shrunken, distorted shape.

There was only one explanation: Rahman had been right. Christopher's transformed blood had the power to heal his vampire flesh, but so much more. He was whole again, but also human. Rahman had finally found his cure but hadn't lived to see it work. Abel sat down on the couch and wept, something he hadn't done since his days as a human. His ordeal was over and more. He'd been returned to the world of men, given a second chance to live his life as a mortal, not a monster.

A new beginning.

Luna X almost shit her pants when Abel walked into the store. He was wrapped in one of her smocks from the coat rack upstairs, obviously the only thing he'd been able to find. It was before noon and the doctor looked as he had when she'd first met him, stood tall and upright on legs of his own without her help. In daytime! The sunlight seemed to sparkle off him as he opened the shop door and stepped inside, seemed almost to follow him in as if it had missed him after so long away and didn't want to part again so soon.

"Luna," he said, laughter in his voice. "What do you think?" He turned as if he were modeling a new outfit, not a fresh body. She stared, and in the same instant realized two things.

Abel Lazarus was no longer a vampire.

She was no longer his slave.

Whatever influence his blood had held over her was gone. Luna X almost gasped at the realization. She'd been so busy all morning that she hadn't even noticed it until he walked in. For the first time in more than twenty years, Luna didn't feel like all her attention was on him. He was in the room but didn't fill the room. It was as if she'd been looking at the universe one way for years and suddenly could see that she'd really seen it from someone else's point of view all that time.

"Luna?"

Abel stared back at her, still smiling. He looked puzzled, until his eyes reflected the panic that overtook her as he suddenly saw what she did. If she wasn't his slave, what was she to him? What was he to her?

He seemed to read her thoughts and reached out to grab her as she slipped past him faster than he could move, which would never, ever have been possible before. That thought scared her more than he ever had, even when he'd fed at her bare, bloody breast after his rescue, not much more than a disembodied head.

Her god had been made mortal, as great a shock as her sudden, unexpected freedom. Abel was too slow to stop her from opening the door and running out and down the street, past the park, with no idea of goal or direction, everything gone from her head but escape and one other thing.

She needed a drink.

CHAPTER 44

Luna X didn't come back.

Abel waited alone in her store, then put together something for his new body to wear from Luna's stock. While he went through the racks, dug through shelves, he wondered where she'd gone, if she was ever coming back, and what he'd do if she didn't. At first he told himself he didn't care, but when she still didn't return he started to fret and grew tired of changing clothes. Abel picked an outfit and left the store. It was still early.

He left the door unlocked, didn't have a key for the store or the office upstairs. Abel had never needed one, had never been able to leave the building without Luna carrying him. There had been few reasons to leave the office, anyway. Only the occasional gallery visits. He didn't watch movies, had never understood their appeal. He'd seen everything in all the museums of New York far too many times, and the current wave of shows was too commercial to interest him.

The office had been his world, more like a prison, as he recovered. His only real entertainment had been walking through the reconstructed memories of his patients, examining the histories of their damaged psyches and looking for ways to repair the damage.

The daytime street had few pedestrians. Most people seemed to be inside, on the job or at home. Those he saw outside sat on benches in the park, read or worked on laptop computers, drank and ate, chatted with one another or on cell phones.

How different it all looked from night. Abel stared. After so long in the dark, he'd forgotten how varied daylight was. The range of color, the way bright flashes of reflected sun caught you off guard when you turned, blinded you until you moved or your eyes adjusted.

He felt the temperature of his skin change as he slid in and out of sun and shade. Abel stepped into doorways and under awnings as he walked down Avenue A to feel it, smelled food from restaurants drift into the street and the scent of flowers from the markets. Sounds shifted as he slid down the sidewalk, music from shop doors fading in and out, people passing with blasting headphones. People talked in low voices, heads together, or shouted across streets to one another. He couldn't tell what they said unless they were near him.

His senses had changed. They were cruder, not as expansive as they'd been as a vampire, but now he had all the sensations of day and night open to him. As his tour wore on, the excitement of his new senses began to wear off like a cheap high. He headed home, wondered if Luna would be there yet, and wondered why he cared.

Was this the downside of being human? Did the burden of their emotions come with his change? Abel tried to pose the question in jest, but found that he asked it in earnest. He felt pain for the first time in generations. His feet hurt and his back ached from his hike. He'd started to remember the pain he'd inflicted on others over his decades as a vampire, pain far worse than sore arches. Each step brought his sins home like he was making his own march to Calvary.

Abel stumbled down Seventh Street as the faces of innumerable victims continued to flash through his head, haunted him with their accusing eyes as he tried to push them away. Now that he'd been saved, given the salvation he'd denied to others for so long, he remembered their pleas for mercy and how he'd ignored them. He felt anguish rise on his way home, passed a church and pushed his way inside to hide his pain.

It was late afternoon.

The church was already dark inside; stained-glass windows provided the only illumination Abel could see at first. The rainbow of light from the multicolored glass held him mesmerized as his eyes adjusted.

He saw a large, dark wood altar at the front with a painted plaster Christ nailed to a cross in its middle. The messiah's eyes gazed heavenward, face transfigured as if in acceptance of his fate. Statues of saints and bishops flanked him on either side. The Virgin Mary and Mary Magdalene were carved in low relief on panels under his outstretched arms. The Virgin gazed up at her son with loving compassion as the Magdalene looked down, as if to reproach the viewer. *This is your fault,* her eyes seemed to say; *He died in agony, because of you.*

Sinner.

Below the Christ's feet was a gold-framed Slavic painting of the Madonna and Child in deep blues and vivid reds, ornamented with gold leaf. The Holy Mother held her right hand to her heart and looked out with sadness, as if she could see the end of her son's life depicted above her. The Christ child was dressed in red robes, cradled in her left arm, a painted puzzle box on his lap. Abel wondered what it signified, knew these paintings were usually allegorical. He couldn't find meaning in it for him, any reason to be drawn inside this church to see it, until he thought of Luna, how she'd carried him for two decades in just this manner, with the same sad love for her godlike child.

She'd played the Madonna for Abel, nurtured him, fed him, and protected him far longer than his real mother and Perenelle combined. Luna X had done more than save his life that night in the subway. She'd helped him build a new one in the years that followed, a life that worked. One he could continue with or without her—except he found that he didn't want it to be without her.

It shocked him to realize that he already missed her after a brief day apart. In the beginning, he'd hated being with her, bemoaned the fact that of all his thralls she'd been the one to find him first. He'd hated her abrasive neediness, her low popular taste in fashion, and her exaggerated awe of him.

Then her sense of worship had faded and she'd begun to treat him like the growing baby she wanted him to be. That had been worse. She'd sewn him custom-fitted outfits as his body developed, grew in irregular directions that made off-the-rack shopping impossible. Even if no one but she could see his true appearance, she wanted him to feel comfortable when he was clothed. Not like a freak.

He thought it was silly at first, felt like he was being dressed up like a pet dog on holidays. Except that the clothes she made for him were more comfortable, and he did feel better in clothes that fit as his body took bizarre new twists over the years. He learned to cast the full-size illusion of whatever outfit she'd made for him, so that when patients complimented his wardrobe they appreciated her true sense of style and he could justifiably give her credit.

When he'd paid to open the shop downstairs it started as just another way to lure potential victims into the building. Before long, local rockers wore her designs on stage and club kids lined up on weekends to be the first out the door in her latest designs. Luna X / Styles had become a hit, slowly growing in popularity.

As long as it didn't draw too much attention to him or his practice, Abel didn't mind, even felt proud that he'd supported the spark of creativity he'd seen in her and fanned it. No one knew her like he did and no one knew him the way she did. There was no need he could express that she hadn't already thought to fill. There was no one else in his life.

Now Luna was gone. He'd always taken her presence for granted. It had been impossible for him to think of her going anywhere. No one he'd enthralled had ever left him. Abel was surprised to find that he felt about Luna X the way Henry Higgins felt about Eliza Doolittle in that musical adaptation of Shaw's *Pygmalion* he'd seen when it opened on Broadway in 1956.

He'd grown accustomed to her face.

Tears filled his eyes again with a sting. He hated the feeling, hadn't wept since his mother's death in 1917, almost too long ago to remember how. But Luna had left him, and now that he was no longer a vampire there was no power on Earth he could use to compel her to come back.

Parishioners knelt in the pews, filed to and from confessionals on one side. It was time for confession. Could this be another sign? Could he somehow make up for his sins, atone and regain his lost Luna? Abel joined their number and knelt down with others seeking repentance. If he was starting a new life, it was better to begin it unburdened of his past sins, to face the world clean, with a blank slate. He would be reborn in Jesus, as his mother had taught him to be.

Father Marek left church early.

He let the younger associate pastor finish up the last confessions for the day. Let him deal with the remaining sins of jealousy between old women or the lustful thoughts of the few teenagers they could still pull in. Marek had gotten his fill of sin for the day, enough for a lifetime.

He hurried into the rectory, locked the heavy wooden doors behind him, and ran to the liquor cabinet. The priest pulled out a bottle of fine old whiskey he'd been saving for a visit from the bishop and opened it with shaking hands. It could have been rotgut for all he cared. He poured a tumbler full, downed it, refilled it, and sat in his chair by the fireplace.

Marek felt sweat that had run down his sides start to cool, drenched his cassock during the man's confession. Not a man. Nothing that could conceive of the things he'd been told could be considered a man.

He'd heard the confessions of murderers and addicts, adulterers and pedophiles, but none of them could compare to the evils he'd heard whispered to him through the screen tonight. Abomination after abomination poured into his ears like poison, so dreadful in conception, so meticulous in execution, that he couldn't stop the man from confessing, couldn't stop listening, couldn't believe it was real.

The priest had sat fixed in the confessional as if by a serpent's gaze. Each confession was worse than the last, and there seemed no end to the inventiveness of the monster's wickedness. The thing on the other side of the screen had finally stopped talking, not because it ran out of material. No. He could go on, he said, but the hour was getting late and he could wait no longer for absolution.

Father Marek gave it immediately and as penance sent him off to make up for his past by being the opposite of the man he had been, someone compassionate and loving. Starting now. It seemed to work and spared him the sight of the thing from Hell who'd transfixed him for the last hour as he left, consoled.

The priest got up to pour another drink and then another, not caring what his fellow pastor or housekeeper would say in the morning. If alcohol had any ability to destroy brain cells, he hoped to kill every last one that remembered what he'd heard and forgiven this day.

Marek prayed to a God he had to fight to still believe in that the man was either completely mad or lying for some insane reason. Sins like that couldn't exist in this world or the next or there was no God, no Devil, in the universe. Only chaos, endless darkness, and the sound of screaming for it to end, a world he couldn't live in.

Not without another drink.

CHAPTER 45

8:43 P.M.—*Central Harlem, 28 July 2007*

Turner hadn't visited the Schomburg in far too long.

He'd been back in Harlem for almost a year and still hadn't paid his respects to his old friend. The 135th Street branch of the New York Public Library had been at the heart of the Harlem Renaissance in the 1920s and 1930s. The staff had hosted readings and events that spread the word of a growing literary movement that included themselves. Almost seventy years after it officially became The Schomburg Center for Research in Black Culture, the building had been redesigned, renovated, and expanded for the twenty-first century.

A reunion was long overdue.

Turner entered the library through the newly redesigned main entrance on Malcolm X Boulevard, with its soaring glass walls and giant video screens. He headed through the main lobby, now spacious, sleek, and modern, to the Langston Hughes Auditorium.

The atrium outside the auditorium was filled with people coming for a panel discussion on the life and work of Zora Neale Hurston. Turner smiled. It was good to see her name draw this big a turnout. She would have been both flattered and bemused.

Harlem had been Turner's home since his first night here, even if he'd had to leave it behind, at times. It was always a pleasure to see the uptown arts crowd on display in full regalia, men and women of all ages, shapes, and backgrounds, professionals and artists, retired and students. They were mostly straight with a splash of gay, in classic styles of the last generation influenced by jazz and Africa, mixed with a wash of pop colors and designer hip-hop fashions on the new kids.

There was the usual scattering of white faces, either fascinated by the place and the period or longtime Harlem residents left over from a time when only white artists and musicians lived uptown. A few were friends of his from back in the day, both black and white, though they didn't know him now. While they had aged, he still looked like he was in his early twenties. Even if they recognized him after so long, they'd never believe he could be the same young man they'd known then.

Turner had reinvented himself again, left New York in the 1970s and returned a stranger almost thirty years later, as he had before. He'd live a decade or two in his beloved Harlem, then leave before anyone became suspicious, and wander the Earth again to search for his identity in the faces of others, looking for a purpose and a point to immortality.

The doors to the auditorium finally opened.

The patient audience filed in across a tile and brass medicine-wheel mural on the floor of the atrium, an artful representation of text from Langston Hughes's first published poem, "The Negro Speaks of Rivers." Turner hadn't discovered it until six years after it came out, when he was nineteen, the same age as the author when he wrote it in 1921.

It spoke to Turner in a clear, new voice and made him want to hear more. He'd found plenty and read other poets like Countee Cullen, and fiction about the scene like *Nigger Heaven*, Nella Larsen's *Quicksand*, and McKay's *Home to Harlem*. He'd burned with the desire to visit their settings in person, to see the art and hear the music that had inspired the writers' work and to meet the people who'd made it. Hard work in Chicago got him train fare to New York in the fall of 1931, despite the Depression, with enough to live on for a few weeks. His fingers kept him here by winning a piano playoff at a speakeasy called Guédé's Place his first night in town.

He'd gotten a job tickling the ivories there that very night and entertained a mixed crowd of blacks and whites, young and old, men who looked like women and women who dressed like men. It was a popular club for all, unlike higher-class joints like Small's Paradise or nightclubs like the

Cotton Club that catered only to whites. Guedé's Place was on 133rd between Lenox and Seventh Avenues on a block called Jungle Alley, where all the real fun was to be had and no one was ever turned away.

It was said that no one could lie in Papa Guedé's. It had a reputation as a bar where only the truth could be told, no matter how painful. Women brought in boyfriends to ask if they loved them. Men brought wives to ask if they were faithful. Many a business deal was sealed or broken there, many a romance begun or ended. Even Turner had found his own love and his own truth at Guedé's, before it burned down that awful last night.

The night he lost Zora forever.

Turner followed the crowd into the auditorium and found a seat in the middle as others filled in the front and the mezzanine. He was close enough to see the faces of the panel, but not so close that he felt they were looking at him.

He sat next to a pretty, young black woman in gold wire-frame glasses, light-skinned with long, dark, curly hair. She would have been called "high yaller" or mulatto in his day. Nowadays, the kids didn't seem to care all that much about what color people were, black, white, or otherwise. It was a blessing that some things had changed. She had a friend next to her; darker, prettier, and styled in a way that seemed to indicate that she knew it. They stared at the first girl's laptop screen as she flipped through black-and-white photos of his Zora.

It caught Turner by surprise at first. He always forgot how accessible almost all information was in the modern age and that personal photographs taken by dearly departed friends a lifetime ago had become part of the public record. He watched the photos along with them and tried not to be obvious. Then one came up he hadn't expected to see here tonight, a photograph so familiar that it brought on pangs of nostalgia and regret that he hadn't felt in ages.

It was a black-and-white picture of him playing guitar on the enclosed porch of a friend's house in Brooklyn. Zora sat on a chair in the shadows to the left of the picture, their host on a seat between them. Zora's face was shadowed, her body in repose. Relaxed, instead of the loud, bigger-than-life broad she played in public. This was the woman that few people saw, thanks to her ability to conceal her true self like a chameleon.

She had called it her party armor: make such a loud entrance that everyone ignored you for the rest of the night, so you could hear what people really had to say and how they said it. This was a photo of the Zora he'd known, the one that had listened, the one that had heard and picked apart the world she wrote down later, alone in her room.

He remembered the moment well. Their male host's close personal friend had taken the photo, more than just a friend according to some. They'd been inseparable for almost three years, despite the other's recent marriage to a woman. It was a rare evening off from rehearsing Zora's show, *The Great Day*, a chance to talk about something other than the musical revue. Music had reared its lovely head anyway, after dinner, over drinks. Zora had sung a song she'd learned on her travels through the South, doing folklore research on a grant from a well-to-do philanthropist with a love of Negro culture.

It was a hoochie-coochie song her wealthy patron might not have appreciated paying to preserve, though authentic. It was a bawdy ballad that inspired a round of jokes from the boys so blue that they'd have been thrown out of any bar in town for telling them. A few drinks and stories later, the four of them had retired from the living room to the porch for a fresh bottle and more music. Turner had closed the evening with a serenade he sang softly for Zora alone, even with others in the room, and it was as he'd reached the end that the picture had been taken.

It reflected the moment, tender, with a touch of sadness. As if they'd had a glimpse of what was to come in the months ahead. If he'd known then what he knew now, he would have grabbed Zora's hand and run, show or no show, taken them both far, far away from Nell, the devil that would consume their lives and love. He must have sighed or exclaimed without thinking, because the girls looked up at him in mild surprise. He smiled.

"Sorry. Didn't mean to spy."

"That's okay, they're public domain," said the girl beside him. She smiled back and angled the screen so that he could get a better look. "I downloaded them from the Library of Congress Web site. They have a lot of Zora photos, recordings, even scans of some of her original typed manuscript pages."

"I'll have to take a look."

Of course, he'd seen and heard them all over the years, long before the photos, recordings, and pages turned out by his Renaissance running buddies were considered historic. Not something he was going to blurt out to a stranger, no matter how fetching. The girl's friend was already staring between him and the photo as she noticed a resemblance.

"You look a lot like the cute guy playing guitar," she said, flirtatious, but sounded like she said it more to keep him talking than with any inkling that he could be the man in the photo.

"That's what caught my eye. Could be a relative. One never knows. My name's Turner. Turner Creed."

"I'm Joie Martin-Johnson. My mom's on the panel tonight." She shook his hand as her friend cleared her throat, loudly. Joie rolled her eyes. "And this is Tasha. . . ."

"Charmed." Tasha held out her hand like a grand diva, as if she wanted him to kiss it instead of shake it, so he did. She giggled as she pulled it back. "You a Zora fan?"

Turner laughed. "I don't know if *fan* is the right word. Let's say, I appreciate."

"I've read everything," blurted Tasha. "Alice Walker got me started with an article she did on her years ago for *Ms. Magazine*. I found it when I was doing research for a paper. It was so sad that she died poor and forgotten."

"Not by everyone," said Turner. He'd done his best to get Zora to let him help her toward the end, but there was no relief he could offer that she was willing to accept. She didn't need money. Friends and neighbors in Fort Pierce, Florida, kept her fed and her bills paid, in exchange for the occasional "consultation." Zora's years of research into voodoo had benefited her in more ways than one.

He looked at the program for the event.

"Who's your mother?"

"Lori Martin. She's writing a novel about Zora."

"Oh?" He hadn't heard about that since his return.

"It's called *Zora's Great Day*, about the year she produced a musical and fell in love with a guy in the company. It's all about her and the lost love of her life, who she wrote *Their Eyes Were Watching God* about."

Turner took a second to process what she'd just said; he couldn't quite believe his ears. Her mother was writing a book about his life, his love? What could she possibly know about it? He didn't know whether to be angry or enchanted.

"I'd like to see that," was all he said.

Joie wrinkled her nose in a most engaging way.

"She's kind of stuck. Rewritten it a few times . . . Of course, I probably shouldn't tell that to a stranger."

"Introduce them after the panel!" said Tasha with a wicked grin and an elbow to Joie's ribs. "Then he won't be a stranger."

"I'd like that," said Turner. "Maybe we can have coffee afterward. I've always been interested in that period." The lights went down as the panel started.

"Mom has a book signing, but, sure," whispered Joie. She closed her computer and sat up.

"Great. I'd love to hear what your mother found out about Zora's secret lover." Which was true. He had enormous interest in what she had to say, and how she said it.

Since it was all about him.

CHAPTER 46

The tab was adding up.

Luna X had drunk her way through happy hour and committed to making it all the way to last call. She hadn't gone a bender like this since her lost month on the road with Guns 'N Roses, back before they got too big, when Axl was still pretty and coke was still cheap. She still wasn't wasted enough to stop screaming inside.

What the fuck happened? Abel was supposed to be healed, whole again, not cured. And why the hell was she sorry that she wasn't his blood bitch anymore after everything he'd done to her? Her tits would never be the same. Not that they'd ever been great, but . . . Luna shook her head.

She had to face it. Being a vampire's victim had made her special. By enthralling her, infecting her with his blood, Abel had made her better than other people, and there hadn't been many reasons in life for her to feel that way. As Adam Caine, then as Abel Lazarus, he'd been her god and had made her a part of something more than human.

With him by her side, wielding his hypnotic power to cloud men's minds, she'd been able to have anything she wanted, had bought their building at a rock-bottom price, filled it with furniture for free. He'd protected her from harm and she'd made sure he was safe. They were more than master and slave, they were a partnership. She knew he felt it, too. *You don't quit a partnership just like that,* she thought, tried to snap her fingers in the air. She needed him and he needed her.

Luna tapped her empty glass, ignored the bartender's cautionary look, and stood, reached out, pulled the bottle from the bar herself, and refilled her glass with tequila. He'd known her since the 1980s and was the only one left downtown who'd let her get away with this. He could tell that something was up, and she knew that he'd make sure she didn't end up in an alley, even if she woke up in his bed.

When she was a girl, Luna had had a guardian angel that watched over her at night. When everyone else was asleep, he'd come in her window, slip under her covers, stroke her with his soft, warm hands and whisper of his love for her, of God's love for her, and how he'd been sent to show her how much God loved her.

The angel had looked a lot like the neighbor boy, but he'd explained that to her. He took on the shape of the neighbor boy when he came in her window so that no one would suspect an angel walked among them. They had to keep his presence on Earth a secret. Luna was part of God's plan, chosen to do great things for her savior. She was very religious—her mother had taught her to be so, as had the nuns—so she had no reason to disbelieve an angel.

The angel had instructed Luna in the Lord's ways every night, and over time she'd learned many ways to satisfy God's naked messenger. He'd told her to be proud of the body God had made for her, stripped her bare, and made her feel beautiful and important like never before. Treasured. In time, her angel had brought other angels into her room to show them all how well she'd mastered her lessons, and she shared her love of God with them all.

It was holy and good, just as the angel had taught her, sweet, sacred nights spent tangled in the limbs of other angels, until her father came in one night and caught the angels in her bed. He mistook them for neighbor boys and chased them out, called the police, and destroyed her covenant with God.

Her angels never came back after that, not looking like the neighbor boy or anyone else, though she saw their faces on the street. A few weeks later, her parents realized that the angels had left her a gift, but wouldn't let her keep it. They drove her to the doctor and compounded their grievous sin by cutting the Lord's seed from her holy womb.

She'd fled that night, packed a knapsack and bought a bus ticket to New York. That's when she became Luna X, when she cut off her family along with her last name.

Luna kept an eye out for her angel and found him, too, in many places, in the guise of many men. Whenever she saw a man look too closely, as if he knew her, she'd ask if he was her angel, and they'd all assured her that they were. They must have been, too, because when she did with them what the angel had done with her in her little bed at home, they said the same things he'd said and cried out to God in thanks. Eyes closed, faces wet, the ever-changing face of her guardian angel, never the same twice.

She'd recognized her angel in Adam when he came home with her roommate, Savannah, all those years ago. He'd looked at Luna with the same power, the same sense of command. After Adam had killed Savannah, he hadn't needed to bite Luna to keep her silent, but he'd done it anyway. She'd hated Savannah and stayed there only for the low rent. Savannah had treated Luna like dirt, like a maid, often worse.

When Luna opened the door and saw Adam feeding at her roommate's slit throat, her blood running down his chest, she'd felt a secret shiver of vindication, as if he'd done it for her to make up for every cruelty Savannah had inflicted. When Adam bit Luna and bound her to him, it only made the moment more magical. In an instant, she'd gone from being a loser to a member of Adam's blood family. She was one of the lucky victims, one of enough use to keep alive.

Luna had called the police, as he'd instructed, told them how depressed her roommate had been for the last few weeks and how she'd covered it up with partying, drinking, drugs, and sex. She knew that Savannah had looked like she was having a great time to everyone else, but at night when they were alone she'd often admitted to Luna how empty her life was.

She'd said that she couldn't admit her true feelings even to her best friends, was spiraling out of control and just wanted to end it all. Luna couldn't believe she'd actually gone through with it.

"She didn't want anyone to know, swore me to secrecy. I was going to call her parents anyway, then I came home and found her. . . ."

Adam had never spoken to Luna after that, once he was safe and the investigation had been closed. He'd disappeared back into his uptown world of wealth and exclusive privilege. Luna had stalked him, followed him at a safe distance, crashed parties to see him, and sneaked into exclusive restaurants where he'd been seen.

When she got the emergency rescue call he'd sent from the subway station, she knew the joy of being needed again. When she was the first to reach him, the one to save Adam, she knew that she had her dark angel back for good and that once he was restored to full power, he'd make everything right.

Life had been better, too. Once she'd gotten his money back from Marlowe's thralls, they'd gone underground, let everyone think he was dead, and bought this house in the East Village. They'd changed his name and she'd taken care of him for these last twenty years while he mended. As much as she hated to admit it, there had been a blessing for Luna in Adam's downfall. Otherwise she'd never have seen him again.

He'd despised Luna the first decade they'd spent together, even though he knew he was helpless without her. He still treated her like a servant. It pissed her off now that she was no longer drugged with love for him, a bottle of tequila in her gut for courage. Even the cruelest master should have some appreciation for the slave who tends to his every need.

Luna finished her last drink and tried hard to believe that the last twenty years hadn't been a complete sham, a waste, that she didn't deserve to get even for losing her youth, her life, to him. Not easy. It was time to go. Luna stood, unsteady on her feet, but firm in her resolve.

She knew what she had to do.

CHAPTER 47

9:34 P.M.—Central Harlem, 28 July 2007

Lori was on the stage of the Langston Hughes Auditorium at the Schomburg Library, still not sure why she was there. She was part of a discussion panel on the life and work of Zora Neale Hurston, but the truth was that despite over a year of research and two radically different drafts of a novel about her, Lori wasn't sure she really understood anything about the woman. Not enough to sit here on stage with renowned experts, many of whom had already expressed mixed opinions about her approach to the book. As she'd expected, the first person at the microphone had asked her to explain herself, yet again.

Zora's Great Day was set at the end of 1931 and told the story of Hurston's passionate affair, between marriages, with a younger man. She'd turned forty-one in January 1932, the month the play opened, but had claimed to be twenty-nine when they met. He'd been only twenty-three. They'd had a relationship that ended suddenly, and she'd never fully explained in accounts of her life who he was, what had happened to him, or why the relationship had ended so abruptly.

In her autobiography she'd talked about a relationship she'd had a few years later with Percy Punter, a Columbia student she'd met at the same time and romanced two years later. Lori had always felt that there was something missing in her account, that Percy had been a great love but not the greatest love of Zora's life. The novel was her fictional account of that true love from Zora's point of view—why Zora had lost him and how the relationship had inspired her most popular and arguably best novel, *Their Eyes Were Watching God.*

"The book's about love and the creative process, how alike they are, how one can feed the other, but also kill it. It's about art and life, but also about death, of a relationship and a dream. It's from her point of view, because you need to see events through her eyes to understand them."

"I heard that you're working on a third draft—do you think your problems have anything to do with being white and trying to get into the head of a black woman? Especially one of a different era?"

Her interrogator was a young black woman in jeans and a dashiki, a clipboard filled with notes in her hand. She'd obviously come prepared, probably as part of some college paper or a magazine article she was writing. Lori had been fielding that question since she'd begun the book, had started it by asking herself the same thing.

"I wish it were that simple. If writers had to be limited to characters who are the same gender, race, age, or anything else as themselves, we'd lose a lot of popular literature, starting with several of Zora's own novels written from a male or a white perspective."

Her answer was so well honed, repeated time and again, in person and in print, that she wondered why anyone who'd done her homework would ask the question. Surely her reply had made it through the grapevine by now.

"No, my problem's less with Zora, more with love. I'm having a crisis of faith in love, as I think she may have had at that point in her life. Zora found her way through it, I'm just having trouble following her lead."

"To a new romance?" There was laughter.

"To a new book; but I think you do have to feel passion to write about it. How does the Cher song go? 'Do you believe in life after love?' I'm not sure I know. When I do, maybe I'll understand Zora better. . . ."

She'd written and rewritten the novel twice already, hated it both times, no matter how different. Both drafts had missed something essential in the story she was trying to tell. There was no spark, no fire, to the love she was trying to describe between her characters. Deep in her heart of hearts, she'd felt it was because she had no use for love anymore; that the great passions of her life were in the past and her future would be solitary.

It wasn't bleak by any means. Her life was filled with loving friends, family, and the occasional roll in the hay with out-of-town editors, professors in town for a conference, or old flames on their way through town to more exotic ports of call. She'd become a kind of sexual stop for aging academics and literati; a local sight that satisfied visitors recommended to friends on their way through New York. It was enough to keep her feeling appreciated.

For once in her life, she felt complete.

There wasn't a void in her life, nothing she missed by being without a partner, hard as that was for her daughter to believe. She had work she enjoyed that paid the bills until this book came along, and a teenager who wasn't nearly as terrifying as she could be. She got along with her child's father, and with her ex-husband and his male partner, so she was balanced and happy in her personal relationships.

Of course, she was dying, but nothing was perfect.

Was that her problem? Was her life so together that there was no reason to stay, no lessons the universe thought were left for her to learn? If so, she could come up with a long list of things she didn't get yet, starting with cancer and other stupid surprises like Steven turning up right now after all these years.

She tried to concentrate on the conversation around her as the other panelists answered questions from the audience, but her mind kept wandering back to Steven. He'd felt good last night. Too good. Looked good, too. He'd cut off his dreads years ago and she missed them, but the short fade he favored now showed off the shape of his head, exposed his face. There was only a sprinkling of gray, just enough to give him gravity. Neither of them was a kid anymore.

So why did seeing him make her feel like she was?

Looking at Steven, she'd felt things she hadn't felt in a while, and wasn't sure she wanted to feel while she was still reeling from the cancer diagnosis. It wasn't that her life was over, but it was definitely moving in a new direction. She wasn't sure where it was going yet and whether or not there would be room for him or anyone else. If they picked up where they'd left off, they would be falling back on the past at the exact moment that she needed to be looking into the future.

Whatever future she had left.

CHAPTER 48

10:39 P.M.—Central Harlem, 28 July 2007

The Lenox Lounge hadn't opened until 1939, years after he'd become a vampire, but Turner had still spent his share of time there over the decades. The walk down Lenox Avenue, from the Schomburg at 135th, Street to the club at 125th, was spent talking about changes in the neighborhood with Lori, Joie, and her friend Tasha. Storefronts were vacant, old businesses driven out by rising rents. They navigated through scaffolding erected around residential buildings under renovation, not for local renters but a new population of affluent owners. Fresh construction towered over existing apartment buildings he'd known since his arrival in 1931. It was a new Harlem since the seventies, but not necessarily a better one in his eyes.

They passed a block-long building that housed a Staples, a Marshalls, and a CVS, major chains that filled 125th Street along with other major chains that had once avoided the area like the plague. The broad boulevard he'd once known as the heart of Harlem had become a temple to big business; smaller, local owners and designers were still there, but struggling to survive when competing against Old Navy and H&M.

Turner led his guests across the street and into the legendary Lenox Lounge, sat them at the bar in front, and ordered them drinks, nonalcoholic for Joie and Tasha once he found out they were only nineteen. Turner shook his head and laughed when he heard. He was old enough to be their grandfather.

That didn't stop him from feeling attracted to Joie. There was something about her that reminded him of Zora in her frankness and energy, but it was no ghost he was chasing. Joie was a living, breathing person, alive in a way he could never be again. Despite the fact that she seemed as interested in him as he was in her, he knew it wasn't a relationship to pursue.

They got back to talking about Zora once they were settled in.

"One thing I never got was why she lied about her age. I mean, I can see taking one or two years off, but ten?" Tasha looked from Turner to Lori, who consulted with each other to see who should answer.

"You want to take it?" said Lori, with a grin. He laughed, could tell she was gently testing him to see what he knew.

"Well. Zora actually had a very good reason, one it takes a while to dig up. It was never vanity. She could be insecure, but not in that way. After Zora's mother died, her father's new wife sent her away. She lived in a series of unhappy situations, some less bad than others, but none she could call home.

"She was saved by a job as maid for an actress in a traveling troupe touring the country. Gilbert and Sullivan, of all things. When the job ended a few years later, she found herself in Baltimore with no education and no future. The city provided free high school to residents. She took ten years off her age at twenty-six to attend high school as a sixteen-year-old."

"They bought that?" Tasha laughed. "I mean, didn't you see that movie when Drew Barrymore did that? I didn't buy it!"

"I don't think she thought she was really fooling anyone. They put her in charge of classes when teachers were absent and she worked her way through school to pay bills. She did make friends, socialized in a way I don't think she'd ever been able to when she had to work just to survive. It was a state of grace, a place she could rest for a while, just grow and be herself. Find herself."

"So she graduated?" asked Joie.

"Yes, graduated, was accepted to Howard, and found enough work to make it through there before going on to Barnard to study anthropology.

First and foremost, her education was in the study of mankind. I think that's what made her writing so clear, so keenly analytical about human nature."

"Why did she keep lying about her age?"

"It wasn't a lie, exactly. It was an excision. In the years before the tour, before school, there was a dark period in her life she never spoke of much. A relationship that crushed her, a part of her life she left behind when she began to see the country and other possibilities. She decided that as long as she'd lost those years, she might as well not go look for them. 'Some years are best left behind,' she used to say. 'No point lookin' for something you don't want to see again.'"

Lori raised her eyebrows.

"I love the way you talk about Zora, like you knew her. You make her very real. You should teach."

"Don't we all in our way," he said with a smile. "Don't let me steal the stage. This is your night."

Lori dismissed that with a wave, looked tired.

"Please. Take it. If this was my night, I decline."

"'Music has charms to sooth a savage breast, to soften rocks, or bend a knotted oak.' There's a show on soon. Stay, and let the music heal your hurting heart." Lori seemed to struggle with her decision and smiled, rueful.

"I would love to hear music and talk more about Zora, but I really don't feel well and must tuck myself in. Joie?"

Her daughter looked at Turner with a grin, then at her friend. "I wouldn't mind seeing the show. Tasha?"

"Duh!"

Lori gave them each a hug.

"I'll see you later. Knock when you get in, even if I'm in bed. Mr. Creed." She turned to him and took his hand. "I place my daughter in your care. It was good to meet you. I hope we talk again soon."

"I'm sure we will. I'll put her in a car as soon as the show is over."

Lori waved over her shoulder as she walked out. Turner could feel heaviness in her, illness. With his vampire senses he could even identify it, but could do nothing for her. Nothing she'd want done, he was sure. It was not his place to ruin the evening for the girls with morbid musings. He put on a big smile and turned back to the girls.

"Ladies! Let the festivities commence!"

Joie floated through the night as if in a fairy tale.

She was the enchanted princess and Turner was her long-awaited prince. She'd never met a guy like him, so calm and assured, a gentleman without being a geek. After the show, they'd walked out and down Lenox, listened to him describe the way the street used to be until he put her and Tasha into a cab and handed her a fifty to pay for the ride.

He'd kissed her hand before he closed the door without breaking contact with her eyes, waved as he watched the cab pull away. Joie stared out the back window at him, turned back around only after he was gone from sight.

"Wow," said Tasha. "I think he liked you."

Joie said nothing, afraid to acknowledge what she felt out loud. Afraid that saying the words would make the feeling vanish like smoke. The cab entered FDR Drive and shot down the East Side to the Manhattan Bridge. The river flowed past as she replayed the evening in her head, saw Turner lean forward to talk about the pictures on her laptop, the way his face had looked in profile in the darkened auditorium when she'd stolen glances at him during the panel. He was so beautiful, so smart. Her heart beat faster, remembering the sound of his deep voice, the low rumble it had caused in her chest when he spoke.

Tasha said something else, but Joie didn't hear it, didn't care what it was. Her friend's comments would be silly jokes, giddy schoolgirl gossip, when Joie was thinking like a woman for the first time. Her head was filled with Turner as it had never been for any other man, not even for Christopher. She was lost in the sight of his lips, the feel of them on the back of her hand, and her secret wish that they had kissed her mouth instead. Sunrise was hours away, but she knew she'd still be up for it. There was no way she could sleep tonight.

Her life had been changed forever.

CHAPTER 49

12:13 A.M.—Red Hook, 29 July 2007

Claire had never seen him so still.

Tom lay on his bed, pale, didn't wrinkle the clean white linens, on his back in white pajamas, silk, as she'd insisted. His eyes were open, stared up at the ceiling without blinking.

Claire had been at his bedside since they'd removed him from the box. Medical personnel had carried him here completely dehydrated and infused him with fresh, whole blood until his heart started to move again. She'd talked to him of their past together and read to him from her favorite books, carried from the burning whorehouse he'd saved her from, *Alice in Wonderland* and Dante's *The Divine Comedy*.

When his tissue was whole and moist again his eyes had opened, but seemed to see nothing. The medical readings didn't change. All evidence said that he was alive, even though he was silent as the grave. Claire stayed beside him, hungry but unwilling to leave long enough to miss his revival.

She read from *Alice in Wonderland*.

"'"Wake up, Alice dear!" said her sister. "Why, what a long sleep you've had!"

"'"Oh, I've had such a curious dream!" said Alice. And she told her sister, as well as she could remember them, all these strange Adventures of hers that you have just been reading about; and when she had finished, her sister kissed her, and said "It *was* a curious dream, dear, certainly; but now run in to your tea: it's getting late." So Alice, got up and ran off, thinking while she ran, as well she might, what a wonderful dream it had been.'"

Claire heard a sigh from the bed, scarcely dared to look up from the book in case she scared him away like a ghost.

"A wonderful dream, indeed," said Tom.

Claire dropped her book and threw herself over him, held back for fear of crushing him with an overenthusiastic embrace. "Are you awake, beloved? Finally awake?"

"You're real, then? I thought my dream seemed quiet. No fires."

"You're finally free."

"Is anyone free?"

He rose from the bed and roamed the edges of the room as if taking their measure. Tom ended on Claire and stared with a beatific smile at her face. He lifted his hands and held her chin in his palms.

"All that is beautiful is in your eyes," he said, and kissed her lips. Claire surrendered, felt the familiar friction of his close embrace, the irritation that told her she was alive and still flesh of some kind, not ageless marble.

"They see everything, hear everything," she whispered into his ear before they parted. He nodded and slipped back into the bed, played the invalid again as she filled him in on what had happened since his entombment in 1937. There was much she had to say that amused him, not the least of which was her tale of Clean Slate's capture of the hundred members of the Veil's Council.

"They are here?"

"Not far away. Nearly all, but Perenelle."

Tom chuckled. "We'll have to pay our respects one day soon. On dear Madame de Marivaux, as well." They stopped talking and stared into each other's eyes in silence while Clean Slate computers recorded nothing but the sound of their shallow heartbeats, pulsing in perfect sync.

Richmond looked at the monitor on his shiny black desktop as Lopez reported in. The mad vampire Tom O'Bedlam was awake, but other than giving him the news of the day, his consort, Claire, had been silent.

"Could they be communicating in some way we can't detect?"

"Vampires can cast visions, but with the dampeners on they can't even do that. No record of direct telepathy. I think there's a simpler explanation, chief."

"What would that be? And don't call me chief."

"They're just fuckin' creepy as Hell."

He looked at the image on his monitor and had to admit she was right about that. Richmond closed the video window with a double tap on the screen.

"Keep an eye on them. She goes nowhere without an escort."

Lopez nodded and left to carry out his orders.

Richmond sat back at his desk and looked out of shaded glass windows at his view of lower Manhattan. He was a native New Yorker, born and bred in Astoria, Queens. He'd grown up without any particular religion. His mother had been raised Methodist, but was married to a man who never went to church and mentioned God's name only when he asked him to damn something. Without any support, she'd given up trying to herd Jonathan and his three brothers to church every Sunday.

Instead of a belief in God, Richmond grew up believing in what he could see and feel and touch. His dad used to say that anything beyond that was just a hustle to get your money.

The winter of 1986 changed all that. He'd seen the face of the real enemy; witnessed the unseen war mankind had raged forever for survival against unnatural forces. Meeting the minions of the Devil had given him faith in an unseen God. He became convinced that there couldn't be a yin without a yang, evil without good, and that if such monstrous things existed in the world, something greater had to exist to defeat them. From childhood agnosticism he'd become a devout believer in his pursuit of a higher good and had never been closer to achieving it than he was today, had never felt closer to God.

Claire had what she wanted, Tom's release. Nicolas de Marivaux wanted a reunion with his wife, but Richmond knew she'd never come in on her own and couldn't let Nicolas out to meet her on the streets. Using the willing Claire as a lure, he could capture Perenelle, a move that would neutralize her as a leader of the opposition and provide motivation for Nicolas to develop a cure. Once they had a cure, the war would be over.

It was all coming together.

CHAPTER 50

1:06 A.M.—*East Village, 29 July 2007*

The aroma of food woke him up.

It was night. Abel was on the couch in his office, stretched out as well as he could be with his restored length. He sat up as the sleep fell from his body slower than it had when he was a vampire. It took a few minutes for the room to come into clear focus. Luna must be cooking. He'd smelled food before when Luna was making meals for herself upstairs. There was something different about it this time, something that it took him a few minutes to realize.

The smell made him hungry.

His feet had stopped aching, which left him free to feel the gnawing in his stomach. Abel hadn't eaten all day, had forgotten that he needed food to drive this new body until now. Hunger pulled him out the door and up the stairs to Luna's floor. Her door was unlocked. He walked inside with a knock.

"Luna?"

There was no answer. Music came from the kitchen, so he walked to the left, following the sound. The lights were on and Luna was hard at work. She had an apron tied over her usual street clothes. Every counter was filled with a platter or a bowl of food. Soup and sauces bubbled on the stove. The oven held a roast rack of lamb, and a pair of Cornish game hens sat cooling on the counter, next to a platter of London broil.

Luna was putting a last swirl of frosting on a chocolate Bundt cake on the wooden island counter in front of her. She looked up as Abel stepped inside the doorway, her face dusted with flour, hair tucked up under a net.

"Hey, sleepyhead," she said with a broad smile. "Wondered when you'd be up."

"I was tired. All that walking. The daylight was so beautiful. . . ." He sat down on a stool next to the island, looked around. "You came back," he said. "I was afraid—"

"Yeah, well," she said, cutting him off. "I figured I been feeding ya all these years, I may as well keep going. I mean, who else would have us, right?"

"Right." He laughed with her and wiped the flour from her cheek. "I guess we're stuck."

She put down the frosting and took his hand. Luna X led him into the dining room and flipped on the lights. The table was as heavily laden as the kitchen counters, with salad, fresh steamed vegetables, sautéed greens, two portions of everything cut and ready to serve, a smorgasbord sampling of international cuisine.

Evidently, Luna cooked as well as she designed clothes.

"I know it's been a while since you ate real food, so I figured I'd give you a refresher course. Guess I got carried away."

He looked at the feast, then back at her, and felt his eyes fill with tears again. It was a damn emotional thing, this being human. He wondered if he hadn't traded one curse for another, far greater one.

"Luna . . ." He searched for words. "When you were gone—"

She stopped him with a hand to his lips as tears ran down his cheeks.

"Me too. It don't make sense, but . . . dammit! You're my boy. My baby. I can't quit you now." She burst into tears, too, and they hugged close, trembled together in the middle of their banquet room, her love for him on display all around them.

"Let's start with oysters. . . ."

"So, what now?" asked Luna.

Abel sat back, his belly stuffed with more food than he'd looked at since he'd died. He had the strangest feeling of fullness that blood had never given him. He'd never been a heavy eater when mortal, but gorging himself this way was a validation of his new nature. Only a living man could have made such a pig of himself.

"We go on. I start daytime sessions for those who want them. But first, I buy a bed." His evening on the couch had left its mark on his all-too-human back. They would go shopping tomorrow, after he'd picked out a room upstairs.

He poured another glass from the latest bottle of wine, which was having the most wonderful effect on his head. It was a weaker intoxication than the blood highs he'd experienced as a vampire, but had its own playful chemistry.

"I own the property, all my bank accounts. They're all legal, as is my accreditation. We go on."

"But the enthralled, now that they're free, will they come back to you?"

Abel sipped his wine and smiled as he gazed into its scarlet depths. Once he'd seen the effect that his cure had on Luna, he'd given the matter a great deal of thought. He had enough dirt on the men and women who'd put him in this position to keep them quiet whether there was a blood bond between them or not. As for as his patients, his strategy lay cleanly outlined in the simplest definitions of the therapeutic process.

If any were brave enough to say that they no longer felt their old connection to him, he'd simply praise their development and congratulate them on passing through the transference stage of their therapy. Now that they no longer saw him in a godlike or supernatural role in their lives, they were obviously well on their way to recovery and in no time at all would be ready to take on the world on their own. If any of them said that they remembered him biting them, feeding on their blood, well, that "delusion" alone would be good for at least six more months of therapy.

By his vampiric command, most of them would have ended the behavior that had brought them to him, and force of habit would keep most of them on the right track after so long. The ones who began to backslide would return for fine-tuning, and he'd use his legitimate, licensed skills to put them back on the right path with time and money. He was still a strict Freudian.

"We'll make do. Let me have a touch more of that strawberry short-cake." Lazarus smiled and started to laugh, softly, then louder. This was the flip side of tears, all that made being human worthwhile.

Luna X joined him as his laughter built and rose to fill the room, not quite sure why, but happy to see him happy. There was no way for Abel to explain all the ironies to her or how glad he'd be to see the coming dawn, how happy he was to be with her, how far he'd come to be here. They howled as if he'd told a joke, when he finally saw that the big joke was life itself.

CHAPTER 51

3:44 A.M.—*East Village, 29 July 2007*

Abel woke up naked on the couch again with another first as a human, the need to pee. He was surprised that it had taken this long and made his way to the bathroom, still a little loose in the limbs from the wine. While Abel stood at the toilet he remembered something else. Neither he nor Luna had ever gone back downstairs to lock the store. Stupid. He'd paid for that stock and was damned if he was going to let some crackhead make a killing off his investment.

He went back to the couch, picked up his jeans from the floor and slipped them back on, pulled on his T-shirt and sneakers. There were padlocks on the metal door that rolled down to lock the shop. He wouldn't need a key to secure them.

Abel walked downstairs and out the front door, propped it open with some junk mail so he wouldn't lock himself out. The shop door was open and the locks would be inside. When he went in to get them, he saw that he was too late. Someone had already ransacked the store. Abel was reaching for the wall switch to turn on the light when he saw movement behind him.

They were still here.

Abel turned, furious. *They'd learn a lesson tonight,* he thought, and stepped forward as they came out of the back of the store, arms filled with clothes. He glared and waved them away with a dismissive gesture.

"Put those back and I'll let you live," he growled.

It took a moment for it to sink in that they were still coming at him, that his words had no effect on them, and that he had no power over humans anymore. Before he could think of a new tactic, one of the two intruders raised something from under the clothes draped over his arm.

Abel couldn't tell what it was until he saw the flashes, heard a pop and then another pop as he was hit in the head, spun, and got another pop in the chest. He tumbled to the ground as they ran away, felt cheated. Abel had thought his life was supposed to flash before his eyes at the end of it, but there was nothing but blood in his eyes, blinding him as he fell to the floor. He heard screams as someone came in.

Luna leaned over him and wept as she tried to stop the bleeding, told him to hold on, that help was on its way. He tried to tell her it was okay. He'd be fine; wasn't he always? All that came out was a garbled, wet sigh as the room around him went dark and blood filled his ears.

CHAPTER 52

7:15 P.M.—*Park Slope, 29 July 2007*

Lori's body ached, but at least this time it was a good pain and she knew it was helping her. Pilates at the local YMCA was one of the few things she did for herself without reservation. It relaxed her and let her erase all thought, no mind, just body, as she threw herself on the floor three times a week and followed orders for an hour. The Pilates instructor gave commands in a firm but gentle voice, guided the class through floor exercises that stretched her out and worked muscles she didn't use behind a desk.

In the first class she'd taken, the instructor had said that Pilates used to be called Contrology because it was about making small, finely tuned movements of the body with precision. For a control freak like Lori, it was perfect. All of her desire to make things go her way could be sublimated into sessions here at the gym. She'd moved from the beginner class to the advanced in only two months and prided herself on her form.

During class the instructor walked around the room, watching and correcting as she moved among them. They all jokingly called her Ilsa, She-wolf of Pilates, because she was so strict, but it was also the reason why her class was full. Lori always felt smug satisfaction in the middle of a difficult maneuver, as they moved through the jackknife or from plank to sideways plank, when the instructor reached out to adjust someone on either side of her, but never Lori. She'd always taken personally the teacher's "Good job!" to the room at the end of each completed move. Today, Lori felt the master's hand on her calf, lifting it as she did her teaser.

"Up a bit more," she said, and moved on, her damage done.

It hurt because it wasn't the first time. Lori had been slipping more and more in the last few weeks as her body seemed to betray her since the bad news. She knew the cancer couldn't be interfering with her workout yet, but the knowledge that her body was breaking down in any way seemed to be bringing on a system-wide revolt, as if the rest of her were fighting for the right to screw her, too.

Her last visit to the doctor hadn't been fun.

There was something perverse about being told you basically had a choice between doing nothing and dying a slow, painful death or going through a long, painful treatment that could kill you just as fast, if not faster. You could either succumb or cheerfully get involved in your own extermination. Lori had too many things left to do, too much she needed to wrap up before she'd be ready to curl up and die, so she'd opted to fight. It didn't matter if they were giving her a stone ax and a club to fight back with instead of a lightsaber and a phaser. She'd do the best she could with whatever she had available.

So, surgery was on her schedule, and once she'd recovered from that she would start chemotherapy, maybe radiation, too. They'd know after surgery. What fun. So she kept exercising. The better shape she was in, the easier it would be, not that any of it would be easy.

She reminded herself that this wasn't her first battle against impossible odds. That had happened in the winter of 1986. Cancer was nothing compared to a subway full of vampires or fighting off zombies in a blizzard. She'd had it worse.

The thought almost made her laugh.

Lori fought back against her lethargy, her depression, pushed through the exercises, and forced her body into line. This was her time, dammit, and she hadn't come here to fail. Joie was out of the house for the evening; Lori was taking a night off from the book, and her plans didn't include blowing off her workout. She felt herself break into a sweat as she worked harder, thought of the dinner, drink, and movie she would have as a treat when she was done.

She was going to earn it.

Steven had spent the afternoon cleaning up the parts of the loft that weren't being rebuilt before he made dinner for Joie. He'd ended in the kitchen, mopped the black-and-white-tiled floor, wiped down the stove and counters, and scrubbed the room into good enough shape to cook in. A remastered release of Miles Davis's album *Sketches of Spain* filled the loft.

He'd been listening to a lot of Miles lately. Steven didn't know why; maybe it was because no one gave mournful horn as well. It echoed his mood. He was in a state of grieving, not for Lori but himself. Something more than a bad five-year marriage had ended in his life. He faced a new beginning, an uncertain future, with no sense of direction. Steven had avoided the phrase *midlife crisis* as long as he could, but here it was, along with a city and a daughter he barely recognized.

Joie arrived just as he started to pull out food, gave him a kiss on the cheek and a bottle of wine from her mother. She sat at the counter while Steven started to work, the way she always did. He'd learned to love cooking in Los Angeles, with an outdoor grill and a city filled with affordable, fresh local produce at farmer's markets. Steven knew that Joie liked eating his meals and, more than that, loved to watch him cook.

It was all art to him, beautiful scents and tastes to engage the mind and body. He'd always said that food and music both hit you on a gut level. You instinctively got it or didn't on first taste or hearing, knew how you felt about either instantly. Both could be put on paper to communicate the same experience from one mind to another across time. He'd never understood why Lori didn't enjoy food the same way as he did.

"Your mom still can't cook?" Steven laughed.

"The closest she comes is paying cash for delivery instead of charging it." Joie stirred her freshly blended smoothie, watched her dad chop and slice ingredients, toss them between bowls and pans as he kept everything in a constant whirl of seasoned smells and sizzling sounds.

"How are you two doing?"

"Friction, when I don't do what she wants; when I'm not who she wants me to be. We fight whenever I stop reading from her script for me."

"The writer's curse." Steven grinned. He knew it well.

"Please! Control freak." She rolled her eyes. "Then, there was that whole latent-lesbian summer."

Steven winced. "Whose?"

"We kind of took turns." Joie smirked as she watched her dad squirm. "Turns out girls aren't any easier than boys. Some things you have to try to know for sure. I think Fritz inspired that."

Fritz Boerum was Lori's ex-husband, a senior editor at *Vogue*. They'd gotten married after a six-month courtship a year after Steven had moved to L.A. She'd insisted that there was no connection. It had taken Fritz a little less than seven years to realize he was gay and move into a condo on the Upper West Side with his new boyfriend, a designer at the magazine. Joie, nearly twelve then, had been the only one of any of them to see it coming.

Even after the marriage was over they'd loved each other too much to end it badly. Lori had even taken Joie on a Caribbean vacation with Fritz and his new life partner, Keith. The minidocumentary Joie had cut from the vacation video, with an added commentary track of what was going through her head, got her an A in her freshman year of film school.

"So Vangie's show didn't shock you?"

Steven laughed loudly. "Baby, I don't want to condescend—"

"But, you will . . ." She made a face at him.

"Downtown's always the same. All that changes are the faces and places, but downtown is downtown. You're not doing anything I didn't do twenty years ago. And you'd better not be doing most of that."

Steven let her have a little more wine as she dished out seconds for them both; broiled chicken with a spicy peanut sauce, fried okra, and Peruvian purple potatoes roasted with rosemary. At nineteen, Joie could handle her wine better than some of his adult friends, and she never drank more than a glass and a half, anyway. He could afford to be European about it. At her age, he'd done worse things than a light Chardonnay.

"Do you believe in love at first sight?"

Steven raised his eyebrows and tried not to smile, because she asked the question so seriously. They were still at the big butcher-block table where they'd eaten in the kitchen. He brought dessert over, fresh cut fruit with homemade sorbet.

"I thought I did, a few times," he said. "Of course, it helps if it hits both at the same time. Otherwise, it turns to stalking." He stopped joking when he saw her staring down into her bowl. "Someone new? I thought you and Christopher had something going."

Please say no. Please say no . . .

"I don't know what's up with Christopher. We're still trying to get through the other day. He's got issues."

Yeah, thought Steven, *I bet he does.*

"So who's the new guy?"

"We met in the audience at Mom's panel. Turner Creed. He's . . ." She trailed off, as if she didn't know the end of her sentence. "I don't know much about him, but he's smart, handsome, and owns his own house. So, Mom's not unhappy."

"Black, white?"

"Dad!"

Steven held up his hands. "Just asking! No judgment."

"Black."

She grinned as he grinned back. He couldn't help it.

"Well. If he feels the same way, you'll know soon, won't you? Give yourself time with him and Christopher. There's a lot you don't know about him, either. No one says you have to rush anything. Get to know them both. Is that advice fatherly enough?"

"It'll do."

Joie helped Steven clean up the kitchen and they talked more about Turner, love, and boys. She didn't ask what was going on with him and her mother, and since he wasn't sure, he didn't bring it up, either. This night was supposed to be about her, not her parents.

He kissed Joie on the forehead and put her into a car service to take her back to Park Slope, even though she insisted that she could walk.

"Shut up. I'm just making sure I get you back to your mom in one piece. Do it for me, even if you hop out a block away. Seriously, man. Don't let her," he said to the driver, and turned back to his daughter. "Go home. Call me when you get there."

"God, you and mom, I swear." Joie rolled her eyes, but she smiled back at him like she didn't mind being his baby girl once in a while. He hoped she would make the right decision and lose Christopher, no matter what more they found out about him. Steven wanted to put that whole part of his past to rest and couldn't do that with Christopher in their lives.

This Turner guy sounded interesting, more like the kind of guy he wanted his daughter to date. There weren't enough black kids out there with a sense of their own history, pre-hip-hop; maybe he'd do her some good. Steven would have to meet him soon to form his own opinion, but he already liked him better than Christopher.

Time would tell.

CHAPTER 53

8:21 P.M.—*West Village, 29 July 2007*

Luna X had been sitting in the waiting room for hours, before the doctor finally came out to give her the bad news. Abel was dead. They'd done the best they could, but it was too late; too much damage to his heart and brain. He would have been paralyzed if he'd lived. There was more, but Luna didn't hear it, didn't care.

Abel was dead.

He'd regained his life, cured of the curse that had brought them together, and lost it all because he'd gone down to lock up her stupid store. She'd almost torched it after they carried him away, stopped herself only because he'd still need the building above it if he came home. She hugged herself tight, rocked on the plastic hospital seat as the doctor told her she had to go to the morgue to identify the body so they could release it to her.

The body. She'd given them her Abel to heal, but his body was all that was left, all she'd get back. Luna X pulled herself together. This wasn't helping her and it wasn't helping Abel. There was still work he needed done. She asked the nurse at the desk for directions and headed for the elevators.

Downstairs, she walked down the long hallway to the morgue. It was such a dull, unexciting view when you thought of who came down this hall. People balanced on the edge of loss or relief, on their way to find out if a body belonged to them or someone else. She knew her answer already.

Luna X pushed open the door and walked inside, talked to a skinny, sleepy, unshaved man in a white coat. He mumbled for her to follow him, didn't bother with condolences. It wasn't his loss. There was a viewing room and he took her in. The body lay on a table, ready for autopsy if requested. She stared at the stained sheet and waited for him to lift it.

"You ready?"

"Yeah," said Luna, even though she wasn't.

The face that came into view was Abel's, all right. She hadn't expected to see anything else. Blood still stained his perfect head, plastered silken hair to his shattered skull. She gasped, felt her throat close up a little. This was not what she'd expected to be doing at this hour. Her body was supposed to be in bed, asleep, and wasn't handling this any better than her mind. She swooned, grabbed the edge of the table to steady herself. Luna looked at Abel again, swore she saw something strange, but couldn't be sure it wasn't an illusion of her grieving mind. She had to be sure.

The man reached forward to steady her.

"I'm okay. Could we have a minute?"

He started to protest; regulations came to his lips and died as she pulled out a handful of bills and shoved them into his hand.

"Five minutes," he said, looked at his wristwatch. "Ten. I'll get some coffee."

As soon as he left the room, Luna pulled the sheet farther down. Abel had been shot in the head and the chest. His skin was still covered in blood, mostly dried except where they'd cleaned it off to perform surgery. Try as she might, she couldn't find any trace of his wounds.

"Shit. I don't fuckin' believe it."

She examined his head and found a dent where the bullet had gone in; then, as she watched, the last of the damage healed over. His skull resumed its previous shape, as if something had been bubbling quietly while he waited for her and only just got to full speed. Luna had to stop herself from screaming with joy as she watched the last break in his skin close, saw the surgical cuts between his stitches heal.

"Luna!"

Abel sat upright with a shout as Luna slapped a hand over his mouth. He looked at her, his eyes wide, questioning.

"No time!" She grabbed surgical scrubs from a dirty pile in a bin and pushed Abel to slip into them as she moved him toward the door. "He'll be back any minute! My God, I can't believe it, I thought you were cured!"

"I'm more! I'm immortal! My God! It's the elixir! The boy's damn blood is still the elixir of life!" Abel almost danced his way into the hall, but she got him dressed instead and guided him out to a door to the fire stairs. He looked down, lifted his smock to look at the surgical stitches, puzzled.

"Later! We have to get out!"

They ran up the steps and out into the street, laughing like two schoolkids playing hooky.

CHAPTER 54

He'd been without love for too long.

Turner was like a man in the desert, no longer able to tell an oasis from a mirage. He knew how stupid it would be to pursue Joie, how stupid getting involved with any human would be, but love was nothing if not stupid.

They say love is blind, but it's not. We run into it with our eyes wide open, fully knowing the folly and helpless to resist it. Turner didn't just fall in love, he leaped, threw himself into it like a pearl diver plunges from a high cliff in hope of finding treasure below.

First and foremost, he tried to remind himself to protect his safety. The Society of the Veil's rules of secrecy aside, he hadn't survived since the 1930s by being careless. Finding ways to live in his Harlem home without drawing undue attention or enslaving his neighbors hadn't been an easy task. It had been a rough neighborhood in the beginning, and the constant police presence had made it harder for him to live a quiet life, undetected by anyone.

Zora had taught him how to harness his new powers, and control his hunger with prayers to voodoo gods she'd first met in New Orleans. His only blood victims had been the criminals who'd brought the police to his neighborhood. A quick visit, a single bite, and once they were enthralled, all it took was a simple command to give them other ways to spend their time than racketeering or drug running.

Anyone who came around wanting to know what had happened to them received the same treatment. When local drug dealers and pimps re-formed overnight, God got sole credit for their salvation from his neighbors. Turner didn't mind, as long as his block drew no undue attention. It was a delicate balance.

In the 1970s, just before he'd left Harlem, a TV news reporter had tried to do a story on how safe his block was. After he'd changed her mind, he'd had to allow trouble in, petty crimes, minor disturbances, enough to keep it from looking too good to be true. Not enough to disrupt his life, just enough to look normal. Mercifully, the whole of Harlem had improved over the years and his sanctuary had become less noticeable.

Turner had picked up where he'd left off on his return, lived the appearance of a normal life here while he decided what the future held. He hadn't made any specific plans. The time he'd spent traveling through Africa for the last ten years and South America the decade before had left him with much to say about the human condition.

He'd considered writing a book, but questioned what he would do with it when he was done. Publish it under an assumed name to keep anyone from tracing it back to him, still alive in a hundred years? At least the ideas would be out there for someone else to follow up on.

It was only since meeting Joie that he'd considered how else he might spend his time in New York. He'd seen the interest in her eyes, but he also knew that his very nature made him attractive to humans. Turner wanted to believe that she'd seen past the glamour of his vampire allure, that she'd been drawn to his true self and not the magic in him. The man who still had a heart, not the creature he'd become.

He'd been so lonely for so long.

It was hard to admit. Joie was the first woman he'd felt anything for since losing the first great love of his life more than seventy years ago. He'd never faced how devastating it had been to lose Zora or why he'd avoided intimacy since then. While she was alive, he had hoped that something could still change between them. Since her death, his heart, heavy with grief, had no room left for anyone else.

To meet this girl at a symposium on his beloved's life and work, to spend an evening talking about Zora to his companions, reliving those days, had opened something in him he'd thought was locked away forever. The past. Not the painful memories of how he'd lost Zora, but how they'd met, the happy days before the inferno. Joie's sense of humor, her deep intelligence, brought back how he'd felt when he'd met Zora Neale Hurston at a Harlem jazz club his first night in town, fresh off the train.

The night his life had changed forever.

CHAPTER 55

11:27 P.M.—Central Harlem, 27 November 1931

Jungle Alley.

Turner didn't know exactly why he'd ended up on this street out of any he could be on his first night in Harlem. He'd been looking for a boarding room when he passed a group of laughing young black people walking down the street. They were dressed up for a night out on the town, two women and three men. One of the women smoked a cigarette as she sashayed down the street and spoke in a loud voice for all to hear, as if she were onstage. A woman smoking on the street was scandalous enough and drew disapproving looks from passersby, but what she said as she strutted alongside her friends was even more so.

"Why shouldn't a woman have the right to love like a man, the same way men do? Take what you want and leave the rest!"

"Zora! I swear, you only say such things to shock," said one of the men. "Who are you to damn romance? Who doesn't love *love*?"

"I don't see any great bargain in it for the average woman," she said. "She's expected to give up her name, her dreams, and her life to take care of a man, while he gets a free maid, cook, nanny, and a whore in the bedroom! All for the price of room and board!"

The men laughed louder than the other woman, who seemed to feel that the comment was somehow directed at her.

"I assure you, my husband gets no maid or nanny in me, Zora," she said. "Though I will admit to the rest on occasion!" That set them off on another round of laughter, which pulled Turner after them like a small boat in a greater ship's wake.

They turned down 135th Street and went downstairs into a club.

There was no name on the sign outside, just a faded painting on wood, a black silhouette of a left hand with the tattoo of an apple on the palm in red. The music drew Turner in after them, the sound of a piano gone mad, jazz rhythms running wild up and down the floor and out the door to the street to invite Turner inside to see its source.

He walked down the steps and inside, stood as close as he could to the piano with his cardboard suitcase in hand. Turner's fingers played along with the music, tapped his thighs without his notice as the light-skinned black man at the piano thrashed it good like he held a grudge. The player seemed to hover above the stool as if in midflight, but his hands did the real flying, back and forth along the keys as the music exploded from the black-lacquered upright piano in front of him.

The audience pounded the floor with their feet, clapped along as the music danced through their heads, and was tossed back to the performer. Their response told him that they were with him, so he picked up the pace, pushed the beat a notch higher, played like he was dueling the Devil. He climbed and climbed, and the audience followed, egged him on. The shouting and stomping stopped as the piano took over the room, filled every inch, reminded everyone that *it was a percussion instrument, not a music box, and you WILL respect me, DAMMIT!* Just when it seemed he could go no higher, he didn't, and stopped cold. They all gasped in the sudden silence and exploded into applause.

"El Greco!" A short black man in a high hat smoked a big cigar behind the bar. As the pianist bowed, the bartender waved at him with a broad smile, spoke with a light Haitian accent. "A hand, ladies and gentlemen!"

The house clapped louder as cash was passed up and stuffed into a brass urn on top of the piano. It was nearly full of crumpled bills already, and Turner realized that he'd walked into a duel, a contest between players to win the pool, the listeners as judges. Turner looked around.

The club was small and had a low ceiling.

The piano was on a stage at the back, under a bare light. Tiny tables dotted the room with cane chairs hiked up close around them, held more people than should have been possible. The club looked a guest or two away from violating the fire code, but, miraculously, as soon as anyone arrived, the same number always left, kept the club under the limit.

Turner had never seen a crowd like this before.

There were blacks and whites mingled throughout, which he'd never seen in Chicago. There were women dressed like men and a few women he was sure were really men, and no one seemed to care. At the bar, a few young men of both races seemed overly interested in one another, stroked thighs and backs with busy fingers as they laughed and whispered. One had arrived with the people he'd followed in. The rest of his party was crowded around a table near the piano.

Turner smiled. He'd found the Harlem he'd come looking for—bootleg liquor was poured from flasks into glasses under the table; a joint was discreetly passed around near the stage, as cigarette smoke filled the air to conceal it. There was a commotion as the audience clamored for more entertainment.

As El Greco stepped away from the piano, the dark man behind the bar quieted the throng. He raised his hands, and Turner saw the tattooed left hand painted on the sign outside, so perfectly inked that if his hand rested palm up on a table, you'd swear he held a real apple.

"Now, now," he said. "Is no one left to challenge the reigning champion? If not, we take a vote now!"

Turner looked around with everyone else and saw no takers as El Greco preened at the bar, drink in hand. He raised his glass.

"Hell, don't let that arrogant prick win again!" shouted someone in the crowd. El Greco flipped him the finger and bowed. The woman who'd been smoking on the street pointed at Turner.

"Get him! I saw his fingers play along with Greco, and he kept up good!" She grinned as she saw Turner's face fall.

"I can't . . . I—" he protested as he was pushed forward by the crowd, almost carried to the piano, his suitcase dropped down by his side. The crowd had started to clap in rhythm by then, stamped their feet as if they called for his blood.

"What's your name, boy?" the bartender shouted over the noise.

"Turner! Turner Creed!"

The bartender gestured grandly. "The challenger, Turner Creed!"

There was a burst of applause, rowdy catcalls, then the room fell into silence. Turner closed his eyes. He played the piano, all right, but only at home for himself. He'd never played in public before. He wasn't sure he could.

The first time he'd ever seen a piano was when he was six, at the house of a white woman his momma cleaned for, and it was only because his momma had to take him with her when she went for her money. The woman hadn't had her pay the day Momma worked and she'd had to make plans to come back on her day off to get the cash, so they could eat.

The piano was an upright and the woman taught piano to neighborhood children to keep herself busy while her husband was at work. One of them was at the piano when Turner and his momma arrived. She'd let them in and asked them to wait a moment while she finished the lesson. The woman went back to the piano and played a selection to show the boy how it should sound. After assigning a piece to practice at home, she walked him to the door and took Turner's mother aside to give her the money she owed her.

While the woman counted out the money, Turner stood by the piano and stared at the keys. They were beautiful, well cared for, the polished ivory soft yellow, the ebony wood deep black. In his head, he could hear the music the woman had just played, and his small hands found the places where she'd put her fingers to make the sounds.

Turner played the piece so that he could hear the resonance in the wood, the way the strings held the notes after the tiny hammers inside the piano struck them. He played it a few times and looked up to see the women staring at him in shock.

"How long has he been studying?" asked the white woman.

"He ain't never touched a piano before, ma'am," said his mother, and the white woman dropped her purse. She had Turner play the piece again and then played other tunes for him. The little boy played them back to her, pitch perfect, didn't just match her performance but added something of his own that gave the melody a bit more lilt, a touch more color.

The melodies grew more complex as she tested his limits, the fingerings harder, but Turner kept up until the woman had to stop, dizzy. There was no limit. She'd laughed, called him a prodigy, and begged his mother to let her teach Turner for free, just so one day she could say she'd been the first to teach him music.

"I see great things for him. Your son is a musical miracle, Mrs. Creed. He has a talent that needs to be nurtured."

His mother nodded and agreed, but knew her son's only hope in this life was to get a skill that could feed him and his family. His father was dead, and even though she'd been seeing a man down the block, marriage was a long way off, if at all. She still had three mouths to feed and no easy way to do it. If there had been money in this music, she might have taken it more seriously, but she was a churchgoing woman who didn't frequent the kind of places that would appreciate Turner's talents.

She did let him come to work with her, though, and take lessons from the lady. Her employer swore that he taught her more than she could ever teach him, but he remembered her as the first person that taught him to love his gift rather than take it for granted.

He never played for anyone else. When his momma tried to get him to play for their neighbors on the church piano, to prove her stories, he froze up. Turner loved making music but could never share it with others, was terrified of playing in front of people to the point of paralysis. He could play only if he was alone, in private, like prayer, heard only from the next room, or at the old lady's house. His miraculous gift ended up as a joke to the community.

Now, he was in front of a room full of people who he was afraid would tear him apart if he didn't play for them. It didn't make it any easier. He sat silent, head down, eyes closed. Turner could hear them breathing like panthers waiting to turn on him. He kept his eyes closed and took a deep breath, pictured the old lady sitting beside him, pretended he was back in her home on her piano, and started to play.

Turner started with the simple melody she'd taught him first, the tune he'd picked out perfectly his first time at a piano. As it tumbled out of his fingers, he threw it to one side, spun the music around, and drifted from classical styling into a dark jazz riff.

He was a man now, no more a child. The music told his listeners that Turner had grown to adulthood in Chicago, a city filled with burned air and the cries of dying cattle, the roar of great engines that drove the masses through the city in trains. The music sped up, slowed, as he painted a picture of his hometown and the river meandering through the middle, tore away the pastoral dream as the stock market crashed, as the economy struggled to survive and the nation went down.

Turner picked up his pace, wove in a thin thread of music that spoke of another place, more hopeful strains from Harlem, tunes that had made their way to him in Chicago, given him courage, and carried him across the country to be here this night. His hands pounded out triumph and glory, the magic of the moment he'd found here only minutes ago with the music, this town, and his place in it.

With them.

As he pounded the keys to a climax, the room broke into cheers and applause. They lifted him up on their shoulders and passed him around the room. El Greco had danced on the keys for them, given them his all, but it had been only flash, fancy finger work and glitter. Turner had opened his heart and the house at Guedé's Place gave him theirs in return, claimed him as their own that night. A white woman in black, petite, with short, dark hair and piercing eyes, swept to his side with the brass urn in her hands.

"You have won, *chéri*," she said, with a French accent and a bright smile. "Now you must claim your prize."

She handed him the urn filled with money, then held him tight and planted a kiss on his lips, her mouth cool and dry. He felt a chill for a moment, like someone had walked on his grave, but the feeling passed as she pulled away.

The crowd hooted, laughed, and clapped as they saw that she'd left her deep red lips painted on his like a brand. The woman hung on his arm, waved for the others to give him more applause. Turner looked around for the woman whom he'd followed in, the one he wanted to thank for getting him up on the stage.

But she was gone, as were her friends, nowhere to be seen.

CHAPTER 56

9:23 P.M.—West Village, 29 July 2007

It had been far too quiet, for far too long.

Perenelle sat in her parlor, reading the evening papers and trying to calm her mind. There had been no news about Clean Slate activity since the Veil's attempt to infiltrate its headquarters in Red Hook. Perenelle distrusted silence. It seldom meant that nothing was happening. She had to remind herself that none of the wars she'd seen over the centuries had moved in anything but fits and starts, one attack spurring retribution weeks later. It was the wait that was excruciating.

Perenelle sighed. She'd had a life once, and love, instead of this mad struggle for survival. For more than six hundred years she'd witnessed historic horrors and had caused more than a few of her own. Before she'd lost Nicolas, she'd at least had a companion to help her keep the world in perspective, but since his loss at the turn of the twentieth century she'd been alone. The Great Depression had coincided with her emotional state as she hit rock bottom. She'd found herself again, found salvation for herself and her kind in the Veil, but hadn't found companionship.

Even Rahman was gone. Though they'd never succeeded in becoming more than intimate friends, at least he'd understood the world she'd been born into, how different it was from this one and the ones to come. Change was the only constant in the universe, and everything changed except her and her kind. No matter how much she learned, how much she tried to tell herself that she'd kept up with the modern age and grown over the centuries, all that had really changed was her wardrobe.

Perenelle was still the same woman she'd been when she died. She'd learned infinitely more about the world and how it worked, had seen more than she could ever have imagined possible in the fourteenth century, but at her core, the person she was, her views of right and wrong, had stayed solid and unchanged. Except for those few exceptionally grim decades of her life when grief had given way to wrath, Perenelle had lived in a frozen bubble, doomed to float through time unaffected by the world around her.

That was the greatest curse of all.

The doorbell rang and she heard Janos go to answer it. He was not as young as he once was and it took him longer to admit guests. As she waited, she wondered who it could be, didn't like visitors dropping in unannounced. No one was scheduled for tonight and no friends had called. Perenelle flipped to the arts section of the newspaper, looked for a review of a new show she wanted to see while she waited for Janos to announce her unexpected company.

"Madame . . ."

Her butler appeared at the study door, his face pale, expression unreadable. If pressed, she would have said that he looked like he'd seen a ghost. When he was gently moved aside by the man behind him, she saw why.

It was the late Adam Caine, in the flesh.

After explaining how he'd survived the chaotic last night in Sheep Meadow Station, Adam, now called Dr. Abel Lazarus, told her that thanks to the elixir in Christopher's body, he was not only human but as immortal as her late husband, Nicolas, had been. He also explained how he'd obtained it.

"I'm still not a terribly nice person. I'm not sure I know how to be." Abel smiled as his cheeks blushed in embarrassment, something that a vampire could never do. "It's going to take time to figure out what all of this means to me. How my life will change."

It was so strange to be in the same room with him after all this time and not feel the presence of another vampire. Perenelle was still in shock, wished the cognac she had been drinking since his arrival could have an effect on her. Enhanced vampire senses enjoyed the scent and taste of vintage liquors far more than humans, but, sadly, only blood intoxicated them.

"Adam—Abel," she corrected. "I'm almost afraid to ask why you've come to me."

"Not the usual reason. I don't need help. Oh, there was a bit of a fuss at the hospital after I walked out of the morgue, but I can buy my way out of that. I wanted to bring you this. . . ." He reached into a shoulder bag he'd brought with him and pulled out a large file envelope. There were three words written on the flap: THE MILLER FAMILY.

"You know about my art projects back when I was Adam Caine, and that Nina and her family were subjects. This is my file on their progress. . . ." He touched it for a moment, his face an odd blend of fond memory and regret. "Now that Christopher is back, I thought it might contain information of use to you in dealing with him. Between us we know all there is to know about him. Someone should have both halves of the puzzle."

Perenelle took the envelope. It was worn and tied with a faded red ribbon. She opened it and flipped through photos, handwritten notes, typed pages that detailed the indignities Adam had visited on the Miller family for more than fourteen years. How he'd met the father in an airport, so proud of his family that Adam had felt compelled to take it all away from him.

He'd destroyed the father's mind, driven him to suicide on Christmas Eve, then planned to come back every seven years to pick off the rest of the family. Seven years later to the day, he'd killed the mother by burning down the family home, saved the son and daughter. Seven years more and Adam fed on Nina for the first time in her Hell's Kitchen apartment, infected her before he killed her and brought her back as a vampire. He forced her to feed on her own child, but she brought it back to life in an attempt to save them both.

There was more: notes on the search for the vampire baby, Adam's attempts to save himself from the Veil, but one piece of information about Christopher's parentage was particularly disturbing. Perenelle looked up, stared at Abel in shock.

"Is this true?"

Abel squirmed like a bad schoolboy forced to confess to his headmistress. "I've already said I'm not a nice person. Back then, I was . . . worse. What I did—I'm sure there's much you've done that you regret."

Starting with your creation, she thought, but stayed silent. She'd been no saint when she'd met Adam and had raised him to be the monster he became. His excesses only mirrored her own, back then, so she couldn't condemn him without damning herself.

"I understand the circumstances. As you say, I've made my own errors in judgment." She glared at him, knew he got her point even if she left it unspoken. "If he finds out, it would break him. Any chance of saving him would be lost."

"Which is why I brought it to you. So you could decide what to do with it."

She shook her head. "This isn't a burden I offered to take on, Abel. I knew Rahman's plans, and God knows he treated the boy as badly as you, but the end result of your combined efforts is not my responsibility."

"I know that, but . . . I didn't know what else to do with the information, who else to trust."

Perenelle looked at the file in her hands, a ticking time bomb. What was revealed here had to be kept secret from Christopher at all costs, but at the same time someone had to know, in case that knowledge was ever needed. She couldn't conceive of what circumstances those might be, but knew that day could come, and if it did, someone would have to be prepared.

"I'll keep it safe while we make the decision about what to do with it, together."

Abel nodded, reached out a hand, and laid it on hers.

"I know I've been more than a trial to you. I know I can never make the past right between us, but I hope we can let it go one day. Not now, maybe . . ."

"One day."

"Will you tell the Veil I'm alive?"

Perenelle shook her head. "The Veil has more important matters to deal with than you." She filled him in on the events of the last few weeks. He looked shocked.

"I'm sorry to hear that," said Abel. "If there's anything I can do, let me know."

She almost laughed at his offer, but reconsidered in light of the circumstances and thanked him. A day-walking immortal could be of use. She stood and led him down to the front door. He stopped before she let him out.

"Perenelle . . . the boy," he said softly. "Do you think he could provide you with a cure as well?"

She couldn't say that the thought hadn't crossed her mind as soon as Abel told her what had happened to him. It would be a major change, one she wasn't sure she could make. Besides that, how would she get his blood? As Abel had? She couldn't knock the boy out and feed on him like that.

There was more reason to hesitate. If she became human in the middle of a war between vampires and humans, what effect would that have? Once word spread, every vampire who found out that Christopher was a potential cure would hijack him, or he'd be hunted down and destroyed by those with no intention of changing back. She hated to think how many mortals would want what his blood had to offer as well. Perenelle shook her head as if to clear it; more secrets, too many to keep covered up. She opened the front door.

"Welcome back, Abel. I wish you better luck in this life than you had in your last." She kissed him on the cheek. "Enjoy the day. Be well. Do better."

He left, and she closed the door, went inside to think.

CHAPTER 57

Turner had found a new home in Harlem.

After the contest, Papa Guedé, the owner and bartender, hired him on the spot as a house pianist. He took Turner's suitcase and set him up in a small room on the top floor until he could find other accommodations. Turner soon discovered that all of Papa's employees lived in the building and all had started work and residency on their first visit to Guedé's Place.

"What can I say? I am a good judge of talent and of character," Papa said, laughing, when Turner pointed out the coincidence. "And no one is ever late for work!"

Turner was still stage shy and could play for the nightly crowd only as long as he kept his eyes closed, sent his mind somewhere else. It became a kind of mystique; someone even started a rumor that he was really a sleepwalker, a somnambulant pianist who played his dreams aloud. The French surrealists were all the rage in intellectual circles and the idea of unconscious art was everywhere. Turner knew nothing of any of that, only that wherever else his mind went when he played, he'd found a place to live and work.

All he had to do now was find the woman responsible so he could thank her. The smoker with the sassy mouth and pretty smile, the one he'd followed into Guedé's that first night.

She showed up a week later with a proposition.

"Hey, piano man!" Zora breezed into the club like a warm wind. It was late afternoon, hours before the evening crowd piled in for entertainment. She grinned at Turner as she sat down at the end of the bar and waved to Papa. "Hey, Papa! You know what I want!"

"I sure do," he said with a smile as he poured her a glass of his best hooch. "And it ain't a drink!"

They laughed as Turner focused on the keys in front of him. He'd dated girls in Chicago, but none of them was like this. Zora was so free and easy that she seemed more like a force of nature than a woman. She picked up her drink and blew over to Turner's side.

"How's it goin'? Looks like you got a steady gig!"

"Yeah," said Turner. "Guess I got you to thank for that."

"Hell no! I just got you up on stage; everything after that was all you!"

"Nonetheless . . ." He played a few notes, eyes down, started to pick out a melody as they talked. She sipped her drink and listened for a while before she spoke again.

"Look," she said. "Here's the deal. I'm working on a show and I could use someone like you. You ever play for the stage?"

Turner felt the blood drain from his face. Playing for the house at Papa's was hard enough, but in a theater filled with people? He shook his head.

"No, miss, can't do that. I got what I guess you'd call stage fright."

"You play here well enough," she said, and lit a cigarette.

"Here's small; I can close my eyes and pretend I'm someplace else. But in a theater . . ." Just thinking of the rows of seats filled with people staring at him and waiting for him to play was enough to make his blood run cold. He shuddered.

"How about if I get you over your stage fright? Make it so you can play for people in public without a care in the world?"

He looked up at her for the first time since she'd sat next to him. Her gaze met his, eyes big enough to swim in, wide, brown, and beautiful. They were eyes that laughed, not at him but at the world, eyes he could tell had seen a lot of life before they'd seen it as the joke she'd decided it was. Her lips smiled at him, full and moist.

"You can do that?"

"Honey, ain't nothin' I can't do," she answered. Looking at her at that moment, he believed her.

"I guess you must be magic, then."

She waggled her eyebrows with mischief.

"Only one way to find out," she said. "Meet me after work and I'll show you. Then you can play for me."

Zora downed the last of her drink and sashayed out, gave him one last look over her shoulder as she hit the door.

"Don't forget!"

"Wait!" he shouted after her. "What's your name?"

Too late. The door swung shut behind her.

"Hell, son," said Papa. "You are new in Harlem if you don't know that yaller gal. That's just good ol' Zora. Zora Hurston. One of them writers always hangin' out here."

Zora *Neale* Hurston? He knew the name in connection with Langston Hughes and some of the other Harlem writers. Turner had even read a few of her short stories, "Drenched in Light" and "Spunk," in black publications like *Opportunity* and the controversial *Fire!!*

Turner had to laugh. He thought he'd found the heart of the Harlem Renaissance, when it seemed the truth was that it had found him. He looked forward to the end of the night, when he'd find out if Zora was a witch, too.

CHAPTER 58

"**'Somehow it seems** to fill my head with ideas—only I don't exactly know what they are! However, *somebody* killed *something*; that's clear, at any rate. . . .'"

Claire read to Tom from her collection of gilt-edged books, more because he liked the sound of her voice after so long apart than because he couldn't read for himself. Fairy tales were a safe way for them to communicate without sharing information with the Clean Slate cameras. Sleeping Beauty symbolized Tom, waking back into the world to take his rightful place by her side. Snow White reminded them of Perenelle, the envious witch who'd poisoned them and torn them apart, who'd be defeated in the end.

She read *Through the Looking Glass* today. Claire found comfort in its convoluted worldview, matched only by Tom's, the way he saw things now still locked away in his head. He'd spoken its name only once, whispered into her ear when he first spoke, before he was sure they were listening.

"Blood World . . ."

She thought about what to do next as she sat by his side, not sure what was going through his head. He wasn't the Tom she'd known. He seemed more sober, not surprising considering his ordeal, but also more focused, singular in his intention. She still wasn't sure if that was good or bad, wouldn't know until he was free to share those intentions with her.

"'Now, *here*, you see, it takes all the running *you* can do, to keep in the same place. If you want to get somewhere else, you must run at least twice as fast as that!'"

So they drifted through the days, one long storybook hour, as they waited for an opportunity to get out and away, to escape, if nothing else. It wasn't much of a life together, but it was all they had for now.

The door opened to admit Jonathan Richmond.

Claire was surprised to see him there by himself, but knew there were cameras everywhere and UV lights built into the entire complex that would reduce her and Tom to ash before they could get across the room to do him any harm.

"We have a plan," he said. "But we need your help."

"To take down Perenelle?"

"To bring her in, yes."

"About damn time." She stood up, closed the book she'd been reading to Tom, and stroked his snow-white hair as he smiled up at her. "Tell me what to do."

CHAPTER 59

Zora was good as her word and showed up at closing time.

"Hey, piano man! Ready for your cure?"

Turner opened his eyes when he heard her voice. Zora popped up with a big grin like a jack-in-the-box beside the piano. Her smile was infectious and Turner caught it spreading across his face before he could stop it. He nodded, finished the last tune, stood up to applause and disappointed hoots from what little audience was left as he walked away from the piano.

"Where we gonna do this?"

"You got a room upstairs, ain't you?" She had a paper bag with her loaded with what must have been her work for the night. He looked at Papa, not sure what he'd have to say about her coming upstairs in his house, but she noticed and smacked Turner's arm.

"Don't worry about Papa! He know I don't mean no harm! Right, Papa?" The bartender looked over at her as he took money for the last drinks before he shut down the bar.

"What you up to now, Zora?" he asked, a twinkle in his eyes. "Don't lead my piano man astray, woman!"

She walked Turner to the stairs in back. "You know I ain't takin' nobody no place they don't want to go!"

"Okay, then! Just don't go raise no Hell under my roof!"

"None you ain't invited in yourself!" She shouted the last back to him as she walked up the stairs with Turner. The steps were narrow and creaked, the boards loose under their feet. Zora went up first, so Turner had a generous view of her backside as it wove back and forth in front of his eyes.

"Enjoy the view while you can," she said. "That's the most you'll see of that tonight." She turned to wink at him as she reached the top, went down the hall to the next flight of stairs. "I figure you're new, so Papa has you upstairs?"

Turner nodded, a lump in his throat, followed her up the next two flights of stairs to the third floor. He nodded toward his room at the end of the hall. She opened the door and stepped inside.

He hadn't had time to do much with his room since he'd moved in. Papa's wife, Mama Brigitte, went through the house each day, swept and left fresh flowers, but each resident was responsible for keeping his room in order.

Turner hadn't brought much with him from Chicago, so there wasn't much of a mess he could make. His cardboard suitcase was stored under the small bed, its contents scattered in the three drawers of the plain dresser next to it. Zora sat on the bed and opened her paper bag.

"Best get down to business," she said. "Don't want Papa saying you didn't get enough sleep to work tomorrow." Zora pulled out two red candles, a small statue of a male saint, and a bowl filled with packets of spices. "You have any water?"

She looked around, saw the vase on the dresser, and pulled out the flowers, poured the water into the bowl.

"Hold out your hands," she said, and set the bowl in his outstretched palms. Zora began to sing softly under her breath, so soft that he couldn't quite hear what it was. As she sang, she sprinkled herbs into the water from the different packets, stopped as she added each to mutter a prayer, and then went back to her song.

Zora took a box of wooden matches from the bag, pulled one out, and struck it against Turner's belt buckle. The flame flared up with the scent of sulfur as she lifted the match from his waist to the candles and lit them. Both candles were placed on the dresser. She lowered her eyes and continued to sing, moved her hands over the bowl of water Turner was holding.

The gestures were strange to him, nothing he'd ever seen before. As she kept singing he could feel the bowl warm in his hands, warmer than his body heat could have made it.

The water began to steam as the herbs soaking in it began to color the water lightly, like tea. Zora's voice rose. Turner still couldn't understand the words but could tell she was singing in French. It sounded like a hymn, like they used to sing in church when his momma took him, a prayer of some kind.

"Papa Legba, ouvrir barrière pour moi passer . . ."

The first was to Legba, then another name, Shango, as if she'd had to start with the first to get to the second. Zora rocked as she sang, bowed over his hands as he felt the heat of the bowl increase against his palms. He watched the water boil. The herbs bubbled and darkened the water. The candles flared up and lightning flashed outside, brightened the room. For a moment, Turner fancied that he saw someone standing behind Zora, dressed in deep red, his face in shadows. The man placed a hand on her shoulders and whispered into her ear in response to her song.

The man's other hand held a double-headed ax by the handle, the sharp blade resting on the floor behind him. As Zora sang a question, he nodded and held a hand over the bowl. Turner could see through the phantom's fingers as if they were smoke or dust. He watched some of the dust fall into the bowl to mix with the herb-saturated water. The brew bubbled like it was on an open fire.

Zora's head fell back and her eyes faced the ceiling, rolled up in her head as her back arched. She held the last note of her song as the apparition in red disappeared in another flash of lightning. Thunder came at the same time as the candles burned hotter than before, melted down in seconds. Turner watched them turn into puddles of wax on either side of the saint as the wicks were doused and the room was plunged into darkness.

"Now! Drink! Drink it all!"

He heard Zora's voice command him as if from a great height. Turner hesitated, feared burning his mouth on hot water that had impossibly boiled by itself in his bare hands.

"Now! Don't let fear make you fail!"

He threw away his doubt, closed his eyes and trusted her, lifted the bowl to his lips and drank. It wasn't hot anymore. The amber brew was cool to his lips and cooler going down, tasted of autumn and Far Eastern places. As he finished it, Turner heard the sound of applause ring in his ears, faint and faraway, but for a change it sounded pleasing instead of like a rain of blows.

Zora lit the lamp by his bed and rubbed her eyes.

"Boy! That work always takes it out of me." She smiled up at him.

"Is that it?" he asked.

"That's it. I'll take my leave now," she said, and held out a hand. He took it and she pulled herself to her feet. "The hour is late and life is short. I know the way out."

Turner didn't know what to make of her. He opened the door to the small room and let her sidle past him to get out.

"Well, thanks, I guess."

"Thank me tomorrow. You'll know what we did, then." Zora started to walk away, turned back and gave him a fast, hard kiss, then spun away into the dimly lit hall. "Tomorrow, Turner! Then you can thank me!" She disappeared down the stairs. Turner shook his head, and went inside to undress for bed, not sure what had happened here tonight.

CHAPTER 60

9:49 P.M.—East Village, 29 July 2007

If there were darker, danker places than The Pyramid Club in the East Village, Perenelle had managed to avoid them so far. It was located on Avenue A, Townsend Burke's territory, and contained all the elements that kept her on the West Side. A smell of spilled beer, sweat, and old cigarette smoke that had lingered since the 1980s, and a clientele that would have done the Bowery proud in its heyday. It was early yet and the club was still nearly empty. She planned to be gone long before it filled up.

Perenelle waited near the door at the bar in front, unwilling to go any deeper until Claire arrived. The front door opened and the girl stepped inside, looked more at home than Perenelle. She slipped off an oversized black leather biker jacket ornamented with silver Mexican Milagros, slung it over her shoulder. The sleeveless dress beneath was black and there was a short string of pearls at her neck, something Audrey Hepburn might have worn in the sixties.

Claire walked straight to the dance floor in back, nodded in that direction for Perenelle to follow as she passed.

She sighed and followed Claire to the back, sat across from the girl at a small table on a low platform. There was a couple slow dancing in the center of the floor, another at a nearby table nursing drinks as they nuzzled each other. Music thudded dully overhead, some popular downtown hit of the eighties.

"What was so urgent you had to meet me in person?"

"I had an idea about getting inside Clean Slate. I don't trust the computer to communicate, after all that's happened. We can't be sure they won't get into our system eventually. I didn't want them finding a record of this."

"I understand."

Claire stared at Perenelle with sad eyes. "I realize we've been at crossed swords for some time, Perenelle, but this is a time to put that aside. Dr. Burke's capture has put much into perspective for me. Since my release by the Veil, he's been my mentor, but more." She looked down, her voice dropped. "All I knew with Tom O'Bedlam was terror and death. Burke showed me another way to face my endless night. I need him to stay on that path. . . ."

Perenelle understood all too well the consequences of losing a partner who kept you committed to a higher vision. Without Nicolas she had spiraled into decades of self-indulgent destruction that ended in 1930s Harlem, the night she reached the depths of her desires, so dark that she had to change or die. She didn't like Claire St. Claire, didn't completely trust her, but could identify with her sense of abandonment.

"Agreed. Let's start fresh."

"I'll get us drinks and tell you my idea."

Lopez listened to the conversation on a Bluetooth headset, sitting in a black van across the street, well out of earshot of even a vampire. Concealed wireless cameras planted throughout the club provided a clear image of everything that happened inside. She checked her monitors, all the video streaming back to headquarters via satellite-phone connection. Lopez had a backup team at the ready in another van, just in case; she didn't want to take any chances, after the debacle on the Upper West Side.

The cameras proved that Perenelle was really there and not just an astral projection. She showed up on video this time, clear as a bell. They'd hoped that if called to a meeting by one of her own, she would let her guard down enough to arrive in person, and their Judas goat had led her into place right on schedule.

Lopez tried not to be too pleased for having thought of using The Pyramid as a trap after her first meeting with Claire St. Claire. It made sense for Claire to arrange a meet here; the club was small, contained, and easy to fill with their own undercover team. It had taken less than an hour to rig the table, and as soon as Claire left for drinks, they could knock Perenelle out and take her in.

That was if everything went according to plan.

Claire stood up.

Perenelle hesitated, chafed at the thought of making an evening of this. Claire had proven her loyalty to the Veil on her missions and Perenelle felt for her loss of Burke, but there was only so much she could bear. While she was willing to give Claire comfort and a shoulder, there was no need to settle in for a night of girl talk over drinks. As Claire moved to go to the bar, Perenelle reached out to stop her.

"No, please, I have another engagement soon," she lied. "Can we just talk?" Her hand gripped Claire's wrist.

The girl looked down as if the touch was all she'd been waiting for to act. Perenelle suddenly had the same feeling she'd had on her way into the Grand Hyatt Hotel, that she was at center stage in someone else's drama. Claire looked up, impatient, pretense of reconciliation gone from her face.

"For fuck's sake! Just do it!"

Perenelle didn't understand what Claire meant or who she could be talking to until she saw one of the dancers point a remote control in their direction. She felt a shock as a powerful force came up through the floor, scrambled her mind, seized up her body, and threw her system into shock.

It had to be the same device Clean Slate had used to disable the Council at the hotel. Perenelle realized Claire's betrayal even as she watched the girl fall with her, the only assurance she had that this would not be fatal. She blacked out as she dropped to the floor, saw the others in the room move in to collect them as the room went dark.

CHAPTER 61

11:33 A.M.—Central Harlem, 6 December 1931

When Turner woke up the next morning, he didn't feel any different. Whatever Zora's ritual was supposed to have accomplished wasn't immediately evident. He got up, washed, dressed, and went about his business. Turner was still hours away from work at the piano and usually spent the day doing tasks around the bar. He scrubbed the floors, wiped down the counters, and brought in ice from the iceman's truck. Working with Papa, the two waitresses, and Mama Brigitte, by nightfall they had the place repaired from the revels of the night before and ready to wreck again.

Turner went upstairs to clean up and put on his performing clothes, a clean white shirt and tie with a secondhand black suit Papa had bought him the first week he'd worked there. He'd decided that Turner's worn street clothes didn't project the image he wanted for the place. If Papa was going to attract a higher-class clientele with his new performer, he needed his piano man to at least wear a suit. They'd work their way up to putting him in a tuxedo.

The suit was a little big, but when it came to playing, better too loose than too tight. Turner sat on the stool, closed his eyes, and warmed up his fingers with a few scales, then rolled into an original tune that had been going through his mind since morning. It was inspired by what he'd heard Zora sing in his room last night, the prayer or hymn she'd used to do her voodoo.

It had a beat that he couldn't get out of his head, so he started there, added the higher notes of a countermelody, her first prayer of supplication. The two wove in and out between his fingers, chased one another up and down the keyboard as he played.

When he reached the end, he was shocked to hear applause. Turner opened his eyes and saw that the room was full. He'd played longer than he'd thought, but, more important, he'd kept playing while customers came in.

He usually flinched at the sound of the first footfall into the room and was weighed down by each step that came after. Once the club was filled, it was all he could do to block out the noise of the crowd, to pretend that he played for himself and himself alone.

Tonight, there was none of that. Instead, it felt like the phantom roar of applause he'd heard last night at the end of Zora's prayer, when he'd finished drinking her brew from the bowl. It had the same pleasing feel, and he accepted their thanks as he had in his waking dream last night.

So Zora's little spell had worked. She was magic after all, beyond the magic that all women were to most men. The thought made him smile. He couldn't wait to tell her the news. Turner went back to the keyboard and played a popular song for the crowd, looked around to see some stop talking to sing along or pay attention, saw for the first time that he wasn't just background music but a show they came to see. His playing was every bit as important to their night out as the drinks and drama. It made him happy and a little proud. Papa had been good to him. If his playing improved business at all, it paid back only a fraction of what Turner owed him.

A dark-haired white woman approached him from the bar, the one who'd presented him with the award he'd won his first night here. She was pale, but beautiful, with small, precise features and eyes that glittered like cracked ice.

The Frenchwoman, Nell.

"*Bonsoir, petit*," she whispered, so low that he was surprised he could hear her above the music and noise of the room. "I've never seen you play so awake. *Merveilleux!* Now, I can look you in the eyes when you play love songs and imagine they are for me."

Turner found her attention flattering, but he knew that most of the whites that flirted with blacks in uptown clubs were just looking for an exotic thrill to tell their friends about. He wasn't interested in being anyone's street tour of Harlem, especially when he was busy chasing Zora. Turner nodded at Nell with a cool smile, didn't want to offend a paying customer, but looked back down at the keyboard and kept playing as they spoke.

"That's what music's for, to let us imagine worlds we'd rather live in."

"*Oui*, indeed. Some can do more than imagine."

She leaned down over the side of the piano.

"I think we are kindred spirits, you and I. We both believe in more than the eye can see and know how to reach it. You hear it inside your head and play what you hear for us. I share my inner life with only a select few."

Turner chuckled. "Ah. Am I so worthy?"

Nell smiled back at him, but her eyes didn't seem to share the sentiments of her lips. There was a coldness there that frightened him, the same cool, calculating look that Turner imagined slave dealers had once used to size up fresh stock.

"Perhaps. Tonight, you seem touched by an even higher power than mine. . . ." She explored his face with her eyes, leaned forward and stared, like she was examining a precious stone for flaws. He felt the pull of her large, liquid eyes, deep as a well. Turner could feel himself falling over the edge into his reflection, sinking deep, deep into her depths. . . .

"If you ask me, the boy's touched all right," said Zora, as she strode up to them from the door. "Touched by genius." As Nell leaned closer to Turner, Zora grabbed him by the arm and pulled him to his feet. "Come on, Papa's given you an hour off. I have people you need to meet."

Turner took the opportunity to break away, left a fuming Nell behind as the audience protested, hooted for Zora to wait her turn. She maneuvered Turner out the door and up the stairs to the street before he could protest.

Not that he would have.

Zora hailed a cab and gave the driver a midtown address as they settled into the backseat.

"I hope I didn't spoil your evening back there," she said, as she lit a cigarette. Turner rolled down his window.

"You actually rescued me. I felt like the main course on tonight's menu." They laughed.

"More like dessert! Well, good, I did you a favor, now you owe me one."

"I owe you for more than that!" He told her about his evening at the piano, his newfound confidence in public, but she only grinned.

"Hell, I never doubted that. Why do you think you're in this cab?" The car stopped at the door of a building on West Sixty-sixth Street. Zora climbed out and thrust money at the man through the window. There was a brief discussion over how much Zora should tip, which she won by threatening to get back in to the cab and ride around the block a few times to get her money's worth if the driver didn't give her back what she asked.

Zora put her change in her bag, pulled out her keys, and led Turner inside and up into an apartment filled with loud black folks. It looked like a celebration had broken out in her absence, with instruments in play and a song in progress. Zora joined in while she hung up her coat and Turner's, corrected their pace and inflection as she walked into the living room, where most of her guests were gathered. There was food and drink out on a table, but despite the easy social look to things, Turner saw that it was a rehearsal and not a rent party.

"Okay, okay, y'all, I'm back now. Let's start at the top."

Turner got comfortable, listened to them as they sang their way through the show, moved to the music as much as they could in the confines of the crowded room, enough to give an idea of what they'd do on an open stage.

He started to get a sense of the show's structure as the men and women in the apartment moved from song to song dressed in their street clothes. Turner tried to picture how it would look on a stage in full costume. The revue depicted a day in a railroad work camp and ended in a night of partying at a jook joint. Turner liked the idea: a faithfully reproduced slice of authentic black lives as they moved from work to play. The troupe reached the end of the script and Zora led them in a round of applause for themselves.

While the performers descended on well-deserved food, poured out drinks, Zora set up plates and cups for her and Turner, then took him out onto the fire escape, away from the noise inside. She sat a few steps above him, sipped her drink between bites of fried chicken and potato salad.

"They're doing their best, but they're nonprofessionals and still don't get what I'm going for. Everybody stiffens up soon as you tell 'em they're going onstage. I don't want holler singing, none of them classic airs. That's all right in its place, but I want my people loose and easy, like they is at home or a bar with friends. The audience should be a part of the evening, not witnesses. This ain't a crime scene, ain't gonna be no questions asked! Just join in and enjoy yourself!"

Turner smiled and didn't say much, didn't need to.

Zora could talk a river of words, her thoughts shifting like currents in the flow. It was like she read from a textbook one minute, rattling off deep observations about historic events or places she'd been, only to hurl grammar aside to make her point with a punch line from a dirty joke or folk tale that sealed the deal as well as any professor could.

Many Zoras slipped in and out of view while in conversation with him, like a full moon transfigured by fleeting clouds. Turner loved the sound of her voice, fast, energetic, with its light southern lilt, but more, it was what she said and how she said it.

She was genuinely funny, as only those who've suffered greatly can be, with a sharp wit developed as a shield against hurt. Her humor was never careless but pointed, aimed at the things she disagreed with in the world, and there were many. This show had been born to address one of her pet peeves.

She'd roamed the South collecting folk tales and studying voodoo rites, but along the way also collected songs from the people she interviewed. She'd spent time in jook joints, railroad work camps, prison camps, sawmills, and heard what the workers sang all day and after hours for one another. Zora started to see the music and lyrics, traditional and contemporary, as a cultural body of work, a vital part of understanding the people she was recording and studying.

No one saw it her way, which didn't stop her from talking about it, and she'd thought a local popular bandleader in New York had gotten her message. Hall Johnson was a friend of hers. She'd given him a collection of songs and notes about how they should be performed.

He'd sat on it for a year, until she finally gave up and put together her own revue, assembled a cast of Bahamian singers who could dance. Hall shined her on for weeks about putting them together with his band, until a mutual friend told her that his manager had put the kibosh on it behind the scenes.

"Guess he was afraid my little show might catch on and his boys would look like the poseurs they are. That's what burns me up. Black music gets popular, white producers start looking for new shows, but nobody wants the real thing. All they want is a carbon copy of whatever sold out the last time, and there's always some damn lowlife Negro ready and willing to give it to them, for a price."

She'd managed to eat all her food and some of his between outbursts, climbed back inside the window to refill her cup without missing a beat in her rant. Turner kept up, followed her in, and refilled his cup as well.

"What they want to see is black folks sanitized for their protection, cleaned up and polished by the maid like fine ebony furniture, no dust, no scratches! Nothing too real. They want the Negro flavor, but don't want it to leave a bad taste in they mouth, okay?"

One of the musicians had started to play a traditional love song on a guitar, smooth and soft. As drums joined in, a few couples drifted to the floor. Turner lifted the cup from Zora's hand and put it on the table, took her by the waist, and moved her out with the other dancers. She didn't stop talking as she put a hand on his shoulder and let him take the other as he clasped her around the waist.

"We have to stop thinking we have to prove ourselves by imitating what white people do, just need to do what we do well and let folks see the value in that. Is that so hard?" She started to quiet down as her head rested on his shoulder. They swayed to the music as the lights were lowered. Turner pulled her closer. She didn't resist, spoke softly.

"So, piano man, what can you do for me?"

He was startled by her frankness, chuckled, and lifted her face with a finger under her chin.

"Whatever you need done," he said.

"We'll have to work around your schedule."

"Anything to accommodate . . ." He leaned down for a kiss and she pulled back in surprise. Turned stopped, realized that what had been said could be heard in two ways and that he might have misinterpreted her. He jumped away.

"I'm sorry, Miss Hurston, I—"

Zora laughed, loud and hard. "No! I'm sorry, Turner. I have border issues. I should have been clearer. I want you to help me with the show, play with us, give us more heart, get my cast to relax and be themselves. I can pay you, even if you do owe me. Just to be clear, the money is only for the music."

Turner felt embarrassed, and she didn't help by letting her grin grow as she approached him.

"Yeah, that's . . . fine," he said.

She stopped in front of him, put her arms around his neck.

"Are we done with work, now?" she asked.

He nodded, his face warm.

"Good. Because I'd like to cross that border again back to where we were." She leaned into his body and laid her cheek on his chest. He was sure she could hear his heart pounding, but she gave no notice as their dance resumed. Once the rush of blood cleared from his ears, he could hear the music again.

Turner put his arms around Zora, glad that he hadn't imagined anything, and let her carry him back into the middle of the floor, any worry about getting back to Guedé's for the rest of the night lost in her warm embrace and her soft lips.

CHAPTER 62

10:56 P.M.—*Red Hook, 29 July 2007*

The room was not what she had expected.

Perenelle had been sure that she'd be taken directly into interrogation, that the first priority of her capture was intelligence and they'd waste no time in starting to torture her for information. Instead, as she came to her senses and lifted her head, she saw that she was in a sterile white room, more like a corporate office than a torture chamber. She wasn't sure why she found that more disturbing.

She was seated at a heavy wooden table bolted to the floor. A wall-wide mirror covered the opposite wall, almost certainly a one-way glass for observation. Her head was still light, but she was fully recovered. Perenelle felt something in the air, a kind of jamming signal. It had to be the house version of the surgically implanted dampening device that Veil operatives had reported in the Clean Slate agent blown up on the Upper West Side.

She noticed a sheet of white paper on the desk in front of her. Perenelle picked it up, saw that it was a letter written in French, and then noticed that it was addressed to her.

> My dearest Perenelle,
> I wasn't sure of the best way to break the news to you of my return. I
> knew that it would come as a shock, no matter what, but how best to

tell you that I had been saved? To unexpectedly see me, face-to-face, after so long, would be too cruel, and to hear the news from anyone else seemed unfair as well.

Though I had no control over the means taken to bring you in, I'm happier than words can express that you are here and that our long separation might soon be over. Forgive me for informing you of my rescue and revival in such a peculiar manner, but love of the power of the written word was always a bond between us. I knew if you read this first it would give you time to absorb the information slowly as you were ready for it. I hope I made the right decision.

If you have any feeling left for me, after so long, if you can welcome me back into your life, I am on the other side of the door. If not I will leave you in peace. You have but to ask me in or not, the choice is yours, and I will respect it. Either way, I remain, eternally yours . . .

Perenelle couldn't believe the signature that followed any more than the familiar handwriting the note was written in, but it was true. She could barely read it through her tears.

"Nicolas de Marivaux."

She could do no more than lift an arm to gesture assent, heard the door open behind her as footsteps came into the room and a warm hand was laid on her shoulder.

"Beloved . . ."

It was still his voice, unchanged after more than a hundred years apart. She would have recognized it anywhere, anytime, no matter how long they had been separated. Perenelle stood and turned, embraced the man she'd taken as her husband in Paris in a chapel in Notre Dame Cathedral on a cold winter's night, the year of Our Lord 1354.

"If we die, we die as one," he'd said, laughing, when he proposed. The plague had raged on in Europe for so long that life had become almost a joke to the survivors. To be lucky enough to be among the living, lucky enough to have found a kindred spirit willing to share the rocky road of life with you, these were blessings not to be taken lightly. She'd accepted gladly and joined him in his life and his work.

He'd been a book vendor then, in one of the stalls along the Seine River, bought and sold rare old books of interest to only the most serious collectors. By some miracle he'd made a enough of a living to support them. Paris had not lost all its curious minds in the king's banishment of the Jews, nor in the many deaths blamed on them by those who encouraged the exile and seized their property. The intellectual population had been decimated by war and disease over the years, but those who remained had questions that could be answered only in books.

It had been the constant flow of a particular class of arcane texts through his hands that had brought alchemy to their door as Nicolas ran across various volumes on the subject, read them, and pursued more as his interest grew.

The idea of spontaneous transformation obsessed him, being able to change lead into gold, death to life, to hold the power of the universe in the hands of a man. His head had filled with ideas beyond any she'd ever heard. The only way not to lose him was to follow, join him on his mad journey into written history as he traced the roots of his mania. She became his partner in all things as she learned the occult sciences that her husband had taught himself.

It was a path whose final destination was the Book of Abraham, bound in brass and soft, fine leather that felt too much like human skin. It had been bought from a Jewish scholar fleeing the king's threatened pogrom, who needed the funds more than his baggage.

Its study led Nicolas to Rahman in Spain as he searched for a translation. That meeting damned Perenelle and her husband to lives beyond measure, gave them centuries to witness the follies and failures of mankind. They roamed the world, looking for a way to restore her humanity, lost because of his mad hubris, his passion to play God.

And still she loved him.

"Am I forgiven?"

She heard the smile in his voice, as she almost crushed him in an embrace she'd waited far too long to give.

"Forgiven? If I could only erase the years there'd be nothing to forgive. For either of us." She released him but kept a grip, as if he might slip away again, the way he had that day on the mountain. He looked so out of place in this room in his new clothes, hair cut in a shaggy, current style. She almost laughed as he sat her down and took a seat beside her.

"You look so modern!" she said, and he blushed.

"Don't tease me. I'm an old man. I do the best I can."

"I would be happy to see you in rags and unshaven." He still looked barely thirty, when he'd really lived for more than six hundred years on Earth, almost seven. She touched his brown hair, only flecked with gray, his smooth cheek, and frowned. "Nicolas, how did this come to be? You're telling me Clean Slate found you in the ice and brought you here?"

He nodded and grabbed her hands.

"They have Rahman's library from his Sheep Meadow Station. His scientific papers and journals cover over a thousand years of vampire history, including your story to him of what happened to me in Tibet."

"And they tracked you down from that? Found you, rescued you, and brought you here? Why? I'm grateful, but I know this has nothing to do with us. . . ."

"They brought me back to find a cure! Beloved, they want to complete Rahman's work!" The words made her blood run colder than usual.

"His experiment that night in New York was the search for a new elixir, a cure for vampirism, and they need me to finish it. I was his partner in Paris, the only one who can understand the Book of Abraham."

"They have the Book?" Her heart sank. She'd hoped that it had been destroyed in the collapse of the tunnel that night as the possessed infant rose from under the earth to pursue them; that its contents had been scattered, lost forever, and no one would ever be tempted to repeat Rahman's experiment again. Another hope dashed.

"It's my chance to save you, once and for all," said Nicolas. "So we can go on with our lives again. Together in the sun."

She ripped her hands from his, pulled away.

"Are you mad? These people are my enemies! They've captured my fellows, committed who knows what atrocities—"

"*They* are your enemies? Would I be standing here if not for them? I understand that they're at war with the vampire world, but can you deny that they have just cause? You've learned to control your appetites, but you have to admit that you're no more than a benign cancer, at best, even when compared to your fellows."

"A cancer? Is that how you've seen me, for all my centuries by your side?"

"I love you for who you are to me, Perenelle, but you deserve better than this existence. You've suppressed the monster in you, but from Rahman's accounts, after I died, even you fell from grace. It's to your credit that you pulled yourself back into the light alone, but your fellows—as you call them—they're monsters. The collected sins of the cells downstairs are unspeakable. I'm offering you a way to leave them behind and rejoin my world."

Perenelle's head reeled, worse than when Clean Slate's device had knocked her out at the club. Until his supposed death, she'd always lived with her husband, outside the society of other vampires. He'd been the perfect mate, with a life span as long as hers, but without the friction vampires usually experienced when around one another, the subtle irritation that kept their hunting grounds spread wide.

It had destroyed her relationship with Adam once he'd become a vampire, had kept her and Rahman apart except for occasional encounters. The vampire "families" she knew all lived in large residences with separate rooms and came together only occasionally. Connections were emotional or political, but no matter how intimate, they all kept their distance, even when living in the same homes.

The exceptions, like Tom and Claire or the junkies who'd protected the vampire baby, had a connection to pain that made the irritation strangely pleasurable. There was sure to be a name for it one day, if psychiatry ever took on the wider world of vampiric dysfunction.

Despite their hermetic nature, her creation of the Veil had bonded thousands of vampires in New York into a community that worked. She'd fought hard to make that happen and sacrificed much. Giving up control of the Veil, which she'd spent most of the last century trying to create, wasn't an easy decision, even in the midst of a war, but she knew it was more than that. Perenelle cared about too many of them and couldn't abandon vampires she'd known for many human lifetimes to Clean Slate for her own self-interest.

"Nicolas, you don't understand. . . ."

"That you prefer the company of killers to mine? No. I don't. What did we do for more than six centuries but look for a cure? Have you lived without me for so long that you've forgotten who and what you are? Isn't restoring your humanity the single most important goal we ever had?"

Perenelle stopped protesting, unable to answer.

CHAPTER 63

It was another great night for *The Great Day.*

Zora's show had brought them together, but work wasn't all that was going well between her and Turner. They'd met each night after rehearsal for over two weeks, gone over notes on performance and how staging could be improved, arrangements relaxed or tightened. It had made sense to meet over food or drinks, and one night when they'd met late, after he'd finished work, it had just made sense for him to stay over.

The first night, he'd slept by himself on the couch in the living room. The second night, she'd ended up on the couch with him after coming out to make sure he was sleeping all right. After that, it had just made sense for him to sleep in her bed when he stayed over. Zora said it saved her money on heat if she didn't have to turn up the gas at night, and he let her say that.

His favorite time with her was now, the morning after the night before, just as the sun was coming up. He was awake and she was awake, but neither would admit it, because that meant a new day had begun and had to get started. So they'd lie there silently, pretend to be asleep in the soft early light, listen to each other breathe, feel each other's heat, the pull of their bodies as the mattress sank in the middle to roll them together.

"You know I'm older than you, right? More than you think." She said it out of the blue, as if he'd asked her.

"Does it matter?"

"Not to me, but I don't discriminate against nobody."

Zora didn't wait for a laugh. She sat up, swung her feet over the edge of the bed, and faced the window. She pulled the sheet with her, wrapped it around her waist like a sarong, and left Turner cold and almost naked on the bed. She picked up a cigarette and put it in her mouth, lit it, without any thought on her part, as if she were sleepwalking.

"I've had years I wouldn't mind losing," said Turner. He sat up and pulled close to her, wrapped himself around Zora's body from behind. "I don't let it slow me down."

"I'm with you there. We all cast ourselves as the heroes or villains of our own lives; make them a comedy or a tragedy. I see no reason to blame God for my poor choice of genres in the past. Done bought me a ticket to a better show. I ain't nobody's tragic Negress. Don't want to be nobody's joke, neither."

She stubbed out the cigarette.

"How about a romance?" he asked.

She brayed. "You one of those types? Get a girl to bed and start fitting her for a ring soon's you in her thing?"

"Zora!" He pulled her down onto the mattress next to him. "You do say some things just to shock."

"Hell no. I mean 'em, too. Ain't that I don't want you here, baby, but don't take it for granted!"

"You'd be lost without me."

"I'm lost with you." The sounds of the rising day drifted in through the closed windows. A popular ballad rose faintly from a radio inside an open window, voices shouted work back and forth as trucks made early-morning deliveries. Zora paid them no mind. The room inside stayed still as she stared into Turner's eyes, serious for a moment. "I had a vision when I was a child."

"Yeah?"

She nodded. In the morning light, her face looked like that of the child she'd been, waking from divine communication. "I saw my life in a dream, laid out in a series of pictures, like the stations of the cross. Each scene was like a trial, something I'd have to face to get to the next, but each would leave me changed in a way I couldn't have been, otherwise. In a way I had to be."

He touched her face.

She looked at him, but seemed to see through him to someplace else. Zora touched his face, but he wasn't sure if it was him she was touching.

"I saw you and your piano. I saw fire and heard music, saw great powers unleashed, out of control, forces I could neither harness nor contain. I saw a night I wished I'd never seen and I saw you fall and rise again." Again she appeared to look through him.

"But I didn't die?"

"What?"

"You saw me fall, but I didn't die."

Zora blinked and looked fuzzy, half asleep, scowled at him like he was the one who wasn't making sense.

"What nonsense are you talking?" she asked. "I'm hungry." Traffic noise rose from the street, angry shouts and horns honking as Zora hopped out of bed and grabbed her robe, went out to the kitchen. He followed. No matter how much he asked while she made breakfast, she denied having talked about any dreams, pictures, or fire, and finally threatened to fire him if he brought it up again.

Turner let the subject drop and left for Guedé's, did his chores, and prepared to go back to Zora's. El Greco was going to cover his early shift so that Turner could attend rehearsal. On his way out the door, he felt a chill.

"*Bonsoir, monsieur,*" said a voice above him.

It was Nell.

Turner nodded politely as he climbed the iron stairs to the street, kept walking when he reached the sidewalk.

"You seem to be in a hurry," she said as she fell in step beside him.

"I have a rehearsal to conduct."

He walked a little faster to discourage conversation, but she didn't take the hint and had no difficulty in keeping up.

"You work so hard," said Nell. "You need a night off."

"I'm sorry, that would be impossible, Miss Nell, for many reasons." Her persistence was becoming annoying. It was only his chivalry and fear for his safety if a cop went by that kept him from stopping to confront this crazy white woman here on the street.

"I say otherwise."

There was a shift in her tone.

When she stopped walking, so did he. Turner stood still, helpless to move as she stepped in front of him and looked up into his face. He couldn't understand why he was frozen in place; since he couldn't see anything but Nell, she had to be responsible.

"I am beautiful, yes?"

He stared down at her pale face, lit bright by the streetlamp above them, his head locked in place like a fly stuck in a spider's web. "Lovely."

"A beautiful woman deserves some consideration, *oui?*"

"Yes . . ."

She reached out and stroked his cheek with cool fingers, chilled by more than the weather.

"Come with me, Turner," she whispered. "Be mine tonight."

Turner nodded, screaming *no-no-no* inside, but it didn't help. He knew he had something else to do, someplace else to be, but it was all drowned in her deep, dark eyes. His head was full of nothing but Nell, and he could no more refuse her than he could deny his own name.

Nell took his hand and hailed a cab.

She was going to kill him.

Hold your temper, they say, keep your temper, rein it in. Zora understood why, because if she released this anger at Turner when he got here, she'd lose him as a conductor, as a lover, and spend the rest of her life in jail for tearing him limb from limb.

He was more than an hour late. Up until now, he'd been a good bet to slip past her defenses in an end run to her heart, but he'd turned out to be another irresponsible lowlife who promised the world and left her holding the bag.

That's how she felt for the first hour.

For the second, she felt cold dread settle in her heart as she pushed her cast through their rehearsal. No matter what she'd said to him at breakfast, she remembered her childhood dream well, even if she didn't remember telling him about it. Zora had seen the nightmare of that image in her head all day.

She'd recognized his face from her dream the first morning she'd awakened beside him. It had almost made her call it all off then, push him out of her heart and her life to save him from being a stone in her path.

Except that she knew it wouldn't be that easy. Not a single vision she'd dreamed that night hadn't come true so far. There was no reason to think that she'd be able to stop this one, no matter how many times she'd been initiated into voodoo in her year in New Orleans. She'd told everyone in New York it was research, but it was her fate she sought to uncover as she trained with true believers.

The "two-headed doctors" she'd met had taken on the riddle of her visions in her training. Though they all had expressed belief in their supernatural origin, none of them had been able to explain them or give her any power over them. They were like divine signposts of change; vivid, lightning-bright moments that made her stop, pay attention, and make a conscious decision to go one way or another with her life.

The crossroads coming up was a big one to face, she knew that, but she hadn't expected it to arrive so soon. She knew her man. If Turner had stood up her and the show, it could only be because he couldn't be here, and that wasn't good. She wrapped out the cast as quickly as she could, put on her coat and hat, and headed uptown to see what had happened.

He'd never been in the West Village.

Turner had lived in New York City only a short while and been kept busy enough at Guedé's that he hadn't had time for sightseeing. Nell's house was a long way from Harlem, in distance and sensibility, but there were similarities. Both neighborhoods had a large population of artists, writers, and musicians who lived on the edge of social convention, pushed the limits of the law and morality. Both neighborhoods had a reputation as dangerous; both were places where someone could get lost and never be found again.

Nell's brownstone was on a quiet side street away from the main-street tourist traffic and local bars. She'd taken Turner inside, unseen, past a carved wooden door covered with frolicsome animals doing some kind of pagan dance. On the second floor was a large parlor with no windows, the floor littered with silken pillows, a grand piano at its center.

The piano was massive, a stallion of an instrument. Its highly polished black lacquer reflected the gaslight in the dimly lit room like a Rolls-Royce limousine under a streetlamp. Turner sat on a long bench. His fingers moved along the keys, playing a soft, slow song, something by a long-dead composer whose name he didn't know. A tune he'd heard once and his hands remembered. It seemed to please Nell.

She lay barefoot across the top of the closed lid of the grand piano, her head near Turner, high heels on the floor. Nell was on her back, letting the vibration of the music resound through her bare skin. Her low-cut, beaded black gown showed off her figure, clung to her body in all the right places.

Turner knew he was drawn to Nell, but it felt false. It was like playing a role onstage, as if he desired her because he'd been told to, no matter what his heart really wanted. He went through the motions, felt his pulse change and his heartbeat race at the sight of her, but when he played, Turner closed his eyes and knew those feelings were really reserved for his Zora, no matter what the thing stretched out on the piano lid made him do.

"Where are you, *mon précieux*? Not here with me."

He opened his eyes to see her face before him, hanging upside down over the keyboard. Her lips were pursed, impatient. The vampire was used to getting her way. That she didn't have 100 percent of his attention obviously annoyed her.

"I was thinking of what else to play. The music seems to please you."

"You please me." She reached out, slipped a hand behind his head, and pulled his face to hers in a kiss. Despite her influence over him, her lips were cold, unappealing. She felt his repulsion and pulled away.

"It's that Zora, isn't it? What spell has she cast to make you resist me?"

"No spell. No magic."

Nell released him and rolled over to her stomach as he started to play again. She leaned forward on her elbows and folded her arms.

"It's love, is it? I've heard that tune before."

Turner kept playing, improvising on the melody he'd played at the bar the morning after his cure. Nell watched him for a while, toyed with her necklace, a long string of flapper pearls. She frowned, put a hand out to stop him.

"I don't like that melody. Play something else. Something that doesn't remind you of her."

He played something from the bar, a blues ballad.

"Love is a lie, you know," she said. "To give your heart away is to lose it forever."

Nell pouted on the piano, glared at him.

"Did you lose your love?" he asked.

"Everyone loses love. It's the nature of the thing. Don't think you're any different."

"I can't help it. . . ."

He smiled at the thought of Zora, closed his eyes again to see her face, then heard Nell snarl and felt her hands grip him. She grabbed the lapels of his suit and stood upright on the piano, lifted him into the air. Turner dangled from his jacket like a doll as he kicked his legs, tried to find enough footing to pull free.

"Can't help it?" she roared. "Then I'll help you!"

She yanked Turner's throat to her lips, opened her mouth wide and tore at his neck with sharp teeth, opened his veins, drank deeply of his blood, and released something of herself into him. His mind roiled like molten wax as he fought for control and lost, felt all love for Zora fade with his will as his world was filled with nothing but Nell, Nell, Nell, and a deep, abiding love for her. The sole thought left in his head was that he had to give her anything she wanted.

Nell was his master.

Turner wasn't at the bar and no one had seen him since he'd left for rehearsal. Zora sat at the bar, didn't bother to take off her coat as she tried to figure out her next move, where to start looking for him.

Papa brought her a drink, her usual. She nodded, downed it, and signaled for another. He brought the bottle with him. It was plain brown with no label, like all the others, kept sorted out by Papa's keen instincts. He refilled Zora's glass and set the bottle down beside her.

"Drowning will not kill all your problems, *ma petite*, but you're welcome to try," he said.

"I need a vision, Papa. I need to see more clearly than ever before."

"This may not be the glass you need," he said. "If you seek clarity, know what you're trying to see."

Zora squinted at him with one eye.

There were many stories about Papa, not the least was that he had more in common with the voodoo god whose name he bore than he cared to admit. Guedé was a god of the common people, coarse, bawdy, and disrespectful of authority. Under his influence, people spoke the truth, said that which they couldn't say on their own about themselves and others.

Papa also had power over the departed, like his wicked and terrible brothers—Baron Samedi, Baron Cimetière, and Baron La Croix—one god with three faces, three names, the Petro Lord of the Dead. There were some who said they were all the same, not just three, but four in one, Guedé's the only face that dared show itself in public without dire consequence.

Papa had found answers for many people who couldn't find them anywhere else. Zora had never had need of his services before, and this was as good a time as any to test them.

"What might it be I need to see, then?"

"You keep asking yourself *what* happened. Perhaps the real question is, *who* happened?"

Papa went to the other end of the bar to serve a customer as Zora sipped her drink and mulled over his words. She knew that Papa never gave a straight reply but always answered the question.

Who happened? What had he meant by that? Zora thought about the people around them, around Turner, here at the bar and outside. One face came to the surface again and again. A face she always saw smiling at Turner from across the room, next to him, whispering into his ear, watching Zora take him away, jealous. Covetous.

Nell. Her envious French rival.

CHAPTER 64

Richmond sat in his armchair in the penthouse with a drink in his hand, looking at his view of the city, his charge to protect. The latest reports were all reassuring. No agents had been lost. Perenelle de Marivaux was safely in custody, reunited with her husband, Nicolas, and he was working hard to bring her over to their side.

Perenelle's home had been thoroughly searched and its contents cataloged. As expected, there had been booby-traps, and her butler had escaped in the confusion, but no matter. Let him tell the others that their leader had been captured. It could only work to Clean Slate's advantage.

By combining Perenelle's diaries with Rahman's records, Richmond realized that he might have assembled the greatest single vampire archive on Earth. Besides helping them in the battle to defeat vampirism, the historic significance of this work made it exciting. He'd captured more than monsters; he'd collected a living document of world history. If they could be persuaded to cooperate, what wonders would they have to tell us about the past?

If Nicolas was successful, if a cure could be found, they had something of real value to offer their captives, a return to humanity and a full pardon. Imagine if all the vampires could be cured and released to live out the rest of their lives after recording their biographies. The mysteries of the past that could finally be solved, the benefit to the future, could give something back for the loss of life and the damage done in the war.

Lopez came in.

"Got something I think you're going to want to see, chief."

"Don't call me chief," he answered; without thinking, he took the large envelope from her hands. It was a standard office file, worn, decades old, with a name written on the flap: THE MILLER FAMILY.

"The name is familiar."

"The baby described in Rahman's notebooks. The subject of his last experiment."

"Ah!" Richmond opened the folder and flipped through its contents, old photographs and sheets of creamy paper with appalling events handwritten on them.

"We've done a bit of research." Lopez grinned, pleased with herself. "The baby survived that last night. It was turned over to Social Services by a couple, Lori Martin and Steven Johnson. The ones who wrote the book on vampires that came out the following year?

"The boy was adopted by a family named Ross and raised in Bridgeport, Connecticut. He left home a few weeks ago and moved to Manhattan to research his past."

Richmond raised his eyebrows.

"Alive? But Rahman's experiment was to re-create the elixir of life. From what his notes say, he would have had to sacrifice the child to extract it. If he didn't—"

"Then the kid is still filled with it."

Richmond's heart raced.

Rahman's records had understandably ended with his life, but Clean Slate had reconstructed most of the events of that last night from news accounts, police reports, and video-recorded debriefings of the soldiers who'd survived the battle in Sheep Meadow Station.

Richmond had known what was done that night and Rahman's progress as he detailed each step of the experiment in his journal, but after that it had all been conjecture. Richmond had hoped that Perenelle could shed some light on that, once they gained her trust and cooperation.

If what Lopez had said was true, the subject of Rahman's work was here in New York, and had to be brought to Clean Slate's headquarters as soon as possible. All their hopes for a cure rested on his shoulders and their ability to re-create what Rahman had tried to do that night.

If Christopher was alive and well, they had what they needed to proceed without translating the Book of Abraham or repeating the infant sacrifice necessary to generate a new elixir. Richmond had never been happy about that aspect of the Work, as Nicolas had revealed it, no matter the greater good. If they had access to the elixir that Rahman had been brewing in the vampire child and that elixir had cured it, they could shave years off their game plan.

"We need him. Get a tactical team together to arrange a meeting."

Lopez nodded and left as Richmond sat back and started reading the file. With or without his cooperation, Christopher Ross was coming in for a visit.

CHAPTER 65

The joint was jumpin', right to Hell.

Zora watched from a seat at the back of the bar.

Nell was perched on top of the piano, kicked her feet up and down to the music and waved an empty champagne glass while Turner played like a fiend, fingers hopping from key to key like drunken grasshoppers. The dance floor was full and everyone had a glass in his or her hand. Turner's wild new music had a scent of sulfur in its fire, but it infused the celebrants' souls with a party madness, a desire to be as intoxicated as the young couple in love appeared to be.

"*An announcement! An announcement!*" Nell shouted over the noise, as Turner's piano slowed to a crawl and quieted. She swung her legs around and stepped down to the keyboard and onto the stool as he steadied her with his hand. She stood up, visible above the heads of the crowd.

"Tonight will be Monsieur Creed's last performance at Papa's—" there were sounds of disappointment and boos, but Nell held up her hands, "*as a single man!* We're to be married tomorrow night! Here on this stage!"

The room cheered and more drinks went around as hands were thrust out from the crowd to shake Turner's, voices extended their congratulations to the groom to be. He accepted them stoically, a smile fixed on his face that looked like it would be more at home on a freshly embalmed corpse.

"Where will you honeymoon?" asked someone in the crowd.

"Upstairs!" said Nell, pointed upward. "You're only a few floors from my Heaven!" There were cheers and rude requests for tickets to that show. She chided them and laughed as her fiancé went back to his keys. He played a love song with a tinge of sadness to it until she smacked him on the shoulder, then his melody brightened into ragtime.

Zora watched the show from the sidelines, unseen by Turner if not by Nell, who stole victorious glances her way every now and then. Turner sat at the piano like a man condemned, head down, as if on his way to the gallows. Only his hands seemed alive, bounced quick as ever across the keys as if possessed.

Papa appeared in front of Zora with a plain brown bottle. He poured her a shot of fresh gin, then lingered instead of whisking it away to serve another customer. Zora knew the look and raised an eyebrow.

"You have somethin' to say?"

"Only that if you choose to step between these two, know you face a battle royal."

"Wouldn't be my first," she said.

"That may be. But this is different, unless you have fought the undead before." His voice was so low, only she could hear it. Zora stared at Papa, then at Nell and back to him.

"She's no zombie."

"We both know zombies are not the reanimated dead, but the enslaved living. I speak of the true undead, the vampire. That which feeds off human life to survive."

He held her gaze, bold as you please, as Zora fought the impulse to laugh out loud. She stopped herself when she saw how serious he was. Zora had known Papa since she'd gotten back to New York, long enough to know his reputation, and knew he'd heard stories of her initiations into voodoo in New Orleans. Ordinary customers seeking a love potion or a charm to right wrongs got harmless sawdust and spices, bags of nothing that smelled pretty, left them placated and did no harm.

Those like Zora, who'd seen the other side, he treated differently. When it came to the higher powers, he'd always treated her as an adept, the only reason he was so frank with her about something as utterly mad as what he'd just said. She'd seen too much to dismiss the possibility that her rival had stolen her man against his will, body and soul. It would explain many things about Nell and her habits. Certainly it explained how Turner could abandon both Zora and her show without a word of apology or explanation, only to turn up tonight engaged to Nell.

"If this is true, how does one combat such a thing?"

Papa shrugged, as he wiped a glass clean.

"If I knew of these matters, and I do not say I do, I'd say that there's a high price for the power to defeat such evil."

Zora sat back, disappointed. *There's a curse on your head, I'll remove it for money?* Was this all that Papa offered, another sleazy sidewalk fortune-teller scam?

"I ain't rich, Papa. Writing don't pay all that well, remember? You can't pay rent with critical praise."

"Not that price," he said with a frown. "For the power to combat something powerful as this, you need to deal with the Petro gods, the guardians of death and beyond. Their price is high, little Zora. Be sure his salvation is worth risking yours."

Zora put her glass down on the bar, done with drinking for the night, maybe for good. She was finally at the next crossroads she'd seen coming and needed to remain clear-headed to decide which road to take.

"Let's talk. No harm in talk, is there?"

His wedding night had arrived.

It was nothing like Turner had ever expected, if he'd given it any thought at all. He stood on the small stage of Guedé's Place in a rented tuxedo, a gift from the house. El Greco sat at the piano, played a light tune as the room slowly filled. Turner felt like a waxworks figure on display, not an actual groom but a clever imitation of one, good enough to fool the eye. People shook his hand and patted him on the back as they offered congratulations of the day, but none of it felt real, as if he were standing in for someone else.

The music shifted to the "Wedding March" before he knew it, and Turner turned to the front of the club to watch his bride's arrival. Nell entered on cue, radiant, a bouquet of white orchids in one hand and a pearl rosary wrapped in the other.

For her wedding dress she wore a midlength ivory lace evening dress, equally suitable for dinner at the 21 Club, with a white lace Spanish mantilla draped over her head to cover her delicate face. Nell glided to the stage, reached his side, and turned to face the house.

"I want to thank you all for coming," she said, with a radiant smile. "It means so much to share this moment with all our friends!"

Turner stood by her side in a daze, still uncertain that she was really talking about them. A local judge stumbled up to the stage. He was one of the club's regular customers, despite its dubious reputation. They kept his secrets and he kept theirs. His honor held a Bible in one hand and a drink in his other as he swayed, struggled to stand upright long enough to perform the civil service.

"Dearly beloved," he said with a swagger. "We are gathered here today, in the sight of this prestigious gathering, to celebrate the union of this man and this woman in holy matrimony. Marriage is not an estate to be entered into lightly, but reverently, with love and discretion—"

There was a great deal of noise made over that, much laughter and ribald commentary. The ruckus went on until the judge turned away from the couple to shush the guests. When he'd quieted them, he turned back to the bride and groom.

"Turner Creed and . . ." he checked a slip of paper in his Bible. "Perenelle de Marivaux. I now duly require you both that if either know any reason you should not marry, that you confess it now."

Nell giggled and shook her head, demurely, looked up at Turner and pretended to await his opinion. He smiled back at her, blankly, thought that there was some good reason that they shouldn't wed, but it was lost, shoved to the back of his head by thoughts of Nell, his beloved Nell, Nell, Nell. . . . Her name tolled like a bell in his head anytime he thought of anything or anyone else. The judge took his silence as assent and went on with the ceremony.

"If anyone can show just cause why this couple may not be joined by law and God, let them speak now or remain silent hereafter."

"That would be me, your honor. I'll be speaking up."

At the sound of her voice, Turner remembered the reason he shouldn't marry Nell, why he couldn't be her husband now or ever. The reason was Zora, who made her way through the drunken crowd, her eyes locked on Nell and ready for a fight.

Zora took a deep breath before she hit the floor, sober as a judge—any but tonight's presiding magistrate. She strode through the mass of well-wishers toward the back of the room and tried to look braver than she felt. The judge glared at her over the top of his spectacles as she approached.

"And what grounds do you have for protest?"

"That the bride is a liar and a thief."

There was a low rumble of confused voices around her as the judge scowled.

"Be that as it may, neither is good enough reason not to marry, or many of these kind folk in observance would have been left at the altar. . . ." He was shouted down and hats were flung in his general direction.

Nell sneered at Zora.

"She's only a woman scorned, your honor. Ignore her and proceed."

"Very well." The judge turned back to the couple. "Do you, Turner Creed, take this young lady to be your lawful wedded wife?" He continued the ceremony as Zora continued forward, chanted as she came, scattered a pungent gray dust on either side of her from a pair of silver rattles. The sound of unseen drums rose to accompany her as the soft whispers of the neighborhood's newly departed dead repeated the prayer with her, summoned to strengthen her spell. She'd prayed most of the night to the gods to raise this power and had held it at bay until needed. Zora's voice rose as she drew nearer to the couple. Nell looked angrier the closer she got.

Gaslights began to flicker as the room went quiet.

Low thunder rolled in the distance, but it was only the sound of the nearby IRT subway, its rumble usually covered by the crowd's roar. The silent guests recoiled from the confrontation as from an impending train wreck, unable to flee or stop the inevitable crash. Nell looked away from Zora and directed her attention to the judge, kept him talking and oblivious to the change in the room's climate.

"As long as you both shall live?"

Turner nodded and mumbled agreement as Nell looked his way. Zora kept walking, shook her rattle and chanted louder, invoked the god she'd chosen to help her, the three-faced Petro Lord of the Dead—Baron Samedi, Baron Cimitière, and Baron La Croix—the kings of the crossroads. Who better to help her do battle with the undead?

In New Orleans she'd learned the difference between the Rado and Petro gods, one good, the other more powerful, but with more potential for evil. There were times when their power was the last resort, but even those who worshiped them feared them. The Petro gods could be persuaded to do good, as long as you were willing to pay the price of service to them. Put payment off for ten years, twenty, thirty, or more, but promises had to be kept or they would have their revenge. Until your service is done, your fortunes will fail you, your family will die, your health will fade, and if it is still not paid, then you will die. Make a promise to the Petros and it will be kept.

Zora had made her deal to save Turner. The price would be paid and kept secret forever, like any good magic. She'd spent the day in ceremonies and sacrifices to be prepared for tonight, felt the strength of the Petro spirits rise and fill her body as she kept up her chant, surrendered herself to the godhead within her.

"Do you, Nell, take this man to be your wedded husband? Will you love, honor, and keep him in sickness and in health, forsaking all others, till death do you part?"

Nell opened her mouth to reply, but Zora was upon them by then, shook the last of the rattle's contents into the air around the vampire. Nell was frozen in midword before she could answer the judge's question. The dust swirled, moved like fog, and joined the mist left hanging in the air behind Zora, a cloud of goofer dust, Papa's own special blend. Mixed by special request for the occasion, it was more than just the usual cemetery dirt: it contained herbs and powders combined to enhance the strength of any magic done with it, a spiritual magnifying glass. It was a powerful weapon that lacked only the courage to use it and a host to channel the power of the gods.

That was Zora's job.

She completed her incantation and a dark rainbow of shadows filled the air around her as the trinity Zora had invoked possessed her and poured the might of the ages into her body. It shook violently, like she'd gripped an electrical line; her skin went taut, her muscles tensed as the power of the gods entered her. She was still Zora, but also so much more: she was Samedi, Cimitière, and La Croix, too, with all the glory of the Petro pantheon behind her.

Zora opened her eyes and saw the room as if for the first time, everything in flawless detail, each object visible in its totality down to the last molecule. Everything made perfect sense to her in a way it never had before, as if she'd been in on the act of creation and had intimate knowledge of every last speck of dust in the room, its essential nature and purpose.

Zora looked upon the vampire and saw the essential truth in her as well. She saw the vampire's true name and spoke it to reveal Nell's real form; uttered words that flung aside the vampire's glamour, her stolen beauty, so that all could see the monster within. A wave of energy from the loa that possessed Zora threw Nell against the wall, away from Turner. She remained pinned to it like an exotic lace butterfly, as the room grew brighter.

The vampire was illuminated in a golden glow, but not from the lamps. The air was filled with smoke and a haze of goofer dust that was the source of the light. The power contained in Zora used it to reach out and pull away the veil of illusion that kept the creature beautiful, stripped away the years it had drained from others to stay young.

Nell shrieked like a banshee as her skin shriveled along with her body as she aged, her borrowed life lost. Decades melted into centuries as she rapidly shrank into what she should have been by now, a dried husk, devoid of life.

Before the curse could be completed, Zora panicked.

She'd become something alien to herself in a way she hadn't anticipated, had given herself over to be ridden by the gods before, but never to the Petro and never anything this big.

The power burned, not her flesh but her immortal soul, altered the essence of who she was in a way she couldn't allow. To use this power was to be changed forever. Zora held back, couldn't surrender completely, felt the gods retreat in rage.

Nell saw her opportunity and fled, threw anyone in her way aside with the last of her inhuman strength. Her final breath was spent calling back to Zora, as glowing dust whirled after her, drove her out into the street.

"You'll pay for this, you nigger bitch! You'll pay!"

The crowd parted to let Nell escape, screamed and fled in her wake, led by the judge as soon as they were released from the spell she'd cast over the room to keep them all complicit. Zora shuddered, dropped to her knees as the spirits left her. She felt like a spent shell still smoking from the gun, lifted her head, and dragged herself to her feet. Zora walked over to the stage to see if she'd succeeded and found Turner limp on the floor, unconscious, or dead.

CHAPTER 66

3:32 P.M.—Park Slope, 30 July 2007

Her cell phone rang.

Joie was in the kitchen, making a meal for her mom, hot soup and a sandwich. Lori didn't feel well today; she was still upstairs in bed. Before leaving the house for the day, Joie wanted to make sure her mom had some food in her. She could see it was Christopher's number on her screen, hesitated before she put down the knife and pushed the button to accept the call.

"Joie?"

"Yeah." She felt her heart beat a little faster at the sound of his voice. Partly because he had that effect on her, partly because she felt guilty about the feelings she'd been having about Turner. "How are you doing?"

He laughed. "I was going to ask you that. I figured, after our fight about Lazarus, you might not want to talk to me yet."

"I understand if you don't like him. He's done okay by me, that's all I'm saying."

Christopher didn't reply, which was just as well. Whatever had happened upstairs between them had shaken him and she couldn't get into the middle of that.

"I just need to make sure things are all right between us."

It was Joie's turn to be silent. Her mind raced through possible responses. She was still attracted to Christopher and didn't know what the whole video-distortion-field thing that Spider had discovered meant, or why dead flowers seemed to bloom when they sat together. A part of her wanted to run like the wind in the other direction, but the rest wanted to understand who he was and what all this meant to her.

She wished that he could be a little more normal, like Turner, just a guy with sex appeal instead of coming loaded down with weird karmic baggage. The only thing she was sure of was that ignoring him wouldn't make any of it go away. She had to do what her mother would have told her to do, if she weren't zonked out on painkillers upstairs: *Don't run away. Confront your fears head-on.*

"Okay, yeah. We should get together, and talk."

She wasn't sure why she'd agreed to see him again, even less sure why she'd agreed that it should be at his apartment. Joie had suggested a nearby café, but Christopher had pointed out that the things they had to discuss couldn't be talked about easily in public. Which was true. She took the subway and was downtown in less than an hour.

"Hi," said Christopher when he opened the upstairs door and led the way in. He looked more serious than usual, which only made him all the more attractive. What was it about the sullen, poetic types that made them so irresistible? She sighed and accepted his offer of a soda as she headed to the front-room mix studio.

Joie dropped her bag on the floor, started to sit down on the couch while he went to the kitchen, and then remembered the weird incident with the wilted potted plants. They were on the windowsill, flowers still in bloom, though it seemed to her that they should have faded days ago. The air in the apartment was hot and thick. The windows were open, but the fan was off. She flicked the switch. The fan was broken; its blade turned slowly, without enthusiasm. Joie sat down on a faux leather armchair next to the sofa, dragged up from the sidewalk a few days ago by Spider. He called it Shopping Streetkea.

"Only one arm is ripped," he'd said. "Gaffer's tape, bitch! It's a free recliner!"

Christopher came in with the sodas and glasses filled with ice. He sat on the couch, didn't seem to care as much as she did about what had happened between them.

"I guess we should start with Lazarus."

Christopher tried to choose his words carefully, but wasn't sure of how to find a good way to say, *Your shrink's a vampire, and he tried to eat me!* For whatever reason, the attack hadn't harmed him, and he still needed to find out more about his past to understand why.

"I may have overreacted. Something happened between us; I could have misunderstood."

Joie looked like the light had suddenly dawned.

"Oh! Oh, my God, did he . . . did he make a pass at you? Or did you think he was? Is that what this is all about?" She looked so relieved that he wished it were that simple. "I can't see him doing that. You must have taken what he said the wrong way, or something he did. He is pretty touchy-feely . . . for a guy."

"I'm sure I did. Let's forget about it for now. But . . ." He couldn't think of any way to tell her to stay away from Lazarus, to warn her of the danger he thought she was in. "Just promise me you'll keep an eye out for anything strange, anything that might make you the least bit uncomfortable with him."

"Christopher—"

He saw her shoulders tense up.

"That's it. No more," he said.

She relaxed. He refilled her glass and his.

"I guess the other thing we need to talk about is the thing Spider found."

"Yeah, I guess . . ."

"First, the vision you had? That's my nightmare, one I've had since I was born. When you told me what you saw, I nearly freaked. I haven't told anyone about my bad dreams since I was a kid. . . ."

He told her everything he knew about his childhood. Growing up in a small Connecticut town where everybody knew him, and knew more about him than he did, for most of his life. He'd been a perfect child by all accounts, but so perfect that he'd been suspect. Even though they'd tried to keep it from him, Christopher had always felt like they thought he was impersonating a good kid and that one day his charming veneer would crack and they'd find him on a roof with a rifle.

When he'd been the most tired of living at home like a ticking time bomb, he'd turned eighteen and been notified of a trust fund left to him by his late, unidentified parents. It wasn't a fortune, but enough to make a fresh start somewhere else. It had taken time for him to work up the courage to come to New York.

"Finding you was like some kind of sign that I'd done the right thing in coming here and taking this apartment with Spider. All this weird history with your parents only makes me feel like we can't ignore whatever's between us. We have to explore and understand it."

"You think there's a reason? Some kind of, what, divine plan?" She scowled, looked like she felt pushed into something against her will.

"No, not that, but there is a connection of some kind that drew us together. You've said so yourself."

He watched her think about it. There was fear on her face, but also wonder and curiosity. Whatever it was, they were part of something out of the ordinary, bigger than life, and there weren't many people who could walk away from that without a closer look.

"Okay, what do you have in mind?"

"Do the video test again, but don't stop, let it keep going."

"Through the nightmare?"

"It's just a dream. I've had it all my life and I'm fine. Really." He smiled. "Maybe not fine, but I'm still here."

She took his hand and stood, sat down next to him on the couch. The camera was already on the tripod, aimed at them. A TV monitor was on the floor next to it. Christopher picked up a remote control from the table and turned both on. They appeared on the TV screen as the monitor warmed up.

Both looked nervous, uncomfortable, as they moved closer and took each other's hands.

"Here we go," Christopher said.

"Through the looking glass," added Joie.

Joie looked at their image on the TV screen and saw the two of them blur into one, glowing, as if their molecules were mingling, burning bright with heat friction. It was the same strange phenomenon they'd seen the first time Spider had tried it, just before the visions had started. Joie didn't feel any different at first, but then she felt an odd ripple run through her head, like someone had just shaken it out and she was suddenly standing somewhere else.

It happened with the speed of a dream, and the world she saw around her felt like one. She could sense Christopher nearby, but couldn't communicate, couldn't see him or herself, only a barren cityscape of abandoned tenement buildings. It was the Lower East Side as she knew it had looked in the 1980s from her parents' old photos. She was on a rooftop. There was a bonfire in a metal drum that burned brightly, next to a ragged band of kids surrounding a baby.

It was unlike any baby she'd ever seen, pale, skin dry as parchment. The child looked frail, but powerful, lorded over them as if it was their master. One of the girls held it close like it was hers, but the look in the infant's eyes made it clear that they were all its slaves.

Then she was on the street, watching a battle between the gang and a single vampire who looked like her therapist. He killed the baby's mother and held up her heart for all to see. The child mourned its loss while the killer escaped and the landscape shifted again.

They were in a subway station now, gloomy, lit by dusty gas lamps on the walls and hanging from overhead, ornate mosaic tile walls darkened by soot. The child sat on top of a pile of live human bodies, all dressed in street clothes as if snatched from the trains, still breathing as it sucked the life from their bodies.

Strange albino creatures with fangs moved over the mound, added more bodies to it, worshiped the child and ornamented it with wreaths of flowers. A tall black man in robes with hair to his waist spoke, read aloud from a leather-bound book with brass fittings, and sent one of the creatures to feed a vial of glowing fluid to the baby.

In its hands the child held a live, severed head with a face that looked like the vampire who'd killed its mother. As she tried to get a better look, the room erupted into warfare. Soldiers and police poured in with civilians, all fighting the monsters in the station. The infant rose into the air and began to glow brighter as combatants fell, their lives sucked into the infant's body. Its health was restored, its cheeks ruddy and pink as it drained the room of life.

Then she was in Central Park, over the ruined crater of a Sheep Meadow covered in snow. She saw her parents, Steven and Lori, decades younger. They retreated from the demon child as it floated in midair, glowed like the sun until the real sun rose. It ignited as the first rays struck, exploded into a ball of energy that filled Joie's vision and blinded her.

In the burning center of the light, Joie saw a series of images: New York reduced to burning rubble, its streets running red with blood; Christopher, comatose, imprisoned in an airtight chamber; saw herself older, with the key to his freedom, twin girls who floated to the walls of his prison like angels and leveled them with a single word. He was freed and came to consciousness, as a red shadow rose to envelop the world in a cloud of blood mist. . . .

Pieces of time flipped through her head; each flash of future history was seared into her memory, planted like seeds to bear fruit later. Every image passed in a moment, but none could be forgotten. They ran together, blended into a chaos that overwhelmed her senses as she felt something else rise, passion, the feeling that her body was bare and touching another, holding someone else wet with sweat as she awoke back in Christopher's apartment, naked in his arms.

He hadn't meant to do it, and didn't remember it, if he had.

Christopher and Joie woke up naked on the couch, sweaty, panting, as if they'd just run a horizontal marathon. She panicked as soon as she saw his naked body, then her own, jumped up and grabbed her clothes as she stood to dress.

Joie didn't say anything as she put her clothes on, just stared at him in confusion, like she didn't understand what had happened any more than he did. He thought she was staring at him and then looked up to see that she was looking behind him, at the plants on the windowsill. Before, they'd been in bloom. Now they were overgrown into something tropical, bigger and wilder than the generic Korean corner-market potted plants they'd been when she came in.

She didn't say anything to blame what had just happened on him, but Joie still left as soon as she was dressed, grabbed the tape from the video camera on her way out without saying a word.

Christopher lay on the couch, depressed, and didn't bother to get dressed. He had nowhere to go. The humidity and hot air kept his sweat from drying, so he lay there, still wet, exhausted by more than the summer heat and their exertion.

The meeting hadn't been a total loss, even if Joie never spoke to him again. If nothing else, she'd accomplished one thing by coming here tonight. Christopher had seen the end of his dream, beyond anything he'd ever witnessed as a child. He knew more than he had before. Unfortunately, only one thing was clear. Whatever nightmare his past might have been, it was nothing compared to what was coming in the future.

CHAPTER 67

11:57 P.M.—Central Harlem, 24 December 1931

Zora had told herself that she was done with love.

She'd been married in 1927, separated a year later, and divorced this July after years apart. It had been a union more impulsive than passionate, the kind that happened after you ran out of everything else to say but, *Will you marry me?*

If the answer was no, at least the awkward pauses and search for conversation would be over. If the answer was yes, well, she'd lived the result of that for a year before she'd quit. She couldn't say for sure why her marriage had ended any more than she could explain how it had begun. All Zora knew was that her poor husband hadn't understood the life of an artist and had rebelled at taking second place to art in her life. It was the problem she'd always had with men. She loved them dearly until work called and she went runnin'.

They weren't always there when she got back.

Zora hadn't fought with her husband. If anything, they'd spent too little time in the same room to disagree. Even when they were together she was usually buried in a book—reading or writing one. Herbert hadn't realized he'd married a woman with two hearts, that only one had time for him and it was the smaller of the two. He'd suffered silently, with notable public exceptions, but the marriage hadn't been fair to him or her. Neither had found what they'd wanted in a mate. In time, they'd accepted it, agreed that love shouldn't last beyond the point where it was pleasurable, and parted to spare each other any more pain. Since then, Zora had courted her muse.

Solitude was easy enough for her.

Men had considered her dangerous enough before, older, educated, independent, and now she could add "divorcee" to the list. It was a wonder that she was invited out in polite society at all, but fortunately, her society was far from polite.

She'd tried to put the New Orleans voodoo research into a publishable form that would make sense to the uninitiated, do justice to her sources, and not give away too many secrets. Not to mention sell well enough to pay her bills while she wrote the next book so she didn't have to kowtow to her patron for money.

There was the show to do, and all that damn business with Langston was still stewing after they'd parted company over rights to their collaboration, her last play, *Mule Bone*. Her life had been complicated enough without love, so she'd sensibly put it out of her life.

Until she'd met Turner.

There was every reason not to love him.

He was more than a decade younger than she was, poorer than a church mouse, and, worst of all, a musician. But he believed in her, in what she believed in, and that her work deserved every bit as important a place in her life as he did. He shared in her work, loved her victories, mourned her losses; and in the little time they'd spent together birthing the show, she'd felt like she'd finally found a soul mate, if nothing else, a man who let her be herself.

Turner was also the most beautiful man she'd ever laid eyes on, inside and out, and when he smiled at her, when he played piano, she felt her heart sing in a way it never had with her husband or any other man. It sang as it did only when she was writing. Surely that was something worth dancing to the edge of the fiery pit to save.

Zora sat by Turner's bedside and doused his fevered forehead with a cool, wet facecloth while he slept. She hadn't found him dead on the club's stage, only unconscious, but he'd been in a coma since last night. The doctor couldn't say why. Turner seemed to be lost in bad dreams, unable to find his way out. It was not the way she would have chosen to spend their first Christmas together. Zora gave him what comfort she could.

The next morning, no one in the club had remembered Turner's wedding night. Either the three-faced Lord of Death had made them all forget before they left her body, or whatever trance the vampire had cast to keep the house quiet had erased its memory of events when lifted. Whichever it was, Papa's club went on as usual, no one the wiser that there had been a supernatural battle there the night before for the soul of her lover.

"Nell . . ."

Turner's eyes opened, stared up at the ceiling. Zora leaned forward, wiped his forehead, and spoke softly.

"No, baby, it's Zora. You're safe now," she said.

His eyes rolled up to her, rolled to the windows, wild.

"No," he said. "She comes. *She comes . . .*"

Zora didn't have time to stand up or get to her defenses before the windows exploded, shattered glass flying inward. She'd been foolish to let her concern for Turner outweigh her plans for defense against another attack. The monster had recovered sooner than she'd expected.

Papa had warned her that vampires have tremendous pride and if humiliated are even more brutal in retribution. He'd told her to finish it off in the club if she was going to challenge it in public, but last night she'd lost control of the force inside her and held back, fearful. Zora had let the vampire get away before her spell was complete; she couldn't afford to make the same mistake again.

Nell must have been waiting out in the cold for some time. She twinkled like a snow queen, frosty silver in the moonlight, lightly dusted with fallen snow and ice crystals as she crept silently into the room, as if on cat's paws. Zora rushed to the dresser for her mojo bag.

The vampire didn't stop her. Instead, she snatched Turner from the bed and gripped his throat in her fangs. He screamed as she bit in, sucked him dry, and threw his body to the floor, all before Zora could work her magic. Zora shrieked Turner's name, dropped her bag, and threw herself on his drained corpse. Nell leaped to the windowsill and crouched there for a moment. Turner's freshly spilled blood ran down her chin, her lips twisted in a triumphant grin to expose sharp, scarlet teeth.

"*Neither of us shall have him now! Only I can raise him, and never will!*

This is better than killing you. To let you live with his loss, as I live with mine!"

Zora wept and cried out Turner's name, over and over, heard Nell's cold voice echo from the streets outside, as she vanished into the icy Harlem night.

"Feel my pain . . ."

CHAPTER 68

8:41 P.M. — *Red Hook, 30 July 2007*

Story time was over.

Claire St. Claire went to the desk of the perky young receptionist who sat outside Jonathan Richmond's office in a neatly pressed one-piece black uniform. She nicely asked to see Richmond with a pleasant, but insistent, smile on her perfect features. Claire knew that the girl was armed, as they all were, and that the place was wired with emergency UV lights that could reduce any vampire to dust. She even suspected that since Richmond had acquired Perenelle, his interest in Claire's survival had likely diminished.

She also knew that he had the weakness of all zealots.

He cared about his cause, not so much the termination of vampires as the salvation of the human race. It was a subtle distinction made by Tom in one of the few conversations they'd had on any subject outside of fairy tales.

It had amused them to spend their only open conversations analyzing their captors. "Let them listen to that," Tom had said, laughing. He'd pointed out that if extermination were Clean Slate's only interest, they'd eliminate all but a handful of their captives. They seemed to see vampires as lost humans and sought a way to save them, welcome them back into the human race and end their curse for good. Tom had enjoyed pointing out that not everyone they offered to redeem would welcome their cure.

"They haven't asked themselves if they'd be willing to step from Olympus to the gutter. What can they offer us to replace godhood?"

Claire had never considered the idea of living again as a mere mortal, with all the weaknesses and vulnerabilities that came with it. The humans were stupid to think that any of them would want a cure. Power was power, and to live without it after so long of getting anything from anyone—how could you face that?

Richmond admitted her into his office after an irritating fifteen-minute wait for no apparent reason, and with nothing she could do about it. Her time inside Clean Slate, with all their high-tech antivampire safeguards, had been sterile, controlled, polite, and strained; utterly impotent, a perfect example of what living life in the real world as a human was like.

No, thank you.

Richmond stood looking at his view, the Manhattan skyline faintly outlined behind him through a glass wall of shaded windows. He gestured to a chair opposite his large black desk, its monitor surface dark. She sat down.

There was a cocktail on his desk. It was evening, after all, though it seemed his job was never done, the disadvantage of living in a penthouse office/residence. She wondered if he ever left the building or if he was some kind of reclusive agoraphobic like Howard Hughes.

"I'm sorry we haven't talked sooner. Since Perenelle's arrival, events have accelerated. We've obtained new intelligence that may hasten a cure. That may be of interest to you. Or not." He picked up his drink with a smirk, confirming that he'd overheard her conversations with Tom on the subject.

"Be that as it may, I believe our deal was that you find Tom, I get you Perenelle, and we go hippity-hoppity home."

Richmond closed one eye and tilted back his head to look at the ceiling with the other as he sipped his drink, obviously not his first. He was being more coy than usual.

"Soon, Claire. We're holding Tom in his best interests. He's been entombed for a long time, longer than you, and your own recovery took weeks, from what Dr. Burke told us."

"You're telling me he's not well enough to go home? He's a vampire. He'll get deader on his own."

"When he's fully recovered, Claire . . . soon."

He nodded to the door as he poured another drink.

Claire would ordinarily have ripped out the throat of anyone who dismissed her like a servant, but, trapped in here, she nodded back and walked out without protest. She went back down to Tom's cell.

"He says you're still not well enough to leave," she said.

"Not to worry," Tom replied. She knew that he could see her fury, but he only smiled, peaceful as a Buddha, and kissed her forehead. "I learned patience in the womb. All things in their time." He lay back on the bed and closed his eyes. Claire sighed, looked through her books for something appropriate, and found the perfect choice in her copy of *The Brothers Grimm*.

CHAPTER 69

Turner was dead.

There was no question. Zora hadn't saved her lover. If anything, she'd brought the wrath of the vampire down harder on him. She lay weeping next to his body for hours, held Turner close as she felt the heat drain from his body. The room was cold now and it was too late for more steam to come up tonight. She'd be lying here until the sun came up, until Papa or the other neighbors came to see how Turner had fared during the night.

They'd find them, take him away, and make plans for his burial. She'd be expected to pick herself up and go on, with her heart torn from her body, her soul trampled underfoot, no worthwhile life left in her.

Zora's entire existence felt like a long, hard road that had led her to this moment, the worst of her life, second only to her mother's death, and still she hadn't seen the fiery vision from her childhood dream. This nightmare was ice, if anything. It seemed like her spirit guides had steered her wrong this time—that, or she'd done something to change her course. Turner was supposed to live, to rise again, and not to die. In her vision he always rose again.

She remembered the vampire's words to her—*Only I can raise him, and never will*—which meant that he could be raised, brought back to life, but only as a vampire. No. Impossible. It was the kind of insane idea that could only be born from the throes of grief, the kind of madness that only love's loss can bring.

Zora tried to push the thought from her head, but her lover lay cold in her arms and each second took him further way from her. If she could pull him back in whatever form, wouldn't that be better than losing him forever? If she could have him by her side as a ghost able to speak her name, look at her with adoring eyes, she would accept that, wouldn't she? How much better to have him there in the flesh, even if slightly cool to the touch, even if only at night?

That decided it. She rose from the bed and went to the dresser for her bag. Zora pulled out what she would need. It would mean another deal with the Petro, digging herself deeper into their debt. The power to banish Nell the first time had taken years off her life. To gain this favor, the price would be even higher.

Zora couldn't begin to imagine what they might ask in return and wouldn't know until the deal was sealed, when they came to her for payment. She had to go back to the question Papa Guedé had asked her the night he'd told her Nell's true nature.

Was Turner's salvation worth risking her own?

Zora looked back at the bed and gazed down at Turner's still face. They were his features, but his body was an empty shell. The man she loved had gone the way of all spirits to someplace she couldn't follow, yet. Would it be so wrong to keep him with her as one of the undead?

She could make it work; find a way to cure him, bring him back to humanity someday. It was the only way not to lose him, to have any chance to save him. This was her crossroads. To bring back her lost love or let him go. If she brought him back, would it still end in fire? Or could she find a way to take him away from here, far from the scene of her vision, so that it could never happen?

There were people she knew in New Orleans, others she'd corresponded with in Haiti, practitioners whose experience and abilities exceeded her own. Even Papa, downstairs, might have a cure. He'd been able to tell her how to banish a vampire, to contact the Petro, so perhaps he knew how to restore Turner to her. Only if she saved him now . . . All rational thought was lost to that one idea, that if she didn't act now, the moment would be lost and she'd lose him forever.

Zora dug through her sack, lit candles and burned herbs, inhaled the sweet fragrances. She offered up her own blood in sacrifice, slit her forearms to fill a bowl to attract their attention and summon them. Her voice rose as she lifted it, called out to the Petro gods as never before, put more need into her prayers than ever. If they'd listened to her last night, if they'd looked upon her kindly then, they needed to hear her now and answer.

She called upon Papa Legba to open the doors, asked mighty Damballah's permission to summon Baron Samedi, Baron Cimetière, Baron La Croix, the three-faced Lord of Death. She spoke the words she'd been taught by Papa Guedé to open the doors to worlds never trod by human feet. With no animals to offer, she sacrificed herself, her life and her fate, in service to them, for Turner.

In answer, all light faded from the room.

The gas lamps stayed high. Their flames simply lost illumination, as the stars and the moon went out, too. The tiny room was flooded with infinite darkness, deeper than any night, so absolute as to dwarf even the vast emptiness of space itself. All sound was swallowed up as well. Zora was left on her knees in the dark, devoid of all sensation but cold.

She kept up her prayer, even though the words couldn't be heard. Zora could still feel her throat move, her lips form the words, as breath passed from her lungs. There was something in the void with her, not living but primal, ancient, called up from vast depths to hear her petition. If ever she had cause to fear in her life, this was the time, but Zora held her ground and kept up her chant. She pictured the object of her desire, her wish actualized, held Turner in her heart and her arms again. Alive and in love, together, forever.

Then she was back in the brightly lit bedroom, warm.

The darkness was gone as if it had never been there, the extraordinary presence she'd felt gone as well. Only she and Turner remained. Zora laid her hand on his chest and felt something, a dull, rhythmic thump deep down inside. Not the beat of a normal human heart, but definite movement. Life.

"I had the strangest dream," said Turner with a sigh, and Zora flung herself on him, locked him in a tight embrace as if he'd been gone for years. "Zora, whatever's wrong with you?"

He put his arms around her and held her as she sobbed.

"Oh, Turner. I've been so foolish," Zora said. She must have fallen asleep and imagined it all, Nell's attack, Turner's murder, summoning the Petro gods to save him. It had only been a terrible nightmare she'd had by his bedside. Turner hadn't been the only one afflicted by fever dreams. She sat up and wiped away her tears to see him clearly. "I had the most awful dream, too. I thought . . ."

Her voice faded as she got a good look at him.

Turner's eyes glittered, too large, too bright, with a strange iciness she'd never seen before except in Nell's when she'd glared at Zora during the wedding. His skin was smooth, but had an odd sheen to it, an almost artificial perfection.

"Yes?"

"I dreamed that you died."

"But I rose again."

"What?" She shuddered, wondered why he'd say something like that.

"That was what happened in your childhood dream, wasn't it? I fell and rose again? That's what you told me."

"Yes, of course," she said. That was what she'd said. Except that there had also been fire and something else she couldn't quite recall. Zora stood.

"I should get you something to eat, now that you're awake."

"Yes. I am hungry." He stared up at her, unblinking. She saw hunger in his eyes unlike any she'd seen before, except when Nell had looked at him in the club. The continued comparisons disturbed her. "Come, sit with me for a while, Zora."

He held out a hand to her and smiled, seductive. Any other time she would have melted into his bed and stripped off her clothes to warm herself against him. She felt no heat from him tonight. She was attracted to him, but not the way she had been before. It felt forced, as phony as his glow of good health. He wasn't healthy. He wasn't well. She wasn't sure what he was, but she was beginning to fear that he wasn't her Turner.

No. It was only the fever, she told herself.

The sickness made him seem different. He was awake, but not recovered. It would take him time to come back from last night's shock to his system. The wounds on his neck were gone, which meant that Nell must be dead and her influence exorcised. Once he'd had time to rest, he'd be good as new, fit as a fiddle.

He had to be.

Papa didn't look at all surprised when he saw them come down the back stairs into the bar. Against Zora's wishes, Turner had put on his suit and shoes and gone down to work as if it were early in the evening and not near closing. She slipped in behind him like his shadow and followed him across the room. Zora sat down at the bar as he went to the piano. There were a handful of customers left finishing up drinks, closing seductions.

El Greco was at the keyboard, idly tinkling away at a popular tune as he hung halfway off his seat, still drunk off free drinks given to play requests. He looked up to see Turner approach and the cigarette dropped from his mouth. El Greco picked it up, adjusted his jacket, and stood. He left the piano without question to sit at the bar. Turner dropped down on the stool and began to play. Papa looked from him to Zora.

"Lord, what you done, girl?"

She couldn't meet his eyes. If she did, he would pull the truth from them and then she'd have to face it, too. Zora knew something was terribly wrong but couldn't admit it to herself yet, wanted to have a few moments, a little time to think she'd won, that she'd gotten back everything she'd asked for and not a monstrous parody of her life.

"You ever read a story called 'The Monkey's Paw,' Papa?"

He frowned. "It is a very old story."

"Be careful what you ask for, they say." Zora felt tears tremble at the brinks of her eyelids. To release them was to admit defeat, so she fought them back, as Turner's music grew louder and faster. On his wedding night it had smelled of fire and brimstone; now it had the stink of death. Not damnation, but freshly turned graves and decayed corpses.

It was a howling tempest of colliding notes that shattered the air to torture his listeners. While Turner's music usually spoke of love and desire, this was a hymn to death and destruction, despair and loss. The music spoke of a bitter, broken city in conflict, the rumbling resentment of down-trodden races and the shrill cry of racist fears, the wails of the starving poor and the dying groans of the bloated rich.

It opened a Pandora's box as all the atrocities of the city spilled out, outrage after outrage, from the first whimper of an addicted newborn's pain to the thin shriek of its last dying breath in old age. Turner's audience covered their ears and fled as they screamed for mercy, begged him to stop, to leave them some last scrap of hope at the bottom of the box to carry home. The melody ended. Turner sat still at the piano.

"She's here."

Zora saw the vampire standing in the doorway. It carried death with it like a storm cloud. Everyone else had left the room, but her, Turner, Papa, and his wife. Nell slid in and stared at Zora.

"Did you think I'd allow you even this meager comfort?" She was on Zora before she could move away, gripped her throat. "I should let him feed on you, but I'd rather finish you myself—"

"Stay your hand, beast," Papa said, interrupting Nell's fury.

Her eyes slid sideways to look at him as she kept her hold on Zora.

"This does not concern you, bartender."

"My house. My rules," said Papa.

He moved a step closer and raised his tattooed left hand. Nell spun without releasing Zora, snapped his neck with her free hand, and let his body drop to the floor. Mama Brigitte screamed and flung herself down by his side.

Turner started to play again, a slow, simple melody, more a dirge than anything else. Nell turned back to Zora, who felt her face flush, her heart beat faster, as if it might be its last chance.

"Turner," she gasped, her throat constricted by Nell's fingers. "Help me!"

He stayed at the piano and stared straight down at the keys. Not even his music changed to indicate that he'd heard her. She could see that his eyes were cold, dead. He was a man without hope. She could see it in his face, his posture. She hadn't raised him, only his body, and he knew it. He was the walking dead, an animated corpse, and in that despair was lost to her, as lost as Papa was to his wife.

The wails of Mama Brigitte had turned to a slow chant, which rose into holy song as she held her hands out over her husband's dead body. Behind

Nell, Zora saw a faint light glow from Mama Brigitte's palms as her husband's corpse lit up in response, brightened, and began to rise from the floor.

The vampire ignored it and tightened her grip on Zora's throat until the light grew too bright to disregard. Nell looked behind her and even her eyes grew wide when she saw what was happening.

Mama Brigitte was more than human.

She was the god Guedé's divine mate in all worlds, who'd possessed the woman who stood by his side while he was in human form. The humans were longtime devotees and had willingly offered themselves and their home as a shelter for the gods on Earth for many years. With the death of her husband's host, Mama Brigitte prepared to leave her mortal guise and called upon their family of gods to release him from his trap of dead flesh so that she could bring him home to their reality.

Turner's tune changed to match Mama Brigitte's cries as her incantation grew in volume and filled the low-ceilinged room like smoke. He played as if he was under her command, echoed the voodoo chant's beat in bass piano thunder as she had her say. She raised the spirit of her true husband from his mortal body and freed Papa Guedé from his earthbound flesh, the human horse he'd ridden while in this world among men.

Zora had seen many things in her time in New Orleans, living with the initiated. During her own inductions into voodoo she'd witnessed strange sights and sounds she couldn't explain away. She'd seen men and women taken by the gods, mounted like horses, and used to speak for them. She'd seen the healthy made sick and the terminally ill cured. She'd seen petitioners' prayers answered as the world was remade according to their desires. Never before had she seen any of the gods she'd communed with face-to-face, exposed, their earthly form shed.

It was a vision of pure energy unbound, as it poured out of the body it had inhabited like lava erupting from a volcano. Zora felt Nell's hands around her throat relax as the vampire released her. She backed away from the being that materialized, as the body that contained it broke apart like an eggshell and fell away to the ground as the luminosity inside it grew brighter.

Mama Brigitte collapsed and fell back on her knees, arms limp at her sides as her eyes rolled up. Her mouth opened and her spirit departed in a cloud of radiant vapor to join that of her husband in his true form as the three-faced Lord of the dead, Samedi, Cimetière, and La Croix. Brigitte and Guedé's spirit bodies mingled in midair like the northern lights as the heat of their incarnation ignited the walls, the furniture, exploded bottles of liquor behind the bar.

All the rumors Zora had heard about the little god Guedé were proved true tonight. He wasn't just a joker and messenger to the gods, brother to the Petro. No wonder he'd been so quick to suggest a deal with them to get what she'd wanted. He was their human face, the one aspect that could identify with mankind enough to bargain, the only part of them that could connect to the earthly world without burning it down with their raw power. Whatever protection there was from that was lost when he left his human host. It was clear that if Guedé was being forced to vacate early, he was taking his bar with him.

The divine fire spread rapidly, turned the room into an inferno in minutes. Turner played on at the burning piano as if it were any other night at the club. Zora gasped for breath, her throat freed, coughed as she sucked smoke into her lungs. She lost sight of Nell, who disappeared to the back of the bar, toward the steps that led upstairs.

Zora struggled to Turner's side, her vision blurred by heat and smoke. Her last strength got her there, but could do no more. She collapsed beside him, sighed his name as she was overcome, felt consciousness slip away as his music continued, piano strings snapping in the heat, the last sound she'd ever hear.

Then she felt strong hands under her back and legs, lifting her up and away from the piano to the front stairs and up to the street. Music still seemed to play in her head, but she realized it was only delirium caused by lack of oxygen to her brain. As she choked her way back to full awareness in the fresh outside air, her head cleared and she saw who'd carried her out. He looked down to see that she was all right, lifted her to her feet, and held her in his arms.

It was Turner.

CHAPTER 70

3:06 A.M.—*Central Harlem, 31 July 2007*

Out of the depths of his despair, Turner's deeper love for Zora had broken through to save her. Would his love for Joie be enough to do the same? It had been days since he'd met her, but he could still think of almost nothing else.

He lay alone on the roof of his Harlem home, at the dawn of the twenty-first century, looking for comfort in the past but finding only pain. Turner stared up at stars that had changed as little as he had in more than half a century since his rebirth. His neighborhood had been transformed since the night Guedé's Place burned to the basement; even his home had been renovated and rebuilt over the years. Everything had changed but him.

His human life had ended that dreadful night in Harlem and his new one began. He'd pulled Zora out of the fire and carried her up to the street at the last minute, just before the building collapsed. He'd regained his humanity before it was too late, come back to himself in time to realize that his lost life wasn't worth sacrificing hers. Their love was all that had brought him back to life as anything but a vengeful demon.

Nothing was left of the building when the fire subsided, though mysteriously no damage was done to the buildings on either side. When it was over, it was as if Papa's building had never been there. As far as anyone uptown knew, Nell had died in the fire. Turner never saw her again. No bodies were recovered from the wreckage, not hers or those of Papa and his wife. The oddly intense heat was blamed for the lack of remains or rubble, which no one believed, but didn't question. In Harlem in 1931, some answers were best left unspoken.

Turner's time with Zora changed.

He moved into her apartment and she taught him to control his vampire hunger with voodoo prayers and meditation. At first she'd fed him fresh animal blood from the downtown meat district to nourish him, sucked from empty wine bottles like he was a baby. As Turner had developed control over his new state, she'd weaned him, taught him to absorb energy from crowds in public places instead, living on a little life from many so he could survive without killing or drinking blood.

He'd been able to stay fairly human, as much as he felt was worth staying, but even after he'd learned to control himself, Zora couldn't stay with him. Turner knew that he'd changed in a way she couldn't bear, no matter how much he'd meant to her. It was one thing to die and come back alive, but to come back as a human parasite was something else. She would always love the man, but not the monster that Nell had turned him into.

She'd sworn it wasn't his fault that they had to part.

There were dark times ahead for her and she had to face them down alone. He'd wanted to help her, sure that she'd brought the evil down on herself to save him, but she insisted she'd seen it all coming in the visions of her childhood.

In the end, it was another joke on Turner, crueler than the childhood curse of a musical talent he couldn't share with others. Zora had gotten him past that, but nothing in her magic bag of tricks could save them from this fate. He wasn't dead, but he'd lost the one person on Earth who had made his life worth living. The other consequences of his change he could endure, but to yearn for Zora's company, to long for her touch when she couldn't stand the sight of him, that was the Hell that Nell had plunged them into, even worse than the one she'd planned.

One day in April, Zora offered him the keys to her apartment and announced that she was going down south on a field trip. The show was over months before, finished alone by Zora while Turner recovered from his death and resurrection. It had played one night to rave reviews, January 10, 1932, on Broadway at the John Golden Theatre, but hadn't raised enough money to keep it going. That forced Zora to take another contract with her patron, Mrs. Charlotte Osgood, to do more anthropological research around the country.

Zora said she thought that time apart would be a good idea for them both. Turner had mastered all she could teach him to survive and retain what he could of his humanity. He was welcome to keep the apartment, but she was going.

She left and did what work she could until she came to a parting of the ways with Osgood in the fall. Zora moved on to Florida, worked on other musical shows, and eventually fell in love with other men, including one she'd met in the cast of *The Great Day* the same year she'd met Turner.

But she was haunted by a painful stomach ailment that followed her to the end, along with other, graver misfortunes to come. Turner always felt responsible. Because she didn't do the service required for saving him, the Petro had exacted their price in punishment over Zora's lifetime. If service to them meant to give yourself over completely for days or weeks at a time while they used your body to wield power any way they saw fit, for good or evil—she'd tasted that, and it was a price she could not pay.

He'd seen Zora only occasionally over the years, never for long, not enough for him or her. They both wanted more, but knew she could never accept what he was or bear to stay with him looking the same, day after day, while she got even older than she felt already.

"Just tryin' to avoid the day somebody calls me your mama and I have to kill 'em," she'd said, laughing, over drinks the first time they met again, hers coffee. She'd stopped drinking after that last night in Harlem, never took it up again. It was in Los Angeles, in 1941, just before America officially entered the war in Europe. Zora had stumbled across him one night at the Formosa Café, a pseudo-Chinese dive restaurant popular with slumming stars. She was in Hollywood, working for Paramount Pictures while she wrote her autobiography.

"You don't have to grow old," he'd reminded her. Turner had made the offer before and she'd always rejected it.

"Oh, no, baby," she said, and blew smoke into the air. "The Petro would enjoy that irony too much. Give me the power to bring you back so you can turn me into another Nell? Uh-uh."

They'd parted a few weeks later, more than friends but not quite lovers, and here he was back where he'd been then. Torn between the right and wrong of love. How selfish was it to expect Joie to love him, as he was, when all he could offer her was the choice to join him or watch him stay frozen in time while she was carried further away from him, day by day? He shut his eyes, wiped the stars and the night sky to instant oblivion. Turner knew the answer, had known it all along, and didn't need memories of Zora to tell him so. It was wrong.

He still wanted to let Joie decide for herself.

CHAPTER 71

7:17 P.M.—*Greenwich Village, 31 July 2007*

Turner had known the writer Amiri Baraka since the early 1960s, when he was still known as LeRoi Jones. It was a detail he didn't mention to Joie when she invited him to a reading by the author at NYU. She wasn't sure who Baraka was, she said, "but he sounds like someone you'd like." Turner brought along a tattered, autographed first edition of the man's early work to lend her and at dinner gave Joie a long rundown of Baraka's literary and political significance, until she started to laugh.

"I didn't get this much my first day in lit class. Why don't you let me read the book, then we'll talk about it?"

They were sitting at Spice, a noisy, trendy Thai restaurant on lower Broadway filled with stylish downtown kids, their friends, and assorted other cute, twenty-something clubsters who wanted to be friends or more. Turner realized that he must look like just another young pseudointellectual academic hitting on a girl he'd just met.

He stammered, embarrassed, both by his enthusiasm in sharing one of his favorite authors with her and by his clumsy attempts to charm her. He was working too hard and it showed. It was humiliating for someone who'd lived three times her lifetime, or would be if she knew.

"Sorry," he said.

"It's okay," she said. "It's nice to see a guy who's into something other than sports or music."

"That would be me." He'd made his excuses for not eating, said he had an upset stomach. She ate while he sipped a whiskey worth the price of a meal.

"How did you get into these writers?" she asked. "I mean, they're all kind of before our time."

"Um. School. Took a course in college that turned me on to the whole Harlem Renaissance era and what came after." He nodded as he answered, as if that would reinforce the lie.

"Where did you go to college?"

"Howard." It had been Zora's school before Barnard and always came as the easiest answer. He'd never had to prove it and relied on his vampiric ability to change the subject anytime someone probed too deeply. He didn't want to do that with Joie.

When she was finished eating, Turner paid the bill and they walked to the NYU building where the reading was being held. Amiri Baraka was on a panel with two other writers, who read and spoke first. His portion of the program was as bombastic as ever, high energy with cutting humor and more honesty about life and politics than many younger writers dared these days.

It's one of the advantages of age, thought Turner, *not to care what people think anymore. I must remember that, no matter what my mirror tells me.* He smiled as they moved up the line to get an autograph on a new anthology for Joie. Baraka saw them, and waved.

"Turner, you dirty old bastard, what are you doing with this pretty young thing?" Baraka asked with a wink at her as he shook Turner's hand, pulled him into a half hug. "Robbing the cradle?"

Baraka was a small terrier of a man in his early seventies, energetic, gray-haired and -bearded, twenty-six years younger than Turner. The year Baraka was born, Turner had been a vampire for almost three years. The writer peered through his glasses to see them more clearly.

Turner had cast a glamour of age over himself in Baraka's eyes to let him see him as if he'd aged, too, rather than as the young man he'd remained. It was a trick that let him stay in contact with his favorite older friends as long as no one around them paid much attention or asked questions afterward.

Joie looked puzzled as they talked like two old men, and Turner let her think it was a private joke between them. It was obvious that they'd known each other for years; he let her draw her own assumptions about how or why. Baraka signed Joie's book "To my good friend's good friend," and made them promise to come by for drinks.

"'Cause I know he never eats!" he shouted after them as they went to the elevator. Joie laughed as Turner winced. The old man always had talked too much.

Turner took Joie for a walk to the West Village that ended in Washington Square Park, strolling past pot-smoking students, musicians, and tourists. They climbed up on a multilayered platform structure for kids to play on during the day, lay on their backs and talked as they stared up at the cloudless night sky.

He took her hand at some point, amazed at how soft and warm it felt in his. It had been decades since he'd held hands with a woman he cared about, far too long for anyone to be alone. Turner tried not to let that drive his desire for her, to keep his attraction based on Joie and Joie alone, not a desperate need for companionship. If this was to continue, it had to be because it was meant to be, not out of his need.

It was getting late.

Turner offered to ride home with Joie on the subway and then take a cab home. It was a stupid romantic gesture inspired by the idea of taking the trip with her, of other people seeing them looking young and in love, feeling their warmth or envy as Joie and Turner negotiated the space between each other like dancers.

"Come on. It'll be one of those movie moments you always talk about."

"We did 'meet-cute,'" she said, laughing. "I'm just not sure I'm ready to go home yet."

"There are clubs on the Lower East Side. . . ." She scrunched up her nose at that idea, so he added, "Or uptown, near me?"

She smiled and nodded; he extended his arm. Joie took it and they headed to West Fourth Street for the uptown A.

On the train, they talked about life, mostly hers.

Turner had to be careful in casual conversation since he didn't have it often. It was too easy to get comfortable and slip up, to mention an event or acquaintance you looked too young to know about. It was easy enough to erase any listener's memory of the moment, but spending his nights altering the past in everyone around him grew tiresome in time. It was easier to stay home and keep his mouth shut.

Fortunately, he thought, *young women liked to talk about themselves. When a man was silent about his past, it just made him seem more attentive, or, at worst, mysterious.*

The train was running local, stopped at the Eighty-sixth Street station and stayed there as overhead speakers told them they were being held and would be moving shortly. Turner and Joie continued their conversation. By habit, his senses had scoped out everyone in the train car when they got on. There were only a few other people in the car, even at this hour. Most looked like they were out for the evening, a few on their way to or from work. He'd paid almost no attention to the meth addict in the corner, half passed out and mumbling to himself. It wasn't until the man lurched to his feet and stumbled in their direction that he became an issue.

"You . . ." he said to Turner as he grabbed the overhead rail for support and leaned down to confront them. "You got a hell of a nerve, sayin' those things about me."

The man was a derelict, red-faced, big, with layers of dirty, worn clothes. His bloated, unshaven face hung over them, flushed, distorted like a Halloween mask, eyes dilated and wild.

Ordinarily, Turner would have sent the lunatic on his way with a mental command as soon as he approached. But he was so busy showing Joie how human he could be that he handled the situation like a man, held his ground, and defended his turf with words.

"I'm sorry, but I'm just talking with my friend. We haven't said anything about you."

"Not her. You." He pointed a dirty, misshapen finger at Turner for emphasis. "You talk about me all the time. I hear it, in here. . . ." He tapped his forehead, swayed back and forth like a cobra, and grinned, like he'd just gotten the joke. Turner would have thought it funny, too, under other circumstances. How often do you hear that your voice is the one in a maniac's head? He examined the man's face, made sure he wasn't an old encounter, someone whose mind he actually had touched and possibly broken. No.

"You better stop," said the man. "Or else."

"I'm not doing or saying anything. I can't be held accountable for what you hear."

"Yeah?" He leaned closer to them, curled the fingers of his free hand into a fist, and held it up. "So, if my hand hit you, that's not my fault either, right?"

Joie grabbed Turner's arm.

"We should go," she said in a small voice.

Turner could smell the toxins in the man's sweat, better than Joie could, knew he was flying high on whatever chemical waste was taking the streets by storm this season. He'd seen the effects of almost all the variants of stimulant addiction over the years and uptown or downtown, they all seemed to end the same way.

The man looked away, muttered to himself as if he'd lost touch with Turner and reality, but seemed to continue the conversation in his head. Turner turned away to comfort Joie, to assure her that they were in no danger—a distraction that was his undoing.

He should have seen it coming. The man's fist went into his pocket and a knife came out, blade first, a box cutter. He slashed at Turner's throat before he could stop him, slashed him twice as Turner shoved the lunatic away, flung him across the car, and grabbed Joie's hand. As the bell rang to signal the closing of the doors, Turner pulled Joie off the train and up the stairs. The train pulled out as Turner kept moving. Joie shouted his name as she trailed behind him. He stopped when he was sure they were away from security cameras and let Joie pull him around to face her.

"My God, Turner! Are you okay?" He stood still and let her pull his torn shirt open to examine the skin underneath, look for the wound. "You need help, we have to—"

She saw nothing and looked again, her face confused.

"Turner . . ."

His shirt was wet, not with what she'd expected to see but with the thick, honeylike fluid that the blood of the infected became after their death and rebirth as a vampire. The skin was healing already, closing up before her eyes, which widened. Turner reached out with his mind and stroked hers ever so gently, just enough to slow her heart rate to normal, to keep down her rising panic as his skin smoothed, any break in the surface vanishing.

She kept staring as her mind struggled to accept it and looked up into his eyes. Turner took her hand as she lifted it away from his chest, held it in his before she could run away.

"Let me explain."

Joie breathed deeply and gulped a few times before she answered, nodded her head.

CHAPTER 72

11:14 P.M.—Central Harlem, 31 July 2007

Thanks to Zora, Turner could play piano for Joie.

His brownstone was a few blocks above 125th Street on the West Side, in an area that was still fairly quiet at night. Turner's antique Steinway baby grand was on the second floor of his brownstone, where he played privately for guests. He'd gotten the house in 1933 as a gift from a notorious bootlegger whose life he'd saved. The man had reformed shortly after Prohibition ended, invested his money in real estate, and used his profits after the Depression to begin a successful career in politics, as so many others had done.

Joie lay on her back on embroidered silk pillows and a colorful Moroccan carpet in front of the fireplace while Turner accompanied his story on the keys. It was a warm night, too hot to build an actual fire, but with her permission he'd shared a sense memory of a roaring blaze, let her see it burning in the empty hearth. It helped to illustrate the truth of what he'd told her, a benign example of his powers.

It had been a long time since he'd been able to talk freely to anyone about his real life instead of maintaining the false faces he'd created over the years to fool people. There had been some advantage to a virtually unlimited life span. His time on Earth had encompassed the most tumultuous decades of life in the United States. He was an eyewitness to the progress of black America and, regardless of the reason, looked forward to what lay ahead.

Since 1932 he'd seen new African nations declare their independence and that continent's rise to power free of European influence, for better or worse. He'd watched the black freedom movement in America develop from the early embers of a dream to a raging passion that swept the nation. Turner had traveled the country as he saw the times changing, worked for all the major movements—CORE, the NAACP, marched with King in Washington in 1963, and even joined the Black Panther Party when it was formed three years later.

He'd talked with Jimmy Baldwin over drinks about his early ideas for *The Fire Next Time* when it was still an essay he was pitching to the New Yorker magazine. He'd read the unpublished first draft of Ellison's *Invisible Man* and read early pages of *Funnyhouse of a Negro* aloud to Adrienne Kennedy so she could hear her words.

Turner had thrilled to seeing Billie Holiday and Lester Young tear it up onstage for the first time, knew they were going places, heard the rise of bebop and the growth of jazz. He'd followed Duke Ellington on tour and hung backstage with Bird, Monk, and Miles. Turner had been a friend to a wide range of modern black artists from Jacob Lawrence and his wife, Gwendolyn Knight, Aaron Douglas, Augusta Savage, and Romare Bearden in the twentieth century, through to Fred Wilson and his partner Whitfield Lovell, Kehinde Wiley, Kara Walker, and Kerry James Marshall in the early twenty-first.

Turner told Joie stories about black film directors he'd met, from Oscar Michaux to Gordon Parks and his favorite, Bill Gunn. They'd met in the early 1970s after Gunn had been hired to make a movie called *Vampires of Harlem* to cash in on the success of *Blacula*. A mutual acquaintance had introduced them when the director was doing research and said Turner was an expert on old Harlem.

They'd enjoyed an evening of conversation and discussed the movie. Turner had told Gunn the truth about himself just for the conversation, then erased his memory of it. Evidently enough had remained to affect his film, renamed *Ganja & Hess*, which became more a philosophical art film about vampires and voodoo than a horror movie. It was the closest Turner had come to telling anyone the truth about himself until tonight.

His powers of persuasion had admitted him to any room over the years and he'd witnessed conversations that had shaped the country and his people. He'd wrestled with how much he could use his abilities to change the minds that changed the world. In the end, he'd chosen the path of non-interference preferred by most of his kind. Vampires weren't human and had no more right to decide the course of human affairs than humans had the right to decide the fate of vampires.

Like a proud parent, Turner had watched black America rise without his help, seen his people stand on their own feet to walk, then run. There were still the internal squabbles that Zora had often written about, but there was also a greater sense of freedom and future potential.

Then he'd watched a young generation raised under hard-won free-doms grow complacent and lose focus, not understanding why parents and grandparents who had fought for their civil rights hated it when their kids called each other "nigger," no matter how it was spelled.

It bothered him that the infinite variety of black culture had been re-duced in the world's view to the harsh, sexist images of mass-marketed mainstream rap videos. In his opinion, the genre had become formulaic, crumbling into decay beneath its brash, boastful surface, the original ideals of the real hip-hop movement lost in the rubble. . . .

"I'm sorry," Turner said with a laugh. "Forgive me. I only feel like an old man when I start judging your generation. I was once more understanding of youth."

He stopped playing. Joie sat up and turned to see if something was wrong. Turner smiled, reassuring, as he walked over to her and extended a hand, pulled Joie to her feet and led her to the door.

"I want to show you something."

Joie followed Turner through his house in a daze.

She wasn't afraid, not just because he'd used his powers to calm her but because no matter what Turner was, she knew he cared about her and her safety. Despite that, Joie had watched enough B horror movies with her dad to know what happened to girls who fell in love with the undead. She'd go along with him as long as she had to, get away, and then decide what to do.

He led her upstairs from the parlor to the top floor. At the end of the hall was a red door locked with a brass padlock. Turner stopped in front of it and pulled out a gold key hanging on a chain around his neck. Joie tensed for a moment, pictured the horrors of Bluebeard's castle on the other side of the door or a collection of aging vampire ex-lovers in coffins like Catherine Deneuve's in *The Hunger.* . . .

It was neither. When Turner pulled off the padlock and opened the door, Joie smelled the rich scent of fresh flowers mixed with smoky incense, herbs, and spices. Soft music played in stereo, gentle drums layered with human voices raised in divine worship. Turner pushed the door open and went inside. Joie followed, drawn in by the profusion of colors and shapes glimpsed within.

"This is my altar room," said Turner. "I keep it sanctified with daily offerings to the gods who keep me feeling human. Their worship was Zora's first gift to me after she brought me back to life. This shrine says more about who I am than anything else I can tell you about my past."

Joie walked deeper into the room in quiet awe.

It felt blessed, holy, like chapels she'd visited in the great cathedrals of Europe on a family vacation. Down one side of the room was a wall of paintings and a long, low table filled with smaller pictures and plaster statues of Catholic saints standing in for Turner's deities. Most were decades old, beautifully crafted.

There was a portrait of St. John the Baptist, representing Legba, the opener who opens the way to the other gods. A statue of St. Patrick with snakes under his heel stood in for Damballah, the highest of the gods, who gave permission for the others to act. On and on, each saint's face concealing another identity, a hidden name of power. In the middle was a carved statue of a woman with outstretched arms holding offerings of flowers, a double-bladed ax blade coming out of her head.

"The ax symbolizes possession by Shango," said Turner. "Shango is my protector, the god of lightning and justice. He gives me the courage and strength to control my lesser appetites."

There were bottles of perfumes and liquors, the best of both, exquisite jewelry of precious stones and rare metals, scented soaps and powders, the scattered currencies of many countries, and everywhere, blooming flowers and lit candles. From the walls hung colorful woven cloths embroidered with mystical figures and magical signs. Clay pots wrapped in fabric or ornamented with beads lined the altar; all were filled with other gifts of fresh picked herbs and dried spices.

It was so much to see, hear, and smell that her senses couldn't absorb it all at once. She took in the essence of the space, a place of peace and a spiritual sanctuary. If this room expressed Turner's true heart, then it was pure and loving.

Turner watched her reaction, took her hands, and faced her, stared into her eyes. If he was ever to have a chance of any future with her, it was now or never.

"Joie . . . I feel something for you I haven't let myself feel for anyone since Zora died. That carries no obligation, but I have to say it. I don't want you to fear me."

"I don't."

"That's because I'm making it easier for you. When you wake up tomorrow without me, you'll know how you really feel, and we can talk again."

Turner called a car service and walked Joie downstairs when it arrived. He put her in, gave the driver enough cash to get Joie home safely, and watched the car pull away until it was out of sight. Tomorrow he'd know if she could accept who and what he was or if she needed to forget him completely. Even during wartime the laws of the Veil still held. No one could know the truth about them.

Not even Joie.

CHAPTER 73

9:08 A.M.—*Park Slope, 1 August 2007*

The sun crept into Joie's bedroom window and woke her up.

She blinked her eyes, tried to register where she was and what time it was, as if she was coming down from something she'd taken the night before. Turner. He'd done something to her head. Had he slipped something into her drink? Last night seemed like a long, strange dream. In daylight, it all seemed impossible, until she opened her bag and pulled out Turner's T-shirt.

It was slashed open at the neck, proof that what had happened was real. Turner had told her to take it for that very reason. As she moved it into the sunlight for a better look, the dried blood on it sparked and burned off with a *whoosh*, like flash paper in a stage magic act.

Joie dropped the shirt to the floor, slapped at it with her slipper to make sure the fire didn't spread, but the flames burned away too fast to do any harm. *Right,* she thought. *Vampires catch fire in the sun. Everyone knows that.* So would vampire blood, even dried. She shuddered. It couldn't be real, but it was.

She went to the bathroom and took a shower, stayed under the hot water longer than needed, to clear her head, as if the water could wash it clean, too.

Joie dressed casually and went downstairs. Lori was in the dining room with a half-empty breakfast plate and the newspaper. She looked up as her daughter came in.

"Look who's awake," she said. "Want something to eat?"

Joie poured a cup of hot water over a teabag.

"No, I'm going to grab food in the city." She added milk and honey, sipped her tea, and watched her mother read the paper, until she looked up at her and glared.

"I feel fine. Go."

Joie laughed and kissed her before she headed upstairs.

"I'll see you later."

She called Christopher from the street, didn't want her mother to know she was still seeing him. It wasn't something she was trying to keep secret. Joie just didn't want to upset her mother any more than necessary, and after their last meeting, knowing that she was with him would upset her.

It had taken her a while to get over their last encounter, between waking up naked and the shock of the full-length dream. She'd had to remind herself that neither had been Christopher's fault, that he'd been driven by the same thing that had taken over her mind. When it came to Turner's revelations, she felt like Christopher was the only one who might believe her and know what to do next.

Turner Creed was a vampire.

It sounded crazy even to think it, couldn't be true, but she knew it was and had seen too much evidence with her own eyes to disbelieve it. She had never thought she'd envy her mother's taste in men, but at least Lori didn't date guys who made TV sets blur out or were undead.

Joie was sure that her parents would never believe her, and Christopher was the only person she knew who'd had any unnatural encounters. She didn't think Turner would hurt her, but still wanted to know how to defend herself. Maybe Christopher had some ideas. It almost didn't matter. She needed to talk to someone about this and it wasn't the kind of problem she could bring to her shrink, no matter how understanding he was.

Christopher opened the door barefoot, wearing a T-shirt and jeans and looking a little sweaty, like he'd been exercising. Seeing him in person, Joie felt a kind of bond, threw herself into his arms and hugged him close. There was something comforting in his lean muscularity, in the way he lifted her from the ground just a little when he had her in a tight embrace.

"I feel so lost right now," she said.

"Welcome to the club," he answered and gave her a brief kiss as they pulled away enough to face each other. She didn't pull away immediately, let his lips linger on hers before they parted. He was still a great kisser, but so was Turner, even if his lips were cooler than Christopher's.

Of course that made sense, now. He was dead.

"Are you all right?" asked Christopher. "What's happened?"

They went to the living room and she told him about her night with Turner, what he'd told her about himself and his past. Christopher stayed quiet until the end, then sighed.

"You don't believe me? That he's a vampire?"

"Oh, yeah, I do. Problem is"—he paused—"so's your shrink."

Joie stared at him and let her mind run over what she knew about Dr. Lazarus, which wasn't much. If Christopher had said this the first time they'd talked about it, she would have left and never have spoken to him again. Things were different now. They compared notes about the appearance of Dr. Lazarus's office, both of which differed from Vangie's description, and on his true appearance. Christopher told her about the attack on him in the office while she was downstairs, waiting.

"This is crazy," she said. "We need help. I can't even begin to wrap my head around all of this."

"That's why I wanted the truth from your parents. The book they wrote—they said it was all fiction, but now we know vampires are real. What if their book is real, too?"

Joie sat quietly and let that sink in for a few minutes. She'd read *Bite Marks* many times over the years. The royalties and rights sales had paid for her home, her early schooling, put clothes on her back, and fed her. It had even made her a minor celebrity in the neighborhood for a while. She knew the story backward and forward. If it was true, then it meant that Christopher's mother had been the victim of a vampire.

Only her parents would know if that had happened before or after Christopher was born, if his immunity to Lazarus's bite was because of his mother's assault or something else, something that could explain the other weird phenomena around him. And why was Joie a part of it? What had happened back then that made her a complement to Christopher, some kind of catalyst?

There were so many questions running through her head and right now only Steven and Lori seemed likely to have any answers. One thing was for sure—she was squarely in the middle, and finding out the answers to Christopher's questions wasn't just for his peace of mind anymore, but her own.

"Okay. I'll go talk to them. They'll tell me or else. Then we'll meet with them together and figure this thing out."

She got up to go, but Christopher held her back.

"What about Turner?"

"What about him?"

He looked up at her. It was clear what he was asking, but she wasn't even sure what her feelings were for Christopher, much less a guy who'd been one of the walking dead since the Harlem Renaissance. Even if he was smart, handsome, rich, and Zora Neale Hurston's ex-boyfriend . . .

She shook her head.

"Not now, Christopher. One question at a time."

Joie passed a couple of movers in black overalls in the hall, carrying a big wooden crate. She backed against the wall at the top of the second-floor landing and let them carry the long box past her and up the stairs before she continued.

"Thanks," said one of the men as they passed. Joie walked outside and let the door close as she stood on the sidewalk for a minute, thinking. She could go straight home to see her mother—so much for not upsetting her—or she could call her father, start with him, and then bring her mom into it. That sounded like a better plan.

She turned to head for the subway and realized she'd left her bag upstairs. Joie pulled her cell phone out of her pocket and punched in Christopher's number to ask him to drop it out the window or bring it down.

Joie turned back to the front door and saw the movers leave the building with the same crate they'd carried in past her. She stepped aside to make way for them, hit Send, and waited for Christopher to pick up. As his phone rang in her ear, she heard a muffled ring from the box that was coming out the front door. It rang in her ear again, then from the box, a distinctive ring she'd heard come from Christopher's phone before.

Joie's body froze.

It's not like there couldn't be more than one phone with that ring, but the movers didn't look like it was their phone ringing and no one else was around. So many weird things were happening that the idea that these men had just gone upstairs and abducted Christopher wasn't out of the question. She let the phone keep ringing, but started speaking, as if her call had been picked up.

"Mom? Yeah, it's me. Sorry I'm late. I'm on my way to the subway now. Okay. One more stop! Bye!" She shut the phone as she walked away and the ringing from the box stopped as soon as she disconnected. She smiled back at the men like nothing was wrong, like she hadn't noticed anything out of the ordinary.

Like her boyfriend wasn't locked in their box.

She wanted to go upstairs to see if Christopher was really gone. He had to be. If she was imagining all this, he would have answered his phone, especially when he saw her number on caller ID. Walking back into the building to see if he was home would only trap her there if the men came back and caught her in the apartment, saw that she knew what they'd done. Her heart pounded as she went into the bakery at the corner and ordered a latte. She watched the street through the big picture window, as the men in black loaded the box into a black van.

The front door of the café was open. Joie kept her phone hidden in her pocket but flipped it open and hit Send again. She heard Christopher's phone ring faintly from the van, as they closed the doors and pulled away.

There were no plates on the van that that she could see, no identification at all on the vehicle. Once the van was gone, Joie pulled her phone out of her pocket and made another call, as she paid for the latte.

"Dad? It's Joie. I think . . . I think someone just kidnaped Christopher." She said it more calmly than she'd expected to, and, to her surprise, Steven didn't question it, told her to come right over. He knew someone who could help. She looked outside again. Now that the men were gone, she'd make a quick check of Christopher's apartment with the super to make sure he was gone, so that she didn't make a stupid mistake. Then she'd go to Brooklyn to fill her father in on everything she knew. Joie picked up the latte, even though she'd only bought it as a cover-up, and got another for Steven. They'd need it.

IV

FULL MOON

All the gods are dead except the god of war.

—Eldridge Cleaver
Soul on Ice
(1968)

CHAPTER 74

3:23 P.M.—*Red Hook, 1 August 2007*

The contents of Rahman's library had been separated into individual pages and cataloged, each held between two vacuum-sealed Plexiglas sheets for safe examination. A single volume could take up feet of space in the master files. At one time, crates of plastic pages had been delivered to researchers at their desks, until the current system was put into place.

It functioned like a jukebox. Codes were punched into a keyboard at sterile workstations, and individual pages were mechanically collected from storage, carried up on tracks by mechanical fingers, and delivered to the researcher, every request cataloged in the system by user ID.

Nicolas had spent the day going through Rahman's notes on his last experiment, in the Reading Room, as it was called, trying to determine where it differed from the one they'd performed in Paris, other than its subject. Now that Perenelle was here, once they got young Christopher's cooperation, they could work with the Clean Slate staff to analyze his blood and hers, look for similarities and differences.

Nicolas knew from years of earlier experiments that his own blood contained no solution and couldn't make others immortal. Only Christopher's blood, the actual elixir, could do that. Perenelle had already told him about Adam's transformation.

Whatever flowed through Christopher's veins obviously had the power to do more than cure a vampire. It gave back the day and all the advantages Nicolas had gained when he drank it, centuries ago, the gifts of longevity and almost instantaneous healing. Richmond said that the boy was the key to ending any further conflict between man and vampire by eliminating the vampiric infection from the planet.

More important, he could return Nicolas's wife to him.

Richmond tapped on the glass between Nicolas and the hallway. He gestured to the door, a question on his face. Nicolas scowled, but nodded. Richmond went to the airlock and entered.

"Why is it I never feel you come to me as a courtesy, but only to keep me working while we talk?"

"Can't it be both?" Richmond smiled in an attempt to charm, but dropped it when he saw that Nicolas was angry. "I understand you've taken issue with our retrieval of the boy."

"You abducted him. You said we would seek his cooperation. Instead, you act like you're Homeland Security. This is not Guantánamo Bay. This is not Gitmo."

"Nice to know that you've caught up on your current events, Nicolas. I'm sure Perenelle has been a great help in that area. Let me explain something . . ." He lifted a remote from his pocket and pressed a switch. The room was flooded with bright white light. Nicolas shaded his eyes.

"This entire complex is wired with high-powered UV lamps as protection against our single greatest threat, vampires. Our only advantage is that there are defensive weapons we can use that don't harm humans.

"We brought Perenelle here to get you to cooperate in our search for a cure. That's our only interest in either of you. If anything interferes with achieving this goal, it will be eliminated. These lights make it easy."

Richmond switched off the UV lights.

The room looked dark as Nicolas's eyes adjusted to the lower illumination. He rubbed his forehead, felt his first headache in six hundred years rising.

"Thank you," he said. "Perenelle told me you'd make our status clear. I should have believed her."

Richmond went to the exit.

"We can't just take his blood like the vampires we're fighting," said Nicolas.

"I know that serving a greater good isn't sufficient excuse for some of our actions. If things were different, we'd do things your way. But we're at war."

Richmond stopped in the airlock.

"I will treat the boy with respect, Nicolas. I'll explain the situation and do my best to enlist him in our cause."

"If he refuses?"

Richmond sealed the airlock and left.

Christopher sat in a black leather chair across from Richmond's big desk, with a strong drink in one hand. It didn't improve his mood. Whatever Richmond's thugs had shot him up with had produced no effect, no drugs did, so they'd resorted to Luna's solution and knocked him out with a punch to the head, tied and gagged him before they threw him into their box.

When he'd heard the knock at the door, he'd figured that Joie had come back for her bag. He'd noticed it on the floor right after she'd left, too late to call her back. Christopher had picked it up and opened the door, only to meet Clean Slate's movers.

Richmond finished pouring himself a drink and turned to face Christopher. He sat back, swirled the ice in his glass before he took a sip.

"I can't apologize enough for your arrival. It was a tactical error made by those no longer in a position to do so. My people have been dealing with the enemy for so long, I'm afraid they forgot themselves and treated you like another combatant instead of a victim."

"You've got that right."

"We need you, Christopher. You're the key to unlocking mysteries you know nothing about. Help us, and I can answer all your questions about your past, about who you are. . . ." He opened a file box and pulled out pages from Adam's files encased in Plexiglas. "What you are. These were recently retrieved in a raid on a vampire leader's home, written by a vampire named Adam Caine."

Christopher sat up and reached for the sheets.

Richmond didn't stop him. The files had photos and notes on his family, about things that had happened to them over fourteen years, as if they'd been under surveillance. His stomach twisted into a knot as he read some of it, misfortunes described before they occurred, planned and executed like some kind of long-term psychological torture.

Richmond watched the boy as he read.

Of course, the file had been censored; key pages considered too emotionally incendiary had been pulled to give them future leverage. What Christopher read should be enough to satisfy his curiosity, yet still be so repulsive that it could even discourage him from digging deeper. More important, it should be enough to convince him of the evils of the enemy, enough to gain his cooperation.

He watched the boy crumble as he learned about the cruelties visited on his mother, uncle, and grandparents, all dead now, a family he'd never know because of the vampire. Richmond offered him another drink while Christopher stared at photographs of his dead mother and her brother, orphaned as he had been by the same monster.

"We're fighting these things, have been since you were a child. What I wanted to tell you myself was that your mother didn't just die. She was killed by Caine and brought back to life as a vampire." He paused. "It gets worse."

Stricken, Christopher nodded for him to continue.

"Caine forced her to feed on her infant child. While Caine was killing her a second time, she called the baby back to life, as a vampire, and then died. But the child escaped."

Richmond told him how a junkie had found the baby and brought it to her home on the Lower East Side. Its vampire blood, mixed with their HIV-infected bodies, had started a plague of mutant living dead. Richmond had been put in charge of a task force working with the National Guard to clean it up and cover it up, the birth of Clean Slate.

"You were that baby, Christopher, and ended up in the hands of a vampire who used you to find a cure with alchemy. Your blood was transformed into the vampire's elixir of life. You were intended for a sacrifice that never happened. Instead, you could quite possibly live forever."

"So I'm not human? Is that what you're saying?"

The boy looked on the verge of overload. His chest heaved as he hyperventilated, struggled to absorb all he'd been told. Richmond dropped to one knee by Christopher's chair, gripped his forearm to ground him, and looked him in the eyes.

"I'm saying that you're better than human, Christopher. And you can help make us better, too."

Christopher released his tears and nodded as Richmond stood and laid a hand on his shoulder.

"Tell me what to do," said Christopher.

CHAPTER 75

5:43 P.M.—*West Village, 1 August 2007*

The house looked more than just deserted.

Steven had been unable to reach Perenelle by phone to tell her that Christopher was missing, so he'd decided to try to find her in person. He'd left Lori to calm Joie down and borrowed her car, driven in so he could make a fast getaway if necessary.

The brownstone looked like no one was home, which wouldn't be unusual if Janos was out. Except that he was never out during the day, when his mistress needed his protection. Lights wouldn't be on yet, and there was no reason for windows to be open, guests to be coming or going. There was no sign of life on the block at all, except for the black van parked diagonally across the side street, in sight of Perenelle's front door.

As he moved down the block, three men in black coveralls came out of the building with packed cardboard boxes. They walked to the black van, put the boxes inside, and went back into the house. Steven drove Lori's car past the building as slowly as he dared.

If he hadn't seen the van he might have gone up to the door and knocked, but after seeing Joie's boys in black, he wasn't about to set himself up as a target. He kept driving. This was looking bad. Steven had no idea who had grabbed Christopher, but it had to have been someone that knew about him and wanted a piece. Someone who had grabbed Perenelle, too.

Without her help, there was no way for them to find out anything. All they could do was report them missing and wait for the police to do nothing. If the kidnappers were the professionals they looked like, there'd be no evidence left behind, no trail to follow. They could even be in collusion with the cops.

Steven made his way east along Canal Street to the Manhattan Bridge. He was starting to sound like some of the old black radicals still in his neighborhood when he'd moved to Fort Greene, talking about "The Man," undercover infiltration, and covert ops. Of course, they'd been proven right about a lot of it when FBI and CIA files were opened under the Freedom of Information Act. The last few years of illegal wiretaps and suspects held by Homeland Security without due process had made it a different world from the one he'd grown up in.

Correction. The world had been this way for a long time. They were just finding out about it. He'd go home to his family and find some way to protect them. Steven sighed. He'd come back to Brooklyn to find himself, he just hadn't expected it to be in the middle of a secret war between man and vampire.

Joie thought she'd cried herself out, facedown in her pillow on her bed like a sixteen-year-old after a bad date. She wanted to strike out at someone, anyone, for what had happened, wanted to jump in and fix everything like her mom always did, and now she saw why that was so impossible. Sometimes things you couldn't prevent or understand happened to people you loved. You just had to accept it and find a way to handle the situation. Christopher had been abducted and Joie didn't know where to begin looking for him. She might never see him again and had to accept that.

Just thinking it sent her into tears again.

Their last chance of finding him was lost when her father came back from the city with the news that Perenelle had disappeared and a black van matching Joie's description had been seen outside. She didn't know who Perenelle was or her connection to Christopher, but she was all her parents had to offer. Now even that hope was gone.

Her cell phone rang and she grabbed it, prayed it could be Christopher calling to say he was all right, it had been some kind of frat prank or mistake. No. Caller ID said it was a private name and number. She answered anyway.

"Hello?"

"Joie Martin-Johnson? I'm calling for Dr. Lazarus. He'd like to reschedule your appointments." It was Luna, the doctor's loopy receptionist.

"Reschedule?" A chill ran down her spine as Joie sat up.

"Yes, the doctor is changing his appointments to earlier hours. Can you see him in the afternoon?"

"Afternoon?" If Lazarus was a vampire, how could she see him in the afternoon? Christopher had seemed so sure of his story. Could he be crazy? Could that explain all this? She snapped out of it. Crazy people don't get carried out in boxes to black vans, they get carried out by guys in white coats to an ambulance. "Is the doctor there?"

The phone was muted, and when it came back on she heard Dr. Lazarus's calm, soothing voice.

"Joie? How may I help you?"

She couldn't help herself. The sound of his voice triggered her trust and she blurted out everything, Christopher's story about his attack, their different views of Lazarus's office, her parents' connection to Christopher's past, his disappearance and Perenelle's. The doctor let her run on as if it were a session, and when she was finished, he spoke quietly.

"This may sound strange, but I can help you. I think I know who has Christopher and Perenelle. Give me your address. I have to talk to you and your parents. And tell them . . ."

"What?"

"Tell them not to be shocked when they see me."

Joie told her parents that her shrink knew Perenelle and could help. That seemed to unnerve them, especially after she gave them his message.

"What's that supposed to mean?" asked Steven.

"Someone we thought was dead is still alive?" said Lori. "Not liking the potential guest list."

Joie answered the door when he got there. It was funny to see the doctor in daylight, even though she'd seen him only a few times. He still seemed uncomfortable with the idea, too, came inside as soon as she opened the door. When she saw her parents' faces when he entered the kitchen, she wished she'd pulled out her camera to capture the reunion.

"Adam Caine. Holy fucking shit," said Steven.

"You're walking in sunshine," said Lori. "How is that possible?"

He sat down at the kitchen table and poured himself a cup of tea from the pot.

"That's what I'm here to tell you. May I?" He gestured to a plate of scones left on the table from breakfast.

"Sure," said Joie.

"It's Lazarus now. Dr. Abel Lazarus."

"You tried to kill us," said Steven.

"You set me on fire. Let's call it even."

Steven and Lori watched him eat the scone like it was an exotic magic trick they couldn't figure out. Abel picked up a knife and they both jumped, then relaxed as he used it to spread jam on the scone after his first bite.

"Your little friend Christopher has an interesting history and I'm afraid it's coming back to haunt us all. Much blood was spilled to save him, and that much blood leaves deep stains."

They listened as he brought them up to date on what Rahman had done to baby Christopher to cure him, all Perenelle had told him about Clean Slate, the secret war between humans and vampires, and how Christopher might be involved as a key player.

"They're probably holding them in Red Hook, but security there is too much for us. I have no powers besides being able to take a bullet. Perenelle could contact the Veil to help us get in, but without her there's no one I can trust."

"You mean a vampire could help us?" asked Joie. "They could contact this Veil?"

"You know one?" asked her mother. Lori looked dismayed.

Joie shrugged and nodded, embarrassed.

"There's someone I can call. . . ."

CHAPTER 76

5:57 P.M.—*Red Hook, 1 August 2007*

The boy had grown considerably since the last time she'd seen him. It was too easy to forget when you lived for centuries that twenty years really was a lifetime. Perenelle stood in the observation room and watched through protective glass as Nicolas drew blood from Christopher's arm. He lay on a reclined examining table and stared up at the ceiling as her husband worked.

The blood looked normal, not at all like the glowing, golden liquid Nicolas had swallowed in Paris to become immortal, fed to her to see if it was a cure. Perenelle reminded herself that the boy hadn't been human when the elixir had been fed to him and that anything could have happened to it in his system over the years. Abel's cure proved that it cured vampirism, but what else did it do? What else was it becoming as he approached the age of twenty-one?

She gave Nicolas a few hours to examine the fluid before she joined him in the lab. Christopher was gone. Nicolas smiled up at her as she entered.

"We've learned a few things. The sample has all the surface properties of ordinary blood," he said. "If I run a simple blood test, I can type it, even look at it under the microscope and it appears normal."

He placed a slide of the blood into a holder, slid it into place, and turned to a computer monitor next to it. Nicolas nodded to an assistant, who went to the keyboard and keyed in commands. The computer screen showed a microscopic view of the slide. Red blood cells squirmed in plasma.

"But if you look at it any closer, change the light spectrum or break it into chemical components, it's not blood or anything close to it."

Under ultraviolet light, the liquid looked like swirling, molten metal, not gold but ruby red. Perenelle stared, fascinated, as at a light show.

"I don't know if the pretense is a deliberate camouflage to escape detection or an adaptation from long-term exposure to the boy's biology."

"Why wasn't this discovered?"

"How? If he was never sick, why test further?"

"What is it if not blood?" she asked.

Nicolas looked like a child on Christmas morning.

"The best description I have is . . . liquid life. It does everything for him that blood would do, but so much more. He's never been sick a day in his life. Whenever he cut himself as child, by the time he got to his mother the injury was gone. I can't imagine what other benefits he gains. Immortality would be only the beginning. I wasn't able to test the original elixir we made in Paris on modern machines, but this seems stronger, more . . ."

"Aggressive?"

He faltered, understood her implication.

"Yes. Aggressive in its defense of life; not the same as the elixir you and I took. I think it's still distilling. Changing. I don't know what that means. I'd like to examine your friend Abel."

"I don't think he'd agree, though that means little here." Perenelle paced the room, irritated. She'd already been a guest here for too long. "Have you exposed it to a sample of my blood?"

"Yes. It has no effect."

"That's impossible!"

"No." Nicolas excused the assistant and pulled Perenelle aside to lab seats at a nearby counter. "The catalyst for the final elixir has always been metabolic. It does nothing on its own, it has to be ingested and digested. The transformation is systemic. Injecting the elixir into your blood is as useless as injecting fertilizer into a plant and expecting it to grow faster."

"So there's no way to test it before I drink?"

Nicolas took her hand.

"All we know is that it cures an ordinary vampire of the need to survive on life and the ability to live in the sun. Abel has the additional benefit of accelerated healing, enough to return from the dead, as I can. But you're different."

"How?" Perenelle wasn't sure she even wanted a cure under these circumstances, still wrestled with her decision, but wanted to know her options. "Are you saying it won't work on me?"

"I'm saying it could do anything. You became a vampire. Afterward, you drank the elixir of life made from a human child. It didn't cure you, but we can't say it had no effect. This elixir was distilled in vampire blood, aged in human flesh. I don't know what it is, only what it's done once, and we don't know what the long-term effects might be."

Perenelle sat back and thought.

"Then there's no decision to make," she said. "I stay as I am until you can be sure."

"I'm sorry, Madame de Marivaux." Richmond entered the room with guards and a medical team. "We can't wait that long."

Nicolas stepped in front of Perenelle, raised his fists to defend her. Richmond stopped him by pulling out his remote control for the overhead UV lights. He pressed a button and the lights went up a small fraction. Perenelle winced, shielded her face against Nicolas's chest until Richmond turned the lights back down.

"Very good. Now. Here's what we're going to do. . . ."

It was a terrible thing to see his wife bound like a lab rat and used as a test subject. The Clean Slate team had her in a biohazard-containment room, wore protective gear as they strapped her to a reclined examining table. They attached sensors to her with wires leading to a bank of machines to measure her responses.

Nicolas stood beside Jonathan Richmond as they watched.

"You're here to be sure that we're doing this with as much consideration as possible for your wife," said Richmond. "It's a privilege, not a right, and can be rescinded as easily as granted."

"What part of consideration involves restraints?"

"For her own protection in case there's a reaction."

"Why are you doing this?"

"There's no other way to know if the elixir will work on her. Not unless you re-create the original formula and feed it to another vampire, but even that doesn't take into consideration any changes in her body over the centuries she's existed. If you were thinking like a scientist, and not her husband, you'd agree. There's no point in waiting.

"The doctors are sure that despite the other serum, the effect will be the same as on her friend, Abel Lazarus. She'll be cured, immortal, like you. Then you can both finish work on the serum free of this distraction and we'll be sure she's on our side and not theirs."

"For God's sake, Richmond—"

Richmond turned to Nicolas and frowned, as controlled as always, revealed only a trace of rage in his voice as he spoke.

"*You dare talk to me of God?* You played God in Paris with the vampire Rahman, a monster you went out of your way to find in Spain. If you hadn't tried to take control of powers best left to God, you and your beloved wife would have lived a long, full human life, died and been buried over six hundred years ago. You have no right to speak God's name, Monsieur de Marivaux, much less invoke his sympathy or intervention on your behalf." He turned away, his jaw clenched.

Nicolas stood for a moment in shock, angry and stunned until the man's words sank in. He sat on a couch at the back of the room, buried his face in his hands, blocked off the sight of his wife strapped to a table. Richmond was right.

It was Nicolas's fault that Perenelle was here. She'd never said it to him, not once in their long life together. All that she was, any offense she'd committed since her death and rebirth as a creature of the night, was entirely his fault. Because of his obsession with alchemy, his desire to wrest the fire of creation from the Almighty's hands, like Prometheus, and give it to mankind.

And how well had that gone? Where were the miracle cures he'd used to save the sick, the brilliant minds he'd preserved for posterity with the elixir of life? Instead, he'd sold his discovery to the highest bidders, cured and prolonged the lives of the rich and venal, all to support his lifelong search for a cure for his wife. A cure for a curse he'd inflicted on her when he brought Rahman into their lives.

Here he'd stood with the answer in his hands and even then he'd hesitated, warned her of possible dangers instead of encouraging her to take the risk. Why? Was he afraid that without her curse she'd have no more reason to stay with him? That he'd be left alone for eternity?

She had every reason to blame him for what she'd gone through with him and the hellish last century without him. Yet, she never had. Would he have done the same if their positions had been reversed? If there was even the slightest chance that this elixir could restore her to humanity of any kind, maybe Richmond was right. If not, it would finally be over, at least for her. All that scared him more were the possibilities that lay between death and a cure.

Anything could happen.

Three ounces of the elixir was the maximum effective dose described in Rahman's records. Everything beyond that was discarded by the body; only the first three caused the change. Abel had drunk at least that much to effect his cure. Clean Slate's doctors had decided to start with that rather than with smaller doses. The elixir might cure human disease in diluted form, but to rebuild her body completely, re-create her as human from vampire, would take the full treatment.

Perenelle listened to them while they discussed what to do with her as if she were a child or not in the room. She was sure Nicolas was nearby, ironically held hostage by his concern for her safety. When the doctors lifted the cup to her lips, she drank, possible side effects preferable to certain death.

Though it looked like blood it didn't taste like it. Perenelle drank the elixir as she marveled at the experience. It didn't have a flavor so much as it seemed to trigger distortions in all her senses as it entered her body. She saw sounds, heard lights, and tasted smells, as a weird shock ran through her body. When she'd drained the cup she lay back, relaxed, and waited to see what would happen. Nothing. The strange sensations subsided and she felt no different.

Then the pain and the screaming began.

CHAPTER 77

10:17 P.M.—Gramercy, 1 August 2007

Turner had had few dealings with the Veil.

He'd voted in elections and had never sought the position of Harlem Bloodline Superior or any other with the Veil, but still knew how to contact them. He filled them in on what he'd heard from Joie. Once they knew that Perenelle had been captured, they didn't hesitate to refer him to the New York Hunt Club for help. This would be a fully sanctioned Veil operation, a rescue mission for their loved ones and any surviving members of the Council.

Lowell Jaeger was founder and president for life of the Club. Turner met him at the bar of their headquarters, a discreet townhouse on Gramercy Park. It was a large old building, one of several private clubs on the park, and looked every bit as distinguished and legitimate as the Player's Club or the National Arts Club.

Jaeger, who appeared to be a slight, dark-haired young man in his late twenties, had founded the organization at the end of 1927 after moving to New York from Los Angeles. He'd been involved in a series of brutal murders there, using others to do his dirty work while he enjoyed the show. Jaeger's last puppet had been a young man named William, who'd kidnaped and dismembered a twelve-year-old girl, the daughter of a banker who'd fired him.

At his trial he'd confessed to other killings, had claimed that an angel named Providence had guided his hand and told him what to do. Everyone had believed he was faking it and trying to plead insanity, but his angel was real. It was Jaeger talking to him in the night, drinking his blood to enthrall and command the young man to kill for him.

Jaeger had tired of the game, abandoned William and his other victims to their fates for the bright lights of Times Square. It was the year that *The Jazz Singer* opened and ended silent film forever, the year Lindbergh flew the Atlantic nonstop from New York to Paris, the year the Columbia Phonographic Broadcasting System went on the air with forty-seven radio stations across the country, the year the Holland Tunnel connected New Jersey to New York. The world population had reached two billion. It was a new age, the Jazz Age.

Jaeger had come to New York to reinvent himself as a new kind of killer and found like minds with similar appetites. It hadn't taken him long to organize them into a pack and arrange outings to hunt down human prey from the fringes of polite society. They'd moved through Central Park and Riverside Park unseen, fed on innocent wayfarers and those using the parks for more nefarious purposes, like hookers and muggers, victims no one would miss or report missing. In time, they'd made their meetings more formal, found a clubhouse and had dinners with live victims, ordered blazers with embroidered club shields for the men, club pins for the women.

They'd fought against the founding of the Veil and rightly saw it as the beginning of a tamer life for vampires everywhere. The attack at the Grand Hyatt had only confirmed Jaeger's worst fears. They'd gotten soft, vulnerable, something their kind should never be.

The only good thing about the war was that it had forced the Veil to unleash the Hunt Club in its own defense. Since the conflict began, its membership had swelled as vampires across the city realized he was being given carte blanche to hunt humans with Veil sanction. Wartime had its advantages.

"I was there the first time we tried to break in with St. Claire in charge. The place is a fucking fortress," Jaeger said. He sipped a glass of fresh blood drained from a nearby thrall behind the bar. A teenage girl and boy stood at the ready, nude, with clamped-off catheter tubes installed in a vein in each of their arms. "Do you have any fresh ideas?"

"Perhaps." The girl offered to fill a glass for Turner. He turned down the invitation. "I understand that there was a more successful Veil operation on the Upper West Side that captured a couple of Clean Slate's vans, some equipment and uniforms?"

"The Trojan Horse bit? Won't they be expecting that again after the last attempt?"

"I'm counting on it. We'll need a distraction once we get in the door to keep them busy until we get downstairs."

Jaeger chuckled and had the boy refill his glass.

"Let me worry about that . . ."

Jaeger drove the black Clean Slate van and pressed his foot to the accelerator as he careened down the street toward their warehouse. Two Veil cars followed in close pursuit. As they approached the building, gunmen leaned out the windows of the vehicle behind them and fired off rounds from automatic weapons as the van swerved back and forth, leaped over the curb to bounce down a slight incline of grass to the corrogated outer door of the warehouse. Jaeger honked the horn and sped up as he aimed for it.

Video cameras outside rotated as they surveyed the scene.

"Moment of truth, people," said Jaeger into his earpiece. "Either they let me in or they don't." He rushed at the metal door and at the last moment it rolled up enough to admit him, slammed down as soon as he skidded to a smoking halt inside.

The van was surrounded by armed guards lined up three deep in a semicircle around the van, obviously prepared for Veil forces to be inside it. Their commander raised a hand to hold them at the ready.

"Come out with your hands up."

Jaeger raised his hands and clasped them on top of his head. One of the guards opened the door to the van. Jaeger lowered his head and stepped out of the van. As he did, a wire attached to his belt pulled free a pin that triggered high-pressure canisters inside the vehicle. Clouds of toxic gas poured out of the van to fill the room in seconds. The armed guards collapsed as Jaeger lowered his hands and walked to the control booth.

Explosions went off elsewhere around the building as Hunt Club members started their distraction right on cue, from the roof and other entrances. The Hunt Club president entered the security booth, went to the console, and pushed aside the unconscious guard. He pressed switches to open the front door and the rest of his team came in wearing gas masks, except for Turner, who was as immune to the gas as Jaeger was.

Jaeger plugged a data card into the computer and punched in a series of codes, got access to the terminal, and started bringing up maps of the complex. Fans sucked the gas out of the room as Steven and Lori pulled off their masks, tossed them into the van. Joie did the same. They assembled next to Jaeger and waited for directions.

"I really wish you weren't here," said Lori to Joie.

"Mom, I'm the only one Christopher trusts. I have to be here."

"I'm with your mom on this," said Steven. "We can handle him."

"Don't count on it," said Abel. "If what Perenelle told you means anything, he's changing. We don't know what we'll find as he approaches twenty-one. What Joie told us about the video experiment means there's something going on and she's a part of it." He brushed off his black coveralls. They all wore uniforms from the Veil's captured Clean Slate prisoners, hoped it would help them blend in as they moved through the complex.

"I'll protect her," said Turner. "You can count on that." He took a gun from the unconscious guard in the van and handed it to Steven.

"Whoa," he protested. "I've fired one gun in my life and I sure as hell can't handle this."

"You will if you want to live." Turner flipped off the safety, showed Steven where it was and how to hold the gun, fired off a round, and handed it to him. He picked up another gun and held it out to Lori. She stared at it for a second, then took it, released the safety.

"Squeeze, don't pull. Isn't that what they always say?" She shook her head and joined Steven beside their daughter.

"Got it." Jaeger waved them over and showed them on the screen where the prisoners were kept. The outer walls still rumbled with the sound of bombs. "We go down this ramp and through here to the holding cells. If we free the Council and disable the Clean Slate internal defenses, we'll have help. Have I said how much fun this is?"

"If I was already dead I'd think so, too," said Steven. "Try to remember that we're not."

Turner got into the van and started the engine. They went down the ramp into the heart of the complex.

CHAPTER 78

Tom O'Bedlam lay on his bed, eyes closed.

Soft music played in the background from a collection of his favorite waltzes on MP3, downloaded to his room's sound system for easy enjoyment. Tom had already learned a great deal about this new world in his short time awake and enjoyed it all. There was so much instant gratification, information was readily available, and there were so many more ways to kill and destroy. All the things he needed to realize his Blood World would be within easy reach once he was free.

Claire St. Claire read to him as usual. Today's selections were from Hans Christian Andersen. The poor little match girl freezing to death as she lit matches she couldn't sell to see visions of the ideal lives of others . . .

At the sound of the first explosion, Claire looked up from the book in her hands, went to the door, and watched Clean Slate guards rush into action.

Tom could place the location of each blast as the sounds drifted in to him through the concrete, like sonic vibrations. Roof, main entrance, sea doors . . . Tom smiled, pictured the resulting fires in his mind, bright, flickering flames licking at walls and bodies.

"Whatever do you suppose is going on?" she said.

He opened his eyes and grinned at her.

"It's opportunity. Can you hear it knocking?"

The sound of mass destruction was like music to him.

Tom stood, took Claire's hands, and pulled her into a waltz. They whirled around the room and laughed. He'd always known their chance would come in time.

Patience was a virtue, the only one he had left.

CHAPTER 79

1:16 A.M.—*Red Hook, 2 August 2007*

The pain stopped.

Perelle had never felt anything like it.

When it stopped, she felt different, stronger. Her body was still in one piece, healthy, better than ever. She didn't know how she knew that or how she knew the exact number of people in the room and each one's exact location, heart rate, gender, size, weight. . . . She laughed and opened her eyes.

The doctors watched her with concern, not sure what to expect. There were four armed guards standing by in the same protective gear as the medical team. They all tensed, poised in the sterile white room for whatever she might do next. All her vampire senses seemed intact; if anything, they were more sensitive. She lay still and breathed deeply, tasted the air as if for the first time. There was something new and different about it.

Or her.

"Nicolas?"

"Here, beloved." His voice came from speakers in the ceiling. She looked to the mirrored wall and knew he was watching from the other side. "How are you?"

"I . . ." she said, and hesitated, not sure she wanted the others to know just how well she felt. "I'm not in any pain."

"I'm grateful for that at least."

Perenelle looked at the doctor nearest her, the one who seemed to be in charge.

"Can you release me?"

He looked to doctors monitoring readouts of her body's response to the elixir and shook his head as they looked back at him in confusion.

"She looks textbook healthy."

"Human or not?" They shrugged. The lead doctor turned back to Perenelle. "We still have a few tests to do, if you'll just bear with us."

"No."

He'd already dismissed her and the answer seemed to catch him off guard in midturn to his team. His head angled back toward her in surprise, as she pulled free of the restraints by raising one arm. The synthetic strap snapped like a ceremonial ribbon announcing her rebirth.

Doctors leaped back as guards moved forward. Perenelle pulled free of the other straps that bound her, swung her feet to the side of the table, and stood up. The floor was solid beneath her feet, her stance strong. She smiled.

"Madame de Marivaux, please sit back down until we've had a chance to examine you." Richmond's voice came from the overhead speakers. He must be observing from outside with Nicolas. She ignored him and started to walk to the door.

The UV lights installed around the room went on at a low setting, one that had been enough to make her cringe earlier. She kept moving, didn't even squint. The lights went up several more levels until ultraviolet light flooded the room at its highest setting. Perenelle stopped to face the mirror, raised her arms, and let her head fall back as if sunning herself. It was amazing. The elixir had worked, but more than merely curing her, it had improved her. She felt a surge of power as it continued to work, changed her into something new, stronger than she'd been in more than six centuries of night.

The lights kicked back down to normal as soon it became clear that they had no effect on her and were only blinding the medical staff. The guards had slipped on protective shades as soon as the light went up one level. They advanced on Perenelle with their weapons drawn. One raised his pistol and she gripped it by the muzzle, pushed it away as he fired. The bullets went through her hand, hurt less than she'd expected them to, and as soon as they passed through her, the wound closed and the skin healed before she could bleed.

The guard fell back, eyes and mouth wide.

Even Perenelle was impressed. She'd always healed quickly, as had Nicolas, but this was virtually instantaneous. The three other guards panicked, started shooting, and hit her repeatedly, but she withstood their fire, advanced, and gripped one of them by the throat. She pulled him close, felt her system join with his as she drained his life. His eyes rolled up as his body went limp and she dropped it to the floor. She rushed at the next guard closest to her, slapped his gun out of his hand, and yanked him close enough to bite his throat by reflex. To her shock, she still had fangs, bit into his throat and drained enough blood for him to pass out.

She released him as the remaining two guards pushed the medical staff back behind them, tried to reload their empty guns as she slammed them into each other to knock them out. The doctors cowered against the opposite wall, as far from her as they could get. Perenelle went to the door as it was opened and Nicolas rushed in from the other side.

"Richmond?" she asked.

"Ran before you grabbed the first guard. He got a call about some kind of crisis upstairs."

"Yes . . . of course." She could hear distant explosions and gunfire that not even Nicolas could hear. He was immortal, but his senses were still only human. "It must be the Veil, trying to get to us. We can help from here."

She went back to the staff.

"Which one of you knows how to operate the dampeners?"

They quaked in terror, but one raised her hand, against her will. Perenelle gestured to the computer.

"Shut down the system. Disable the UV lights. Keep them off."

The woman whimpered, shook her head, and wept. Perenelle stepped closer and stared into her eyes. The technician's face changed, softened, as she smiled, looked like she suddenly got a joke Perenelle had told. She smiled, cheery, went to the keyboard, and typed a series of codes into a series of windows. When she was done, Perenelle could feel a change in the room. The signal was off, and if the woman had followed directions, so were the overhead UV lights throughout the complex. At least now the imprisoned Council members and their rescuers had a fighting chance.

She turned back to the others.

"I want you all to stay here and be quiet. Don't tell anyone what we've done or where we've gone." She could feel their compliance, knew that they would do as she commanded. Though she hadn't even touched them, she had the same degree of control it usually took infection to achieve. Whatever the elixir had done, however it had interacted with the old elixir still in her body, the result was that she was unlike any vampire or human she'd ever met, mortal or immortal.

Nicolas stared, stunned.

"How . . . I don't understand any of this."

"We can analyze it later. Somewhere else."

CHAPTER 80

1:23 A.M.—*Red Hook, 2 August 2007*

The dampeners were off.

Claire could tell as soon as it happened. The irritating low-level buzz that had nagged at her since she arrived like the whine of a dozen hungry mosquitoes around her head had stopped. It was blessed silence, sweet peace, and so much more.

She went to the door and stepped out into the hall.

Two armed guards stood there as always, the honor guard that followed her everywhere in the complex. They stared straight ahead, impassive, and made no attempt to communicate with her, stoic as the Buckingham Palace guard.

Claire smiled, walked up to one, and stood in front of him.

"Hello," she said. She slid closer, coyly looked back over her shoulder with a grin. "See that guard over there?"

The man nodded, just a little, enough for her to know she'd taken control.

Claire leaned closer and whispered into his ear, soft and seductive, "I want you to shoot him for me."

The other guard looked up at one of the dampeners to see that the status light was red, not green, and raised his gun a second too late to defend himself. Claire's guard took him down with a quick burst of automatic-rifle fire and then lowered his weapon.

Claire threw her slender arms around his neck and pulled him down until she could reach his throat with her teeth. She bit hard, deep into his jugular, and drank long, satisfying gulps of fresh blood coupled with the precious life she'd been denied while she cared for Tom. Her head swam with the intoxicating pleasure of it as she slowed to save some for Tom, spun the guard into the room and to his bedside.

"A treat, my love, and good news," Claire said as she tossed the semiconscious guard onto the mattress. "We're free." Tom leaned down, lifted the man's neck to his lips, and took the last of his blood and life.

His eyes met Claire's as he fed, brightened as he prepared to leave with her. Tom released the body, rose, and walked to Claire's side, his bright teeth stained red with blood. He embraced her and their lips met, the kiss sweetened by their victim's blood as their tongues entwined. They pulled apart and strolled out the door hand in hand, Claire's books in a leather bag, left their rabbit hole for the real world above.

CHAPTER 81

1:48 A.M.—*Red Hook, 2 August 2007*

This was crazy.

The most dangerous thing Joie had done up until now was to go skiing on a beginner slope with friends from high school without lessons. That had ended only in a broken ankle. This adventure could go wrong in so many more ways that she wished she were back home with that cast on right now, pain or no pain.

The explosions outside kept the building busy, as hoped. She heard the thudding rumble of distant blasts as groups of guards rushed past them in all directions. None took any time to question the Veil's makeshift rescue squad as they moved deeper into the complex. The halls were brightly lit and long, seemed to go on for miles. Joie sensed Christopher, didn't know how, but as they went through the halls she could tell how close they were to him.

"This way," she said as Jaeger hesitated at a convergence of corridors. They trusted her instincts, followed her as she went to the right. She got to a door and touched it, knew that Christopher was on the other side.

"Here," she said, and opened it.

Joie stared inside, surprised. In the middle of overlit corporate sterility, they'd found an oasis of comfort. Richmond had obviously gone out of his way to make his hostage feel at home. The walls were deep blue, the floor was carpeted, the lighting low. Any fears they might have had that Christopher was being tortured or bled dry were erased when they saw the big-screen TV, Playstation 3, leather couch, and waterbed.

Christopher looked up from big pillows on the floor, controller in hand as Call of Duty 4 raced by on the wall-mounted HDTV screen. The sounds of gunshots and explosions filled the air from speakers around the room.

"Joie!" He leaped up, ran to her, and they embraced. Turner scowled but said nothing. Steven and Lori stepped back outside to keep watch with Jaeger. "What are you doing here?"

"You were kidnapped—we're here to rescue you! Didn't you hear the noise?"

He looked baffled.

"I thought it was the game. Rescue? No, it was all a mistake. These people are okay, they told me the whole truth about my family. They're just trying to save us."

"Salvation for some, extermination for others," muttered Turner, as he peered outside.

"No, a cure . . . Who is this guy?"

"Turner, don't—"

"Turner?" Christopher bristled. "This is Turner? The guy's a fucking vampire! What are you doing with him?"

Abel Lazarus walked in.

"We have to get out of here. I think the Hunt Club got carried away, we have an all-out war on our hands out here."

Christopher's jaw dropped. Joie winced. Her doctor's appearance at this moment wasn't going to help.

"Lazarus? What the fuck is this? Are you working for them? What did they do to you?"

"Christopher, I can explain everything, we just have to get you out of here."

"I'm not going anywhere with these bloodsuckers."

"He's not a vampire anymore."

"No? Not since he *fed on me?*" He bellowed the last at Lazarus, who sighed, annoyed, and went back outside.

"Christopher, please—" Joie tried to calm him. She heard the noise from the hall increase as the battle around them grew, and it was only a matter of time before they were trapped in here.

"No! Clean Slate are the good guys, Joie, not the vampires you're with! They're controlling your mind! Making you see things their way when all they want is to feed on us, fuck with our heads! Do you know what they did to my family? What they did to me? You want me to go with *them*?"

"Joie," said Turner.

He looked into the hall as Lori and Steven pushed their way in. They looked to Joie for answers.

"What's going on? We're on a timetable here!" said Steven.

"He thinks we're the bad guys," said Turner, impatient.

"Are you shitting me? I'm out there with a damn machine gun in my hands," said Lori. "This is not the time for debate! We can sort out who's good and bad at home."

Christopher stood still.

"I'm not going."

Joie grabbed his arms.

"You don't understand."

"I understand that a vampire like him wiped out my family and left me an orphan," he said, glaring at Turner. "I understand that they're a plague on this Earth and need to be eliminated by any means necessary. Cured or killed."

"Leave him be," said Turner. "Let's find the others and get out." Steven and Lori went back into the hall. Turner held a hand out to Joie. She hesitated a moment too long.

"Fuck you! You're not taking her anywhere!" Christopher lunged at Turner. Joie moved with him, grabbed at the back of his shirt as he hit Turner and knocked him to the ground.

"Stop it! Christopher! Stop!"

They rolled on the floor. Turner had been caught off guard, before his superior strength and speed could give him the advantage. Christopher had him in a headlock. Joie threw herself on his back and pulled at his shoulders. The idea of having two guys fight over her always sounded better than it really was. Lori ran to her daughter's side.

"Joie! We have to go! Now!"

Joie felt her mother's hands on the back of her black coveralls, grabbed at Turner and tried to pull him away from Christopher as they rolled over. Lori fell and the four of them were in a pile on the floor. Joie's head swam as she felt her skin warm up, the same strange feeling she'd felt when she sat next to Christopher on the couch. This time, instead of blurring a video image, she saw her skin and Christopher's start to glow, growing brighter as Christopher got angrier and she became more frantic to stop him.

She tried to stop it, but all she could do was think that if Turner wasn't a vampire, none of this would be happening, and as her heart pounded louder and faster the light enveloped them all, brightened the dark blue room, flared up and vanished in a flash as Christopher swung at Turner's face and connected.

The light faded and they were all left stunned for a moment, as if whatever reaction it had caused had just caught up to them. Joie felt tired, like she'd just run a race. Christopher stared at her, dazed, like he felt the same way. Lori was already on her feet, on her way to the door. Turner was face-down on the floor, unmoving.

Joie saw him and gasped.

"Turner!" She rushed to his side and rolled him over. His eyes were closed, his nose bleeding. He opened his eyes, looked up at her blankly for a moment. "Your nose . . ." she said.

"What?"

He blinked at her a few times and reached up to his face.

"It's bleeding," said Joie.

"That's impossible." Turner pulled his hand away and looked at his own blood, baffled, then woke up completely and flinched. "Shit! That hurts! That can't hurt. . . ."

She helped him to his feet and then turned back to Christopher. She knew as soon as she saw the look in his eyes that she'd lost him, that as far as he was concerned she'd betrayed him as soon as she'd gone to Turner.

"Christopher . . ." She reached out to him.

He shook his head, clenched his jaw as he flushed red, his eyes angry. Lori helped Turner to the door. Gunshots rattled down the hall, sounded closer. Joie took one last look at Christopher, but he'd turned his back on her. There were so many things she wanted to say to him, but this wasn't the time or place. She could either stay here or leave him behind and get out with her family. There was no way to force him to go.

All she could do was hope that the people he trusted had told him the truth and would protect him, that there would be time for her to connect with Christopher later to make things right between them. She made her decision, helped Lori get Turner out the door and let it close behind them.

CHAPTER 82

Tom O'Bedlam and Claire fairly skipped down the halls.

His body was as strong as ever, and even though he'd shared only the one guard with Claire, he was positively invigorated. Richmond's professed concerns for his health had obviously been greatly exaggerated. The sound of growing battle around them reminded Tom of the Blood World of his dreams and filled him with a sense of hope that it wasn't just a fantasy but a delightful premonition.

As they passed a particular door, Claire stopped and spun in a pirouette, with an angelic smile on her delicate porcelain features. She pulled him to it.

"Wait. You mustn't miss this!"

Tom resisted her tug, kept an ear on the battle above them.

"My dear. Is this distraction worth the risk?" he asked her.

"Risk? Now that their damn electronic interference is gone, we can dance any of them on our strings. Here is a once-in-a-lifetime opportunity for you. A parting gift." She slipped an ID card taken from one of the dead guards into a slot beside it. The door slid open and Tom followed her inside.

It was a large, circular room two stories tall.

The walls around them were bomb-proof floor-to-ceiling glass, the space on the other side divided into cells. The doors to each were on the outer wall, so there was no way into the central chamber from any of them. It was a safe vantage point from which to observe or question the occupants, a holding tank big enough to accommodate one hundred cells in all, fifty on each level, custom built to contain one specific population.

The Hundred, the High Council of the Society of the Veil.

There were empty cells; only those who hadn't been eliminated after questioning or sent elsewhere for testing remained imprisoned here. There were more than eighty left, weak but defiant. Their captors hadn't gone out of their way to humiliate the vampires, had left them their clothing and their dignity. Tom saw many familiar faces as he strolled along a metal-grate walkway around the room, perfectly preserved features he'd love to see ground under his heel.

Claire trailed behind.

"How lovely! All my old friends come to see me off." They obviously couldn't see him or they would have responded with more than the mild discomfort they exhibited, like uncomfortable zoo animals. Tom chuckled and looked around. "Surely there's some means of communication? I'd hate to leave without saying goodbye."

Claire hopped to a console in the middle.

Tom had been in a box since 1937 and still found color television a major mystery, but his Claire had been awake and paying attention for the last twenty years and enjoyed showing off her technical prowess. The bombs she'd made for the New York Hunt Club were still keeping things lively upstairs. It took her no time at all to figure out how to bring up the lights in the central chamber so that he was visible from all the cells. She pressed a switch so that they could hear sound from the cells and broadcast to the prisoners.

There was a satisfying collective gasp from those who'd been present when Tom was entombed, jurors at his condemnation. He bowed.

"My friends, it has been too long. Forgive my neglect."

"My God, Claire, what have you done?"

The voice echoed from overhead speakers. Tom's eyes glittered, shot around until he spotted the face to match it, his creator, savior, and nemesis.

Dr. Townsend Burke.

"Only what you should have done first, Father," said Tom.

"Don't call me that."

"No? But you're Pygmalion to my Galatea, Doctor. Would you deny your own masterpiece? Art only appreciates over time." He stood before the glass wall of Burke's cell, rubbed his hands together at the sight of his Judas sealed in a jar like the star of a small boy's bug collection.

"You, most of all, should appreciate my increased value, having locked me away for safekeeping."

There was a collective wail from the remaining assembly, as if they were all aware of how vulnerable they were and didn't need a reminder that he might bear them ill will. Some wept for their lives, others offered treasures or begged to join him if he would spare them. Only Burke refused to cower or plead. Tom glanced at Claire, waved a finger across his throat, and she cut off sound from all the cells but Burke's.

"We should have disposed of you," he said.

Tom's jaw dropped, he clutched his chest and reeled, feigned pain in his heart and rolled back to face the doctor with a bright smile.

"We all make mistakes."

Tom joined Claire at the console. The others could still hear him, even though he spared himself their prattle. This conversation was to be had with Burke alone.

"I understand why you wished never to see me again, Doctor. But why free my Claire into your care? Why take over her tutelage?"

Burke stared into Tom's eyes, sadder than any human could become in one lifetime. Tom sneered. Burke had taken an eternity of possible pleasures and reduced it to gloom, made a curse of the gift of infinite freedom. What he saw as weakness Tom saw as power, which had always been the wall that divided them.

"Her curse was my fault, like yours. If I had never made you, you could never have made her. You were a mistake, Tom, an irrational act that unleashed more madness than I could ever have imagined. I couldn't save you, but I couldn't let her pay the price for my mistake any longer. I thought I could give back the life you took away, hope for a future of more than blood and insanity."

Tom turned to Claire and considered her carefully.

She met his gaze, her expression unreadable.

"Well. Noble intentions. The good doctor's had a little more than twenty years to work his magic. I had only fifteen. What say . . ." He turned back to Burke. "We let her decide your fate."

Burke faced Claire and nodded.

She looked from him to Tom, hesitated as she looked down to the control panel. Her hands were folded in front of her.

"My life has been a long, painful journey, Dr. Burke. I have never known where it would lead me." She looked up at him. "When it brought me Tom, he was better than what I had. When you freed me and took me into your home, it was better than imprisonment. It has not been unappreciated.

"I've seen many changes over the last century." She trembled. Her eyes seemed to well with tears as she spoke. "The year I was interred, vampires were a savage lot, wild and free. Since then, you, Perenelle, and others like you convinced them that we didn't have to be hunters chasing down prey, but could be farmers tending crops instead, feeding on humans like symbiotes instead of parasites.

"You've turned vampires into vegans that live off residual scraps of life from busy streets, subways, and theater crowds. Convinced them that they don't have to kill to live, that blood is just another addictive drug to quit. I've always understood what you wanted for me, Doctor. What you wanted. Peace. Contentment. To be at one with the universe."

She began typing on the computer keyboard.

"These are all good things. I want them, too. What you've never understood is that I am at peace. I am content. I am at one and Tom is my universe. Ever since the night he made me the divine goddess that I am." Claire pushed Enter and the glass cell walls darkened to protect observers. She looked up and grinned at Burke, her green eyes glistening with tears, not of sorrow but of suppressed laughter. Her shoulders shook with mirth.

"My time with you was only Purgatory until I earned my place in my sweet Tom's Heaven, and we're off to find it. You, Doctor? Burn here in Hell with the rest of the hypocrites."

She pressed another key and the ultraviolet lights in the cells farthest from Burke went up to full luminance. There had been a lock-out command put in place from somewhere else but she'd hacked her way through it easily. Panicked figures inside the cells farthest from them beat smoking fists and heads against the glass or cringed against the doors of their cells as brilliant artificial sunlight burned down on them like the Sahara's hottest day.

Claire flipped the sound back on to hear their screams as they died. Burke glared at her in helpless fury as the UV lights clicked on around him in cell after cell, two by two on either side of the circle, closing in on him from either side. She'd programmed the controls to delay each ignition to prolong Burke's agony, forced the doctor to watch each of his fellows perish first, making him the last to die.

It was simple, elegant, but cruel, executed with tools found at hand, a brilliantly improvised revenge for all the years Burke had treated her like his own Eliza Doolittle. Tom laid his hand on Claire's. He'd chosen well.

She was truly his perfect partner.

The doctor's eyes stayed on them as the white lights finally illuminated his cell and seared his pale flesh until it smoked. He stared at them in rage without eyelids until his eyeballs burned away and turned to dust as his face flamed off with his hair and skin. Muscle and bone combusted to ash in seconds, like all those trapped around him, and his clothes dropped to the floor, empty.

Tom took Claire into his arms again, kissed the girl on the forehead like an approving parent before pulling her back out the door to the hallway and freedom.

CHAPTER 83

It was astonishing.

Perenelle's new senses gave her a clear mental image of the complex's layout, helped her guide Nicolas away from the worst of the fighting and up toward the surface. Along the way she'd sensed the location of the captive Council members and then felt them suddenly fade away, as if they'd been wiped out one by one. The sensation was so vivid that she was sure there was no point in looking for them, moved as fast as she could to get herself and Nicolas out to meet the others.

Then she felt someone she knew. Abel.

She hadn't been able to detect him when she was a vampire, but whatever she'd become, she could not only tell who was in her area but could tell if they were mortal or immortal, human or vampire. Abel was with a group of humans and vampires, which meant he must be part of the rescue team. She steered Nicolas in his direction.

They found them in the halls a floor above them.

"Abel!" Perenelle called out as she spotted him. Lowell Jaeger, the leader of the New York Hunt Club, led them along with Steven, Lori, and a young woman who had to be their daughter. A young black man was with her, his face familiar, one she knew but hadn't seen in a long time, not since . . . *No.*

Not since Harlem, 1931. Life was filled with far too many cruel ironies. To meet the man she'd most wronged just when she had found her long-lost love was the worst of them. He looked up and recognized her at the same moment she remembered him.

Turner Creed.

Turner felt better than he had when he'd picked himself up off the floor after Christopher had punched him in the face, but not by much. While they ran, Joie tried to explain to him about the energy field generated when she was near Christopher, about the dead flowers blooming, but none of it made sense as she blurted it out between explosions and the sounds of gunfire.

All he knew was that he was suddenly, impossibly, human and everything had changed. He was disoriented, relearning how to react with his new senses, limited as they were. It was like walking under water. Everything was muffled and slowed.

Joie was busy guiding them out of the building when Jaeger got a call from others telling him that the cells where the Council had been held had been found filled with dusty remains. Their mission was officially over and they were pulling out with survivors. As they reached the next floor, they ran into two more Veil members, a man and a woman.

"Perenelle!" said Lori. "You found us!"

The woman greeted the others, then looked at Turner with an expression that puzzled him until he realized what she must have—that they weren't strangers. He felt his heart pound, his blood rise as he slowly recognized the demon that had torn his life apart seventy years ago, had killed him for spite and left him for dead until Zora raised him as a vampire. Nell, the inhuman thing that Zora had banished in 1931, the one he'd thought had perished in the fire at Papa Guedé's.

"*Monster!*" he yelled, barely able to contain his rage. "You bitch! We risked our lives for *you?*"

To be stripped of all his power just before meeting her after all these years, that was the most sadistic joke of his life. Joie held him back and looked shocked as she saw fury explode out of him at the sight of the woman they knew as Perenelle.

Nell stepped forward, raised a hand, and he felt his rage fall away like rain as she linked with him, but did not feed. He calmed, knew his anger in his mind, but couldn't feel it in his body. His heart slowed, his head lightened, all taken from his control. Turner trembled, knew he'd done this many times to others over the last seven decades, but hadn't felt the influence of a vampire over him since the last time Nell had controlled his mind to take him away from Zora and make Turner her slave, then victim.

"Be calm. I understand your rage and it's justified, but this is not the time or place. Once we are safely away, you will have your justice."

Turner stared and was forced to take her at her word. The eyes he looked into were not the same as those he'd faced down in Harlem during the Great Depression. She was a woman who'd seen much since then and perhaps had changed, like he had. He relaxed, backed down, and turned to the others.

"How do we get out?" Turner asked.

"We don't. Not here." Jaeger looked up from the phone in his ear. "The guards recaptured the main exit above us. Our only other way out is back down out the river exit."

"No. Too much risk." Steven shook his head, looked at Lori and Joie with concern.

Turner stepped forward.

"Give me a moment. I prepared for this possibility, but I need time to summon our salvation." He squatted on his heels, bowed his head, and chanted softly, "*Papa Legba, ouvrir barrière pour moi passer . . .*"

His words ran together, grew louder. He'd spent the night before in prayer and offering to the gods who protected him. Even if he'd become human, that didn't end his long association with the loa. Seventy years of service still counted for something. Shango had promised him protection and he called on that aid now, as Zora had taught him, called upon Legba to open the line to Damballah to place the call, and sang his way through to Shango for the power to escape.

The others watched him, too familiar with unnatural powers and supernatural beings to doubt him or interrupt. Two floors above them, an armed squadron of Clean Slate guards stood between them and freedom. If Turner offered any chance of getting out, they'd take it.

Then the god answered his call.

Turner felt a sudden charge in his skin and hair, the electric presence of the deity in his flesh, and lifted his lids to see the world through the eyes of a higher being. He felt whole again, more than mere man, saw and heard things his human mind never could have. Turner knew he was in the back-seat, Shango driving, sat back and watched the god lift his body from the floor to his feet as he moved toward the ramp to the surface. Inhabited by divinity, he strode forward with sure confidence that nothing could stop him as he led them the two flights up to the exit.

The guards at the top were many and saw them coming, but that meant nothing to Shango. He was the god of thunder and lightning, the god of swift justice, and with a wave of his hand thunderbolts dropped from the ceiling to strike them down. He raised both arms and electricity filled the air, threw the squadron shaking to their knees, shocked them to their very cores. As they fell, Shango directed his power at the massive inner metal doors that blocked his way to the outside, ripped them from their hinges with crackling energy, and threw them aside. Metal screamed, and the cor-rogated outer door crashed to the ground as Turner led the way.

Steven, Lori, and Joie ran out, followed by Jaeger and Abel, with Peren-elle and Nicolas not far behind. Turner stood outside the building, eyes still illuminated by the presence of the god inside him. Lightning bolts pounded down around them, struck the massive building over and over as the genera-tors inside it died, provided the last distraction needed to get the last of their team out of the rest of the building. Turner dropped to the ground, felt the loa leave him as the thunder and lightning continued, the god keeping his promise until the end.

Steven and Abel ran to the street to wave in transport. Turner felt Joie's hands on his face, opened his eyes as she examined him with concern. For a moment, as consciousness faded, Turner thought he saw Zora's smiling face instead of Joie's. Zora gazed down at him, proud and happy that he was alive and well again, a man, even if no longer hers. She'd kept him alive on Earth long enough to find a cure. He kissed her and said goodbye for the last time.

She'd saved him after all.

CHAPTER 84

2:27 A.M.—*Red Hook, 2 August 2007*

It was not Jonathan Richmond's best day at work.

Lightning hit the building, one strike after another. The power went out, and as the emergency power went on, it was killed, too. Battery-powered emergency lights clicked on, lit the hallway with a dim green glow as Richmond made his way to the nearest emergency stairs as quickly as possible. He should have had Lopez with him for protection, but she was busy trying to clear the last of the enemy from the premises. He had to get to the safe room on his own.

Richmond had spent the last hour on the phone with the mayor, the police chief, and several state agencies, persuading them to let him handle the situation here. The last thing he needed during a vampire invasion was New York's finest blundering in with SWAT teams and tear gas to make a bigger mess of things. They didn't know what they were really dealing with, and it would be even harder to cover up afterward with a squadron or two of trained eyewitnesses taking it all in.

He'd figure out an explanation to feed the public later. Maybe an industrial accident that blew up tanks of chemicals, which would explain the explosions and give them an excuse to quarantine the area while they concealed evidence of the truth and repaired the damage to the building. That worked. One problem solved already. He was good at thinking on his feet.

Richmond got to the stairway door and pushed it open, saw two familiar figures on the green-lit other side. He recognized them instantly and moved back into the stairwell a moment too late. They'd spotted him with delight and advanced to pull him into the hall.

Tom O'Bedlam and Claire St. Claire.

"How rude of us to leave without thanking our host!"

Tom slid up to him, dapper and agile as Fred Astaire with a sparkling grin on his pale face. He slicked back his snow-white hair with one hand and gestured with the other. Claire slipped behind Richmond and gripped one of his wrists, connected it to the other with a snap, and held them together behind him. Richmond didn't bother wasting words on them. These weren't creatures that would listen to a plea for mercy. He took a different tack.

"I can help you."

Anything to survive, long enough to betray them.

"Yes, you can."

Tom was on him in a flash. He bit deep into Richmond's throat before he could say more, drank and infected him with his tainted spit. Richmond felt it burn through his system as it entered his mind, took control as he felt all resistance to the devil at his neck vanish, turn to grudging admiration that blossomed into love, then worship. He lost all thought for his mission, didn't care about anything anymore except the commands of his new master, Tom.

It was everything he'd ever feared it would be.

And better.

Tom released Richmond and let him drop to the floor as Claire released his wrists. He stared down at the man for a moment as Claire stepped back to the stairs, scented the air like a wild animal ready to run at the first trace of the hunter.

"Not so fast, sweetness. Stay thy flight . . ."

He folded his arms, tapped his jaw, thought, and remembered the lessons of his womb. There was death and destruction here, but in that chaos was opportunity.

Here was the head of an organization with extensive international resources, files on all of Tom's kindred around the world, and the trust of presidents and kings. The complex was in disarray; the dampeners and UV lights that had kept Tom and Claire from escaping were out of commission. All he had to do now was move to the center of the web and become the spider.

It was his old plan to take over New York reborn, the one foiled in 1937, which had put him in a box for seventy years. Here was a chance to complete that clever notion, appearing like magic from nowhere as if predestined. The chance to take charge of Clean Slate instead of New York and use it to further the larger, worldwide plans born in his iron womb, if he could seize the moment.

Tap, tap, tap.

He tapped his chin as he'd pounded on the inside of the vault after he was locked in for days until he'd realized that it was useless, that they were serious and he was locked in forever. He'd tapped on it after that, made the only sound he could in the silence, meditated on it and used it to sharpen his senses, keep them working in isolation in the endless dark.

Tap, tap, tap.

Sound. Sensation. The hope that someone would hear.

He'd had time in his womb to master a universe that extended as far as his mind and body. His mind had constructed the endless boundaries of Blood World for him to explore, a rich, violent landscape to keep his consciousness occupied, focused, strong, but his body had become equally adept at following his will.

Vampires had always had the ability to disguise their appearance, to look older or younger as camouflage and alter their features or coloring. He'd gone far beyond that in his tomb, had mastered control of his flesh to the point that he knew he could mimic Richmond's features, fool even the security cameras in the complex that could see through ordinary vampiric illusions of the mind. He'd keep Richmond on hand, alive, hidden, as a living database who'd gladly answer any questions about how things were done for his new master.

Tap, tap, tap.

He'd have just enough time to establish himself as the new head of Clean Slate without their knowledge, to rig the detectors and dampeners to look operational while he and his associates came and went as they pleased, slowly taking control of the pertinent heads of departments. In time, he could influence the governments he worked for, infiltrate their operations with his own agents and begin changes in global economies and politics to lead to his vision of the future, the birth of his Blood World.

They'd found a new home after all.

Like little Dorothy in Claire's copy of the *Wizard of Oz*, they'd overlooked what was under their noses all the time. There's no place better than where you are. It had taken the invasion by the Veil to point out what was already within their grasp. Tom explained his plan to Claire and she laughed as they led Richmond back upstairs to his penthouse-headquarters.

They found a convenient room in the suite where they could keep him secret from the others, and Tom took on the man's appearance as his own, went to Richmond's bedroom and put on one of his custom-made Italian suits, a monogrammed silk shirt, and a hand-woven tie. His new guise complete, Tom poured a drink and sat down in Richmond's armchair to survey the chaos below.

Claire was at Richmond's desk with his password codes, freely given, swiped her fingers across the surface to bring up his control console and started reconfiguring the Clean Slate system to work for them. Tom smiled over at her.

"I'm so impressed by your mastery of these technical toys, love," he said. "I was never very mechanical." He sipped his scotch, a predictably good one. She grinned back at him, happier than he'd seen her in days.

"I had to do something to fill the years without you."

Tom blew her a kiss, spun his chair back around to watch the Clean Slate guards chase off the last of the intruders.

The walls below were breached, smoked despite the system-wide extinguishers that had quenched the flames. Explosions still went off deep below as the fires reached gasoline fuel tanks for their trucks, oil for generators.

The air above was filled with black smoke, their view of the city obscured. Sirens rose in the distance as the fire department came to tend to the flames, regardless of any instructions Richmond might have given the city administration. The scene was a catastrophic panorama of chaos and devastation that bordered on apocalyptic. Tom raised his glass to the view and drained it, smashed it against the shatterproof window. He let the shards of glass lie scattered where they fell, reflecting the disorder outside like a hundred crystal balls revealing the future.

Tom sighed and leaned back in the chair. His chair now, just like the complex, Clean Slate Global, and soon the rest of the world. His world, to shape as he saw fit.

For the first time since he woke up, Tom felt at home.

CHAPTER 85

5:37 A.M.—*Park Slope, 2 August 2007*

The sun would be up soon.

Turner hadn't seen a sunrise in more than seventy-five years, and didn't know if he anticipated or dreaded witnessing the first of many for the rest of his mortal life. No matter how spectacular or special this one was, there would soon come a day when dawn was routine, just another thing that happened, like eating meals or making bowel movements. A day when he paid more attention to what he got done in a day than how it had begun. If he was afraid of anything, it was that his newfound humanity would lose its novelty too soon, that he'd find it too easy to take for granted. Turner pulled the quilt he'd taken from a downstairs linen closet tighter around him, felt the night's chill for the first time since his last sunrise. The trapdoor behind him swung open and Perenelle stuck her head up, wary.

Turner stared at her for a long time, then sighed.

"Come on."

She climbed up the ladder to the roof and sat cross-legged next to him in the same clothes she'd been wearing when she'd been abducted. Neither she nor Nicolas had been back to her home to change yet, preferred to wait until daylight to survey the damage done by Clean Slate's invasion. Turner didn't look at her but studied the sky instead, silent.

"When we first met, I was a mad thing," said Perenelle. "The pain I caused was the pain that I'd experienced and I had no right to inflict it on you.

"I know it means nothing to say that what I did that night made me realize how low I'd sunk. It made me leave New York, work hard for long years to pull myself back up to a semblance of humanity again. I know there's no apology great enough, but I am sorry for the loss I caused you."

"Nell . . . I'm no priest. I can't offer you absolution."

"I know that," she answered. "I just needed to say it."

He shivered. Nell didn't feel the cold, like he did. Turner wanted to shove her off the roof to the street below. In her current condition, it probably couldn't kill her, but it would express his feelings well enough.

They sat in silence. The stars twinkled overhead, but he didn't see them as brightly as he had when he was a vampire. Perenelle watched him.

"Do you miss it? The vampire's eye?"

He shrugged. "It's so little to be human. We're so clumsy, so slow. Most of the beauty in the world escapes us because we can't see it or won't see it. I'm going to have to cram lifetimes of experience into the few decades I have left ahead of me. I can't tell you how fragile, how limited I feel from how I felt last night.

"But I'm alive," he said. "I'm human. I feel, breathe, eat, I piss and shit. I love. It's a miracle more amazing than any of the wonders I've seen since you killed me and Zora brought me back. I wouldn't trade it away, not even for true immortality."

He turned to her for the first time, marveled at how much she looked like the woman she must have been before she'd died, instead of the dead white porcelain doll he'd met in Harlem.

"No," she said after a moment, their eyes locked. "I suppose not. It's a day I may never see again."

"I guess there's some justice in that," he said softly, and looked away. Perenelle said nothing, seemed to lose patience with his company, and shifted in her seat.

"When is this thing, anyway?"

"Six-o-one A.M." Abel came through the trapdoor with a bottle of champagne and tulip flute glasses from Lori's kitchen. "I looked it up on the Internet. I can't think what we ever did without it."

Abel climbed up without invitation, sat down beside Perenelle and passed out glasses, popped the cork on his bottle, and filled them.

"I've done a few sunrises by now, but couldn't help joining the newbies to see the looks on your faces. Where's your noble husband for this grand occasion?"

"He told me very sweetly that we'd have many dawns to share together and that I should have this one for my own as a moment of private contemplation. I suppose that's out." Turner shrugged, smiled as she glanced at them both. "I think he really just wanted to sleep in. It was a long night." They all laughed and clinked glasses.

"To a new day," said Abel. "For us all."

"A great day," said Turner, thought of his lost love and the new one waiting for him downstairs, one that was possible now. They sipped their wine and turned to the sun as it made its first appearance of the day, as it had so often without them. It came slowly. The sky brightened before the sun made its actual appearance, like footlights rising to set the stage for the star's introduction.

Spotlights came on and the entire cast of dawn appeared in full regalia for the main performance, clouds lit pink and turquoise from below, stars and moon fading into night skies that retreated offstage into the wings in seconds, gave way to day. The shining disk of the sun rose majestically over the Brooklyn brownstones and buildings that lay before them, poured golden light down as it floated above the horizon, awaited applause. Their faces were lit up, warmed by the sun without flame, without fire.

It was morning and they were still alive.

No more hiding from the dawn. No more living trapped in night. Turner remembered a corny old saying and laughed. As lame as it was, he felt it for the first time and couldn't help saying it as they raised their glasses again.

"To the first day of the rest of our lives."

Joie lay in bed, watched sunlight creep up the wall of her room as she wondered where Turner was, if he was enjoying the sunrise of his first day as a man. Again. She couldn't get the idea out of her head. He'd been a vampire when she'd met him, then she and Christopher had cured him in a flash of light, just like that. If only he hadn't stayed behind at Clean Slate, lost faith in her. There were so many questions she had about him and her connection to him. Perenelle was the only one who might be able to answer them now.

She rolled onto her belly, buried her face in the pillow. There were more-immediate concerns. What was she going to do about Turner? Beyond everything else they'd shared, last night had been an experience beyond them all. What did he think of her now that he knew she wasn't quite human? Or was she? What was she? Until last night, she'd thought she knew. There was a knock on the door, light but firm.

"Yes?"

"It's Turner."

Joie felt her heart leap at the sound of his voice, her stomach twist as she caught her breath. Her first thought was that she had to look like shit, and then she rolled her eyes. Vanity wasn't an attractive feature. He didn't love her for her looks if he loved her at all. Did he love her? Did she love him? Joie panicked, then stopped, sat up, and wrapped the sheet around her. This was Turner, not some guy she'd met last night at the mall. She knew this man; and she was not a schoolgirl anymore.

"Come in," she said. Turner opened the door and smiled.

"I should give you time to get dressed."

"Just shut the door." She waved him in. He sat next to her on the bed. The sun lit a halo around the back of his head. She took his hand. "How was it?"

He shrugged, laughed.

"There are no words. I could play the dawn for you on the piano. But words . . ." He shook his head and looked down. "I don't understand what's happened, or how you did it."

She started to speak and he gently put a finger to her lips. Joie sat back and smiled at his old-world gesture. It was easy to forget his real age until he did things like that.

"I want to thank you. I lost nothing I'd ever asked for and regained everything I lost."

"It scares me, Turner. I don't understand how I'm a part of whatever this is."

"I know. Whatever it is, we'll get you through it. Your mother's making breakfast downstairs and sent me to fetch you. She's been asking me about Zora all morning, now that she knows the truth."

"Don't let her drive you crazy." Joie laughed. "That book has been her curse for two years, you must seem like salvation."

"It's fine. I've wanted to tell someone the story for so long that I like the idea of her writing it all down. Maybe it will help me to see it all in print from beginning to end. I don't think she knew she'd be writing a vampire novel when she started, but she's taking it well."

They laughed, and when the laughter died out it left them in an awkward silence. The moment they'd put off was here. Joie knew they had to stop worrying about what they were and decide who they were to each other. Their fingers twisted closer as Turner leaned toward her. Joie tilted her head by reflex, leaned forward to meet him, and their lips touched, pressed together in a long, soft kiss, better than any she'd gotten from Christopher. Turner had only kissed her hand when he was a vampire. This was their first real kiss and she felt it in every part of her body.

Joie pulled him down, lost in loving him as if she'd found her other half. Whatever bond there was between her and Christopher, it wasn't this. She could tell that Turner felt the same. He'd gotten back not only his life but his heart, and now he gave it to her. Without thinking, they slipped off what little clothes they had on, slid under the sheets, and made sweet, slow love in the morning summer sun, as if they'd done it a thousand times before, as if they'd never stopped.

Perenelle slipped back into the living room sofa bed with Nicolas. He stirred and snuggled back against her as she curled around him from behind. She blew into his ear and he smiled.

"Not again, you lusty bitch," he said with a sigh and a chuckle. "You can't make up for centuries of celibacy in one night!"

"You have the stamina of a dozen men. A thousand." She giggled and pulled him closer. "I'm not asking for anything the elixir hasn't given you."

Last night they'd made love for the first time since her transformation. While she was a vampire, any sexual feelings had been channeled into the act of feeding, the vampire's method of reproduction. Human sex had no real sensation for her, as it did for Nicolas. Their love had been chaste for centuries, an affair of the heart and mind. Now her body felt human sensations again. Whatever else she might be, Perenelle had been completely reunited with her husband, body and soul.

She stopped her flirtatious play and snuggled against Nicolas as he fell back asleep. His chest rose and fell as she luxuriated in the heat of his body, hers rising in return. She could still feel the snake coiled within her, a last trace of the vampire she had been. The ability to reach out with her mind and join to his, make him see anything she wanted him to, and leave him drained of life, of blood. It was not a comforting feeling.

She wasn't human and she wasn't an immortal like her husband and Abel. The combination of the old and new alchemical elixirs in her body had turned her into a strange hybrid between immortal and vampire. She could face the day, but had all the power of the night at her command. Despite her fears, it was the best of all possible worlds. If the war wasn't over yet, at least she was better equipped to fight it. But all that was far away. Perenelle let herself relax and share the bed with her husband.

There was plenty of time for war later.

CHAPTER 86

6:56 P.M.—*Red Hook, 2 August 2007*

Jonathan Richmond had been a compulsive note taker.

He'd documented all his actions in a daily digital diary on his computer, which gave Tom a full briefing on all his activities for years. Any records before that were safely stored away on disk for future review, the rest in his mind, under Tom's control.

Tom was a quick study. Claire had shown him how to read Richmond's records on the desk computer and he'd spent hours reading them in reverse chronological order. By the end of the night he'd been caught up on the last five years, briefed enough to carry out his impersonation with the staff.

He'd kept his communications during the day brief, claimed minor injuries in the battle that kept him in his quarters to recover. He'd ordered Lopez to send Christopher to his office and then finish securing the facility. She could report to him when he was done with the boy. Richmond's second-in-command had only the briefest hesitation, not enough to make him suspicious, accepted her orders and did as he asked.

Tom sat in Richmond's chair with Richmond's face as the boy walked in. Christopher looked at Tom for a second, almost as if he could see through his facade. The look faded. The boy could see through ordinary vampiric illusion and was immune to their mental influence, but Tom's disguise was the physical reshaping of his features. The boy couldn't disbelieve the evidence of his own senses, no matter what his instincts told him.

He sat down. Tom looked serious.

"I'm sorry about last night. We should have been better equipped to protect you, but they took us by surprise with more force than we thought they could muster."

"It's good they did. I needed to see the truth."

"Yes." Tom slid a hand across his desktop. Icons popped up across its glossy black surface and he clicked on one to bring up thumbnails of video clips from security cameras. "The truth. You've seen a file on your family, written by the vampire who tortured them to death."

"Yes. Adam Caine."

"He disappeared in the eighties and was presumed dead, but we ran the footage in last night's invasion through facial-identification software and came up with several matches. Do you recognize this man?"

Tom stroked a thumbnail and it blew up into a window of edited video, shots of Abel Lazarus moving through hallways of the complex. Christopher looked at him, puzzled.

"Yeah. That's Lazarus, Joie's shrink. The one who bit me? They say he's cured now."

"Yes, we heard. He's actually Adam Caine."

Tom brought up several clippings from magazines, photos of a red-haired man identified as Adam Caine at art-world events, at downtown clubs in the late eighties. Christopher gaped.

"He's the one? He was here in front of me?"

Tom laid a hand on Christopher's shoulder.

"That's not all. There were pages excised from his files when you saw them last. It's time you understand everything your so-called friends have kept hidden from you."

Tom opened a desk drawer, lifted out several pages of Adam's handwritten records sealed in airtight sheets of archival Plexiglas. He put them on the desk and let Christopher pick them up. The boy read them and his face contorted as he digested the words on the two pages, dissolved into tears of stunned disbelief as he screamed, bellowed his rage and smashed the sheets down on the desk, pounded them until the plastic broke and freed the paper to be ripped apart, shredded so that no one could ever see the words again and hold them against him.

Christopher collapsed to the floor. Tom poured a glass of scotch, carried it around the desk, and crouched by the boy's side to hold it out. Christopher took it as he regained enough composure to hold the glass.

"They lied to you," said Tom as Richmond. "What was done, what you are becoming, is a threat to them. They see you as an abomination, not the god in training you are, and want to destroy you. We can save you from them. We can help you find justice."

His world had ended.

It was so much worse than he'd ever dreamed possible. Christopher felt scraped raw inside. Anything that held the last of the darkness at bay had been shredded, each truth he discovered about his past another knife cutting it free.

Wasn't it bad enough that his mother had been slain by a monster for sport and that he'd been raised from the dead as a vampire baby to be used in an ungodly experiment? The truth was that he'd been cursed long before that, a bastard child of incest.

His father was his mother's brother.

The vampire Caine had made Jim rape his sister, Nina, blind to the truth. She'd run away, pregnant, to give birth to Christopher in New York, kept her secret to the grave. Only Adam Caine had known, and he'd written it down in his diary like another vacation memory.

Christopher was sickened, wished he could tear his innocent spirit free from his corrupt flesh. Why had he begun this search? Why hadn't some knowledge deep in his psyche stopped him from starting a journey of fucking mythic proportions, a classic Greek tragedy that could only end in tears, with him laid low for vultures to feed on?

Richmond helped him to his feet and into the chair.

Christopher barely heard what he said and it really didn't matter. He couldn't face any of them again if they knew this about him. Not Steven and Lori, definitely not Joie. They had lied to his face when he'd begged them for the truth about his parents, his past, and maybe he could understand why now.

It was still a betrayal.

Richmond offered him a place to stay, a salary, a purpose, a future, when he felt he had nothing left to live for. It was too easy to say yes, to stay here and heal as they rebuilt the facility. To be part of something bigger than himself, a cause he could lose himself in. He shook hands with Richmond, wished that booze had an effect on him as he took another drink and pledged his all to Clean Slate and their mission.

Whatever it was, he was part of it now.

Christopher left after he'd finished his drink, apologized for the mess, and went back to his room to think about what he'd just learned. Tom could feel the lad's confusion and pain, the perfect foundation for the building to come. Blood World's lesson was that change is incremental. The process of breaking down to rebuild applied to individuals as well as to systems. Rebuild a man and he rebuilds his world. Rebuild enough men and they rebuild the entire world. Christopher was the first of many and the key to it all.

Tom sat back with the satisfied feeling of a good opening move in chess, the perfect gambit that lets you see the rest of the game unfold before you, every move after it inevitable and in your favor.

Lopez came in after the receptionist announced her.

"Good news, chief. Our prisoners were vaporized, not escaped. At least that saves us rounding them up."

"I suppose that's good news of a sort," said Tom. "Have you taken a full inventory?"

"Yeah. All present and accounted for, except Tom O'Bedlam and Claire St. Claire. We have alerts out."

"They can't have gone far. You know the procedures. We should salvage something from this debacle." He put Christopher's glass back on the bar and poured another drink for himself.

They didn't call her the White Witch for nothing.

Lopez sensed that something was wrong as soon as she walked into the room. As soon as she knew who wasn't accounted for, she knew she had to keep an eye out for anything out of the ordinary. With the complex's defense systems down and still getting back online, she knew that anything could happen. Lopez wasn't relying on the recently repaired hall dampeners. She wore a portable unit, and had passed out as many as she had to squadron leaders, but knew the battery lasted only a few more hours before she'd need a recharge.

Because it was working now, she knew that Richmond wasn't a vampiric illusion. Her mind was clear and sharp, but something told her that this wasn't right. He hadn't responded to her "chief" crack, and though that could be dismissed under the circumstances, she didn't think so.

She gave Richmond a full report, brought up windows on his desktop screen to show him footage of damage and repairs. He responded in all the right ways, but automatically, as if mouthing lines without knowing their meaning. As she talked, she thought, *What if Tom O'Bedlam could change his shape, enough to fool the eye and cameras?*

What if the active lights were lit on the dampener drives, but weren't really working? Not hard to pull off, if you took control of the techs that ran it, during the blackout. They'd been in here all morning for meetings before finishing repairs. Tom would have had time to do that while the defenses were down, if he'd captured Richmond and knew who did what at Clean Slate.

The shaded windows that protected his office from outside surveillance could act as a sun shield as well. There was no reason the vampire couldn't conduct business as usual from Richmond's desk during the day.

Maybe not all the cells were occupied when the ultraviolets in them went off. Maybe the incineration of the surviving members of the Hundred wasn't an accident but a cover-up. She'd done enough of those over the years to know the signs. Done to cover up the biggest absence of all, the hole filled by Tom and Claire, in the hope that they'd assume they were killed as well.

What if they hadn't run at all, but burrowed deep inside the building, into its heart? Lopez finished her report to Richmond, headed for the door, and delivered one last test to be sure.

"Okay, chief. Catch you later."

No response. Lopez grinned at him as if nothing was wrong, turned, walked out the door, and kept walking. She got in her car, left the complex, and drove as far and fast as she could from Clean Slate headquarters. Going home to pack would only give them warning that she was leaving town. There wasn't much there she'd miss and she could call a neighbor to free her cat. She'd gotten it off the streets when it climbed in her window one night for food and stayed; it could go back no problem.

Intuition aside, common sense had told Lopez a long time ago to make sure she had an easy out from this life. It wasn't the kind of job you retired from with a gold watch. She'd outlived most of the crew who'd started with her, and the ones who'd lived—well, she wouldn't call that a life. Bodies smashed beyond repair, brain damaged, or worse. She had money and other resources the job knew nothing about, not even Richmond, put aside against a day when she might have to drop everything and run, for any reason.

As head of Clean Slate Tom had access to world leaders and files of secrets that could sway any one of them, if he didn't just bite them, and take charge as soon as he got in the room. She had read the dossier on him. Tom O'Bedlam had no limits. That was why she'd hit the road.

If the worst-case scenario was being played out, if the organization really had been taken over by vampires and she was the only one who knew, she had to spread the word and start some kind of movement to take Clean Slate back. Given what he had to work with in Richmond's place, if Tom really was in control of the organization and all its holdings, her safety was the least of her concerns.

The world was at his mercy.

EPILOGUE

New York City
15 August 2007

I have been in Sorrow's kitchen and licked
out all the pots. Then I have stood on the
peaky mountain wrapped in rainbows, with
a harp and a sword in my hands.

—Zora Neale Hurston
Dust Tracks on a Road
(1941)

CHAPTER 87

It was late afternoon and cool for summer.

Lori felt better than she had in a while, even though she'd thrown up this morning. She sat in the doctor's office and waited for Sherrie to come back with her results after a quick physical. It had been a routine presurgery checkup before the operation later in the week, but after a few minutes of examining her, Sherrie had ordered X-rays and blood tests.

The doctor came in with a folder, her face unreadable.

"Well," she said. "You're full of surprises."

Lori looked at her, not getting it. Sherrie wasn't the kind of doctor that usually liked to play games.

"What's up?" asked Lori.

She'd known Sherrie socially since moving to Park Slope, and she'd been her gynecologist for more than ten years. They'd seen each other through a lot of life's adventures, but she'd never seen an expression on her face like the one she wore now.

"Do you believe in miracles, Lori? Because that's all I can say we have here." She pulled out X-rays. "There's no trace of any tumors. The cancer's gone. I've ordered more blood tests, but if you compare this to one taken a few weeks ago, there's a radical difference even the amateur eye can see."

Lori looked at them and saw that Sherrie was right. Even she could see it. The tumors were gone. Whatever Joie and Christopher had done that had cured Turner of vampirism had cured her of cancer. She wanted to laugh, knew she could never explain it to Sherrie or anyone else.

"What did you do? Did you see someone, eat something? Chinese herbs? Prayer? Voodoo?"

Lori waved a hand, still overwhelmed.

"No, nothing. I don't understand it either."

"Well, here's something you can understand. Another miracle. I didn't even think to check first or I would never have ordered the X-ray."

Lori looked at the page Sherrie slid across the table to her. It was a pregnancy test. The result was positive. She was pregnant?

"No!"

"Yup. Congratulations. You beat the odds on all counts."

Lori opened her mouth with no idea of what to say. She was going to be a mother at forty-eight? The only reason she hadn't bothered to use protection when she'd rolled into bed with Steven was because her ovaries were coming out in a week.

Never take anything for granted.

How was she going to explain this to Steven? Or Joie? Pregnant. The laughter started again and Sherrie joined in, not knowing how really funny it all was.

The test was positive.

There was a little plus sign right there on the plastic indicator, no ambiguous colors to misinterpret, just yes or no, pregnant or not, and she was pregnant all right. She wasn't sure if it was Christopher's or Turner's. The answer to that made a big difference in her life and her child's, not to mention theirs.

Joie sat on the toilet seat at home with the pregnancy test in her hand, not sure what to do next. A long time ago she'd decided that if she were ever pregnant, she'd have the baby. Her feeling had always been that she wouldn't have sex with anyone she didn't love and whose baby she wouldn't want to raise, married or not.

Now that the moment was real, it was bigger than she'd realized. She'd never considered abortion, but if the baby was Christopher's, would it even be human?

She remembered the visions they'd shared at his apartment when they mind melded, the first time they'd had sex. After his childhood nightmare, she'd seen visions she couldn't forget of a future that still scared her. A moving tableau of images of a world in chaos, breaking down, ruled by a madman, the city in flames. If their child was going to be involved in any of that, she wanted to spare them both. Was that so wrong?

Joie stuck the test and wrapper into her pocket, decided to throw it away outside the house. She'd keep the news secret from her parents and Turner until she was sure what it was she was going to do.

She just hoped it wouldn't take more time than she had.

It was the boy's twenty-first birthday.

Perenelle stared out the front window of her home, a vacant look on her face. She'd reclaimed her brownstone, finally made it a home with Nicolas. Janos had returned to put things right. There were precious paintings and books missing, gifts from her favorite impressionists and a few early abstracts from her old friend Picasso. They graced the Clean Slate vaults now. She was grateful that Janos had escaped harm and counted herself lucky that they hadn't burned her home to the ground and sown the earth with salt as they'd done in earlier ages, elsewhere.

Nicolas kissed her on the back of the neck.

"You're thinking of Christopher?"

"He's twenty-one today. I can't help but wonder if Rahman was right, if he's changing, becoming something more than human." She remembered the sight of the child a little over twenty years ago, controlled by Rahman's spirit as it rose from under ground, pushed aside the concrete and stone walls of the subway station and earth above it as it rose to the surface in a bubble of force.

It had flown, levitated in midair with no effort, and manipulated matter with its mind. Imagine that power brought to maturity in the hands of an angry adolescent who felt betrayed and abandoned. Did Richmond have any idea of what he was dealing with? Perenelle doubted it.

"All we can do is wait," said Nicolas. "If he inherits that kind of power, we'll know soon enough."

Perenelle took his hand as he laid it on her shoulder and stared out into the night with her. He was right. All they could do was wait, prepare for the worst, and hope for the best.

Some things never changed.

Christopher woke up to the sounds of "Happy Birthday."

He'd fallen asleep after lunch and had almost forgotten that it was his birthday. His sense of time was getting lost inside the complex. Without windows, there was no real day or night. He spent most of his time in the lab, being tested, or in the gym, working off his rage.

The song came out of the ceiling intercom speakers.

He got up and stretched as Richmond's voice ended the song.

"Christopher! Come to level four. We have a surprise for you." The door opened and Christopher walked out and went to the elevators, went up two levels to the fourth floor. Two guards met him and led him to a door. Christopher yawned. He'd been sleeping a lot the last few days, felt odd and achy, like he was getting the flu. The door slid open and he stepped through.

There was a short hall through a kind of airlock. Christopher looked around when he got past the inner door. The room was bare, round, and glossy black, walls, floor, and ceiling.

"Mr. Richmond? Hello?"

The door behind him slid shut and locked with a hiss. Christopher realized that the sound wasn't from the closed door but from vents in the room. The air was being sucked out.

"Hey! Richmond!"

He shouted, raced around the room looking for an exit, but there were no windows in the chamber and only one door. He pounded on it as the air was siphoned out until he found it harder and harder to breathe. With no more air left to shout, Christopher fell to his knees and then to the floor, unconscious.

As soon as the boy was out cold, a team of technicians in sealed, red oxygen suits entered through the airlock, kept the air seal inside intact. A rectangular black platform rose from the floor of the room to waist height, lifted Christopher up with it. The team stretched him out and stripped him bare, attached wireless broadcast probes to his skin, and installed needles in the veins of his arms. They were attached to tubes that ran to a robotized collection system that allowed the research staff to draw blood samples as needed without entering the chamber.

Tom and Claire watched it all on monitors from his desk in Richmond's office. He sat in his big chair wearing Richmond's face, never dropped the mask anymore. Claire perched on the back of his chair like a raven as she looked over his shoulder.

"It seems Rahman's elixir may not be done steeping. Richmond's journals were quite clear about the boy's twenty-first birthday and the possible hazards. Drugs don't work on him, but the solution was simple." Tom explained his plan to Claire as they watched the operation. "Vampires don't need to breathe, but immortals do—he can't die, but reducing his oxygen does knock him out. This will keep him quiet until we're done."

Christopher was the key to realizing Tom's Blood World.

He'd seen all the surveillance tapes and witnessed what the boy's blood had done to Perenelle when she drank it. She'd faced the light of a dozen suns and walked away without a tan, all the powers of a vampire intact. That wasn't what had happened to her protégé, Abel. Tom had to find out what made her different.

Research on Perenelle and Christopher's blood would give Tom the power to improve his social saboteurs. With the power to enslave humans, control their minds, and walk in daylight, his forces would be invincible as they changed the world.

He'd be invincible.

Tom shut off his desk-screen views of Christopher's unconscious body, locked in stasis. To succeed, he'd have to reproduce the original elixir Perenelle and Nicolas had made in Paris with Rahman. That meant getting them to translate the Book of Abraham from Rahman's library. They'd also have to sacrifice a human child again, which he knew they'd refuse to do, but in time he'd find a way to persuade them. He'd said it before and was sure he'd find reason to say it again.

Patience was the only virtue he had left.

ACKNOWLEDGMENTS

My first novel had a long journey to completion, but this one was written in a year, right on the heels of the first. It was a very different writing experience, moving swiftly through a familiar landscape with sure footing, instead of hacking through underbrush and paving the road as I advanced. I want to thank a few of the people who got me to the end.

As before, thanks to my energetic editor, Monique Patterson, who sealed the deal in the first place and made this book possible. She has been an invaluable midwife to my first two babies, and I will be forever grateful.

Thanks to the members of the bi-weekly Other Countries writing workshop, an ever-changing cast, but in particular the core ensemble: Len, Kevin, Robert, James, Dadland, Gary, Tod, Anton, Tabb, Sur Rodney, and Wayne, with apologies to any I missed. Your thoughtful comments helped me refine what was less than clear in this novel, and your appreciation of chapters that worked was much-needed when I was working in a critical vacuum.

Thanks to my friend Kurt Vega for playing Yoda to my Luke while I re-established my credentials as a geek who can generate his own online content by putting together my book's web life to let the world know about the Testaments. And thanks to Sandrine Colard for her last minute French corrections.

A belated thanks to my friend Christian Villalba, who said "What about the Hindenburg?" when I said I was looking for a critical historic event in the 1930s to build the birth of the Veil around. Your high school obsession fed perfectly into mine, and helped make the first book for me.

Thanks to those I thanked in the first book, for all the same reasons, especially Linda Lutes, Victoria Sanders, Benee Knauer, and God. Last but most certainly not least, thanks to the late great Zora Neale Hurston, who I hope is laughing down at my use of her in this book. I'd heard of her since high school, as a leading name in the pantheon of Harlem Renaissance writers, but one I'd never read. I knew her books in the same way people know familiar landmarks they never visit.

I began *Blood Pressure* knowing I wanted a vampire created during the Harlem Renaissance, and that I wanted to incorporate voodoo in the same way I did alchemy in the first book. That led me to Zora's work on the subject. From there I read her autobiography, more about her life by others, read her fiction, and fell in love with the woman. Once I hit the Harlem streets in the 1930s it was impossible to avoid her and Zora's voice was so strong in my head by then that bringing her into the story became irresistible. I underestimated the degree to which she would take over, but if I claim to know anything about the woman, I should have expected it.

I have in no way attempted a historically faithful representation of Zora, her times, or her work but rather to capture a spiritual and aesthetic essence drawn from my study of them, a kind of dream Zora if you will, moving through a fantasy landscape based loosely on facts. As Zora made a fiction of much of her own life, rearranging or reinterpreting events to suit points she wanted to make, I've made my own fiction out of a little known period in her life. I apologize to her for liberties taken, though I think they'd amuse her.

Zora's work was the basis for my depiction of voodoo in this book, and while I did additional research, have stayed with her spellings of names and her vision of the religion as drawn from *Tell My Horse* and *Mules and Men* in creating my own mythology based on it. My depiction of the gods and their world in this work are not meant to accurately depict voodoo as it's practiced daily by believers, so much as capture a small part of the heart of a larger and rich religion. I can only hope voodoo has fared better here than the Catholic Church generally does in horror literature.

I have taken liberties here as well, incorporating hoodoo ritual into voodoo as the "street" side of the larger religion, in the same way popular superstitions like burying a statue of St. Joseph upside down near a house to sell it are performed by otherwise devout Catholics today. Rather than trying to explain the specific differences between the two, I chose to blend them into aspects of the same body of belief. On these and all other matters of "fact," I beg the indulgence of the more scholarly.

Pleasant dreams,

—Terence Taylor
Brooklyn, 2009